PRAISE FOR
Come Sundown

"[Roberts] is moving into more complex and darker storytelling, to terrific effect."—*Kirkus Reviews* (starred)

"A firecracker read." — *The New York Post*

"With its take-no-guff heroine, and a compelling plot of spine-tingling suspense, this is quintessential Roberts."—*Booklist*

"...what makes this novel most engaging is Roberts's ability to suffuse her story with rich details of one family's life, as well as sizzling doses of romance and mystery."
—*Publishers Weekly*

"...an engrossing read."—*Bookpage*

"Romance and suspense are Roberts's specialty. She delivers both in *Come Sundown*."
—*Shelf Awareness*

Also by Nora Roberts

SERIES

Irish Born Trilogy
BORN IN FIRE
BORN IN ICE
BORN IN SHAME

Dream Trilogy
DARING TO DREAM
HOLDING THE DREAM
FINDING THE DREAM

Chesapeake Bay Saga
SEA SWEPT
RISING TIDES
INNER HARBOR
CHESAPEAKE BLUE

Gallaghers of Ardmore Trilogy
JEWELS OF THE SUN
TEARS OF THE MOON
HEART OF THE SEA

Three Sisters Island Trilogy
DANCE UPON THE AIR
HEAVEN AND EARTH
FACE THE FIRE

Key Trilogy
KEY OF LIGHT
KEY OF KNOWLEDGE
KEY OF VALOR

In the Garden Trilogy
BLUE DAHLIA
BLACK ROSE
RED LILY

Circle Trilogy
MORRIGAN'S CROSS
DANCE OF THE GODS
VALLEY OF SILENCE

Sign of Seven Trilogy
BLOOD BROTHERS
THE HOLLOW
THE PAGAN STONE

Bride Quartet
VISION IN WHITE
BED OF ROSES
SAVOR THE MOMENT
HAPPY EVER AFTER

The Inn BoonsBoro Trilogy
THE NEXT ALWAYS
THE LAST BOYFRIEND
THE PERFECT HOPE

The Cousins O'Dwyer Trilogy
DARK WITCH
SHADOW SPELL
BLOOD MAGICK

The Guardians Trilogy
STARS OF FORTUNE
BAY OF SIGHS
ISLAND OF GLASS

The Chronicles of the One
YEAR ONE
OF BLOOD AND BONE

Nora Roberts & J. D. Robb

REMEMBER WHEN

J. D. Robb

NAKED IN DEATH

GLORY IN DEATH

IMMORTAL IN DEATH

RAPTURE IN DEATH

CEREMONY IN DEATH

VENGEANCE IN DEATH

HOLIDAY IN DEATH

CONSPIRACY IN DEATH

LOYALTY IN DEATH

WITNESS IN DEATH

JUDGMENT IN DEATH

BETRAYAL IN DEATH

SEDUCTION IN DEATH

REUNION IN DEATH

PURITY IN DEATH

PORTRAIT IN DEATH

IMITATION IN DEATH

DIVIDED IN DEATH

VISIONS IN DEATH

SURVIVOR IN DEATH

ORIGIN IN DEATH

MEMORY IN DEATH

BORN IN DEATH

INNOCENT IN DEATH

CREATION IN DEATH

STRANGERS IN DEATH

SALVATION IN DEATH

PROMISES IN DEATH

KINDRED IN DEATH

FANTASY IN DEATH

INDULGENCE IN DEATH

TREACHERY IN DEATH

NEW YORK TO DALLAS

CELEBRITY IN DEATH

DELUSION IN DEATH

CALCULATED IN DEATH

THANKLESS IN DEATH

CONCEALED IN DEATH

FESTIVE IN DEATH

OBSESSION IN DEATH

DEVOTED IN DEATH

BROTHERHOOD IN DEATH

APPRENTICE IN DEATH

ECHOES IN DEATH

SECRETS IN DEATH

DARK IN DEATH

LEVERAGE IN DEATH

CONNECTIONS IN DEATH

Anthologies

FROM THE HEART

A LITTLE MAGIC

A LITTLE FATE

MOON SHADOWS

(with Jill Gregory, Ruth Ryan Langan, and Marianne Willman)

The Once Upon Series

(with Jill Gregory, Ruth Ryan Langan, and Marianne Willman)

ONCE UPON A CASTLE	ONCE UPON A ROSE
ONCE UPON A STAR	ONCE UPON A KISS
ONCE UPON A DREAM	ONCE UPON A MIDNIGHT

SILENT NIGHT

(with Susan Plunkett, Dee Holmes, and Claire Cross)

OUT OF THIS WORLD

(with Laurell K. Hamilton, Susan Krinard, and Maggie Shayne)

BUMP IN THE NIGHT

(with Mary Blayney, Ruth Ryan Langan, and Mary Kay McComas)

DEAD OF NIGHT

(with Mary Blayney, Ruth Ryan Langan, and Mary Kay McComas)

THREE IN DEATH

SUITE 606

(with Mary Blayney, Ruth Ryan Langan, and Mary Kay McComas)

IN DEATH

THE LOST

(with Patricia Gaffney, Mary Blayney, and Ruth Ryan Langan)

THE OTHER SIDE

(with Mary Blayney, Patricia Gaffney, Ruth Ryan Langan, and Mary Kay McComas)

TIME OF DEATH

THE UNQUIET

(with Mary Blayney, Patricia Gaffney, Ruth Ryan Langan, and Mary Kay McComas)

MIRROR, MIRROR

(with Mary Blayney, Elaine Fox, Mary Kay McComas, and R. C. Ryan)

DOWN THE RABBIT HOLE

(with Mary Blayney, Elaine Fox, Mary Kay McComas, and R. C. Ryan)

Also Available . . .

THE OFFICIAL NORA ROBERTS COMPANION

(edited by Denise Little and Laura Hayden)

COME SUNDOWN

NORA ROBERTS

St. Martin's Paperbacks

This is a work of fiction. All of the characters, organizations, and events portrayed in this novel are either products of the author's imagination or are used fictitiously.

COME SUNDOWN

Copyright © 2017 by Nora Roberts
Excerpt from *Under Currents* copyright © 2019 by Nora Roberts.

Interior photographs by Bruce Wilder

All rights reserved.

For information address St. Martin's Press, 175 Fifth Avenue, New York, NY 10010.

Library of Congress Catalog Card Number: 2017002672

ISBN: 978-1-250-12309-1

Our books may be purchased in bulk for promotional, educational, or business use. Please contact your local bookseller or the Macmillan Corporate and Premium Sales Department at 1-800-221-7945, ext. 5442, or by e-mail at MacmillanSpecialMarkets@macmillan.com.

Printed in the United States of America

St. Martin's Press hardcover edition / June 2017
St. Martin's Griffin edition / April 2018
St. Martin's Paperbacks edition / April 2019

St. Martin's Paperbacks are published by St. Martin's Press, 175 Fifth Avenue, New York, NY 10010.

10 9 8 7 6 5 4 3 2 1

For Jason and Kat,
the best of traveling companions

PART ONE

A Journey

So, when a raging fever burns,
We shift from side to side by turns;
And 'tis a poor relief we gain
To change the place, but keep the pain.
—Isaac Watts

PROLOGUE

— *Western Montana, 1991* —

Alice Bodine relieved herself behind a thin screen of lodgepole pines. She'd had to trudge through knee-high snow for the screen, and her bare ass (with the dragonfly tattoo she'd had inked in Portland) shivered in the wind that soughed like the surf.

Since she'd walked a solid three miles on the back road without seeing a single car or truck, she wondered why the hell she'd bothered.

Some habits, she supposed as she hitched her jeans up again, just didn't break.

God knows she'd tried. Tried to break habits, rules, conventions, and expectations. Yet here she was—hardly three years after her self-proclaimed emancipation from everything usual, all the ordinary—dragging her half-frozen ass home.

She shifted her backpack on her shoulders as she high-stepped into her own footprints to get back to the sorry excuse for a road. The backpack contained all her worldly possessions, which included another pair of jeans, an AC/DC T-shirt, a Grateful Dead sweatshirt she'd taken off some forgotten guy back when she'd first gotten to Los Angeles, some soap and shampoo she'd copped during her mercifully brief stint cleaning rooms at a Holiday Inn in Rigby, Idaho, condoms, her stash of makeup, fifteen dollars and thirty-eight cents, and what was left of a nickel bag of pretty decent weed she'd swiped from a guy she'd partied with at a campground in eastern Oregon.

She'd told herself she was aimed toward home due to her lack of funds and the very idea of cleaning up some jerk's cum-stained sheets ever again. And there was some acknowledgment of how easy it would be to become one of the dead-eyed women she'd seen hooking on the shady side of so many streets in so many towns she'd passed through.

She'd come close, she could admit that. You got hungry enough, cold enough, scared enough, the idea of selling your body—it was just sex, after all—for the price of a meal and a decent room seemed okay.

But the truth was, and there were times she faced the truth, there were some rules she wouldn't break. The truth was, she wanted home. She wanted her mother, her sister, her grandparents. She wanted her room with her posters all over the pretty pink walls, and the windows looking out to the mountains. She wanted the smell of coffee and bacon in the kitchen in the mornings, the feel of a horse under her at a full gallop.

Her sister was married—hadn't it been the stupid, altogether *traditional* wedding that had set her off, that was the last straw? Reenie might even have a kid by now, probably did, and was probably still as goddamn perfect as ever.

But she missed even that, even the annoying perfection of Maureen.

So she walked on, another mile, with the worn fleece

jacket she'd bought at Goodwill barely holding off the cold, and the boots she'd had for more than ten years slapping the snowpack on the skinny shoulder.

Should've called home from Missoula, she thought now. Should've just swallowed her pride and called. Her grandpa would've come to get her—and he never lectured. But she'd envisioned herself striding up the road to the ranch—maybe even swaggering up that road.

How everything would stop, just stop. The ranch hands, the horses, even the cattle in the fields. The old hound, Blue, would lope out to greet her. And her mother would step out on the porch.

The Prodigal Returns.

Alice's sigh puffed out a stream of warm breath, whisked away in the stiff, cold wind.

She knew better, had *known* better, but snagging a ride in Missoula seemed like a sign. And it took her within twelve miles of home.

She might not make it by nightfall, and that worried her. She had a flashlight in her pack, but the batteries were iffy. She had a lighter, but the thought of making a camp without tent or blanket, with no food, with the last of her water gone two miles back had her pushing on, harder.

She tried to imagine what they'd say to her. They'd be happy to see her—had to be. Maybe they'd be pissed at her for taking off the way she did, with no more than a snotty note. But she'd been eighteen, and old enough to do what she wanted—and she hadn't wanted college or the prison of marriage or working some pissant job on the ranch.

She'd wanted freedom, and she'd taken it.

Now she was twenty-one, and making the *choice* to go home.

Maybe she wouldn't mind working on the ranch so

much. Maybe she'd even think about taking some college classes.

She was a grown woman.

The grown woman's teeth wanted to chatter, but she kept moving. She hoped her grandparents were around— and felt hard twists of guilt because she couldn't be absolutely sure Grammy or Grandpa were still alive.

Of course they are, Alice assured herself. It's just been three years. Grammy wouldn't be pissed, or not for long. Maybe she'd scold some. Look how skinny you are! What on God's green earth have you done to your hair?

Amused at the thought, Alice pulled her ski cap down snug over the short cap of hair she'd bleached out as blond as she could manage. She *liked* being blond, liked the way the more glamorous color made her eyes read greener.

But most of all she liked the idea of being enfolded in one of Grandpa's hugs, of sitting down to a big meal— Thanksgiving was almost here—and telling her whole stick-up-the-ass family of her adventures.

She'd seen the Pacific Ocean, had strutted along Rodeo Drive like a movie star, had twice worked as an extra for an actual movie. Maybe getting real parts in real movies turned out to be a lot harder than she'd imagined, but she'd *tried*.

She'd proved she could be on her own. She could do things, see things, experience things. And she could do it all again if they gave her too much grief.

Annoyed, Alice blinked and swiped at the tears flooding her eyes. She wouldn't beg. She would not beg them to take her back, to take her in.

God, she just wanted to be home.

The angle of the sun told her she'd never make it by nightfall, and she could smell fresh snow in the air.

Maybe—maybe if she cut through the trees, across the fields, she could make it to the Skinner place.

She stopped, tired, torn. Safer to stay on the road, but heading across the fields would cut off a good mile or more. Plus, there were a couple of cabins, if she could remember her way. Bare bones for wilderness vacationers, but she could break in, get a fire going, maybe even find some canned food.

She looked down the seemingly endless road, then over the snow-buried fields, toward the snowcapped mountains rising into a sky going gray-blue with dusk and the oncoming snow.

Later, Alice would think of that indecision, that few minutes of hesitation standing in the bitter wind on the shoulder of the road. The few minutes before she took a step toward the fields, the mountains, that would have taken her into the lengthening shadows of the pines, away from the road.

Though it was the first sound Alice had heard in more than two hours—other than her own breathing, her own boot steps, the wind shuddering through the trees—the rattle of an engine didn't register at first.

When it did, she scrambled back through the snow, felt her heart leap at the sight of the pickup chugging its way toward her.

She stepped forward and, rather than sticking out her thumb as she'd done countless times in her journeys, waved her arms in a signal of distress.

She might have been gone for three years, but she'd been born and bred a country girl. A Westerner. No one would drive by a woman signaling for help on a lonely road.

As it eased to a stop, Alice thought she'd never seen

anything more beautiful than that rusted-out blue Ford with its gun rack, tarp-covered bed, and a TRUE PATRIOT sticker on the windshield.

When the driver leaned over, rolled down the window, she had to fight off tears.

"Looks like you need some help."

"I could sure use a ride." She gave him a quick smile, sizing him up. She needed that ride, but she wasn't stupid.

He wore a sheepskin coat that had some years on it, and a Cutter-style brown hat over short, dark hair.

Good-looking, Alice thought, which always helped. Older—had to be at least forty. His eyes, dark, too, looked friendly enough.

She could hear the line-dance beat of country music from the radio.

"How far you going?" he asked in that western Montana drawl that sounded like music, too.

"To the Bodine Ranch. It's just—"

"Sure, I know the Bodine place. Going right by it. Hop on in."

"Thanks. Thanks. I really appreciate it." She swung her backpack off, hauled it in after her as she climbed in the cab.

"You have a breakdown? I didn't see anything on the road."

"No." She settled the backpack at her feet, nearly speechless with relief at the warmth pumping out of the truck's heater. "I was heading in from Missoula, hitched a ride, but they had to turn off about six miles back."

"You been walking six miles?"

In bliss, she closed her eyes as the ice cubes that were her toes began to thaw. "You're the first truck I've seen in about two hours. I never figured on walking all the way. I'm really glad I don't have to now."

"Long walk, and for a little thing like you on her own. It's coming on dark soon."

"I know it. I'm lucky you came along."

"You're lucky," he repeated.

She didn't see the fist coming. It was so fast, so shocking. Her face seemed to explode from the blow. Even as her eyes rolled back, she slapped out.

She didn't feel the second blow.

Moving quickly, thrilled the opportunity had simply fallen into his hands, he hauled her out of the truck cab, rolled her limp body into the bed of the truck under the tarp.

He bound her hands, her feet, gagged her, then tossed an old blanket over her.

He didn't want her to freeze to death before he got her home.

They had more than a few miles to travel.

CHAPTER ONE

— Present Day —

Dawn bloomed, pink as a rose, tinting the snow-drenched mountains with delicate color. Elk bugled as they swam through mists on their morning pilgrimage, and the rooster crowed his insistent alarm.

Savoring the last of her coffee, Bodine Longbow stood at the kitchen door to look and listen to what she considered the perfect start of a November day.

The only thing that could make it better was one additional hour. Since childhood she'd wished for a twenty-five-hour day, had even written down all she could accomplish with just sixty minutes more.

Since Earth's rotation didn't accommodate her, she made up for it, rarely sleeping beyond five-thirty. When dawn broke, she had already completed her morning workout—a precise sixty minutes—showered, groomed, dressed for the day, checked e-mails and texts, eaten a breakfast of yogurt, which she was trying to convince herself to like with granola that she didn't like any better than yogurt, while she checked her schedule on her tablet.

Since her schedule already lived in her head, the check wasn't necessary. But Bodine believed in being thorough.

Now, with the predawn portion of the day in the bag, she could take a few moments to enjoy her morning latte—double espresso, whole milk, and a squirt of the caramel she promised her inner critic she'd wean herself off of eventually.

The rest of the household would pile in soon, her father and brothers from checking on the stock, getting the ranch hands going. Since it was Clementine's day off, Bodine knew her mother would sail into the kitchen, cheerfully and perfectly produce a Montana ranch breakfast. After feeding three men, Maureen would put the kitchen to rights before sailing off to the Bodine Resort, where she served as the head of sales.

Maureen Bodine Longbow was a constant wonder to her daughter.

Not only was Bodine dead sure her mother didn't actively wish for that extra hour a day, she obviously didn't need it to get everything done, to maintain a solid marriage, help run two complex businesses—the ranch and the resort—while continuing to enjoy life to the fullest.

Even as she thought it, Maureen breezed in. Her short, roasted-chestnut hair crowned a face pretty as a rosebud. Lively green eyes smiled at Bodine.

"Morning, my baby."

"Morning. You look great."

Maureen skimmed a hand down a narrow hip and the trim, forest-green dress. "I've got meetings on top of meetings today. Gotta make an impression."

She slid open the old barn door that led to the pantry, took a white butcher's apron from the hook.

Not that a pop of bacon grease would dare to land on that dress, Bodine thought.

"Make me one of those lattes, would you?" Maureen asked as she fastened the apron. "Nobody makes them as good as you."

"Sure. I've got a meeting straight off this morning with Jessie," Bodine said, referring to the resort's events manager of three months, Jessica Baazov. "About Linda-Sue Jackson's wedding. Linda-Sue's coming in at ten."

"Mmm. Your daddy tells me Roy Jackson's crying in his beer over the cost of marrying off his girl, but I know for a fact Linda-Sue's ma's determined to pull out every stop, and then some. She'd send that girl down the aisle to a celestial chorus of angels if we could provide it."

Bodine meticulously steamed the milk for the latte. "For the right price, Jessie'd probably manage it."

"She's working out real well, isn't she?" With an enormous skillet on the eight-burner range, Maureen began frying up bacon. "I like that girl."

"You like everybody." Bodine handed her mother the latte.

"Life's happier if you do. If you look for it, you can find something good about anybody."

"Adolf Hitler," Bodine challenged.

"Well, being what he was, he gave us a line in the sand most never want to cross again. That's a good thing."

"Nobody's like you, Mom." Bodine bent from her superior height—she'd passed her mother's five-three at twelve, and had kept going another five inches—kissed Maureen's cheek. "I've got enough time to set the table for you before I go."

"Oh, honey, you need breakfast, too."

"I had some yogurt."

"You hate that stuff."

"I only hate it when I'm eating it, and it's good for me."

Maureen sighed, lifting the bacon out to drain, adding more. "I swear, sometimes I think you're a better ma to yourself than I ever was."

"Best mom ever," Bodine countered, taking a stack of the everyday plates from the cabinet.

She heard the racket seconds before the back door opened. The men in her life piled in along with a pair of dogs.

"Mind you wipe your boots."

"Oh, now, Reenie, as if we'd forget." Sam Longbow took off his hat—nobody ate at Maureen's table wearing a hat.

He stood six-three, most of it leg, a raw-boned, handsome man with silver wings sweeping through his black hair, with character lines fanning out from the corners of deep brown eyes.

He had a crooked left incisor, which Bodine thought added charm to his smile.

Chase, two years Bodine's senior, hung his cattleman's hat on the peg, shrugged out of his barn jacket. He'd gotten his height and build from his father—all the Longbow siblings had—but in face and in coloring, he favored his mother.

Rory, three years her junior, combined the two with deep brown hair, lively green eyes in a twenty-two-year-old version of Sam Longbow's face.

"Can you make enough for one more, Mom?"

Maureen arched her eyebrows at Chase. "I can always make enough for one more. Who's the one?"

"I asked Cal to breakfast."

"Well, set another plate," Maureen ordered. "It's been too long since Callen Skinner's been at our table."

"He's back?"

Chase nodded at Bodine, headed to the coffee machine. "Got here last night. He's settling into the shack, like we talked about. A hot breakfast'll help that along."

While Chase downed black coffee, Rory added generous doses of milk and sugar to his own. "He doesn't look like some Hollywood cowboy."

"A disappointment to our youngest," Sam said as he washed his hands in the farmhouse sink. "Rory hoped he'd walk around with jangling spurs, a silver band around his hat, and polished-up boots."

"Didn't have any of them." Rory snagged some bacon. "Doesn't look much different than when he left. Older, I guess."

"Not a full year older than me. Save some of that bacon for the rest of us," Chase added.

"I've got more," Maureen said placidly and lifted her face when Sam bent down to kiss her.

"You look pretty as a candy box, Reenie. Smell just as pretty, too."

"I've got a morning full of meetings."

"Speaking of meetings." Bodine checked her watch. "I have to go."

"Oh, honey, can't you stay to say hey to Callen? You haven't seen that boy in near to ten years."

Eight years, Bodine thought, and had to admit she was curious to see him again. But . . . "I just can't, sorry. I'll see him around—and you, too," she said, kissing her father. "Rory, I need to go over some things with you at the office."

"I'll be there, boss."

She snorted at that, aimed for the mudroom, where she'd already put her packed-for-the-day briefcase. "Snow's coming by afternoon," she called, bundling into her coat, hat, scarf, and, pulling on gloves, walked out into the cold morning.

She was running a minute behind, so she walked briskly to her truck. She'd known Callen was coming back, had been at the family meeting about hiring him on as head horseman for the ranch.

He'd been Chase's closest friend as long as she could remember, and had wavered between being the bane of her existence to her first secret crush, back to bane, back to crush.

She couldn't quite remember which category he'd been in when he'd left Montana. Now, as she drove over the corrugated snowpack of the ranch road, it occurred to her he'd been younger than Rory when he'd left home.

About twenty, she calculated, no doubt pissed and frustrated at losing the bulk of his birthright. Land, she thought now, her father had bought from the Skinners when—if you said it politely—his father had fallen on hard times.

He'd fallen on hard times because he gambled any good times away. Dead crap as a gambler, she'd heard her father say once, and as addicted to it as some are to the bottle.

So with the land he'd surely loved down to less than fifty acres, the house, and a few outbuildings, Callen Skinner had set off to make his own way.

According to Chase, Cal had done just fine, ending up wrangling horses for the movies.

Now, with his father dead, his mother a widow, his sister married with a toddler and another baby on the way, he'd come back.

She'd heard enough to know that what Skinner land

remained wasn't worth what was owed on it from mort-
gages and loans. And the house stood empty, as Mrs.
Skinner had moved in with her daughter and family in a
pretty house in Missoula where Savannah and her husband owned a craft shop.

Bodine expected another meeting soon about buying
the last fifty acres, and as she drove she weighed whether
that parcel would work better for the ranch or resort.

Fix up the house, she mused, rent it to groups. Or for
events. Smaller weddings, corporate parties, family re-
unions.

Or save that time and expense, tear it down, build from
there.

She entertained herself with possibilities as she drove
under the arching Bodine Resort sign with its shamrock
logo.

She circled around, noting the lights on in the Trading
Post as whoever caught the first shift prepared to open for
the day. They had a trunk show this week with leather
goods and crafts, and that would lure in some of the late-
fall guests. Or with Rory's teams' marketing blast, draw
in non-guests who'd stay for lunch at the Feed Bag.

She pulled up in front of the long, low building with
its wide front porch that housed reception.

It always made her proud.

The resort was born before she was, at a gathering with
her mother, her grandmother, and her great-grandmother—
with her grandmother, Cora Riley Bodine, driving the
train.

What had started as a bare-bones dude ranch had
grown into a luxury resort that offered five-star cuisine,
personalized service, adventure, pampering, events, entertainment, and more, all spread over more than thirty

thousand acres, including the working ranch. And all, she thought as she got out of the truck, with the priceless beauty of western Montana.

She hurried inside, where a couple of guests were enjoying coffee in front of the massive, roaring fire.

She caught the fall scents of pumpkin and cloves, approved as she waved a hand toward the desk, intent on reaching her office and getting organized. Detoured to the desk when Sal, the perky redhead Bodine had known since grade school, signaled her.

"Wanted you to know Linda-Sue just called to say she'd be a little late."

"She always is."

"Yeah, but this time she's saying it instead of just being it. She's going by to pick up her mother."

The solid foundation of Bodine's day suffered its first crack. "Her mother's coming to the meeting?"

"Sorry." Sal offered a sorrowful smile.

"That's mostly Jessie's problem, but thanks for the heads-up."

"Jessie's not in yet."

"That's all right, I'm early for the meeting."

"You always are," Sal called out as Bodine veered off, taking the turn that led back to the resort manager's office. Her office.

She liked the size of it. Big enough to hold meetings with staff or managers, small enough to keep those meetings intimate and personal.

She had a double window looking out on stone paths, a portion of the building that held the Feed Bag and the more exclusive Dining Hall, and fields rolling toward the mountains.

She had deliberately arranged her grandmother's old

desk with her back to that window, avoiding distractions. She had two high-backed leather chairs that had once graced the office in the ranch house, and a small sofa—once her mother's and now reupholstered with a sturdy weave in a strong summer blue.

She hung her coat, hat, and scarf on the coatrack in the corner, smoothed a hand over her hair—black as her father's, worn in a long, straight tail down her back.

She had the look of her grandfather—so his widow always said. Bodine had seen photographs, and acknowledged her resemblance to the young, doomed Rory Bodine, who'd died in Vietnam before his twenty-third birthday.

He'd had bold green eyes and a wide, top-heavy mouth. His black hair had had a wave to it while hers ran ruler straight, but she had his high cheekbones, his small, pugnacious nose, and the white Irish skin that required oceans of sunscreen.

But she liked to think she'd inherited her grandmother's canny business sense.

She went to the counter that held the pod machine that made tolerable coffee, took a mug to her desk to go over her notes for her first two meetings of the day.

As she finished up a phone call and an e-mail simultaneously, Jessica came in.

Like Maureen, Jessie wore a dress—a sharp red in this case, paired with a short leather jacket the color of top cream. The short, high-heeled boots wouldn't last five minutes in the snow, but they matched the red dress as if they'd been dyed in the same batch.

Bodine had to admire the slick, unassailable style.

Jessica wore her streaked blond hair pulled back in a sleek coil as she often did on workdays. Like the boots, her lips matched the dress perfectly and suited her slashing cheekbones, her slim, straight nose, and her eyes of clear, glacier blue.

She sat as Bodine finished the call, taking her own phone out of her jacket pocket and scrolling through something.

Bodine hung up, sat back. "The coordinator for the Western Writers Association's going to contact you about a three-day retreat and farewell banquet."

"Do they have dates? Numbers?"

"Projected number nincty-eight. Dates are January nine arrival, departure on January twelve."

"This January?"

Bodine smiled. "Their other venue fell through, so they're scrambling. I checked and we can work this. We slow down right after the holidays. We'll hold the Mill for them, for the meeting rooms and banquet, and the number of cabins she requested for forty-eight hours. The coordinator—Mandy—seemed organized, if a little desperate. I've just now sent you, my mother, and Rory an e-mail on the particulars. Their budget should work."

"All right. I'll talk to her, get a meal plan, transportation, activities, and so on. Writers?"

"Yep."

"I'll alert the Saloon." Jessica made another note on her phone. "I've never organized an event for writers that doesn't run a big bar tab."

"Good for us." Bodine wagged a thumb at the little coffeemaker. "Help yourself."

Jessica simply lifted the Irish-green Bodine Resort insulated cup of water she carried habitually.

"How do you live without coffee?" Bodine wondered, sincerely. "Or Coke. How do you live on water?"

"Because there's also wine. And there's yoga, meditation."

"All of those things put you to sleep."

"Not if they're done right. You really should do more yoga. And meditation would probably help you cut back on the caffeine."

"Meditation just makes me think about all the other things I'd rather be doing." Leaning back, Bodine swiveled her chair side to side. "I really like that jacket."

"Thanks. I went into Missoula on my day off, splurged. Which is nearly as good as yoga for the mind and spirit. Sal tells me Linda-Sue's going to be a little late—news flash—and her mother's coming with her."

"That's the latest. We'll deal. They're booking fifty-four cabins for three days. Rehearsal dinner, wedding, wedding reception, basically taking over Zen Town the day before the wedding in addition to the other activities."

"The wedding's only four weeks away, so that's not much time to change their minds, add more fluff."

Bodine's wide mouth tipped into a smirk. "You've met Dolly Jackson, right?"

"I can handle Dolly."

"Better you than . . . anybody," Bodine decided. "Let's go over what we've got."

They went over the list top to bottom, and had moved on to a smaller holiday party event the week before Christmas when Sal stuck her head in the door.

"Linda-Sue and her mom."

"Be right there. Wait, Sal? Order up some mimosas."

"Now you're talking."

"Smart," Jessica said after Sal popped out again. "Fuss over them and soften them up."

"Linda-Sue's not so bad. Chase dated her for about five minutes in high school." Bodine rose, tugged her dark brown vest into place. "But mimosas never hurt. Let's soldier up."

Pretty, curvy, easily flustered Linda-Sue paced the lobby with her hands clasped between her breasts.

"Can't you just see it, Mom? Everything decorated for Christmas, the trees, the lights, a fire going like now. And Jessica said the Mill's just going to sparkle."

"It better. I'm telling you we need those big candle stands, Linda-Sue, at least a dozen. Gold ones, like I saw in that magazine. Not the shiny gold, the classy gold."

As she talked, Dolly scribbled on a page in the brick-thick, bride-white wedding binder she carried.

Her eyes looked slightly mad.

"And red velvet—dark red, not bright red—laid out on the path from where the sleigh stops instead of white. It'll show off your dress better. And I'm telling you we need a harpist—wearing red velvet with that classy gold trim—to play while people are coming in to get seated."

Jessica drew in a breath. "We're going to need more mimosas."

"I hear you." Bodine pasted on a smile, stepped into the breach.

Bodine gave the classy gold wedding forty minutes, then escaped. In the three months since Jessica had filled the slot as events manager, she'd proved herself more than capable of handling a fussy mother and a dithering bride-to-be.

In any case, Bodine had a meeting set with the food and beverage manager, needed to answer a couple of questions from one of their drivers, and wanted to cross a discussion with their horse manager off her list.

The winding, hilly gravel road from her office to the Bodine Activity Center (the BAC) ran nearly a half mile, but the minute she stepped outside into that apple-crisp air, she decided she wanted the hike rather than the drive.

She could smell the snow now, judged it would start to fall before mid-afternoon. But for now, the sky hung pale blue under the crowding clouds.

She walked by a couple of the little green Kias they provided to guests during their stay (on-property use only), then turned onto the narrow gravel road and saw no one.

Fields spread on either side, buried in snow. She spotted a trio of deer loping through it, white tails flashing, dark winter coats thick.

The cry of a hawk had her gaze lifting to watch it circle. Falconry ranked high on her three-year-plan for the resort, and she'd made progress in that area as she came to the end of year one.

The wind whipped snow off the ground, sent it swirling around her like sparkling dust while her boots rang on the iron-hard ground.

She spotted movement near the BAC, some of the staff out with a few of the horses in the sheltered paddock. The warm smell of horses carried to her, as did the scents of oiled leather, hay, and grain.

She lifted a hand in greeting as the man in the heavy barn coat and brown Stetson glanced over. Abe Kotter patted the paint mare he'd been brushing, then walked a few steps to meet Bodine.

"Gonna snow," she said.

"Gonna snow," he agreed. "Had a pair outta Denver want a ride. They knew what they were doing, so Maddie took 'em out and about for a bit. Just got back."

"Just let me know if you want to rotate any to the ranch, switch out."

"Can do. You walk down from the main?"

"I wanted the walk, the air. But you know, I think I'll saddle one up, ride it back, go around to see the ladies of Bodine House."

"You tell them hey for me. I'll saddle you up, Bo. Three Socks could use a ride. You'd be saving my old bones."

"Old my ass."

"I'm sixty-nine in February."

"You say that's old, you'll have my grannies taking some shots at your bones."

He laughed, stepped back, and gave the paint another rub. "Maybe so, but I'm taking that winter break like we talked about. Heading to see my brother in Arizona, me and the wife. Right after Christmas, and through to April."

She didn't wince, though she wanted to. "We'll miss you and Edda around here."

"Winters get harder when the years add up." He checked the paint's hoof, pulled out a hoof pick to clean it. "Not so much call for trail rides and such in the winter. Maddie can step up, manage the horses for a couple months. She's got a good head on her shoulders."

"I'll talk to her. Is she inside? I've got to go in, talk to Matt anyway."

"In there now. I'll get Three Socks ready for you."

"Thanks, Abe." She started out, walked backward. "What the hell are you going to do in Arizona?"

"Damned if I know except stay warm."

She walked around inside the building. Starting in spring right through till October, the big, barn-like space would hold groups gearing up for white-water rafting, ATV jaunts, trail rides, cattle drives, and guided hikes.

Once the snow got serious, things tended to slow down, and now the space echoed with her boot steps as she crossed to the curved counter and the resort's activities manager.

"How ya doing, Bo?"

"Doing, Matt, and that's enough. How about you?"

"Quiet enough we're catching up on things. We've got

a group out cross-country skiing, another shooting skeet. Family group of twelve's taking a trail ride tomorrow, so I gave Chase the word on that. He said Cal Skinner's back, and going to handle that end."

"That's right."

She talked to Matt about inventory, replacing gear and equipment, then pulled out her phone with her notes to discuss additional activities for the Jackson wedding.

"I'll be sending you an e-mail with all the details. For now, just make sure you block all this out, pull in whoever you need to cover it all."

"I got it."

"Abe said Maddie was in here."

"She's in the ladies'."

"Okay." She glanced at the time on her phone before pocketing it. She wanted that ride to see the grannies, then really had to get back to the office. "I'll wait a few."

She wandered to the vending machine. Jessica was right—she should drink more water. She didn't want water. She wanted something sweet and fizzy. She wanted a damn Coke.

Damn that Jessie, she thought, plugging in the money and taking out a bottle of water.

She took the first annoyed swig as Maddie stepped out of the restroom.

"Hey, Maddie."

Bodine headed over to the horsewoman. She thought Maddie looked a little pale, a little tired around the eyes despite her quick smile.

"Hi, Bo. Just back from the trail."

"I hear. You okay? You look a little peaked."

"I'm fine." After waving it away, Maddie puffed out a breath. "Do you have time to sit a minute?"

"Sure I do." Bodine gestured to one of the little tables scattered around the room. "Is everything okay? Here? At home?"

"It's great. Really great." Maddie, a lifetime friend, sat and pushed back the brim of the hat that sat on the chin-length swing of her sunny blond hair. "I'm pregnant."

"You're— Maddie! That's great. Isn't it great?"

"It's great and it's wonderful and amazing. And a little scary. Thad and I decided, why wait? We only got married last spring, and the plan was to hold off a year, maybe two. Then we said why do that? So, we dived right in."

She laughed, then tapped Bodine's water. "Can I have a sip of that?"

"Take it all. I'm so happy for you, Maddie. Are you feeling all right?"

"I puked three times a day the first couple months. First thing in the morning, lunchtime, and dinnertime. I get tired quicker, but the doctor says that's how it goes. And the puking should let up altogether pretty soon—I hope to God. I guess it has, a little. Just now I was queasy, but I didn't barf, so that's something."

"Thad must be doing backflips over the moon."

"He is."

"How far along are you?"

"Twelve weeks come Saturday."

Bo opened her mouth, closed it again, then took the water back for another gulp. "Twelve."

After sighing out a breath, Maddie bit her bottom lip. "I almost told you straight off, but everything says how you should wait to get through the first three months, the first trimester. We haven't told anybody but our parents— you just have to tell them—and even then we waited until I had four weeks in."

"You sure don't look pregnant."

"I'm gonna. And truth is, my jeans are so tight in the waist already, I've got them hooked up with a carabiner."

"You do not!"

"I do." To prove it, Maddie lifted up her shirt, showed Bo the little silver clip. "And look at this."

Maddie lifted her cap, bending her head to show a good inch of brown roots bisecting the blond. "They don't want you dyeing your hair. I'm not going to take off my hat until this baby comes, I swear. I haven't seen my natural-born color since I was thirteen and you helped me color it with that box of Nice'n Easy."

"And we used some to put a blond streak in my hair that ended up looking like a slice of neon pumpkin."

"I thought it looked so cool. I'm a blonde in my heart, Bo, but I'm going to be a pregnant brunette. A fat, waddling-around, peeing-every-five-minutes brunette."

On a laugh, Bodine passed the water back. As she drank, Maddie stroked a hand over her as-yet-invisible baby bump. "I feel different, I really do, and it's a kind of wonder. Bodine, I'm going to be a mother."

"You're going to be a terrific mother."

"I've got my mind set on that. But, well, there's another thing I'm not supposed to be doing."

"Riding."

With a nod, Maddie drank again. "I've been dragging my feet there, I know. Jeez, I've been riding since I was a baby myself, but the doctor's firm on it."

"So am I. You went out on the trail today, Maddie."

"I know it. I should've told Abe, but I thought I should tell you first. Then he's talking about how I can take over for him while he's gone this winter. I didn't want to say because he really wants this trip, and I could just see him putting it aside."

"He won't put it aside, and you won't be in the saddle until you get the all clear from your doctor. That's it."

Biting her lip again—a sure sign of anxiety, Maddie twisted and untwisted the cap on the water bottle. "There's the lessons, too."

"We'll cover them." She'd figure it out, Bodine thought. That's what she did. "There's more to the horses than riding, Maddie."

"I know it. I already do some of the paperwork. I can groom and feed and drive the horse trailer, drive the guests to the Equestrian Center. I can—"

"What you can do is get me a list, from your doctor, of the dos and the don'ts. What's on the do side, you do— what's on the don't side, you don't."

"The thing is, the doctor's awful cautious, and—"

"So am I," Bodine interrupted. "I get the list and you stick to it, or I let you go."

Slumping back, Maddie sulked. "Thad said you'd say just that."

"You didn't marry an idiot. And he loves you. So do I. Now, you're going home for the rest of the day."

"Oh, I don't need to go home."

"You're going home," Bo repeated. "Taking a nap. After the nap, you're calling your baby doctor, telling him—"

"It's a her."

"Whatever. You tell her to make up that list and send it to you, to copy me. Then we'll go from there. Worst thing, Maddie, you switch a saddle for a desk chair for a few months." Bodine smiled. "You're going to get fat."

"I'm kind of looking forward to it."

"Good, because it's gonna happen. Now go home." Bodine stood, leaned over to give Maddie a hard hug. "And congratulations."

"Thanks. Thanks, Bo. I'm going to tell Abe before I leave. Tell him you've got it all covered, all right?"

"Do that."

"In fact, I'm telling everybody. I've been dying to since I peed on the stick. Hey, Matt!" Rising, Maddie patted her belly. "I'm pregnant!"

"Holy shit!"

Bodine had time to see him boost himself right over the counter and run over to lift Maddie off her feet.

Parents got told about babies first, Bodine thought as she went back outside. But there was a lot of family around here.

CHAPTER TWO

Α s she rode, Bodine worked out what had to be done,
what could be done, and what made the most sense
to do. Losing two of her key horse people, one until spring,
one for a solid eight months, created a puzzle. She had the
pieces; she just needed to find the best way to fit them into
the whole.

Snow trickled, thin and scant for now, a harbinger of
what would come. She liked the smell of it, the way a
hawk glided through it overhead, and a fat rabbit hopped
up, vanished, hopped up, as it raced across a wide, white
field.

She nudged Three Socks into a quick, bright trot then,
reading him, let him stretch it into a lovely, rolling lope.
She spotted one of the maintenance trucks rumbling down
the road from the High Timber Cabins, and gave herself
and her mount the pleasure of taking the longer route
around, where the world opened up to the view of white
mountains rising up into a soft and pale gray sky.

For a while, she let her mind empty. She'd solve the
puzzle, fix the problem, do what had to be done.

She rode past the white tents of Zen Town, up the rise by the snuggled cabins they called Mountain View Estates, and wound around again to the road toward her grannies' house.

It sat back from the road, leaving room for the gardening they both enjoyed, a white dollhouse with fancy blue trim, big windows to let in the views, and generous porches, front and back, for just sitting.

She rode the gelding around the back to the grannies' little barn, dismounted. After giving him an appreciative rub, she tethered him.

She walked through the thin snow to the back porch, where she industriously wiped her boots on the mat.

The scent of something wonderful simmering on the stove caught her the minute she stepped inside. As she unbuttoned her coat, she walked to the pot to sniff.

Chicken and leeks, she mused, inhaling. What her grammy called Cock-a-Leekie.

She glanced around. The eat-in kitchen opened to a sitting area with a cushy couch, a few easy chairs, and a huge flat-screen.

The grannies loved their shows.

Some daytime drama with a pair of impossibly beautiful people currently played. She spotted the needlepoint basket—Grammy's—and the crocheting basket—Nana's—but neither of the women.

She checked in the guest bedroom/home office, found it tidy and empty.

She stepped out where a sitting room with its fireplace simmering like the soup bisected the two little bedroom suites.

She started to call out, then heard her grandmother's voice from the right.

"I fixed it! Told you I'd fix it."

Cora strode out of her bedroom with a shiny pink toolbox in one hand. She smothered a squeal, slapped a hand to her heart.

"Sweet baby Jesus, Bodine! You scared the life out of me. Ma! Bodine's here!"

Tools rattling, Cora hurried over to hug Bodine.

UGG slippers, the scent of Chanel No 5, a body so slim and agile it belied her years clad in Levi's and a soft, chunky sweater her own mother would have knitted.

Bodine drew in her scent.

"What did you fix?"

"Oh, the sink in my bathroom was leaking like a sieve."

"Do you want me to call maintenance?"

"You sound like your grammy. I've been fixing what needs fixing most of my life. Now I fixed the leak."

"Course you did." Bodine kissed each of Cora's soft cheeks, smiled into the sharp blue eyes.

"You got something needs fixing?"

"I'm going to be short two horsemen, but I'm working on fixing that."

"That's what we do, isn't it? Ma! Bodine's here, for God's sake."

"I'm coming, aren't I? No need to shout."

While Cora had let her hair—worn in an angled wedge—go to salt-and-pepper, Miss Fancy's stubbornly remained the red of her youth.

At a few months shy of ninety, she might admit to moving somewhat slower than she once had, but she was proud to say she had all her teeth, could hear anything she damn well wanted to, and only needed cheaters for close work.

She was small, more round than plump. She favored shirts or caps with statements she surfed for and bought off the Internet. Today's read:

THIS IS WHAT A
FEMINIST LOOKS LIKE

"Prettier every time I see you," Miss Fancy said when Bodine hugged her.

"You just saw me two days ago."

"Doesn't make it any less true. Come on and sit down. I need to check that soup."

"It smells amazing."

"Needs another hour or more if you can stay."

"I really can't, I've got to get back. I just rode by to see you first."

Miss Fancy stirred her soup while Cora put away her toolbox.

"Tea and cookies then," Cora decreed. "There's always time for tea and cookies."

Bodine reminded herself she was eating healthier, avoiding sweet snacks, empty carbs.

"Cora and I baked snickerdoodles last evening." Miss Fancy smiled as she set the kettle on a burner.

Why did it have to be snickerdoodles? "I could take time for a cookie. You sit down, Grammy. I'll make the tea."

She got the pot, the cups, the leaf strainers, as neither woman would lower themselves to having a tea bag in the house.

"Y'all are missing your show," Bodine pointed out.

"Oh, we've got it recording," Miss Fancy told her, brushed it away. "It's more fun to watch in the evenings and zip right through the commercials."

"I've tried explaining to her the show doesn't have to be on and running to record, but she won't believe it."

"It doesn't make a lick of sense," Miss Fancy told her daughter. "And I'm not taking chances. I heard that Skinner boy's come back from Hollywood, and working on the ranch."

"You heard right."

"I always liked that boy." Cora set a plate of cookies on the table.

"Good-looking as they come." Miss Fancy took a cookie. "With just enough troublemaker in him to make him interesting."

"Chase, and his serious ways, was the better for it. And you were sweet on him," Cora said to Bodine.

"No, I wasn't."

The grannies exchanged almost identical smirking looks.

"I was twelve! And how do you know?"

"Had the pining eyes." Miss Fancy patted a hand over her heart. "Hell, I'd've been sweet on him myself if I'd been younger, or him older."

"What would Grandpa have had to say?" Bodine wondered.

"That married and dead aren't the same. We were married sixty-seven years before he passed, and the both of us were free to look all we wanted. Touching, now? That's when married and dead are the same."

On a laugh, Bodine brought the tea to the table.

"Tell that boy to come by and see us," Cora demanded. "A good-looking man perks the day up."

"I will." Bodine eyed the cookies.

She'd eat healthy later.

By the time Bodine finished for the day, the snow was falling fast and thick. She found herself more than grateful for the cookies in the afternoon, as she'd missed any excuse for lunch and now ran very late for dinner.

By the time she parked the truck back at the ranch, she

was ready to eat whatever was at hand—after a glass of wine.

She shed her outdoor gear in the mudroom, hitched up her briefcase, and found Chase in the kitchen pulling a beer from the refrigerator.

"Beef stew on the stove," he told her. "Mom said to keep it on warm till you got here."

Red meat, she thought. She was trying to cut back on red meat.

Oh, well.

"Where is everybody?"

"Rory had a date. Mom said she was going to soak the rest of her life in the tub, and Dad's probably in there with her."

Instantly Bodine tapped the heel of her hand on her temple. "Why do you put that in my head?"

"The look in his eye put it in mine. I believe in sharing." He waggled the bottle he held. "Want a beer?"

"I'm having wine. A glass of red wine every day's good for you. You can look it up," she insisted when he smirked at her.

Maybe she poured with a very generous hand, but it was still *one* glass.

"So, Maddie's pregnant."

"How the hell do you know?" Annoyed, she drank wine with one hand and scooped stew into a bowl with the other.

"Maddie texted Thad how she told you, and just about everybody else within shouting distance, so he told me. And just about everybody else within shouting distance. I was waiting for it anyway."

"Waiting for it? Why?"

"It's a look in the eyes, Bodine. It's in the eyes—and a

couple comments here and there about fatherhood and such."

"If you suspected as much, why didn't you pin him on it?" Annoyed, she gave Chase a hard poke in the side. "If I'd known a few weeks back, I could've hung on to one of the seasonal horsemen. And look who I'm talking to," she said, grabbing a spoon from the drawer. "Never-Ask-a-Question Charles Samuel Longbow."

"The answer comes around anyway. I'm taking my beer in the other room, by the fire."

Sticking the spoon in the stew, Bodine followed him. Like her brother, she sat on the big couch, putting her feet up on the table.

"I called every seasonal I knew could handle being in charge. I need more than a rider. The handful I tried all have winter work already." She ate stew, mulled on it. "I've got a few weeks before Abe's gone to the damn desert, but I don't like putting somebody up front I don't know, I haven't had a good chance to train. I've got Ben and Carol, but as good as they are, they're not managers."

"Use Cal."

"Cal?"

"Yeah, he can switch back and forth easy enough. He's as good as it gets with horses, and he's a manager. You get too squeezed, Dad and I can fill some holes. Rory, too, or Mom. Hell, Nana can take trail rides. Rides pretty much every day anyway."

"I went by to see her and Grammy today. Rode Three Socks. When Nana found out, she wanted to ride him back to the BAC for me. Got a little put out when I wouldn't let her because of the snow. She shouldn't be taking trail rides in the winter."

In his deliberate way, Chase nodded, drank more beer. "She could do lessons."

"Yeah, I've thought of that. She'd like it. Well, if I can pull from the ranch on this, at least while Abe's gone, it would save me from finding somebody else. You're not completely useless, Chase."

"Me?" He swigged some beer. "I've got untapped uses."

"I don't suppose those uses run to where we come up with about ten miles of red velvet, a dozen gold candle stands—five feet high—and a female harpist in a red velvet dress."

"For now, those remain untapped."

"Linda-Sue's wedding. Her mother came with her today, and added or changed or complained about every damn thing. A waste of mimosas," Bodine muttered.

"You wanted to manage the place."

"Yeah, and I love it, even on days like this. Besides, the velvet and the harpist and the gold? They're Jessica's problem. The fact she didn't tell Dolly Jackson to shut the hell up proves I was smart to hire her."

"Never figured she'd last this long." Happy with his feet up, he studied the snow falling free outside the window. "And she hasn't gotten through a Montana winter yet."

"She'll last. Why wouldn't she?"

"City girl. East city."

"And the best events manager we've had since Martha retired five years ago. I don't have to check and recheck everything she does."

"You do anyway."

"Not as much as I did." She looked out the wide window as Chase did, watched the snow fall against the dark. "We're in for about a foot. I better text Len, make sure we're getting the roads plowed."

"Check and recheck."

"That's my job." Bodine shifted her gaze to the ceiling. "Do you really think they're up there in the tub together?"

"I'd bet money on it."

"I don't think I can go up there yet. I think I'm going to need another glass of wine first."

"Get me another beer while you're at it." His gaze followed hers upward. "I'd just as soon give them another half hour before I head up myself."

Bodine spent most of the next day checking the roads that wound through the resort, approving proposals, putting others on the back burner, and fast-tracking a request for new linens for cabins.

She'd just settled in to review the winter promotions— brochures, mailers, website, Facebook, and Twitter— when Rory strolled in.

He dropped into one of her chairs, sprawled out as if he planned to stay there awhile.

"I'm just taking a last pass at the winter promotions," Bodine began.

"Good, because we've got a new one to plug in."

"A new what?"

"Idea." He glanced back with a smile when Jessica came in. "Here she is, my partner in crime. Mom's tied up, but she'll swing in if she gets loose."

"What's this about? The brochures are scheduled for printing tomorrow, and the spread on the website's due to go live next week."

"A few days later isn't going to matter."

Knowing that was exactly the wrong way to approach Bodine, Jessica gave Rory's arm a pat—and a pinch— before she sat. "I think we can build on the interest we've generated in the last two years on the Cowboy Cookery event and the Bodine Rodeo."

"The Bodine Rodeo's our top-selling annual event," Rory added. "But only about twenty-five percent who participate or buy tickets stay with us, eat in our restaurants, drink at our bar, use our services."

"I'm aware, Rory. The bulk of the rodeoers have their own campers or RVs, or they bunk in motels. A lot of the ticket sales are for locals. The June Rope 'n Ride doesn't generate the same ticket revenue, but pulls in more bookings. Some of it's just the season."

"Exactly." He pointed at her. "Winter season, what have you got? You got snow. And more snow. People coming here from out East or California, they want a cowboy experience, the trail rides, the chuck wagon, buffalo burgers, and they want it with a thick coat of luxury."

At home in a sales pitch, Rory crossed his fancy Frye boots at the ankles.

"You got some who come wintertime, scoot around on snowmobiles or like to snug up in a cabin and have a massage, but three or four feet of snow puts them off, so we lose that potential revenue. Why not use the snow to add revenue?"

Bodine had learned—though she could admit it had taken a while—not to look at Rory as her baby brother when it came to marketing.

"I'm listening."

"Snow sculpture competition. A weekend event. Broad pictures? We'll say four categories. Under twelve, twelve to sixteen, adult, and family. We award prizes, get the local media to cover it. And we offer a discount on cabins to participants for a two-day stay."

"You want people to build snowmen?"

"Not snowmen," Jessica put in. "Though that would be an option. Snow art, sculptures, like they do with sand sculpture competitions in Florida. You grid off a few acres, have a section for kids, supervised by staff. You serve hot chocolate and soup."

"Snow cones."

"Snow cones." Rory shook his head at his sister. "I should've thought of that."

"We provide tools—shovels, spades, palette knives, that sort of thing," Jessica continued, "but the competitors have to come up with their own ornamentation, if they want to. We hold a meet and greet Friday night, assign locations, kick it off nine sharp Saturday morning."

"You're going to need activities for the younger kids," Bodine considered. "Short attention spans, right? And they'd need to get out of the cold with something to do, foods, snacks. Adults, too, not planned activities, but a lot of them might want breaks."

"We set up a buffet in the Feed Bag. Maybe some heated tents for neck and shoulder massages. I can work out activities for kids." Jessica frowned. "Stick with the winter theme. We could offer sleigh rides for an additional fee. We have a party, with entertainment, Saturday night, announce the winners, award the prizes."

"I like the concept, but you're going to have to refine the details, the sales pitch, and the price points pretty quick. Get some photos. Snow Sculpture *Extravaganza* works better than *competition*."

"Damn it, it does," Rory agreed. "I guess that's why you're the boss."

"And don't you forget it."

"Let me start on those details." Pocketing her phone, Jessica stood up. "Rory, how about we put our heads together in about an hour and nail it all down?"

"I can do that." He watched her go, turned back to smile at his sister. "She sure smells good."

"Seriously?"

With his million-dollar smile beaming, Rory wiggled his eyebrows. "Seriously good."

"She's too old for you—and too classy."

"Age is just a state of mind, and I got plenty of class when I need it. Not that I'm looking to go there," he added. "Just saying what is." He pushed to his feet. "You know, I can market the hell out of this."

He could, she thought. And he would. "See that it pays for itself," she warned him.

"Bean counter."

"Daydreamer. Get. I've got work."

More of it now, she thought, looking back at her computer screen and the current layout of the brochure.

They'd need to change the layout with this addition to their promotions and events, and do all of that with enough lead time to draw solid bookings.

She picked up the phone to contact the designer.

Rory and Jessica—with an assist from Maureen—were as good as their word. By five o'clock, Bodine had a fleshed-out proposal on her desk and a mock-up of a design, the language, the price points.

Tweaking it, approving it, getting the approved copy to the designer added another hour, but she counted it well worth the time.

As she left for the day, she looked toward the Dining Hall, scanned the cars and trucks in the lot. Several Kias and a good number of SUVs, trucks, and cars from outside diners.

Good enough.

She wanted her own dinner, and some quiet time when she didn't have to have the answers. Maybe an early night.

After she pulled up at the ranch, she grabbed her brief-case and walked into the mudroom outlining an evening agenda in her mind:

Glass of wine.

Dinner.

Long, hot shower.

A couple hours inside a book.

Sleep.

Sounded just perfect.

She caught the scent of—pretty damn sure—Clementine's lasagna, and decided there was a God.

As Bodine walked into the kitchen, Clementine—all six rawboned feet of clear-your-plate-and-don't-give-me-no-sass-no-nonsense—let out one of her cackling laughs.

"Boy, you haven't changed one smidgen of one inch."

"Nothing in this world or the next could change my deep and abiding love for you."

Bodine knew that voice, the smooth, sly charm of it, and looked to where Callen Skinner leaned against the counter, drinking a beer while Clementine loaded up the dishwasher.

CHAPTER THREE

He'd changed a smidgen of an inch, Bodine thought. He'd been on the skinny side of lean when he'd left. He'd filled out some. Long legs and narrow hips gave him a rangy look, but he'd broadened out in the shoulders, fined down in the face.

It had always been a good face, but now the angles were sharper, the jaw firmer. He wore his hair, which was the shade of a winter deer hide, longer than she remembered, so it curled a bit around his ears and over the collar of his shirt.

She wondered if his hair still took on streaks from the sun when he left his hat off more than ten minutes. He turned his head, looked straight at her, and she saw his eyes were the same: that deceptively calm gray that could take on hints of blue or green.

"Hey there, Bodine."

Clementine swung around, stuck her fists on her bony hips. "About damn time. You think I'm running a cafeteria? You're lucky there's a scrap left for you to eat."

"Blame Rory. He's the one that dumped work on me at the end of the day. Hey there, Callen."

"You wash your hands," Clementine ordered. "Then sit yourself down at the table."

"Yes, ma'am."

"Want a beer?" Callen asked her.

"She'll want a glass of that red wine she's taken to drinking 'cause it wards off heart problems or some such thing. That there," Clementine said, pointing.

"Is that so? I'll get that for you." Callen sauntered over, got a wineglass, poured while Bodine dutifully washed her hands.

"You eat this salad." Clementine heaped some into a bowl, drizzled something on it, tossed it. "And don't give me any lip about the dressing."

"No, ma'am. Thanks," she added when Callen handed her the glass.

She sat, took the first sip of wine, then as Clementine whipped a napkin over her lap, picked up her fork. "You sit down there and keep her company, Cal. Half the time late to supper and eating alone. Half the time! There's a plate keeping warm in the oven, and see that she eats every bite."

"I'll do that."

"You want some more apple pie?"

"My darling Clem, I'm sorry to say I've got no place to put another."

"Well then, you take a nice slab of it over to the shack when you leave." She gave him a pinch on the cheek, and his grin flashed like a summer lightning bolt.

"Welcome home. I'm going on now." Instead of a pinch on the cheek, Bodine got a light slap on the back of the head that ended in a caress. "Every bite, young lady. I'll see you in the morning."

"Good night, Clementine." Bodine let the door of the mudroom close before she let out a sigh, picked up her wine again. "You don't have to sit here and watch me eat."

"Said I would. I swear I'd run off and marry that woman for her bite alone. Her cooking'd just be a bonus." He took a slow pull on his beer, watching Bodine over it. "You got prettier."

"You think?"

"I see. You always were pretty, but you added to it. How are you otherwise?"

"Good. Busy. Good and busy. You?"

"Glad to be back. I wasn't sure I would be, so that's a nice bonus, too."

"You haven't had time to miss Hollywood yet."

He rolled his shoulders. "It was good work. Interesting. Harder than you think—harder than I thought when I jumped into it."

To her mind the best and most satisfying work usually was. "Did you get what you needed from it?"

His eyes met hers again. "Yeah."

"I know it's been a couple years, but I want to say I'm sorry about your father. And sorry I wasn't at the funeral."

"Appreciate it. I recall you were sick, flu or something."

"Or something. Three days of it. Sickest I've ever been, and I don't look to repeat it."

"While we're at the sorrys, I'm sorry about your grandpa—great-grandpa. He was a good man."

"About the best. How's your ma, Callen?"

"Doing good. Better off where she is, with a grandbaby to spoil, another coming. We're selling off the rest of the old place to your daddy."

Bodine picked at the salad. "I don't know if I should say I'm sorry."

"No need. It doesn't mean anything to me. Hasn't for a long time."

That might be true, she thought, but it had still been his birthright. "We'll make good use of it."

"I reckon you will." He got up, took her plate out of the oven. "And look at you, Bodine," he said as he set the plate in front of her. "Running the whole damn resort."

Since Clementine wasn't there to give her the beady eye, Bodine added a few good grinds from the pepper mill.

She liked the heat.

"I don't do it by myself."

"From what I hear, you all but could. I did some work for you today," he added. "Chase figured it'd be best if I went over and worked with Abe, since it's been some years, and get a feel for the operation."

She'd known—only because Chase had thought to text her, after the fact. "Did you get a feel?"

"Got a start of one. So I'll tell you, if you want to hear it."

He waited a beat. She shrugged and ate lasagna.

"I agree with Abe on how you should hire another horseman. It's true enough you can pull from the ranch, but you'd be better with somebody over there who sticks over there. I can take over for Abe easy enough by the time he leaves next month, but you're still one short."

Since she agreed with the logic, couldn't argue with the advice, she nodded. "I'm working on it. I just haven't found anybody yet."

"It's Montana, Bodine. You'll find your cowboy."

"I'm not just looking for a pair of boots." She gestured with her fork, and on that stood her ground. "If I didn't know you, you wouldn't be filling in for Abe."

"Fair enough."

"But I do know you. Maybe you know somebody back in California who's after a change of scene."

He shook his head, studied his beer. "Change of scene's built in, as you go where they need you. And the money's too good if you are. I could call in a favor, but I wouldn't feel right about it, asking somebody to give up that pay to do some trail rides and lessons, muck and groom."

His gaze lifted to hers. "Why did I?"

"I didn't ask."

"Yeah, you did. It was time to come home." Then the lightning grin flashed again. "And maybe I missed you and your long legs, Bodine."

"Mmm-hmm." The sound was both amused and sarcastic.

"I might've, if I'd known you'd gotten prettier."

"I might've missed you back if I'd known you'd filled out that skinny build."

He let out a laugh. "You know what I realize right now? I did miss you. I missed this kitchen, too. Though, boy, it's got some fancier touches since I was in it last. Barn doors on a pantry big enough to rate them. A big-ass shiny stove, and that faucet coming out of the wall. Clementine says it's to fill the pots that go on it."

"The grannies got Mom hooked on those home improvement shows. She all but drove Dad crazy until she talked him into redoing it."

"There's more I missed. I'd like to go by and see Nana and Miss Fancy."

"They'd like that. You got all you need in the shack?"

"More than. It's fancier, too, than it was back when Chase and I would sneak in there to plot our adventures."

"And locked me out." Still just a little bitter about that, she realized.

"Well, you were a *female*."

She laughed at that, at his cleverly horrified tone. Maybe she'd missed him a little, too.

"I could ride as well as both of you."

"You could. It annoyed the hell right out of me. Chase said you lost Wonder a couple winters back."

Bodine had ridden, loved, and groomed the sweet-going mare since they'd both been two. "Just about broke my heart. Six months before I could pick another for mine."

"You picked well. Your Leo's got brains, and spirit. Want another glass of that wine?"

She considered. "Half."

"What's the point in half of anything?"

"It's more than none."

"Sounds like settling." But he rose, got the bottle, set it on the table. "Looks like you've about cleared your plate, so I've done my duty by Clementine. I should get on."

"You want that pie?"

"No. If I took it, it'd be sitting there, trying to seduce me into eating it, and I'd never get any sleep. It's good seeing you, Bo."

"You, too."

When he left, she sat a moment, taking stock, absently rubbing the penknife she carried in her front pocket— always. The one he'd given her for her twelfth birthday.

Maybe, just maybe, she still felt a little of that crush. Just a light flicker of it.

Nothing she needed to worry about, nothing she wanted to act on. Just a little flicker at seeing the man he had become from the boy for whom she'd had teenage heart flutters.

It was good to know it, acknowledge it, and set it neatly aside.

She picked up the wine bottle, poured precisely half a glass.

It was more than none.

— 1991 —

He ordered her to call him *Sir*. Alice memorized every line of his face, the exact timbre of his voice. When she escaped, she'd tell the police he was about forty, white, around five-feet-nine, maybe a hundred and fifty pounds. Sort of sinewy and very strong. He had brown eyes, brown hair.

He had a puckered scar on his left hip, about an inch long, and a splotchy brown birthmark on his right outer thigh.

He often smelled of leather, beer, and gun oil.

She'd work with a police artist.

She'd had more than a month to curse herself for not paying more attention to the pickup. Even the color didn't stick in her memory, though she thought—mostly thought—faded, rusty blue.

She couldn't give them his license plate, and maybe he'd stolen the truck anyway. But she could describe him from his cattleman's hat right down to his scarred Durango boots.

If she didn't manage to kill him first.

She dreamed about that, about somehow getting her hands on a knife or a gun or a rope, using it to kill him the next time she heard that cellar door open, the next time she heard those boots come heavy down the steps to her prison.

She had no idea where she was, whether she was still

in Montana, or if he'd driven her to Idaho or Wyoming. He could have flown her to the moon for all she knew.

Her prison had a concrete floor, walls covered in cheap paneling. It had no window, and only the single door up a shaky flight of open steps.

She had a toilet, a wall-hung sink, a skinny shower with a handheld sprayer. Like the air in the room, the water in the shower never approached warm.

As if to provide her privacy, he'd tacked up a ratty curtain to separate the toilet area from the rest.

The rest was ten paces square—she knew because she'd paced it off countless times, straining against the shackle clamped to her right leg that prevented her from climbing more than the bottom two steps. It held a cot, a table bolted to the floor, a lamp bolted to the table. A bear climbing up a tree formed the base for her light and the forty-watt bulb.

Though he'd taken her backpack, he'd left her a toothbrush, toothpaste, soap, shampoo, and orders to use them, as cleanliness was next to godliness.

He'd provided a single scratchy towel and a washcloth and two thankfully warm blankets. A copy of the Bible sat on the table.

For food, an old wooden kindling box held a box of Cheerios, a partial loaf of white bread, small jars of peanut butter and grape jelly, a couple of apples—as Sir claimed they kept the doctor away. She had a single plastic bowl, a single plastic spoon.

He brought her dinner. It was the only certain way she knew another day had passed. Usually some sort of stew, but occasionally a greasy burger.

She'd refused to eat the first time, screamed and raged at him instead. So he'd beaten her senseless, taken her blankets. The next twenty-four hours, a nightmare of pain and chills, convinced her to eat. To keep her strength up so she could escape.

The bastard rewarded her with a chocolate bar.

She tried begging, bribing—her family would give him money if he let her go.

He told her she was his property now. Though she'd clearly been a whore before he'd saved her on the side of the road, she was his responsibility now. And his to do with as he pleased.

He suggested she read the Bible, as it was written a woman was to be under a man's dominance, how God had created woman from Adam's rib to serve as his helpmate and to bear his children.

When she called him a crazy son of a bitch, a fucking coward, he set aside his own bowl of stew. His coiled fist broke her nose before he left her weeping in her own blood.

The first time he raped her she fought like a mad thing. Though he beat and choked the fight out of her, she fought, screamed, begged against every rape, day after day until the days blurred together.

One of those days he brought her a slice of fried ham cut up into bite-size pieces, a heap of mashed potatoes with red gravy, a scoop of mushy peas, and a biscuit. He even provided a red checkered napkin folded into a triangle, shocking her speechless.

"It's our Christmas dinner," he told her as he settled to eat his own meal on the steps. "I want to see you eat with appreciation what I went to some trouble to make."

"Christmas." Everything inside her flooded and trembled. "It's Christmas?"

"I don't hold with all that gift-giving nonsense or the

fancy trees and whatnot. It's a day to celebrate Jesus' birth. So a good meal's enough for that. You eat."

"It's Christmas. Please, please, God, please, let me go. I want to go home. I want my ma. I want—"

"You shut your mouth on your wants." He snapped it out and her head jerked back as if from a blow. "I get up from here before I finish this meal, you'll be sorry. You mind me and eat what I give you."

She used her spoon, managing to shovel up some ham and chew it even though her jaw still ached from the beating he'd given her a few days before.

"I'm so much trouble to you." Over a month, she thought. She'd been in this hole in the ground with this maniac over a month. "Wouldn't you rather have someone—a helpmate like the Bible says—who could take care of you? Cook for you?"

"You'll learn," he said, eating with a deceptive calm and patience she'd already learned to fear.

"But . . . I can cook. I'm a pretty good cook. If you let me go upstairs, I could cook for you."

"Something wrong with that meal you're eating?"

"Oh, no." She ate some of the gluey potatoes. "I can tell you went to a lot of trouble to make it. But I could take on that trouble, do the cooking and cleaning, be a real helpmate."

"I look stupid to you, Esther?"

She'd stopped shouting her name was Alice weeks before.

"No, Sir! Of course not."

"You think I'm so stupid, so weak to the seduction of a woman, I don't know you'd try to take off if you go up those stairs?"

His mouth twisted. His eyes went to that terrible dark.

"Maybe you'd try shoving a kitchen knife in my gullet first."

"I'd never—"

"Shut your lying mouth. I'm not going to punish you as you deserve for saying I'm stupid because it's the birth of Baby Jesus. Don't try my patience on that."

When she subsided and ate in silence, he nodded. "You'll learn. And when I deem you've learned enough and good enough, I might let you upstairs. But for now you got all you need down here."

"Could I ask you for something, please?"

"You can ask. Don't mean you'll get."

"If I could have the gloves and another pair of the socks that were in my pack. It's just my hands and feet get cold. I'm afraid I'll get sick. If I caught a chill, I'd be more trouble to you than I already am."

He gave her a long, silent study. "I might consider that."

"Thank you." The words wanted to stick in her throat like the food, but she forced them out. "Thank you, Sir."

"I might consider it," he repeated, "if you show me the proper respect. Get on your feet."

She set the paper plate on the table by the bed, rose.

"You take off your clothes and lie down on that bed I gave you. I'm going to take what's mine by right, and this time you don't fight me."

She thought of the chilblains on her hands and feet, the constant cold. He'd rape her regardless. What point was there getting beat up on top of it?

She took off her sweatshirt, the shirt she wore under it. Her heart was too dry for tears now as she took off the socks she'd all but worn out from pacing the concrete floor. She tugged her jeans down, stepped out of the left leg, shoved the rest down to the where the shackle clamped her ankle.

She lay down on the cot, waited for him to strip, waited for him to lay his weight on her, to shove himself inside her, to pant and grunt, grunt and pant.

She thought that was the moment that broke her, when she submitted to rape for a pair of socks.

But when she thought back on that night, after she knew the year had turned, as she bent over the toilet sick and dizzy every morning for a full week, she knew it hadn't been that moment.

Her breaking point was the moment she knew she carried his child.

She feared telling him; feared not telling him. She thought of suicide, for surely that was the most humane choice for herself and what he'd planted in her.

But she lacked the spine and the means.

Maybe he'd do it for her, Alice thought as she huddled on the cot. When he found out she was pregnant, he'd just beat her to death. And it would be over.

She thought of her mother, her sister, her grandparents, her uncles and aunts and cousins. She thought of the ranch, how it would look like a postcard in the January snow.

They wouldn't look for her, she reminded herself. She'd locked that door herself, burned that bridge, cut that line.

And they'd never find her in this rat hole.

She wished she could tell them she was sorry she'd lit out the way she had. So angry, so full of herself that she hadn't cared about how they'd feel. Hadn't believed they'd care.

She wished she could tell them she'd been coming home.

When she heard the door open, heard the boot steps, she shuddered. Not in fear as much as resignation.

"Get your lazy ass out of that bed and eat."

"I'm sick."

"You'll be more'n sick you don't do as I say."

"I need a doctor."

He grabbed her by the hair, yanked her up. Screaming, she covered her face. "Please, please. I'm pregnant. I'm pregnant."

The grip on her hair tightened as he jerked her face up. "Don't you try any of your whore tricks on me."

"I'm pregnant." She said it calmly now, sure she was facing death. Struggling to be ready for it. "I've been sick every morning for six straight days. I haven't had my period since right after you brought me here. I missed in December, now I'm coming up on when I'm due for January. I lost track of the time until you said it was Christmas. I'm pregnant."

When he released her hair, she sank back down on the bed.

"Then I'm right pleased."

"You—what?"

"Something wrong with your hearing, Esther? I'm pleased."

She stared at him, then just shut her eyes. "You wanted to get me pregnant."

"We are to go forth and multiply. It's your purpose on this earth to bear children."

She lay still, pushed resignation aside, let a splinter of hope through. "I have to see a doctor, Sir."

"Your body is made for this purpose. Doctors just buffalo people to get rich."

He wants the baby, she reminded herself. "We want the baby to be healthy. I need prenatal vitamins and good care. If I get sick, the baby inside me gets sick."

That heat, that mad heat flashed into his eyes. "You think some cheating doctor knows better than me?"

"No. No. I just want what's best for the baby."

"I'll tell you what's best. You get up and eat what I brought you. We'll dispense with relations till we're sure it's well planted in you."

He brought her a little portable heater and an easy chair. He added a small cooler to the room, where he stocked milk, raw fruits, and vegetables. He fed her more meat than before, and made her take a daily vitamin.

When he felt she was healthy enough, the rapes continued, but with less frequency. When he hit her, he kept it to open-hand smacks on her face.

As her belly grew, he brought her big, billowy dresses she hated, and a pair of slippers she shed grateful tears over. He tacked a calendar to the wall, marking off the days himself so she watched the days of her life crawl by.

Surely he'd let her upstairs once the baby came. He wanted the baby, so he'd let her and the baby come upstairs.

And then . . .

She'd need to take time, Alice calculated as she sat in the easy chair near the stingy heater while the baby kicked and stirred inside her.

She'd need to make him think she'd stay, she'd be obedient, that she was broken. And when she got a good lay of the land, when she could plan the best way to get out, she'd run. Kill him if she got the chance, but run.

She lived on it, the baby coming, the baby opening the door to escape. A means to an end—and nothing else to her, this thing he'd forced inside her.

When she was upstairs, when she had regained her strength, when she knew where she was, when Sir's defenses were down enough, she'd get away.

This Christmas she'd be home, safe, and the bastard

would be dead or in prison. The baby . . . she couldn't
think of that.

Wouldn't.

At the end of September, in her eleventh month of captivity, her labor started as a nagging ache in her back. She
paced to try to ease it, sat in the easy chair, curled up on
the bed, but it didn't ease. It spread, rounding to her belly,
coming harder.

When her water broke, she began to scream. She
screamed as she hadn't since the first weeks in the cellar.
And, like those weeks, no one came.

Terrified, she crawled onto the cot while the pains
came harder, closer together. Her throat cried for water,
driving her up between contractions to draw some from
the sink into one of the Dixie Cups he'd stocked for her.

Ten hours after the first pain struck, the door up the
stairs opened.

"Help me. Please, please, help me."

He came down fast, stood frowning before he shoved
his hat back on his head.

"Please, it hurts. It hurts so much. I need a doctor. Oh
my God, I need help."

"A woman brings forth children in blood and pain. You
ain't no different. It's a good day. A fine day. My son's
coming into this world."

"Don't go!" She sobbed it out as he started up the steps.
"Oh God, don't leave me." Then the pain robbed her of
anything but a wailing shriek.

He came back again with a stack of old towels more
suited for a rag heap, a galvanized bucket of water, and a
knife in a sheath on his belt.

"Please call a doctor. I think something's wrong."

"Ain't nothing wrong. It's Eve's punishment, is all." He tossed her dress up, stuck his fingers into her so fresh pain erupted.

"Looks like you're about ready. You go ahead and scream all you want. Nobody's going to hear you. I'm going to deliver my son into the world. Deliver him with my own hands, on my own land. I know what I'm doing here. Helped birth plenty of calves in my time, and it's about the same."

It would rip her in two, this monster he put in her. Mad with pain, she struck out at him, tried to roll away. Then simply wept, exhausted, when he left her again.

She fought again, screaming herself hoarse when he came back with a rope, tied her down to the cot.

"For your own good," he told her. "Now, you start pushing my son out. You push, you hear? Or I'll cut him out of you."

Drenched in sweat, buried in exhaustion, Alice pushed. She could never have resisted the urgent need to even with the pain tearing at her.

"Got his head, look at that fine head. Already got some hair, too. You push!"

She gathered all she had left, screamed through the last, unspeakable pain. When she went limp with exhaustion, she heard a mewling cry.

"Is it out? Is it out?"

"You birthed a female."

She felt drugged, out of her own body, saw through the glaze of tears and sweat he held a wriggling baby, a baby slick with blood and goo. "A girl."

His eyes when they met Alice's were flat and cold, and struck her with fresh fear.

"A man needs a son."

He put the baby on her, dragged some twine out of his pocket. "Put her on the breast," he ordered as he tied off the cord.

"I . . . I can't. My arms are tied down."

His face a cold mask, he yanked the knife out of his belt. Instinctively Alice arched, struggling against the rope, desperate to wrap arms around the baby to shield it.

But he sliced the cord, then the rope.

"You need to pass the afterbirth." He fetched another bucket while the baby's cries grew in volume, and Alice tucked hands around the infant.

The new pain caught her off guard, but it wasn't as bad as before. He dumped the placenta in the bucket.

"Shut up her caterwauling. Clean her up, and yourself, too."

He started up the stairs, took one last look back. "A man needs and deserves a son."

After he slammed the door, Alice lay in the soiled bed, the baby crying and wriggling against her. She didn't want to nurse the baby, didn't know how anyway. She didn't want to be alone with it. Didn't want to look at it.

But she did look, looked and saw how helplessly it lay against her, this thing that had grown inside her.

This child. This daughter.

"It's okay. It'll be okay." She shifted, wincing as she sat up, as she cradled the baby and guided its mouth to her breast. It rooted a moment, its long eyes staring blindly, then she felt the tug and pull as the baby suckled.

"See there, yes, see there. It's going to be all right."

She stroked the tiny head, crooned, and felt impossible love.

"You're mine, not his. Just mine. You're Cora. That's your grandmother's name. You're my Cora now, and I'll look out for you."

He left her for three days, and she feared he wouldn't come back. With her leg shackled she couldn't get to the door, couldn't find a way out.

If she'd had something sharp she might have tried cutting off her own foot. Meager supplies began to dwindle, but she had towels for the baby, the washcloth she rinsed and soaped again and again to keep little Cora clean.

She sat in the easy chair, the baby in her arms, singing songs, soothing whenever Cora went fussy. She walked the baby, kissed her downy head, marveled at her pretty fingers and toes.

The door opened again.

Alice held the baby tighter as he came down, carrying a sack of supplies.

"Got what you need." He turned, looked at the baby in her arms. "Let's see her."

Even if she could rip out his throat with her teeth, she couldn't break the shackle. She needed to calm and charm him, so she smiled.

"Your daughter's pretty and perfect, Sir. And she's such a good baby. Hardly cries at all, and only if she's hungry or messy. We could sure use some diapers, and some—"

"I said, let me see her."

"She's just now fallen asleep. I think she has your eyes, and your chin, too." No, no, she didn't, but a lie could calm and charm. "I should have thanked you for helping me bring her into the world, for helping me make her."

When he grunted, crouched down, Alice relaxed just a little. She didn't see that beating look in his eyes.

But he snatched the baby so fast, Cora woke with a shocked cry, and Alice sprang from the chair.

"She looks healthy enough."

"She is. She's perfect. Please, I can stop her crying. Let me just—"

He turned away, strode toward the stairs with Alice flying after him, the chain banging the concrete until it went taunt. "Where are you going? Where are you taking her?"

Half-mad, Alice leaped onto his back; he swatted her off like a fly, strode up the stairs. Stopped to look back as she dragged uselessly at the shackle.

"Got no use for daughters. Somebody else will, and pay a fair amount."

"No, no, please. I'll take care of her. She won't be any trouble. Don't take her. Don't hurt her."

"She's my blood, so she won't come to harm from me. But I've got no use for daughters. You'd best give me a son, Esther. You'd best do that."

Alice dragged on the shackle until her ankle dripped blood, screamed until her throat burned like acid.

When she collapsed on the concrete floor, weeping in absolute despair, when she knew she'd never see her child again, that's the moment she finally broke.

CHAPTER FOUR

— Present Day —

With the addition of the writers conference and the snow sculpture event now on the books, and the various holiday events and specials geared to pump up interest through Valentine's Day, Bodine walked her way through résumés and recommendations from various managers.

She earmarked her own choices—the new college grad looking for a position in hospitality, the recent empty nester with previous experience in housekeeping, the young horseman looking for full- or part-time work, a couple applications for waitstaff, an experienced massage therapist who'd just relocated out of Boulder.

She culled through a few more, weighed priorities.

They needed another housekeeper, as Abe's wife, Edda, would leave that slot empty when they headed to Arizona. And the applicant looked solid. They could certainly use another cowboy, and more waitstaff.

She considered the college grad, who seemed open to whatever position she could get. Solid résumé, good grades, local girl.

Armed with her folder, she set out to hunt up Jessica.

Bodine found her in the Dining Hall, heads together with the restaurant manager.

"Great. Two people I want to see. Jake, I've looked over those two waitstaff apps you sent over."

"Carrie Ann gave them her stamp," he said, referring to their eagle-eyed waitress of twelve years.

"So I see. You've got my okay if you want to bring them on. It'll give you time to see if they hit the mark before the holiday bookings."

"Good enough. We square here, Jessica?"

"Same page, same line. I think the Hobart event's going to hit every mark. I appreciate it, Jake."

"You bet. I'll see about starting the new staff this week."

When he walked off, Bodine turned to Jessica. "How would you feel about taking on an assistant/intern?"

"I've got Will." Alarm flickered in the cool blue eyes. "You're not taking Will away?"

"No, adding one. Potentially. She's the niece of a friend of my mother's—but," Bodine continued, "she's got good qualifications. Majored in hospitality, took a job at a hotel in Billings after she graduated, but her mother took a bad spill last month, and she came home to help out. She wants to stick closer to home. She's young, but she's got excellent references. She strikes me," Bodine said. "Feels like you could train her the Bodine way."

"You're the boss."

"Well, true enough, and I'm going to hire her on regardless. But if, after you look over her résumé, you'd rather not take her on in your area, I'll put her in activities or sales to start off."

"I'll look over her file." Jessica took it from Bodine. "Have her come in for an interview."

"That works. Let me know when you can, soon as you can."

"I will." Setting it down, Jessica anchored it with her tablet. "Have you talked to Rory?"

"Not since breakfast. Why?"

"We've got two bookings for the Snow Sculpture Extravaganza."

"Already? It just went on the website this morning."

"That's right." With a smug smile, Jessica toasted with her water bottle.

Bodine tapped her folder on her palm. "Looks like I'd better get busy hiring more fill-in winter staff. Can I ask you something?"

"Sure."

"Why do you wear heels every day when you spend as much time running around here as sitting down? Probably more time," she amended. "They have to hurt by the end of the day."

Jessica's eyebrows rose; her gaze dropped down to Bodine's feet. "Why do you wear gorgeous boots every day? We wear what we are, Bodine."

Bodine glanced down at her smoke-gray Dingos with the buckles running up the sides. They were sort of gorgeous. "I am my boots."

"And your Levi's, and most days—like this—your snappy vest. I do admire your collection of snappy vests."

Amused, Bodine tugged at the hem of the thinly striped blue and green vest. It could be considered snappy, she supposed.

"They're my compromise between a suit and just jeans."

"Works on you."

"Well." Bodine tossed her hair—in a long braid today—over her shoulder. "I'm going to take my gorgeous boots and snappy vest over to talk to Abe. I've got an application here for him, too, and another for Zen Town." She started off, turned back. "I'd be crying in those shoes of yours inside two hours."

"You're tougher than that."

"On the inside," Bodine qualified, "I'd be crying."

She grabbed her coat and hat from her office. According to her schedule, Abe should be finishing up a pair of lessons at the Equestrian Center.

She hopped in her truck for the ten-minute drive winding through the resort, out to the road toward the center.

She wandered inside the big ring to the smell of horses and the sound of a nervous giggle.

"You're doing fine, Deb, just fine. Heels down, Jim. That's the way."

Frowning, she stepped closer, and saw Callen rather than Abe mounted and running a lesson.

Couple of novices, no doubt about that, but Callen had them under control.

The man could sit a horse, she mused. Just as easy as another might sit a Barcalounger.

He had the novices on a couple of reliable hacks—though the bay they called Biff could be as lazy as a teenage boy on a summer morning. He plodded along under the man while the nervous giggle rode the cooperative Maybelle.

"Ready to try a little trot again?" Callen asked them.

"Oh gosh, I guess." The woman looked across the arena at Jim. "I guess, huh?"

"Let's go for it."

"Tell 'em what you want," Callen advised.

Asses hit leather hard enough to make Bodine wince,

but both students managed to circle the entire ring at an easy trot.

"Go ahead and go around the other way. You've got it now. Give him a nudge there, Jim. He'd rather stand than walk. That's the way."

Callen took his own horse—a gorgeous buckskin Bodine didn't recognize—in a tight circle to keep both riders in view. When he spotted Bodine, he tapped the brim of his hat.

"You ready to try a canter? Elbows down, Deb," he instructed when they jerked up on another giggle. "You can do this. Show her what you want."

"I'm a little—okay." Lips pressed in a tight line, Deb rocked in the saddle, and let out a squeal when the mare smoothed out into a gentle canter. "Oh my God! I'm doing it. Jim!"

"I see you, babe. We're riding!"

They circled twice, and though the woman swung back and forth in the saddle like a metronome, she had a huge smile plastered on her face.

"Ease them back now, that's it, all the way down to a walk. You did great."

"Can we do it again? Time's up," Jim added with a glance at his watch. "But—"

"Once more around."

"Yeehaw!" he said and, with some enthusiasm, had Biff reluctantly loping another circle.

Grabbing a mounting block, Bodine started across the soft dirt as Callen dismounted. He held a hand up to his horse, who blew out his lips, then stood hipshot with the reins tossed over his neck.

A little breathless, a little flushed, Deb beamed down at Callen. "Jim bribed me into this with a pair of boots I fell for in the shop back at the resort. I can't believe how much fun it was! How do I get down?"

With a laugh, Callen held Deb's mount. "Just swing your leg over, slide off. The block's right here."

Clumsy but game, Deb got her feet on the block, then grinned at Bodine as she stepped off. "Hi! Do you work for Cal?"

"This is the boss lady," Callen told her. "We all work for her."

"Oh! It's so nice to meet you." Deb stuck out a hand. "We had the best time, didn't we, Jim? I went from never being on a horse in my life to a—What was it, Cal?"

"Canter."

"That's it. Oh, I'm going to be sore for a week, but I can't wait to do it again. Let's do a trail ride, Jim."

"Sign us up." With slightly more grace than his woman, Jim dismounted. "Or I will. I got the resort app on my phone. That's a hell of an idea. Jim Olster."

"Bodine Longbow."

"Oh, even your name sounds like Montana. I love it here. We just got here yesterday, and I love it. Would you take a picture? Would you mind?" Deb pulled out her phone. "Of me and Jim and Cal and the horses. I love your hat. Now I have to have a hat, too. I like that flat-brim style. We're going shopping, Jim, and celebrating in the Saloon. I rode a horse!"

Bodine took pictures, ending with one of Deb pressing her cheek to the mare's.

As they left, Deb still chattering, Bodine walked the mare to the rail to uncinch the saddle. "I'd say there's a pair of satisfied customers."

"Then some. She must've really wanted those boots. Her hands were shaking when they came in."

"We carry some really nice boots. Where's Abe? He's on the schedule for the Olster booking."

"Ah, Christ." Callen hefted a saddle from horse to rail. "You didn't hear yet. His wife had some chest pains, so—"

"Edda? Chest pains? What happened, where is she?" Even as she peppered out the questions, Bodine yanked out her phone.

"Slow down. I got a text from him about halfway through the lesson. It looks like she had a little heart attack."

Bodine nearly had one herself. "A—a—*little*?

"Mild's what I got. They're keeping her in the hospital for now, but she's stable. I was here when he got the call. She was out—her day off, right?—with a couple of lady friends, and started having chest pains. I told him to go, I'd cover for him."

"I appreciate that, I do, but somebody should have called me."

"Abe was a little distracted—out of here in a flash. I was a little busy making sure the customer didn't faint on me."

"Right, you're right." To calm herself, she pulled off her hat, swatted it against her thigh as she paced back and forth. "I just—I need the details. She's stable? You're sure?"

"Abe said—here's a quote: 'She's squawking about going home. But they're keeping her overnight, doing some tests.'"

"What kind of tests? Why would you know?" she said before he could answer. "I'll look it up. I'll look up what they do, and I'll call him."

Calmer with a plan somewhat in place, she put on her hat again. "What else is on Abe's schedule?"

"There's a trail ride coming up," he said before Bodine could pull it up on her phone. "Carol can take it. And a weekly lesson at four."

"That'd be Lessie Silk, she's twelve. I can take that myself."

"I've got it," he assured her. "Chase knows where I am."

"Okay. All right. I'm hiring another hand. I've got someone to interview. I was going to talk to Abe about it, but I'm just going to call him up—the new hand—have him come in. If he's not an idiot, we'll take him on."

She'd contact Abe, get details on Edda. Call the applicant, schedule an interview, and since Edda was in charge of housekeeping, she'd adjust the schedule herself, as Edda wasn't going to come back to work until her doctors gave her an all clear.

"Got it worked out?" Callen said after a moment.

"I will have. Mild, you said?"

"That's the word Abe used, same as he used *stable*."

"Okay." Bodine blew out a breath, steadied. "Who's this handsome boy?" She rubbed the unfamiliar buff-colored gelding's neck.

"This is Sundown. My better half. Sundown, meet Bodine."

Callen swept a finger down, and the horse bent his forelegs, bowed.

"Now, aren't you the clever one?"

"Smartest damn horse I ever met." Callen tapped Bodine's shoulder. Sundown eased closer, laid his head where Callen tapped.

Laughing, Bodine hooked an arm around Sundown's neck. "How long have you had him?"

"Since he was born—at sundown—four years last May. I was helping out a friend, between projects, and his mare delivered this one. Love at first sight. I bought him on the spot, and when he was weaned and ready, he came with me."

Callen wrapped the reins securely around the saddle horn. "Want to show off, Sundown?"

With a toss of his head, the gelding trotted out to the center of the ring.

"Rattlesnake!"

At Callen's call, Sundown reared, hooves striking air. "Backstabber." Dropping his forelegs, Sundown kicked his back legs high. "Do-si-do." Brightly, the horse danced laterally left, swung his hindquarters around, danced right. "Pretty filly."

Amused, impressed, Bodine watched as a kind of gleam came into the horse's eyes before he did the equine version of a manly swagger back to Bodine.

"Kiss the girl."

Sundown lowered his head, rubbed his blowing lips over Bodine's cheek.

"You are a charmer," Bodine said, pressing her own lips to the gelding's cheek. "You trained him? You always had a way, but this is really something."

"I picked up some tips from the experts on my travels, but I'm working with prime here. Absolute prime."

"I sure wouldn't argue." And love, the sort she knew very well that bloomed between horse and human, shined in Callen's words.

"Do you do any trick riding? You used to do some."

The quick grin Callen aimed had—by Bodine measure—a hefty dose of flirt in it.

"Want me to show off now?"

"I'm just thinking how we get a lot of families, a lot of kids on the weekends, and more yet when summer comes. A little show in the paddock by the BAC, some fancy riding, ending with the tricks he can do? They'd eat it like ice cream."

"Maybe."

"Say a half hour, and another half hour to let the kids ask questions, pet the horse. You'd get paid extra. If you want to think about it, I'll see where it would best fit."

Sundown butted Callen's shoulder as if to say: I'm in!

"I can think about it."

"Good, then we'll talk. Do you need help with the horses?"

"I can manage well enough."

"Then I need to get back." She started out, turned, walked backward as she spoke. "You're a good teacher, Skinner. I never figured you for the patience."

"I spent some time developing it."

"Considerable, I'd say."

When she turned around again, Callen admired her long legs until she moved out of sight.

"Patience ain't everything," he said to his horse. "Maybe next time *I* should kiss the girl."

Sundown let out a sound no one would have mistaken for anything but a laugh.

Bodine squeezed all she could into the rest of the day, and the morning after.

She made her calls, her appointments. With the rare move of closing her office door, she assured herself of enough uninterrupted time to adjust the schedule to compensate for having Edda and Abe off the roll, at least for a few days.

It pleased—and relieved—her that not a single soul she shifted around complained.

After begging a container of chicken soup from the Dining Hall kitchen, she made the trip out to see Abe and

Edda. Heated the soup herself to make sure they ate, while Edda insisted she was fine.

Once Bodine got home—missing dinner yet again— she snagged the pork chop meal out of the warmer, settled down with it and her laptop to run a last check on the people she hoped to hire.

She ate with one hand, worked the keyboard with the other. And looked up with her mouth full when her mother came into the kitchen.

Bodine said, "Mmm."

"I thought I heard you come in. You oughtn't to work so late all the time, my baby."

Bodine swallowed. "Everything went to hell. I'm fixing it."

"You always do. I just got off the phone with Edda. She sounds a little tired, a little sheepish about it. I think I'm going to have some of that wine, too. She told me you went over there with soup, warmed it up for them."

On her way to get a glass, Maureen paused to kiss the top of Bodine's head. "You're a good girl."

"Scared me. She always seems so . . . sturdy. She's not going to need surgery, but she's got to take medication. And make some lifestyle changes. Diet, exercise."

"We'll see she takes better care of herself." After sitting, Maureen poured her wine, added a little more to Bodine's glass. "That goes for you, too. More sleep, regular meals. Ma and I—and your dad—didn't start up the Bodine Resort to see you work all day and half the night."

"Special circumstances."

"Aren't there always?" Maureen said in her placid way.

"No, really. But I'm working right here to smooth it out. I've got five people coming in tomorrow—I work fast—for interviews. And one more coming in the day after."

"Six? Jessie told me she was talking to Chelsea tomorrow. I have something to say there," Maureen added.

"I know she's Jane Lee Puckett's niece, and I know you and Mrs. Puckett go back."

"More than that, though that has weight. Jane Lee's been a sister to me since my own . . . since my own took off the day after my wedding and broke our mother's heart."

Maureen took a deep sip of wine, then a deep breath. "She's family. I won't remind you she changed your diapers, and Chase's and Rory's come to that, the same as I changed her children's. That's family, and that matters."

"I know that, Mom."

Maureen simply aimed a look—the one that could, and did, shoot down any protest, explanation, or excuse. "That's not all I have to say about it. Chelsea's smart and bright and well-mannered. She gave up a good job to come back home when her family needed her. That's quality. So it seems to me you'd be foolish not to hire her."

She held up a hand before Bodine could speak. "It's your decision to make. We put you in charge because you're smart and bright, and fairly well-mannered yourself. And you not only wanted it, you worked for it. But that's what I have to say about it."

"I think it's important that Jessica interview her, and have some serious say in anyone we hire to work with her."

"That's why you're in charge, too. Because you're right about that. I expect Jessie's no fool, and won't disprove that with Chelsea. Five more?"

"Waitstaff, housekeeping, a horseman, and a masseuse. We don't necessarily need the extra at Zen Town right now, but it would give her time to learn how we do things. And I liked her application. The others are necessary, most especially the housekeeping and horses. In fact, I could use another qualified instructor for the ring, as Abe's taking some time now to tend to Edda, and that's just what he should do. I could ask Maddie to come in once or twice a week, just for lessons, but I worry she'd overdo something."

"Try her once a week, and make it clear you'll boot her if she overdoes anything or gets on a horse."

"That's a good compromise." One she'd have come up with if her brain hadn't been on overload all day. "Callen took Abe's lessons again today. I walked in at the tail end of one yesterday, and was surprised at how good he was at it. I never thought of him as a teacher."

"Hidden depths?" Maureen smiled. "He was never as wild as some wanted to think. And Cal was one of the some."

"Maybe. I was more impressed with his horse, a young buckskin gelding. He does tricks."

"I heard about that, but I'd like to see for myself."

"I asked him to think about doing some performances at the BAC paddock. Adults would love it, and kids would go crazy for it."

"You're always thinking, Bo."

"It's why I'm the boss."

The next morning, Bodine met with the housekeeper applicant at nine sharp. She liked what she saw, what she heard, so she called one of the housekeeping staff in to give the applicant a tour of an empty cabin.

"Beth will bring you back when you're done. Come see me after, Yvonne, tell me what you think."

Bodine shifted from her office to the Dining Hall, where her manager was interviewing a hopeful waiter. The applicant looked younger than his twenty-one years. He wore a white dress shirt with a string tie tight around his nervously bobbing Adam's apple.

Their longest-running waitress sat across from him, arms folded, gaze narrowed. "We do things a certain way around here, and that way is work. Don't have a table to serve, you bus another. Things are slow, you do setup, fill condiments. What you don't do is lollygag."

"I'm a hard worker, ma'am."

"Maybe you are, maybe you aren't. I show lollygaggers the door right quick. Why do you want to work here?"

"I need a good job, ma'am, to save up to go back to school, get my college degree."

"Why do you have to go back? Why aren't you still there?"

He flushed a little, face turning pink under his straw-colored hair. "My folks helped out as much as they could, and I worked at the Bigsby Café, like it says in my résumé. But it's costly, and I need to work, save up, to go back and finish. The Bodine Resort's a fine place to work, and it's closer to home than Missoula."

Bodine saw Carrie Ann soften, but doubted the poor boy did. "Did you keep your grades up?"

"Oh, yes, ma'am."

"What're you studying?"

"I'm majoring in education. I want to teach. Elementary level. I . . ." He flushed deeper. "I want to help form and inform young minds."

"Is that so?"

"Yes, ma'am."

Carrie Ann let out one of her *harrumphs*, cut her gaze toward Bodine. "I'm going to take you over to the Feed Bag, show you some ropes. You don't prove to be an idiot, you'll come back here and talk to Sylvia in HR about your paperwork."

"Uh—I— Are you hiring me on?"

"Unless you prove to be an idiot. Get your coat on. It's cold out."

She rose, walked over to Bodine. "He'll do."

"I'll tell Sylvia to be ready for him."

When she started off to do just that, she ran into Jessica coming out. "Bo, perfect. I want you to meet Chelsea."

"We've met," Chelsea said.

Bodine studied the pretty, doe-eyed brunette. "I'm sorry, I don't remember. I know your aunt and uncle."

"I had my thirteenth birthday party here. You took us on our trail ride. I got my first real kiss from a boy I thought I'd marry and have six kids with after that ride, so it sticks in my memory."

"What happened to the boy?"

"It turned out he just liked kissing girls, something my thirteen-year-old self didn't understand or appreciate."

"It's nice to see you again."

"Bodine." Jessica put an arm around Chelsea's shoulder. "I love her. I want her for my own."

"I don't think you mean you just like kissing girls, so I'm assuming you're hired, Chelsea."

"Thank you, both of you. I want you to take note I'm not jumping up and down and squealing, which demonstrates my maturity and decorum. Because inside, I'm doing just that. Oh! And there went a cartwheel!"

That got a laugh out of Bodine.

"I really want to work here. I really think I can do good, creative work here."

Chelsea paused when Rory strolled toward them with another man at his side.

"Looks like the Beautiful Women Club's in session," Rory said.

"My brother Rory—sales and marketing. This is Chelsea Wasserman."

"You're Jane Lee's niece." Rory shot out a hand. "She always says how pretty you are, but I figured she was being a doting aunt."

"Chelsea's coming on as an assistant in events," Jessica told him. "So you'll be seeing more of her."

"Glad to hear it. Oh, Bo, this is Esau LaFoy. Sal said you've got him down for your ten o'clock."

"Yes, I do."

"I'm just a little early. I'd be happy waiting out in the lobby until you're finished and ready for me."

He wasn't much older than the new waiter, Bodine mused, but she didn't think he'd blush. His eyes, a hazel that edged toward green, stayed steady and respectful.

"No need for that. Come on into my office." She gestured, led the way.

Though they had some wear on them, he'd shined up his boots. He also wore clean Levi's with a Western-style checkered shirt, a fleece-lined denim jacket, and a black ridge top hat, which he took off, politely, and set in his lap when he took the chair she offered.

"So, Esau, you're from the Garnet area."

"I am, like my daddy, and his daddy before him. Most call me Easy, Miss Longbow."

"Easy. You've done some traveling."

"Here and there. I followed the rodeo awhile, picked up ranch work when I needed. The names I gave you in that file you got there will tell you I know how to work, and I know horses."

"Why did you give up the rodeo circuit?"

"The fact is, I couldn't much afford to keep with it. It's costly if you don't hit in the money regular, and I took a couple of hard spills. On that, my pa's getting older, and

I come to realize if I got laid up, he wouldn't have anybody to help him out when he needed. We got a few acres some south of Garnet. He's a tough bird, and takes pride in it, but in some years, maybe he won't be able to do all he does."

"The work here can be sporadic during the winter season. You might not get forty hours a week."

"I'll take what I can get."

"Do you have your own mount?"

"Not right now, as I had to sell him off. I could maybe get one if you want."

He smiled when he said it, showing a chip in his left incisor and a kind of dopey, affable charm.

He has a good face, Bodine thought. A little tough, a little weathered, like a lot of cowboys who spent hours in the saddle, under the sun, in the wind. He kept his hands still. They showed the kinds of calluses she expected from someone who worked with horses.

She'd already had a background check run, and he'd come up clean. High school dropout, but as he'd said, and those in his file confirmed, he knew horses.

"It's not required for you to have your own mount. We have our stock, and we bring on more in the spring. Have you ever taught horsemanship?"

He opened his mouth, shut it again, and took his time. "I want the job, so it's hard to say no. I can't say I've spent much time showing anybody how to ride. Was a girl I met in Abilene I showed some riding to, but that was for fun like. Mostly people I've spent my time with know."

She couldn't call him the brightest bulb in the lamp on the basis of the interview, but he struck her as polite, honest, and amiable enough.

And she was in a bind.

"It's more than working with horses, tending tack,

feeding, and grooming. We cater to our guests, and some won't have been on a horse before, or not in years. Trail rides are popular, and those who lead guests out have to learn themselves: How to match the horse and rider, how to watch on the trail to make sure a guest who doesn't know a horse from a giraffe doesn't get into trouble—and has a good experience."

"Horses are easier to figure than people, but people aren't that hard, seems to me, if you pay attention."

"I can't argue with that. Why don't we go over to the Equestrian Center, you can have a look at that part of the operation, and we'll meet up with our head horseman."

He rose. "I'd be pleased to."

CHAPTER FIVE

Bodine managed to get home in time for dinner, avoiding Clementine's wrath and spending the best part of an hour filling her family in on the new hires while they ate.

"You rounded up a lot in one day," Sam commented, sipping at his nightly after-dinner two fingers of whisky.

"One more tomorrow, but every one of the hires wanted the job, presented well, and passed muster with the respective managers." She glanced at Chase. "With Abe out, I had Callen take a look at LaFoy."

"He'd know what to look at."

"LaFoy." Sam frowned in thought. "I don't think I know any of that name around here."

"He's from around Garnet."

"Can't place the name."

"Well, we'll see how he works out, but before I left him with Callen, I had a good look myself. How he handled himself, handled the horses, interacted with Callen and Ben, who was working at the time. Before I left them I told Callen to let me know if he had any reservations.

Since he didn't, I hired LaFoy. And I took your advice, Mom, and talked to Maddie about doing a weekly lesson."

"I think that's going to work out fine. And I'm happy you liked Chelsea. She's going to be an asset, you mark my words."

"I did like her. Jessie, on the other hand, loved her. And I liked that she stayed on for a couple hours, getting her feet wet. Shows initiative."

"You told us Mrs. Puckett's niece was smart," Rory put in. "You didn't tell us she was hot. Really hot."

"Down, boy," Bodine muttered even as Maureen wagged a finger.

"You keep your hands and your charming self to yourself, Rory Carter Longbow."

"But my charm, it just can't be contained."

"I've got plenty of rope in the barn to hog-tie it if we need to." Chase finished the meal as he'd started the day, with black coffee. "I ought to let you know I talked with Abe this evening."

"How's Edda?" Bodine asked.

"She's doing all right, but this whole business scared him. He's thinking of taking Edda to visit with their son and his family for a week or so over Thanksgiving. And he's thinking about spending a couple weeks with their daughter for Christmas."

"He didn't say anything like that to me," Bodine began.

"Well, let me finish it out. It seems their kids are pushing for it, and more yet, it came clear to him that once he comes back to work, she's going to do the same. He says he doesn't see a way to stop her. He wants her to have a good stretch of time first, and this, and the trip to Arizona would do that."

"I can understand that, but—"

"He came to me before you," Chase went on in his

quiet steamroller style, "because he wanted to know if I was clear with you putting Cal on in his place, since we hired Cal for the ranch and it wouldn't just be here and there, or filling a hole now and then, but full-time managing until spring."

"Yes, but—"

Chase just lifted a finger, which had Bodine rolling her eyes.

"What I said was this: Cal's an asset here. But the way things are, he'd be a bigger asset to the resort, so— and Dad agrees—we're fine with letting you have him through the winter if that's what works. On the condition that that's what Cal wants, too, as it's not what he was hired on for."

Bodine waited, exaggerating the pause. "That it?"

"Yeah."

"Do I have any say in it?"

Chase shrugged. "Your say comes in after, seems to me. If we said no, we're keeping Cal here, that would be that. If Cal says no thanks, you hired me for this not that, same thing. So your say comes in after that's settled one way or the other."

Bodine drummed her fingers on the table. "And what did Cal have to say about it?"

"Haven't gotten to that, as I talked to Abe then got called in to dinner. I figured to run it by him in the morning."

"I'll do the running by, thanks all the same."

"Fine with me. Don't know why you'd get your back up about it."

In answer, Bodine put on her sweetest—and scariest— smile. "I'll explain it then. Abe should have come to me, as I'm being asked to hold two key positions open from November until April. That's one. He should have come to me to discuss whether I approved taking Callen Skinner as my full-time horse manager from now till April—which is just what you should've told him. Then I decide on all that before—*if* I decide yes—I come to you and Dad and ask if you can let me have Cal for this length of time. Given that's yes, I ask Callen if he'd agree to that."

Chase shrugged again. "Looks to me like we got to the same point, and maybe a little quicker."

"Quicker's not the point." Frustrated, and a little insulted, Bodine threw up her hands. "The ranch and the resort are separate entities. That was the smart and practical decision made back when Nana decided to expand the dude ranch. There's paperwork involved, a salary to negotiate, a job description, a contract."

"You'd have all that either way," Chase pointed out.

"Aw, Bo's just steamed up because Abe came to you instead of her."

Maureen aimed a cool look at her younger son. "She's right to be. The men may outnumber the women at this table, but that doesn't give you more weight. And right is right. Abe should have gone to his boss, and that's Bo. I'm going to attribute that mistake to his stress and worry over Edda. I hope you'll do the same, Bodine, and give him some understanding on it."

Anger deflated, a little. "I can. I do. But—"

"The ranch and the resort are like you say." Sam continued to sip his whisky. "They're separate. Your grandmother was smart enough to see, all those years back, that your uncles weren't going to be able to put in all the time and work needed to run a ranch of this size, and none of their boys—or girls"—he added with a glance at his wife—"showed any interest. So she worked up the dude ranch, saw how she could draw on that and keep the working ranch."

He took his time, sipped his whisky. Not a person sitting at the table would have thought to interrupt.

"Then after I came into it, she put her head together with her mother and yours, and came up with big plans. No question we've got smart, forward-thinking women in this family, and we have two business enterprises that provide us with the life we want to live, in the place we want to live it. And they both honor your granddaddy's memory. But they're not just business enterprises, and we're never going to forget that."

"No, sir," Bodine said. "I don't forget that."

"I know you don't, though there are times I miss seeing you around, in the paddocks, in the stable, in the barn. A man can miss his girl."

"Daddy."

"He can miss her and be proud at the same time. What we can't forget, and don't, is what we have, what we've made—starting with your grandmother—is a community, and a family. Abe's worried about his wife, and doing everything he can to take care of her—whether or not she wants it. And knowing Edda, she's put up some fight over it. I don't think he meant any disrespect to you by talking it out with Chase first."

"He probably didn't." But Bodine still aimed a stare at Chase.

"I just talked to the man, and now I've told you what's what. You just let me know what you decide."

"I'll do that." She rose. "I'm going to take a walk, figure out how to handle all this."

Rory waited until Bodine was safely out of earshot. "Jeez, what's the big deal? *Mucho sensitivo*. It's just—"

He broke off and withered under his mother's stare. "Until you work in a man's world without a penis, you can

hush about it. You can think about that while you help
Clementine clear and wash up."

"Yes, ma'am."

Within five minutes, Chase sat alone with his father at
the table. "I just talked to the man," Chase said again.
"And I'm offering to let her have, if he's agreeable, our
best horseman—one we just acquired—for a solid four
months."

"It's a balancing act, son. Women, business, family. It's
all a balancing act. How about you and me go out on the
front porch, smoke a couple of cigars, and complain about
women? Doing that now and again helps the balance."

"I'll get my coat."

Bundled in her own coat, Bodine walked off the lingering mad in the cold, clear air. Overhead, the countless
sweep of stars shimmered as pinprick lights in an indigo
sky. The moon, nearly full, sailed—a round, white ship
over quiet seas.

The air around her moved briskly, carrying the scent
of pine and snow and animal. She heard a cow low, an
owl call, saw the slinking shadow of one of the barn cats.

The two happy mutts, Clyde and Chester, raced around
her for a while; then, since she didn't seem interested in
play, they raced off to find their own fun.

As the mad cleared, she used the room to lay out a plan
for what to do next. She'd need to speak to Abe and Edda,
and since her father was right about community and family, she needed to rid herself of resentment before she
did. Once rid of it, she still needed to make it clear that
the buck started and stopped with her.

She'd need to make one of the housekeeping staff temporary head. Otherwise, she'd end up dealing with the
scheduling and minor issues every week. Potentially daily.

And she needed to prepare herself, to have another plan waiting in the event that two of her key people decided to retire altogether rather than come back.

The idea made her sad, just sad. Abe and Edda had been key staff at her grandmother's early incarnation of the dude ranch, and had stuck with them through all of the changes, all of the expansions.

She could and would find qualified replacements, if necessary. But they wouldn't be Abe and Edda, and for some reason, accepting that made her feel lonely as well as sad.

She turned toward the stables instead of the shack. Callen could wait a bit longer.

After unlatching the big door, she walked inside, inside the scents of horses, hay, manure, grain, liniment, and leather.

As she walked down the wide, slanted concrete, some equine heads on either side poked out from their stalls. Some blew a greeting, but she continued on where one was watching her, waiting for her.

"Hey there. There's my boy." She rubbed the cheeks of the Appaloosa she called Leo due to the leopard spots over his white hide.

He butted his head against her shoulder, looking at her with his sweet, fascinating blue eyes.

A man could miss his girl, she thought. A horse could miss his girl, too.

"I'm sorry. I haven't been around much, I haven't been paying attention. The last couple weeks . . ."

She shook her head, went inside the stall, took up a brush to run it over his flanks.

"No excuses. Not between us. You know what? Tomorrow we'll ride to work. You can visit the resort horses for the day, and we'll have a good, strong morning ride. And a good, strong ride home again tomorrow night. I've missed you, too."

She pulled a carrot out of the pocket Leo was nibbling at. "You always know. Just don't tell anybody."

While he crunched, she laid her head on his neck. "I'll figure it out, right? I've got it half figured already. I'd still like to boot Chase in the ass, but I've got it half figured."

She gave Leo a couple of quick rubs. "I'll see you in the morning. Bright and early, too."

Since the idea of a good, strong ride pleased her, she wandered out of the stables, scratching a few more heads on the way, before aiming her steps toward the shack.

Small, rustic with its cedar shakes and little front porch, it stood a muscular stone's throw from the main house, and an enthusiastic spit from the bunkhouse.

Originally it had been built with its peaked roof and square windows for the dude ranch. A few other cabins that once were scattered through the trees had been scrapped for supplies in the building of the resort. But they'd kept the shack, for the occasional overnight guest, for storage, as a very unofficial playhouse.

And now for Callen Skinner.

A horseshoe knocker graced the barn-style front door, but Bodine used her knuckles to knock while she watched the smoke pump out of the chimney on the bunkhouse side of the shack.

Callen pulled the door open, stood in the backwash of light. He said, "Howdy, neighbor."

"Howdy back. Got a minute?"

"Got plenty of them. Did you eat yet?"

"Yeah, I just . . . Oh." When she stepped in, she saw the plate on the table. "You're eating. We can do this later."

"Nothing wrong with now." To prove it, he shut the door behind her. "Want a beer?"

"No, I'm good."

He crossed back to the table, picked up a remote, and switched off the old black-and-white movie on the TV.

It was a small, efficient space, holding the kitchen and living areas, which had been spruced up nice enough by her mother. The bedroom rayed off the kitchen with a bathroom so tiny she wondered how he managed to shower without banging his elbows and knees.

"You going to sit?"

"I really hate to interrupt your dinner."

"You won't if you sit and talk while I eat it. Take off your coat. The stove keeps it warm enough."

The little potbelly in the corner did its job, Bodine thought, tossing her coat on the back of the living room chair.

She sat across from him at the square two-seater table. "You cook?"

He cut a bite from a fried-up rib eye. "Enough to get by. I could've had dinner in the bunkhouse, but I had some things I wanted to get done."

A folder sat beside him, closed now.

"Just in the neighborhood?" he asked her.

"As it happens. I like this neighborhood."

"Me, too."

"You didn't get in touch to tell me LaFoy was no damn good, so I hired him."

"You said to get in touch if he was no damn good, and he didn't strike me that way. He's good with the horses, knows his way around, appears to listen when you talk to him, and got on fine with everybody else when we toured around. We had a couple come by just to look at the horses with their preschooler. He was polite and personable. I figured that did the trick, though I wouldn't say he's sharp as an average tack."

"Well, I had the same take, so that's good enough." She sat back, sighed. "Here's the thing, Skinner. It seems Abe's not coming back until spring. He's worried about Edda, wants to keep her from doing much for a while, so he's taking her to spend time with family here and there, to keep her occupied."

Listening, Callen sawed off more steak. "Sounds like a good idea, considering."

"We talked about you going back and forth, filling in, filling in more come January, but that's not going to work now."

"You need to plug that hole all the way."

"I do. Dad and Chase both say if you want to switch over to the resort for the winter, that's fine with them. If you want, you and I can talk about salary, as you'd move off the ranch books officially and onto the resort's until Abe comes back. If you don't want that, as you came here to work the ranch's horses, that's fine, too. If that's the case, I'd just like you to keep filling in until I can hire somebody to plug that hole."

He scooped up some mashed potatoes, washed them down with beer. Said, "Hmm."

"I've been doing the scheduling for that area and for housekeeping since Edda got sick. I can pull from the staff I have to fill the housekeeping position, but I can't pull from the BAC and Equestrian Center for a horse manager. Even if Maddie wasn't pregnant, she's not a manager. Not yet anyway. And I don't think she much wants to be. So I'd have to go outside for it. I can do that if you don't want to take it on."

He ate some, thought some. "Can you lay out the details? Salary, yeah, but duties, responsibilities, what kind of autonomy's involved if it's official? Temporary, but official."

"Absolutely." It set her mind at ease he'd ask rather than jump to either yes or no. "If you give me your e-mail address, I can send it all to you. In writing."

"You can have my e-mail." He rattled it off. "But if you don't have every detail inside that head of yours I'll eat my hat. And I like wearing it."

She considered a moment. "Beer in there?" She wagged a thumb at the refrigerator, then waved him down before he could stand to get it for her.

She pulled out a Moosehead, popped the top in the open mouth of the bull bottle opener on the wall. And took a long sip.

"I like beer." She took another pull. "I like wine fine, but, boy, there's nothing like a cold beer."

She sat, and ran through the job description, the duties, the responsibilities, the expectations, who reported to whom, the liabilities, the resort policies.

It was a long list. She paused, drank more beer.

"Are you sure you don't want this in an e-mail?"

"I've got it. Most of it makes sense."

She intended to send the e-mail anyway.

When she named the salary, he ate more steak, mulled it over.

"Seems fair enough."

"Good. Do you want to take some time to think about it?"

"Just want to clear it with Sam and Chase."

"I told you they'd cleared it already."

"You did. But you didn't hire me on here, they did. I'd like to get their go-ahead in person. Since I expect they'll give it, just as you said, I don't need any time. I'll take you up on it. Though it causes me some hardship for a few months."

"Hardship? How?"

Taking a pull of his beer, he gave her a long study over the bottle, gray eyes assessing. "Well, it's a tricky business to make a move on you when you're my boss. Sister and daughter of my bosses, tricky enough, but doable. Straight-up boss, that's something that'll take some figuring out."

She eyed him over her own beer. "We've both got too much to do for you to be putting any moves on me—or for me to have to dance around them."

"Never too much to do for that." He gave her an amused and considering study. "How good a dancer are you?"

"I'm very light and quick on my feet, Skinner. And I really need this to work, so don't complicate it."

"It's not my fault you grew up so damn pretty. How about this: You and me make a date. First of May, that's a good day. Spring's come around, and you won't be my boss anymore. I'll take you dancing, Bodine."

The fire crackled in the old potbelly, a reminder of heat and flame.

"You know, Callen, if you'd given me that flirtatious look and that smooth talk when I was twelve going on thirteen, my heart would've just stumbled right out of my chest. I had such a crush on you."

Now his grin didn't flash. The smile came slow and silky. "Is that so?"

"Oh my, yes. You with your skinny build, half-wild ways, and broody eyes were the object of my desperate affection and awakening hormones for weeks. Maybe even a few months, though at the time it seemed like years."

She gestured with her beer. "The fact that you and Chase considered me a nuisance at best only added to the secret longing."

"I expect we were mean to you half the time."

"No, I can't say you were. You crushed my adolescent heart with mild disdain, which is just how boys of fourteen and fifteen look on girls of twelve. And like a girl of twelve with a first crush, I got over it."

"I had more than a couple moments of interest in your direction when you hit about fifteen."

Surprised, she took a slow sip of beer and decided to use his own words. "Is that so?"

"You took your time blooming, but you got it right. I noticed that." He rose, got himself another beer, held up a second in offer. She shook her head. "Hard not to notice, or squash the interest. But that would've put me at, what, about eighteen. And at eighteen I was already thinking about when I'd light out and make my fortune. Added to it, you were my best friend's little sister."

"That's never going to change."

"But you're not so little anymore. And that three years or so difference between us, that doesn't matter once you grow up. Plus, I'm back."

"Did you make your fortune, Callen?"

"I did well enough. More, I did what I needed to do. I learned what I needed to learn. Now I'm back, and for good."

When her eyebrow winged up, he shook his head.

"I'm done lighting out, done needing to. This is my land. It's not about the owning of it, but waking up in the morning knowing you're where you want to be, having good work to do and good people around you."

His words struck a chord with her. "You lost most of the broody."

"A good part of the pissed off, too, seeing as they went pretty much hand in hand. Now, about that date."

With a half laugh, she set down the beer and rose. "I'll send you the week's schedule. It'll change because some guests wait until they're here to book a riding lesson or a trail ride—and the sleigh rides we'll have going starting next week."

She walked over, shrugged into her coat. "If you have any questions about how to work it, shoot me an e-mail back. Or come into my office."

"That's not a yes or no on the first of May."

She smiled. "It isn't, is it? Thanks for the beer," she added, and strolled out.

On a low chuckle, Callen patted a hand over his heart. One of the biggest appeals, to his way of thinking, of a sassy, contrary woman—especially one with a good, sharp brain—was the challenge presented.

He'd never been able to resist a challenge.

By the time Billy Jean rang up the last tab and finished the routine closing of the Saloon, her feet were barking like her mother's irascible Jack Russell terrier.

She looked forward to getting off them, sliding into bed even if it was alone, since she'd shown her boyfriend (cheating, lying, no-good bastard) the door a few days before.

More, she looked forward to adding the night's tips to her Red Dress Fund.

She'd found it while doing some online shopping and had fallen in lust. She visited it in her shopping cart every day; and by her calculations, tonight's tips would allow her to click Buy.

One hundred and forty nine dollars and ninety-nine cents.

A lot of money for a dress, she thought as she shut off the lights. But not for *this* dress. Plus, it was a reward for hard work, and a symbol of her new status as a single woman.

She'd wear that red dress her next night off, maybe head on down to the Roundup for some drinking and dancing. Then they'd see what's what, she decided, with lingering bitter thoughts of her ex.

She wandered out into the cold. Heard the crunch of her boots on the gravel stir up the quiet. She'd let the last group of customers linger a little longer than she should have. But those tips, those tips added up.

And she could sleep half the morning if she wanted.

She just loved working the last shift.

She got into her car—a secondhand compact SUV she'd be paying off for what right then seemed forever. But it got her where she wanted to go and back again.

She headed away from what they called Bodine Town, with its restaurants and shops and offices, wound her way on the unpaved roads, snaking by woods and dark cabins, onto the bumpy corrugation that jostled her kidneys and made her wish she'd stopped in the ladies' before she'd locked up.

But once she got to the paved road, she could hit the gas. Her little car could move like a jackrabbit, and at this time of night, the road would be clear as a summer morning.

About fifteen minutes, she told herself, and she'd be home.

Then her car bucked, made a couple of coughing noises, and died.

"Well, goddamn it! Goddamn it, what is this!"

Snarling, she turned the key, pumped the gas. And when nothing happened, smacked the wheel.

What the hell was she supposed to do now?

She sat a moment, eyes closed, until she could gather herself. After slamming out of the car, she yanked up the hood. Cursing again, she stomped back to grab a flashlight out of her glove compartment.

She could change a tire—and had. She knew how to add water to a radiator, gas to the tank, and check battery cables. Other than that, she might have been staring at a rocket engine.

She left the hood up, paced over to kick the front tire before digging her phone out of the purse she'd left on the front seat.

Her first instinct was to call Chad—the cheating, lying, no-good ex. Then she remembered they were exes. She considered calling one of her divorced parents, but neither of them lived that close by.

She toyed with doing a search for a twenty-four-hour road service or calling her friend Sal. Sal was closer, but—

She heard an engine, saw the swish of headlights, and thought: Thank God!

When the truck slowed down, stopped behind her car, Billy Jean hurried over to the driver's window.

He said, "Looks like you need some help."

She gave him her best smile. "I'd sure appreciate it."

— *1992* —

Another Thanksgiving came and went. Alice knew the days by squares and numbers on the calendar. He hadn't taken that way—yet. She marked time by it, and tried, tried so hard to imagine herself at home, around the big table in the dining room.

Ma making two big turkeys—one for the ranch hands. If she tried hard enough, she could smell it scenting the kitchen. Grandpa would grill beef, too, and Grammy would glaze a ham. Her favorite.

And all the trimmings, too. Mashed potatoes and

sweet potatoes with marshmallows, green beans, brussels sprouts—*not* her favorite. Biscuits and gravy.

She'd make the cranberry sauce. She liked watching the berries pop as they boiled up. Reenie would make deviled eggs. They took time, and too much patience.

And just when you thought you couldn't eat another bite? All those pies!

She imagined herself as a little girl, sitting beside her sister at the kitchen table, making little tarts with the leftover pie dough.

Ma humming as she rolled out more.

But even as Alice's lips curved, the images wouldn't stick. They flickered and faded away until she was lying on the cot in that terrible room, the irons heavy on her leg, and her arms empty.

He'd taken her baby.

Though her milk had dried up—painfully—the phantom ache in her breasts remained, a terrible reminder.

She escaped into sleep—what else did she have? In sleep she tried to go back home. Thanksgiving turkey, riding a fast horse while the sky exploded with sunset light.

Would she ever see the sun again?

Putting on lipstick, buying a new dress. Lying out under the summer stars with a boy who wanted her.

Would anyone ever touch her with care and sweetness again?

She willed herself into her bedroom. Pink walls and movie-star posters, the windows bringing the sky and mountains to her.

But when she opened her eyes, her reality weighed like lead on her soul. Four dull walls, a concrete floor, and a locked door at the top of a set of steep steps.

No, she'd never see the sun again, its rise or its fall. Her world had no window to bring it to her.

No one would ever touch her with care or sweetness. Because only Sir existed. Only Sir, who pounded into her every night. And when she screamed because her body hadn't healed from childbirth, he pounded harder and slapped her into silence.

She'd never see her bedroom again, so pink and pretty, or sit around the big table at the ranch and share Thanksgiving dinner with her family.

She'd never hold her little baby girl again. Her Cora with the tiny pink fingers and toes.

The loss of it all, the emptiness inside her at the loss of a child she hadn't believed she'd wanted and had loved so much, so quickly, smeared every thought like fetid smoke.

She ate because when she refused, he poured soup down her throat, dragging her head back by the hair, pinching her nostrils closed. She washed because when she stopped, he beat her and scrubbed her with cold water and a hard brush until her skin broke and bled.

She begged for her baby. She'd be good, she'd take care, she'd do anything if he gave her baby back to her.

She's somebody else's problem now.

That's what he'd told her. He had no use for daughters.

She hoped he'd beat her to death, but he seemed to know just how far he could go.

He wouldn't let her die as she wanted. Just let her die, let her slide away into sleep where she could sit on the front porch rocker, looking at the mountains while she sang to her baby.

If she'd had something sharp, she'd have used it to slit her own throat. No, no, his first, she thought—all but dreamed—lying on the cot, eyes shut tight so she didn't have to see her prison.

Yes, she'd kill him first, then herself.

She wondered if she could somehow sharpen one of the plastic spoons he brought her with her meals. Or her toothbrush. Maybe her toothbrush.

She could try, she would try, but God, she was just so tired.

She only wanted to sleep.

As her mind drifted she imagined tearing up her sheet, making a noose. There was nothing to hang it on, but maybe if she tied it to one of the steps, wrapped it tight enough around her neck, she could choke herself.

She couldn't go on this way, couldn't wake day after day, night after night in this terrible place, knowing he'd come down those stairs.

Worse, even worse than the brutality, the rapes, were all the endless hours of aloneness. An aloneness that grew deeper, wider, blacker, without her child.

She made herself get up, studied the sheet with dull, listless eyes.

Should she tear it into strips, braid the pieces? Would that make it stronger for what she needed?

So hard to concentrate when every thought had to fight through a fog. She toyed with the sheet, looking for weak spots, easy-to-tear spots.

The concept of killing herself seemed no more frightening than solving a routine math problem.

Even less so.

But she had to wait, she reminded herself. He'd come down soon. Wait until after he leaves again. Killing herself might take some time.

Today, she thought with a tired sigh. She could die today.

Escape.

She stood again, but this time the room swayed.

No, she realized, she swayed. And her stomach pitched.

She barely made it to the toilet, dropping to her knees as that pitching stomach emptied.

Clammy, queasy, she caught her breath, sicked up more.

Tears came as she curled on the floor, breathless, shivering. Tears of grief, and a strange kind of joy.

She heard the locks *thunk*. Heard his boot steps—heavy, heavy.

Shoving herself up, bracing on the sink, as her head still spun a little, she faced him.

She found her hate again as the long fog lifted into a terrible clarity.

Placing a hand on her belly, still saggy and loose from giving birth, she found a reason to live again.

"I'm pregnant," she told him.

He nodded. "It best be a son this time. Now clean yourself up, and eat your breakfast."

CHAPTER SIX

— Present Day —

In the apple-crisp morning, with the eastern sky abloom with rose and gold, Bodine shouldered her briefcase and strode toward the stables.

She heard the chickens humming the way they did while Chester and Clyde had their morning wrestling match outside the bunkhouse. The dogs broke off their tumbling to race to her, tongues lolling, eyes bright—as if they hadn't seen her in a month.

Nothing much started the day off with a laugh like a couple of madly happy dogs, so she rubbed and scratched them into insanity until they picked up their wrestling match.

She waved to a couple of out-and-about ranch hands, spoke casually to a couple more busy mucking stalls in the stables.

She stopped short when she saw Callen in his sheepskin jacket, comfortably worn boots, and dung-brown Stetson settling a saddle on the impressive Sundown's back.

"Going for a ride?" she asked him.

He glanced over. "Sundown needs to stretch his legs, and I can use him at the resort today."

"He's an asset. He can go on the books, too, if you want."

"No need for that." While Callen cinched the saddle, the horse turned his head, nipped the hat off Callen's head. "What have I told you about that?"

Sundown merely stuck his head over the low door, offering Bodine the hat.

"Why, thank you. It's a nice hat."

"It won't be, if he keeps playing with it. Something you need?"

"I've got what I need, and that's a horse of my own who needs to stretch his legs. I'm riding to work this morning."

"It's a good morning for it. I'll wait for you. We might as well ride over together. Can I have my hat back, boss?"

She passed it over to him as she turned to walk to Leo's stall. Heard Callen's frustrated "Now, cut that out."

As she saddled Leo, she wondered if she could teach him a couple of tricks. With his fondness for carrots and peppermint treats, bribery could work.

She heard the stable hands hooting with laughter. When she led Leo out, she saw why.

Sundown sat on the concrete run with the patient air of a man taking a break in an easy chair, while Callen leaned against the stall door, scrolling through his phone.

"That horse beats all, Cal," one of the hands called out. "He beats all to hell and back."

Callen looked over, smiled at Bodine. "Ready?"

"I am. Are you?"

Callen pushed off the door, took Sundown's reins. "Let's get going." The horse pushed to his feet with the same indolent ease as his owner.

After a short study, a little nose snorting, the horses apparently deemed each other acceptable.

In the stable yard, Bodine swung into the saddle. "I had a route in mind, one that'll give Leo a good run."

"That'll work."

They started at a walk, warming muscles, as the light brightened and the sky blurred from rose to blue. The crisp air moved in the light wind, fluttering over her face, smelling like a winter potpourri of snow and pine.

"Did you get a chance to look at the schedule?" Bodine asked him.

"Yep. I see the farrier's coming around tomorrow, and the vet the day after. I'll make myself known to them. The new man's starting this morning, so I'll keep an eye on him, see if we were right about taking him on."

"Next week's Thanksgiving."

"I heard that."

"We get a lot of groups and families over that long weekend. I thought we might try out that little show, if you're agreeable. Nothing we'd advertise off-site, just a little bonus for people already here."

"I guess we can see how it goes."

"I'll schedule it."

They rode down an incline, across a narrow ravine, and up again where a herd of deer slipped silent as spirits through the woods. The tops of the lodgepoles whooshed in the wind.

"Time to stretch those legs." Bodine nudged Leo into a gallop.

Cold slapped her cheeks as Leo's hooves rang over the road. He kept his ears up, his head high, showing her he enjoyed the ride as much as she. Callen rode beside her, his horse matching Leo's stride as if harnessed in tandem.

When the road forked, Bodine turned right, slowing to a canter, then an easy trot. Reveling in the ride, the air, the morning, she tossed her long braid over her shoulder and decided she wanted more.

"We can take the trail up and around." She gestured to the track through the trees marked by the Bodine shamrock brand. "It's a pretty winter ride, and it'll take us to another good stretch before we split off."

"Lead the way. Chase and I rode these trails now and then as boys, when your father cut him loose for a couple hours. I remember when you added those cabins we just passed."

"It's quiet enough you can forget they're there."

They wound up where the snow was piled thick and clung like white fur to branches. Off the trail she spotted signs of deer and fox in prints and scat. "You can just smell the smoke," she added, "from the cabins where guests are up and have a fire going. But mostly, it's just air."

"Why'd you take the office instead of the horses?"

"I'm good at it." She turned in her saddle, looking back at him. "I'm good at horses, but there are plenty who are good with horses. I like managing all the moving parts, making sure they run smooth day after day. Or making it seem like they do even if we're scrambling where the guests don't see. Also, I guess I like never knowing exactly what I might be dealing with on any given day, but making an agenda, clicking off the boxes so I know most of what's coming and can figure out the rest."

She turned back again as the track began its descent. "I do miss the horses, that everyday and anytime connection. I'm going to start riding to work more than I have been."

She gave Leo a pat on the neck. "Guests will get a kick out of seeing that—the general manager riding around. Sets a tone."

"Always thinking."

"Oh, I am."

Laughing, she swiveled around again as the horses stepped back onto the road. "My mind's a busy place, Skinner. I like riding and letting it empty out for a time. Are you up for another gallop?"

"Sugar, I'm always up for a gallop."

"I just bet you are." She shouted, *"Cha!"* and sent Leo racing. Once again, Callen had his horse matching her speed and rhythm.

She was glad she'd taken the long way, the roundabout way. It meant some doubling back, but she had the time.

On impulse, she took the turn away from Bodine Town.

Just a few minutes more before she aimed for the office, for the workday, for the agenda. Even as she told herself it was time to stop, time to turn back, she spotted a car stopped on the side of the road.

She thought little of it, nearly didn't stop.

She dropped to a trot. "We need to . . . Wait a minute. That looks like Billy Jean's car."

She walked her horse up to it. "It is her car."

"Who's Billy Jean?"

"She works at the Saloon. Bartender, server." Bodine dismounted. "She must've been working last night, I'd have to check. It looks like she had a breakdown."

Frowning, Bodine looked through the window and felt a stab of real alarm. "Her purse is on the seat. She wouldn't just leave her purse on the seat."

"Hold on." Callen dismounted, handed Bodine the reins of both horses, and walked around the car. Bodine yanked her phone out of her jacket, scrolled through for Billy Jean's number.

"Bo."

"Wait, wait, I'm calling her. Maybe she just . . ."

She trailed off as she heard the opening riff from Michael Jackson's hit. Billy Jean's signature song.

"That's her ring. That's her ring. What—"

"The phone's on the ground over here. And it looks like somebody's trampled through this snow, into the trees."

"She wouldn't do that." Though Bodine could see as clearly as Callen the disturbed snow and brush. Then she saw more.

Her gaze landed on the shape, the dark blue jacket barely an instant before Callen's did the same, but Bodine leaped and ran before he could grab her.

"Bo. Damn it. Wait."

"She's hurt. She's hurt."

He caught her, dragged her back. With snow up to their knees, they struggled until she got an arm loose enough to punch.

"Let go of me, you stupid son of a bitch. She's hurt."

With no choice, he clamped his arms around her. "She's past hurt, Bo. Stop it. Stop it now. You can't help her."

Fury and fear spewed through her like a sickness. "Get your hands off me. I swear, I'll kill you."

He only tightened his hold. "You can't touch her, do you hear me? It won't do any good and might do some harm. She's gone, Bo. She's gone."

Desperate, she fought him another few seconds, then stopped. Just stopped, with her breath tearing out, smoking away, her body quivering.

"I need to see. I won't touch her if . . . I need to see. Let me go."

He eased his hold, shifted so he was no longer blocking the body from her. "I'm sorry. I'm sorry, Bo."

"She . . ." *She's gone.* Callen's words echoed in her head, and the awful truth of them struck her heart, her guts. "She hit her head on that rock. She hit her head. There's a lot of blood. She . . . Let go. I'm all right. Let go."

When he released her, she kept her gaze on Billy Jean's face, took her phone out again. "Will you call nine-one-one, Callen?" Maybe her voice came out raw, but it came out steady. "You do that, and I'm going to get our security to—to—block off the road here. To block it off so nobody comes near."

"Let's go back to the road and do that."

"I'm not leaving her."

She had to think, to take steps, to do what came next. While it was too early—thank God—for guest check-ins or checkouts, many employees used this road to get to work if they lived off property.

She ordered security to block the road, both sides for half a mile, to everyone but law enforcement, called for a staff member to bring the keys to the closest unoccupied cabin.

"I don't think I should tell them why." Still knee-deep in the snow, Bodine stared at her phone. "I don't think I should do that yet. I should call my parents. They need to know, but . . . Billy Jean's parents, they live . . . near Helena. No, no."

She had to press the heel of her hand to her forehead, somehow shove the information out of her brain. "Her mother lives near Helena. They're divorced. Her father . . . I can't remember. She has a brother somewhere. In the navy. No, no, he's a marine."

When Callen said nothing, she snapped at him, "It's important."

"I know it is. I didn't know her, Bodine, but that doesn't mean I don't know it's important. The sheriff's on the way, and you can tell him how to contact her family."

"I need to talk to them." Everything inside her felt hot

and dry, just scorched. "She worked for us. She was one of us. I need to talk to them, too. Somebody was chasing her. You can see where . . ." She looked back, saw the trenches in the snow. Where someone had chased Billy Jean.

And where Callen had come after her, to stop her.

"I messed that up," she murmured. "I plowed right through, and I'd have grabbed on to her, moved her, if you hadn't stopped me. It's a crime scene, that's what it is. I know enough to know you're not supposed to go stomping around a crime scene."

"You saw a woman lying in the snow. You saw blood. You were thinking of her, not a damn crime scene."

Thinking of her—a friend, an employee, a woman with a rollicking laugh. And not thinking at all, Bodine admitted.

She couldn't allow herself to do that again.

"I'd've made it worse. It can always be worse, and I'd've made it worse." She had to take a long breath before she could look at him. When she did, she saw the bruise forming just under his right eye. "I'm sorry I hit you. I really am."

"You're not the first, I don't expect you'll be the last."

Still, she gave the bruise a light brush with her fingertip. "You can put some ice on it once we . . . The cabin. Need to get the keys once they bring them down to Mike— security. The police can use it if they need to. They'll need to get our statements, maybe talk to whoever saw her last before she left the Saloon."

Think, think, she ordered herself as her insides quivered. Make an agenda, tick off the boxes. "And . . . I don't know what else. I can't seem to get my brain in order."

"It's working well enough from where I'm standing."

"Maybe you could walk on up, see if they got the keys to Mike yet."

"You're not leaving her. I'm not leaving you. Bodine. Walking back to the road, right there, isn't leaving her."

She glanced back. They'd left the horses, just left the horses standing in the road.

"You're right. We need to secure the horses," she said, starting back. "And we need to get them to the BAC. When they're done with us, the police, you could ride Sundown and lead Leo."

"I'll take care of it."

Even as he gathered the reins, Callen turned toward the sound of an approaching car. He steered the horses to the far side of the road, grateful the police had responded faster than he'd hoped.

He wanted, above all, to get Bodine away from there, away from standing in the snow, looking at the body of a dead friend.

The black truck with the county sheriff's department emblem on the side stopped a few feet short of Billy Jean's car.

Callen watched the man get out. The broad-shouldered, defensive lineman's build, the cream-colored hat over short, straw-colored hair, reflective sunglasses over eyes Callen knew to be cold, hard blue. Square-jawed, thin-lipped, he turned his head enough to give Callen a ten-second stare before moving toward Bodine.

Callen thought, Fuck me, and secured the reins to a branch before crossing the road again.

"It's Billy Jean Younger," Bodine said. "She's one of our bartenders."

Garrett Clintok nodded. "Sheriff's on the way. I'm going to need both of you to stay clear. Heard you'd come back, Skinner."

Not sheriff, at least. "Hadn't heard you were deputy.

Bodine's had them send down keys to that cabin right up there. I'm going to take her and the horses up there."

"You're going to wait until I say different." He looked down at Callen's jeans, boots. "You went right on out there, compromised the crime scene."

"I did that," Bodine said quickly. "I saw her and I didn't think, I just tried to get to her. Callen stopped me. I'm sorry, Garrett, I just reacted."

"Understandable enough. Did you touch her?"

"Callen stopped me before I got to her. I could see— Anybody could see she was gone, but I just reacted."

"Her phone's on the ground, the other side of her car," Callen added. "We didn't touch that, either. Deputy."

"I really would like to get inside, just sit down. Maybe have some water." Bodine shifted, just a little, just enough to put herself between the men and the ugly vibrations in the air. "I'm feeling a little shaky. Do you think Callen could go down to where I have Mike blocking the road, get the keys? We'd be right there. Big Sky Cabin. We didn't want to leave her alone, but now that you're here . . ."

"You go ahead. I don't want you talking to anybody about this yet, not until we get a handle on things."

"Thanks. Thank you, Garrett."

They crossed the road together, got the horses, began to lead them up the road.

"You played him like a fiddle."

Bodine sighed. "I don't care for playing the weak-kneed female, but I'd forgotten how the two of you butt heads."

"I butted back, that's different."

The cold edge in his voice made her want to sigh. "Maybe so, but I didn't see the sense in having a pissing match with Billy Jean lying there twenty feet away. Since I'm supposed to be weak-kneed, go on and take the horses up to Mike. Ask him to have somebody come and take them in. I'll wait on the porch in a damn rocking chair."

Inside a half hour she'd made coffee; they had a fire going. And she'd paced about two miles circling the living area of the cabin.

It didn't do her nerves much good when instead of the sheriff, Clintok walked in.

"I know this is a hard time for you, Bo. Why don't you sit down for a bit? I'm going to take your statement in just a little while. Skinner and I are going to talk out on the porch first."

"The sheriff's here. I saw the trucks out the window."

"That's right. They're doing what needs to be done, just like I am. Skinner?"

He jabbed a thumb at the door, stepped out again.

"Don't provoke him," Bodine warned.

"My breathing provokes him."

Callen walked out. Clintok leaned back against a porch post, nodded. "Let's hear your side of it."

"That's an interesting way to put it. We were riding to work," he began.

"You and Bodine? You do that a lot?"

"First time, but then I haven't been back long, and only started working at the resort officially as of last night."

Tipping down his sunglasses, Clintok aimed those hard eyes over them. "I heard you were working at the Bodine Ranch."

"Things changed."

"They fire you?"

Don't provoke him, Bodine had asked, but doing so held too tempting. Knowing how to get under Clintok's skin, Callen smiled a little. "Logic says if they had, I wouldn't be working at their resort. We were riding to work," he said again.

"Whose idea was that?"

"I'd say mutual. I was planning on it. She was planning on it. We ended up planning on it at the same time."

"Looks like you took a big detour. Quicker ways to get from the ranch to the resort on horseback."

"We wanted a ride."

"Who picked the route?"

"Bodine."

Clintok's mouth twisted into a nonverbal *Liar*. "Uh-huh. How well did you know Billy Jean Younger?"

"I didn't know her. I never met her."

"Is that so?" Now Clintok hooked a hand in his gun belt. "You're working at the resort, but you never once met her."

"That's right, seeing as I just started there."

"Where were you last night, Skinner?"

"I'm living on the Bodine place, and that's where I was."

"In the bunkhouse?"

"No, I'm in the shack."

On a long, slow nod, Clintok stepped closer, crowding Callen's space. "Alone then."

"Most of the time. Bodine and I had a conversation and a beer last night, pertaining to me taking over for Abe Kotter while he's gone."

Rather than move back, Callen simply edged forward. "Are you seriously trying to wind what happened to that girl around to me? Does it stick that deep for you, Clintok?"

"I know what you are, what you've always been. Did Billy Jean get a piece of you there when you went at her? She give you that eye?"

"I never met Billy Jean. Bo gave me a shot."

"Now, I wonder why she'd do that."

"Ask her."

"Be sure I will." With his mouth twisted in a sneer, Clintok tapped a finger on Callen's chest. "You're back here a handful of days, and we've got a dead woman. You're back here a handful of days, and you want me to believe you never once stepped foot into the Saloon at the resort and made yourself known to the good-looking woman working the bar? I know bullshit when I smell it, Skinner."

"Seems to me you're shoveling that shit so deep you'd be hard put not to catch a whiff. There's a boot scraper by the door, if you don't want to go tracking it around behind you."

Clintok's face went red as boiled beets, a transition Callen knew—from past experience—generally presaged a sucker punch.

"Go on, follow through with that." Callen's invitation blew as cold and stiff as the wind. "We'll see where we end up."

Clintok's teeth set—Callen would have sworn he all but heard them grinding. But the deputy backed off.

"You can go on to work, for now. Don't make any traveling plans."

"I'll leave when Bodine does."

"I told you to move along."

Deliberately Callen walked down the porch, sat in one of the rockers. "Now, tell me what law I'm breaking."

Clintok's right hand closed into a fist. "It won't take me long to deal with you. That time's coming."

But he walked inside, leaving Callen sitting in the rocker.

"There's coffee," Bodine said immediately.

"I wouldn't say no to that." Clintok, the red still

staining his cheeks, sat at the long table in the kitchen area. "Would you know if Billy Jean was working last night, and when she'd have left?"

"She was working, and I can't be sure exactly when she left, but it would've been after midnight. We leave closing up to the staff, as long as they're available until midnight. It could've been as late as one. Then there's closing up. So I can only say she'd have left somewhere between twelve-thirty and one-thirty."

She set coffee in front of him, sat herself. "I really need to tell my parents about this, Garrett, and some of the staff."

"In a bit. We got our own men blocking off this area, so you can tell yours to go on once I get your statement here."

"All right."

"Now, what were you doing riding with Skinner way over this way? Did he ask you to take the long way?"

"No. I wanted to give my horse a good run. I haven't had him out for over a week. It's why I left early this morning, and when I ran into Callen saddling his own horse, we rode together."

"His idea?"

"God, I don't know, Garrett." Weary, half-sick, she shoved at her hair. "It was just the natural thing to do. We're leaving at the same time, going to the same place."

"All right, but—"

"Look." She was done with the weak-kneed ploy. "I know you've got a deep dislike for Callen, but that's beside the damn point here. We left the ranch together, and I decided how we'd get to the resort. I wanted a good ride. I started to head in, but I just wanted a little more, so I took this road to get another gallop in, and I saw Billy Jean's car. I didn't think that much of it, except she must've had car trouble and called somebody to come get her, but then I saw her purse still in the car, and I got worried. I called her. I took out my phone to call hers, just to check. And . . ."

Now she had to take a moment. She rose and poured a glass of water. "I heard—we heard—her phone ring. I know her ringtone. And her phone was on the ground, lying in the snow, and then I saw . . . I looked over where you could see somebody'd been going off the road, walking or running through the snow, and I saw her coat. I saw her. I told you, I just reacted, and I started running, trying to . . . to get to her, and Callen grabbed me, told me to stop. That I couldn't help her."

"Now, how did he know that?"

"Oh God, Garrett, anyone could see!" Anger reared up, through the weary, through the sick. "I just didn't want to see, to believe, so I tried to get away. I even punched him, but he held on until I calmed down. I don't know why you're letting some idiot high school feud make you try to point fingers his way, but I can damn sure tell you, whoever did that to Billy Jean wasn't Callen Skinner."

"I got a job to do." Clintok pushed to his feet. "And unless you can tell me you know just where Callen Skinner was when this happened to Billy Jean, I'll point where I need to point. You ought to be careful of him. You can go on into work if that's where you're going. The sheriff'll come around to talk to you himself when he's done here."

When he walked out, Bodine snatched the coffee off the table, dumped it down the sink. "Male, dick-measuring, ball-swinging, chest-puffing *bullshit*."

She swung around when Callen came in. "And I don't want to hear any of it out of you."

"All right."

"The pair of you want to ram antlers and paw the

goddamn ground? There's a woman dead. A woman I hired. A woman I liked. A woman with family and friends, and . . ."

"There it is," Callen soothed when Bodine covered her face, began to shake. He went to her, wrapped arms around her. She didn't fight him this time, stayed stiff only for a moment. Then leaned in, let go.

"She was a friend of mine. She was a friend."

"I'm sorry." He pressed a kiss to her temple, stroked a hand down her back. "I wish there was more to say, but that's all there is."

"I need to do something. I'm better if I know what to do."

"You need to take a minute. That's doing something, too."

"Crying's just annoying. Crying doesn't do anything."

"Sure it does. You empty something out so you can fill it with something else."

"Maybe, but—"

She turned her head just as he turned his. Their lips met.

Bumped, she'd think later. Really just bumped— unplanned, an accident in timing and direction. Maybe they lingered together a few seconds, but it wasn't remotely an actual kiss.

Still, she jerked back. "That—that's so disrespectful."

"It wasn't meant to be."

Stuck between frustrated and embarrassed, she waved her hand in the air, swiped at her wet cheeks as she paced away. "Wasn't you, wasn't me. Just happened. It's a horrible morning, horrible, and it just happened. I need to get to Bodine Town. My mother should be in by now. I need to tell her about this. We need to . . . God, we need to figure out how to tell everyone."

She pressed her fingers to her eyes. "You need to get to the BAC. We're shorthanded enough there."

"Why don't I call Chase, tell him what happened? Seems like he and your father should come over here. You're going to want your whole family when you tell everybody."

On a long expelled breath, she dropped her hands. "You're right, you're right, and I should've thought of that. We'll have Mike take us in. Clintok said the police are blocking things off now."

She closed her eyes a moment, drew her shoulders straight again. "Okay, I know what I have to do. Let's get going."

CHAPTER SEVEN

The family gathered at Bodine House, spread out in the pretty living room with its dozens of framed photographs and its simmering fire. After insisting her mother sit, just sit, Maureen passed around the coffee.

If they'd been at the ranch, Bodine thought, a family meeting would take place at the big dining room table. With her mother fussing just as she was now.

Because fussing kept her calm. Bodine could relate, as doing something, most anything, did the same for her.

They'd chosen the meeting site because the family needed to stay close, and Bodine calculated she couldn't spare more than a half hour away from her office.

She needed to tend to her people, deal with the fallout and grief already reverberating through the resort.

"What can we do for her family?" Miss Fancy sat, back erect, in her favorite chair. "I knew her—a hardworking, fun-loving girl. But, Bodine, you'd have known her best. What can we do for her family?"

"I'm not sure right now, Grammy. Her parents are divorced, have been, I think, a long time. She has a brother in the marines, and I don't know where he's stationed. I'll find out. Her mother's in Helena, as best I know. I'm just not sure about her father."

"If her family comes here, we need to put them up somewhere as private as we can, take care of them."

"No question of it," Cora agreed. "Bodine, you'll need to block off two cabins so we'll have them if needed. And choose a driver for them."

"I've blocked the cabins already." She had an agenda, tried to organize what could and should be done. "For a driver—while they might rent cars, I think one of us should be available for driving them wherever they need to go. I think we should do that rather than one of the staff."

"That's a good thought," Maureen told her. "We also have to tend to our resort family. Billy Jean . . ." Tears swam into her eyes so she took a moment to settle the ones that rose to her throat. "She was well liked. Such an outgoing girl. We need to address, and soon, the grief and the shock, and the fear, too. We don't know what happened yet, but people are going to be speculating and worrying on top of mourning one of our own."

"I think we should bring in a grief counsclor."

At Rory's suggestion, Chase turned his head, stared.

"I don't see people wanting to talk about all this with some stranger."

"You wouldn't," Rory agreed. "And other stoics wouldn't. But some would, more than you might think. We're a company, and as a company, we should offer counseling to our employees."

"I may be of Chase's mind about talking things through with some counselor," Sam began, "but I can see Rory's point here. We should find somebody who has a good reputation for this, and provide it. People can decide for themselves on it."

"I'll look into it." Doing so was already on Bodine's list.

"No." Cora shook her head at Bodine. "You're going to have enough on your plate. I can find the right person for this."

"I'm not being cold or callous." Rory scowled into his coffee. "And I'm as pissed off as I am sad. I still can't get my head around it, and I'm not sure I will even when we find out what the hell happened. But we've got to think about a press release, how we answer reporters, not to mention how we answer guests."

"I'm working on it," Bodine assured him. "Until we know what happened, it's best we say the truth first. We're all shocked and grieving over the loss of one of our own. And we're cooperating fully with the investigation. There's just not much else to say at this point."

"I can talk to some of the staff. Nana's right," Rory continued, "about you having so much on your plate."

He'd know what to say, Bodine thought. And he'd know when to just listen. Rory had such heart and the ability to read what a person needed often before that person knew themselves.

"That'd be helpful. As this goes along, Jessica and I will refine official statements, and work out what everyone— not just us, but everyone—should say to guests, to reporters. You could help with that, too, Rory."

"Why her?" Chase asked. "Why Jessica? She's events, isn't she?"

"Because she's smart and she understands perceptions. She stays calm and on message, but she knows how to adjust when circumstances change."

Bodine sat cross-legged on the floor, looked up at him and his doubtful frown. "Have you got a better pick for it?"

"I don't see why you'd want somebody who barely knew Billy Jean, and works on parties. But it's your decision." He moved his shoulders.

"That's right."

"Dad and I have to settle down the ranch hands. It doesn't make sense." Anger eked through. "It just doesn't make any damn sense why someone would go at her that way."

"We don't know that's what happened." Bodine held up a hand before Chase could bite at her. "I think it has to be what happened, but we don't know. Until we do, you have to tell everyone at the ranch the same as we're telling everyone at the resort."

He stared at her until the hot anger in his eyes cooled. "It had to be an awful thing for you, finding her like that. I'm glad you weren't alone when you did."

Because the image of Billy Jean's body flashed into her mind, Bodine only shook her head and looked away. At a knock on the door, she rose quickly. "I've got it."

She opened the door to find Sheriff Tate dutifully wiping his boots on the mat.

"Bodine, how are you doing, honey?"

Bob Tate had a robust build and a weathered, ruddy face. She'd known him all of her life, as he was friendly with her parents and liked to tease he'd kissed her mother once before her father got up the gumption.

"It's a terrible day. A hard, terrible day."

"I know it." He gave her a quick hug, then a pat on the back. "I stopped in over at the office, and that pretty blonde from out East said you and your family were all over here. I'm going to need to talk to you, honey."

"I know. Let me take your coat."

"Don't you worry about it." He stepped into the living room. "Miss Fancy, Mrs. Bodine." He took off his hat. "I'm sorry to have to come into your home like this."

"You're always welcome here, Bob." Cora rose first. "I'll get you some coffee."

"I'd sure be grateful for it. Maureen, Sam, boys."

"Rory, get Sheriff Tate a chair." Miss Fancy gestured toward her daughter's bedroom. "How's Lolly doing?"

"She's got me on a diet." He smiled as he said it, eyes crinkling. "A man could starve to death in his own house. Thank you, Rory."

He sat in the chair Rory carried out, puffed out a breath.

"What can you tell us?" Sam asked.

"The fact is, I can't tell you much right now. We're doing all we need to do, and I can't speak frankly on that. I need to ask Bodine some questions."

Cora stopped on her way back from the kitchen, coffee cup in hand. "Do you need us to leave?"

"No, ma'am, no, there's no need. It could be, as you all knew Billy Jean, you may have something to say that might add to the picture. But, Bodine, you're the one who found her. Along with Cal Skinner."

"Yes, sir. We were riding to work together—horseback," she qualified. Though, of course, he knew.

"You took a roundabout way. Cal suggested that?"

"No. I did. I had the lead."

He lifted his eyebrows, but nodded.

She gave him the details, as she had to Garrett Clintok. Tate stopped her when she got to Billy Jean's phone.

Nodding, Tate flipped through a little notebook. "Cal suggested you try to call her."

"No. When I saw her purse was in the car, I got worried, so I called her cell. She doesn't have a landline. And I heard her ringtone. About the same time, Cal said for me to come around the car and look. And we saw her phone on the ground, and that torn-up path through the snow.

Then I saw her, and I tried to run over to where she was lying in the snow. I thought she was hurt, I tried to tell myself that, but the truth was I could see—anybody could see—it was too late. Callen stopped me, held me back."

Watching her, Tate tapped a stubby pencil against his notebook. "Did he go up to her?"

"No. He held on to me, got me calmed down enough till he could make me understand—I just didn't want to understand—that we weren't supposed to touch her, or anything."

"I'm told Cal has a black eye. Did he have that this morning when you started out for work?"

"No, because I gave it to him. I was half-crazy, fighting to get loose, and I landed one on him before I got ahold of myself. And I see what's happening here." She spoke coldly now. "And I've got something to say."

"You go ahead."

"I told Garrett as clearly as I'm telling you what happened and how. If he told you differently, he's lying."

As if to tamp things down, Tate tapped a hand in the air. "Well, Bo, I'm aware there's some bad blood between Cal and Garrett."

"Clintok poisoned it a long time ago." Chase got to his feet, slow and easy. "It got poisoned when we were no more than kids and Clintok dogged Cal, hounded him. He was goddamn relentless. Sorry, Grammy, but that's the word for it. He poisoned it when he and three of his asshole friends . . ."

When he paused again, Miss Fancy waved a hand. "Wait until you're done to apologize for your language in the parlor."

"It's what they were as they jumped us when Cal and I were camping down at the river. The three of them holding me down so Garrett could pound on Cal. But it ended up with Cal pounding on him, and getting the better of him before Wayne Ricket—you remember him?"

"I do," Tate said, "seeing as back when I was deputy, I hauled him into a cell more than once, and as sheriff I had a part in putting him away for five years for aggravated assault."

"He jumped into it, so it was two against one. But that only left two on me, and I had some mad worked up. We licked them. After, Clintok settled for hard words—didn't have much else, as a couple of the gut punches Cal landed had Clintok puking like a sick dog. I'm saying, if he could find a way to beat Cal down, even if it's steering you into thinking he'd kill a woman, he'd do just that."

Piece said, Chase sat again.

Tate sat silent a moment, studying his little book. "I appreciate the information. All right then, Bo." Tate turned back to her. "What happened next?"

"Cal called you, and I called our security, as I had my wits about me again, so they could block off the road and keep anybody from coming along. Clintok got there first, and it was clear he wanted to push at Callen, so . . ."

She blew out a breath. "I said how I needed to sit, have some water, and I'd arranged for the office to send down the keys for the near cabin. I wasn't in the mood to have the two of them snapping at each other with Billy Jean lying over there."

"That was a smart way to handle it. I've got some details to get yet, and I need to talk to Billy Jean's direct supervisor and whoever was working with her last night."

"That'd be Drew Mathers. I've talked to him and the bar staff. You'll need to do that, too, but I can tell you: Billy Jean sent the others home about twelve-thirty. She had three couples still in the bar—four of them came in as friends, and the other couple got friendly, so they stayed on. I can't tell you for sure what time she closed down and left, but I can give you the names of the people who were in the bar after twelve-thirty."

"That would be mighty helpful. She had a boyfriend, didn't she?"

"They broke up. A couple of weeks ago. Chad Ammon. He's one of our drivers, doubles as bell staff. He's off today."

"Is that Stu Ammon's boy?"

"It is."

"And would you know who did the breaking?"

"She did. He cheated on her with a girl out of Missoula—and a girl from Milltown before that—so she showed him the door. I want to say—and I know you'll need to talk to him, too—Chad is absolutely slippery when it comes to women, but there's not a mean bone in his body. And he was about as upset about getting the boot as he'd have been nicking himself shaving. Just something that happens."

"Was she seeing anyone else?"

"She was, how'd she put it? Taking a breather from . . ." She glanced at the grannies. "A certain anatomical part. I saw her almost every day, and she'd have told me if she'd shifted her mind on that."

"All right then. I appreciate you laying all that out for me, Bo." After tucking his book in his pocket, Tate got to his feet. "That was fine coffee, Mrs. Bodine. I'm going to leave you all alone."

"Are you going over now?" Bodine asked him.

"I am."

"If I could go over with you, I can get the people you need to talk to, set up a place for you to do that."

"That'd be helpful."

He waited for her while she got her coat. She glanced back at her family. Nothing more to say for now, she thought, and went outside with Tate.

"I know you can't say what you can't say," she began, "but it's clear somebody went after her. I don't know why she stopped where she did, how it happened, but it's clear she was scared enough to run, and that means she was running from something. Someone."

"There's more to do before I can say whether or not that's the case. Officially."

"I'm asking if I should put on more security."

"I don't know that that's necessary. But when something like this happens, people are going to be spooked until the answers come out. I think you should do whatever you feel's right."

A woman she knew was dead, and on her land, Bodine thought. She wished she knew what felt right.

As he loaded a docile mare into a trailer, Callen spotted the sheriff's truck heading down the road toward the BAC.

He'd been expecting it.

He lifted the trailer gate behind the pair of horses, stepped toward the shelter where Easy LaFoy was grooming another horse.

"Going to put you to work later," Easy told the gelding. "So you get your lazing around in now."

"Easy, I'm going to need you to take these horses down to the center. We got a lesson in about an hour. Maddie's going straight there for it."

"I ain't finished here, boss."

"It's all right, I'll see to it. You get these two down there, saddle them up. Just say to Maddie that she's to remember the rules. You can take your lunch while the lesson's going on."

"Okay, boss." He stepped out of the shelter with Callen as Tate pulled up. "I guess he's here about what happened to that girl. Awful thing to happen."

"Yeah. You go ahead." And Callen walked over to meet Tate.

"Cal." Tate nodded. "How's your mom doing?"

"She's doing fine. She likes having a grandkid right under her feet to spoil."

"I got one coming myself."

"I didn't know that."

"Yeah, first one, due in May. My wife's half crazy already buying those onesies and teddy bears." Tate paused, watched Easy maneuver the truck and trailer. "That a new hand?"

"He is, but then, so am I."

"Not the welcome back anybody'd want. How about you go over it for me?"

"Can we talk while I work? We've got a six-person trail ride coming up this afternoon."

"We can sure do that." He walked with Cal to the shelter and the horses, and Callen picked up where Easy had left off.

As he worked, Callen relayed everything from meeting Bodine in the stables to finding the body.

"You rode up White Tail Trail?"

"Yeah. This weather, it's like riding through a movie. Picture-perfect."

"You'd know about that. Movies."

"I guess."

"Have you had a drink in the Saloon here since you've been back?"

"Nope. I've been busy, and I've got beer back at the ranch. I'd never met the woman." And would never forget her. "I can't prove I didn't decide to drive over this way in the middle of the night, and go after some woman I'd never met, but it sure would be a change in habit for me."

Despite the circumstances, Tate's lips curved a little. "You got in some tussles here and there as I recall."

"With boys and men," Callen agreed easily, even though he heard Clintok's influence in the line of questioning. "The kind of tussling I did with girls and women? That's of a different nature, and always by mutual agreement."

"I've never heard otherwise." Tate gestured to Callen's eye. "Looks like you've had a recent tussle. That's a decent black eye you're sporting."

"I've had better. Bodine . . . She just wanted to get to her friend. She couldn't think outside of that, and I couldn't let her. So, yeah, you could say we tussled, and she caught me. She's got an admirable right hook."

"This how you told it all to my deputy?"

"I did."

Tate waited a beat, another. "Don't want to add to it?"

"There's nothing to add."

"I've got a story to tell you." Tate dug a pack of gum out of his pocket. "The wife nagged me until I quit smoking." He offered the pack, and Callen took a stick out. "Anyway, I was saying. There was a poker game one night, over at the Clintoks' spread. The missus was visiting her sister, took the little girl along, so it was just Bud Clintok and young Garrett at home. He'd've been about twelve, I guess, at that time. Your dad was there."

Callen's eyes stayed flat gray as he nodded. "He usually was if there was a poker game."

Or a horse race, or a sporting event to bet on.

"That's a fact, though he had his stretches where he

held that devil down. But this wasn't one of those stretches. It's not speaking ill of the dead to say Jack Skinner had a weakness. But there wasn't mean in him. That night, he was having a run of luck. Raking it in. Lot of drinking going on, a lot of swearing and betting and smoking— which I dearly miss."

Tate sighed, chewed his gum.

"Last pot, it came down to your dad and Garrett's. Now, Bud had been losing almost as much as yours had been winning that night. This was a rich pot, and Bud, he kept raising. Jack, he kept raising right back. About five hundred dollars in there when Bud ran out of money. He says he'd put something else in. Your dad, half joking, says he could put the pup in. This dog, no more than a four-month-old pup, had taken to Jack. Jack said the pup was his lucky charm. And Bud says that's fine. And they laid the cards down.

"Bud, he had a heart flush, eight through queen. And Jack? Four deuces."

Pausing, Tate shoved back his hat, shook his head. "Four deuces, and that was that. Jack took the pot, but he wouldn't take the pup. That pup belonged to the boy, and there was no meanness in Jack. He said he'd rather Bud buy him a steak dinner, and that's where they left it. Everybody went home, a little drunk and lighter in the pocket but for Jack—and myself, as I broke even, and that was as good as a win under the circumstances."

Tate looked away toward the mountains, then straight into Callen's eyes. "I heard how somebody shot that pup dead the very next day. Now Bud, he can be a hard man, but he'd never have put a bullet in a pup."

Callen could see it, had seen that mean in Clintok even back when they were twelve.

"Why did you take him on as deputy, Sheriff?"

"He served his country, and he came back home. I figured, from what I could see, Garrett had outgrown that streak of mean. I'm not saying he can't ride the line now and then, but I can't say I've had cause to complain about him, either. But him and me? We'll be having a talk, because a woman's dead, and nobody who works for me is going to use that to satisfy an old grudge."

"I've got no issue with him. If he stays out of my way, I'll stay out of his."

"That's how we'll keep it. You give your mother my best when you talk to her next."

"I will."

Alone with the horses, Callen gave some thought to bitter young boys—he'd been one—and to a father who'd never been mean, but weak enough to lose everything. Including his son's respect.

In her office, Bodine pushed through the steps, handling the work that couldn't be put off, but stopping everything whenever one of the resort crew came in for comfort or with questions.

She worked through it with a fist in the pit of her stomach and a headache brewing behind her eyes.

Jessica paused in the doorway, tapped her knuckles on the doorjamb.

"I'm sorry to interrupt."

"No, it's okay. I was going to come get you in a bit anyway. Saves me the steps."

"Have you eaten anything?"

"What?" Momentarily blank, Bodine rubbed at her stiff neck.

"That's what I thought." Taking charge, Jessica simply picked up the phone on Bodine's desk, pushed the extension for the kitchen.

"Hi, Karleen, it's Jessica. Would you send a bowl of the soup of the day and some chamomile tea down to Bo's office? Yeah, that'd be nice. Thanks."

"What if I don't want soup?" Bodine said when Jessica hung up.

"You'll eat it because you're smart enough to know you need it. The same as Rory is, and your mother."

Bodine worked up a smile. "Are you taking care of us?"

"Somebody has to. You look worn-out, and I happen to know there's been a steady procession of people coming in here today looking to lean on you, like there's been in Rory's office, and Maureen's. But more streamed in here."

"Big boss."

"That's right. They need you for comfort, so you need soup. Now, tell me what I can do to help."

"I've been working on a couple of things, and . . . Didn't you have a consult on the Rhoder Company's conference set for right about now? And an interview today?"

"I rescheduled them. It wasn't a problem. We've had a death in the family."

Now Bodine's aching eyes burned with tears. As she pressed her fingers against them, Jessica turned back, shut the door. "I'm so sorry, Bodine. I didn't know Billy Jean very well, but I liked her. Let me take some of this off your hands. I know Sal generally picks up your slack when you need it, but . . . she's a wreck right now."

"They were really good friends. I could use your help with a couple things. And I know you've got plenty on your hands right now, too."

"Chelsea's every bit as good as you and I thought she'd be. Adding her to my team's freed me up enough I can take some time."

"I can fill it. First, I've written up a statement for the press. I've already had to use it twice with reporters who've called about what happened. I want to make sure it hits the right notes."

"I'd be happy to look at it."

"We need one for guests, too. Those who are here, those who are booked and might contact us about this. I've got that drafted up. You didn't know her very well," Bodine added, "so you'll be more objective. I'm not sure I haven't gone too far toward the brisk and brief because she was my friend and I'm overcompensating."

"All right."

"And finally, we need to hold a memorial for her. Here. I spoke with her mother already." Bodine paused, blew out a breath. "We offered them cabins here, and drivers, whatever they need, but they're going to stay in Missoula, and they're going to take her back to Helena, back home, when they can. The memorial will be for all of us, all of us, resort and ranch and anyone around who knew her and wants to come pay respects."

"Let me take that. I'm not being flippant when I say a memorial's an event, and events are my area. You just tell me when you want to have it, and where on the property, and I'll put it together."

Grateful, Bodine let that weight slide away. "I think it has to be indoors, as we can't trust the weather. The Mill's the best place."

"I agree." Jessica rose at the knock on the door, opened it. "Thanks, Karleen, that's just perfect."

She brought the tray to the desk, set it down. "Eat."

"Stomach's in knots."

"Eat anyway."

On a weak laugh, Bodine picked up the soupspoon. "You sound like my grammy."

"A towering compliment. Give me a general idea of what you want, and I'll work the details."

Flowers, because Billy Jean had loved them. And country-western music. As she sketched it out, Bodine ate. The soup had been a good choice, as it sort of slid right in and down without much thought.

"I think we'd need to have it open for four or five hours, with someone from the family there. We can work that out," Bodine said. "But I'd want to give everyone who works here a chance to come in, spend a little time, and there's no day coming without bookings. I thought about shutting down for a day."

Jessica, still taking notes, didn't bother to glance up. "Then you thought about ruining the plans of people who'd not only booked a cabin but maybe airfare, taken off work."

"It wouldn't be right. But everyone needs to have the chance to come in. It'd be easier to do at the ranch, but—"

"She was resort family."

"I can't get it straight in my head." Though her throat clogged, Bodine pushed the words through. "I can't get that this could happen straight in my head. It's not that we never have trouble. A guest getting a little out of hand or staff getting bitchy with each other or even some tussles at an event. But something like this? I can't get it straight in my head."

"Bo? Sorry." Rory came to the door. "Mom needs a minute if you've got it."

"Sure. I'll be right there. Jessie, maybe you can just use my desk, go over those statements. That'll be something done." Bodine brought them up on the computer, rose. "I'll be back in a minute."

Jessica took the desk chair, read over the statements. Straightforward, but maybe just a little too brisk, maybe just a little forced.

She shifted to the keyboard, began to type suggestions.

"Bo, I want to . . ." Already halfway across the office, Chase stopped. "I thought it was Bo."

"She had to step out a minute." Jessica rose. "Chase, I'm so sorry."

"Appreciate it." He took off his hat, held it in his hands. "I'll get out of the way, let you eat your lunch."

"It's not mine. I had to, apparently, channel Miss Fancy and get Bodine to eat something. She'll be right back. Why don't you sit down? I'll get you some coffee."

"I'm coffee'd out. Never thought to hear myself say that." But he did sit, a bit heavily. "Ah, is she holding up all right? Bodine?"

He looked tired, even a little pale, she thought, and realized she'd never seen him look either before. Jessica came around the desk, took the other guest chair. "You look tired—and don't appreciate me pointing it out. But Bodine looks exhausted."

"She'll need to run everything," he stated. "Plan everything, talk to everybody."

"She will, and is. Still, I think working is getting her through the first hard shock, but the fact is, everybody's leaning on her. She looks pale and worn down, and hasn't had time to grieve herself, or even come to terms."

He said nothing for a moment, just stared down at his hat.

More than pale and tired, she thought. He looked unspeakably sad. "Have you eaten?"

"What?"

"Apparently I'm pushing the soup today. I can order some for you."

"No, I . . ." He simply stared at her for a very long beat. "I'm good. I . . . I gave Bo a hard time about you."

"About . . . me?"

"When she said she was going to ask you to help out with the statements and all that."

Absorbing that, Jessica pushed at a pin, though it hadn't been loose, in the smooth coil at the back of her neck. "Because I'm not from here."

"Not from here, haven't been here long, and . . ."

"And?"

"Doesn't matter. I came to apologize to her. She was hurting, and I could see it, but I took a little swipe anyway. Because I was mad." He scowled down at his hat again. "Just mad. Still am."

"Is this how you look mad?"

"Depends." He glanced up. "On what I'm mad about. Bo thinks you're the one to go to for this, then I've got no reason to say otherwise."

Jessica nodded, crossed her high-heeled feet at the ankles. "Since you opened the door . . . What's your problem with me? We both know you have one."

"I don't know. Maybe it just takes me time to get used to people."

"People like me?"

"People altogether." He hesitated a moment, then shrugged. "There's a good reason I work the ranch and Rory works the resort. I'd go crazy dealing with people all damn day."

"Well, if you figure out the problem with me is more than me being human, let me know. Maybe we can work it out. I'll go let Bo know you're waiting."

Chase cleared his throat as she started out of the office. "Do I have to apologize to you, too?"

She turned her head, skewered him with a look. "Depends," she said, and left.

PART TWO

A Purpose

Hold to the now, the here, through which
all future plunges to the past.
—James Joyce

CHAPTER EIGHT

— 1995 —

Alice—her name was *Alice* whatever he called her—gave birth to a son.

He was her third child, and the only one Sir allowed her to keep. The second baby, another girl, had been born only ten months after the first. A little girl she'd named Fancy because she'd come with a pretty down of red hair.

When he'd taken her baby away, her second daughter away, up those stairs, she refused to eat or drink for nearly a week, even when he beat her. She tried to choke herself with the bedsheet, but had only passed out.

He'd forced food into her, and feeling her own body crave it, she died a little. He gave her three weeks after childbirth before raping her again. Within six, she conceived a son.

The birth of the boy she named Rory for the father she'd never known changed things. Sir wept, laid a kiss on the baby's head as it squalled and wailed. He brought her flowers—the purple pasqueflower that bloomed in April all around the ranch.

They said *home*, and had the rusty knife of hope carving into her.

Was she still home?

He didn't come to take the baby away, instead brought her milk, fresh vegetables, even a steak. To keep her milk strong and healthy, he said.

He stocked her with diapers and wipes and baby lotion, a plastic tub and baby wash. When she asked—carefully— if she could have softer towels for the baby, he provided them, and a windup mobile, of animals and an arc, that played a lullaby.

For months he didn't strike her or force himself on her. The baby was her salvation, sparing her from beatings and rapes, giving her a reason to live.

Emboldening her to ask for more.

He came to see the baby, bring her food, three times a day. The midday meal had been an addition after Rory was born. She'd come to gauge the time of day by his visits.

Preparing for the breakfast visit, she nursed the baby, washed him, dressed him. He'd taken his first steps only the night before, and she'd wept with pride.

A new hope burned in her. Sir would see his son walk the first time, would allow them to go upstairs, allow her to take the baby outside, to walk in the sun.

And she would see the lay of the land. She would begin to plan how to take her child and run.

Her child, her precious boy, her salvation and joy, would not grow up in a cellar.

She washed herself, brushed her hair that was now nut brown and past her shoulders.

When he came down the stairs with a plate of runny eggs and a couple of overdone slices of bacon, she sat in her chair, bouncing the baby on her lap.

"Thank you, Sir."

"See that you eat all of it. Waste not, want not."

"I will. I promise, but I have a surprise for you." She stood Rory on his sweet, chubby legs, kissed the top of his head. He clutched her fingers for a moment, then let go and took four wobbling steps before he sat on his butt.

"He can walk," Sir said quietly.

"I think he may be walking early, but he's just so smart and sweet." She held her breath when Sir went to Rory, stood him up again.

And Rory, hands waving, giggled as he toddled across the floor.

"He'll be running before you know it," she said, pushing cheer into her voice. "Boys need to run. It'd be good for him to have more room—when you think it's right," she said quickly when Sir turned those dark, hard eyes on her. "To get some sun. There's—there's vitamins in sunlight."

He said nothing, but bent and picked up the baby. Rory tugged at the scraggly beard Sir had grown during the last months.

It killed her, every time he touched the baby. She had a knot of terror and despair tight in her belly. But she made herself smile as she rose.

"I'll share breakfast with him. He likes eggs."

"It's your job to give him mother's milk."

"Oh, yes, and I do, but he likes solid food, too. Just little bits. He's got five teeth and another coming in. Sir? I'm remembering what my own mother said about fresh air, and how you need it to stay healthy, grow strong. If we could go outside, get that fresh air, even for a few minutes."

His face as he held the baby turned to stone. "What'd I tell you about that?"

"Yes, Sir. I'm just trying to be a good mother to . . . our son. The fresh air's good for him, and for my milk."

"You eat that food. He's got more teeth coming in, I'll get him something to gnaw on. Do as I say, Esther, or I'll have to remind you of your place."

She ate, said nothing more, told herself to wait a week. A full week before she asked again.

But in three days, after she'd eaten the evening meal, nursed the baby, he came down the steps again.

And stunned her by showing her the key to her leg shackle.

"You heed what I say now. I'm going to take you out the house, ten minutes, and not a second more."

She quivered as that rusty knife of hope slashed jagged through her heart.

"You try yelling, I'll break your teeth. You stand up."

Docile, head down so he wouldn't see that flicker of hope in her eyes, she rose. The hope died when he looped a rope around her neck.

"Please, don't. The baby."

"You shut your mouth. You try to run, I'll snap your neck. You do just as I say, and it may be I'll let you go out for that fresh air once a week. You don't obey me, I'll beat you bloody."

"Yes, Sir."

Her heart shook in her chest when he fit the key into the lock and, for the first time in four years, the weight of the irons dropped from her ankle.

She made a soft, throaty sound, an animal in pain as she saw the raw, red, circling scar above her foot.

His eyes were bright black moons. "I'm giving you a gift, Esther. Don't make me sorry for it."

When he shoved her forward, she took her first step without the shackle, then another, her gait uneven, a kind of shambling limp.

She held Rory close, struggled her way up the stairs.

Run? she thought as her shaking heart grew heavy. She could barely walk.

He tugged the noose tight at the top of the stairs. "You heed me, Esther."

He opened the door.

She saw a kitchen with a yellowing floor, a wall-hung cast-iron sink with dishes stacked in a drainer beside it. A refrigerator no taller than she was, and a two-burner stove.

It smelled of grease.

But there was a window over the sink, and through it she saw the last dying lights of the day. The world. She saw the world.

Trees. Sky.

She tried to pay attention, take a picture with her mind. The old couch, a single table and lamp, a TV like she'd seen in photographs—a kind of box with . . . rabbit ears, she remembered.

Wood floor, empty walls, log walls, and a small, empty fireplace made out of mismatched brick.

He nudged her toward the door.

So many locks, she thought. Why would he need so many locks?

He opened them, one by one.

Everything—her plans, her hopes, her pain, her fear—fell away as she stepped outside on the short, sagging porch.

The light, oh, the light. Just the hint of the setting sun sliding behind the mountains. Just a hint of red against the peaks.

The smell of pine and earth, the *feel* of air moving over her face. Warm, summer air.

Trees surrounded her with a scraped-up patch of ground where vegetables grew. She saw the old truck—the same one she'd so foolishly climbed into—an old washing machine, a tiller, a locked cattle gate with barbed wire forming a toothy fence around what she could see of the cabin.

She started to step off the porch, lost in wonder, but Sir yanked her back.

"This is far enough. Air here's just like out there."

She lifted her face as tears of stunned joy rolled down her cheeks. "Oh, the stars are coming out. Look, Rory, look, my baby. Look at the stars."

She tried to tip the baby's head up with her finger, but he only grabbed on to it, tried to gnaw.

It made her laugh, kiss the top of his head.

"Listen, listen. Do you hear the owl? Do you hear the breeze going through the trees? Isn't it beautiful? It's all so beautiful."

As he babbled and gnawed, Alice tried to see everything at once, absorb everything.

"That's enough. Go back in."

"Oh, but—"

The rope dug into her throat. "I said ten minutes, no more."

Once a week, she remembered. He'd said once a week, too. She went inside without a sound, and this time saw the shotgun on a rack over the empty fireplace.

Was it loaded?

One day, please God, one day she'd try to find out.

She limped back down the steps, amazed the ten minutes had both exhilarated and exhausted her.

"Thank you, Sir." She didn't think—couldn't think—of what it meant that the humble words didn't burn her throat as they once had. "Rory's going to sleep better tonight for getting that fresh air. Look there, his eyes are drooping already."

"Put him in his bed."

"I should feed and change him first."

"Put him in his bed. He wakes up, then you do that."

She settled him down. He barely fussed at all, and quieted when she rubbed gentle circles on his back. "See that? See how good that was for him?"

Once again, she kept her head down. "Did I do everything you told me?"

"You did."

"Can we really go outside once a week?"

"We'll see about it, if you keep doing as I say. If you show me you're thankful for what I give you."

"I will."

"Show me you're thankful now."

Keeping her head lowered, she closed her eyes tight.

"You've had more'n enough time to heal up after birthing the boy. And he's eating solids so he don't need your milk the same as he did. It's time you do your wifely duties."

Saying nothing she walked to the cot, pulled the baggy dress over her head, lay down.

"You've gone to sagging here and there," he said as he stripped. Leaning over, he pinched her breasts, her belly. "I can tolerate such things." He climbed on top of her.

He smelled of cheap soap and kitchen grease, and his eyes held that wicked, burning light she knew too well.

"I can do my duty. You feel my staff, Esther?"

"Yes, Sir."

"You say: 'I want my husband to use his staff to take mastery over me.' You say it!"

She didn't weep. What did words matter?

"I want my husband to use his staff to take mastery over me."

He rammed into her. Oh, it hurt, it hurt.

"Say: 'Take what you will of me, for I am your wife and your servant.'"

She said the words as he pounded and grunted, as his face contorted with a horrible pleasure.

She closed her eyes, and thought of the trees and the air, of the last rays of the sun, and of the stars.

He kept his word, so she made the trip up the stairs and onto the porch once a week.

When the baby was a year old, she worked on the nerve to ask him if she could fix him a fine meal to repay him for his kindness. To celebrate Rory's birthday.

If she could convince him, then show him she was obedient, she might get to the shotgun.

He came down with her evening meal, picked up the baby as always.

But this time, without a word, he carried the baby to the steps.

"Are we going outside?"

"You eat what I brought you."

Fear made her voice sharp. "Where are you taking the baby?"

"Past time he was weaned. Time he spent more time with his father."

"No, please, no. I've done everything you said. I'm his mother. I haven't nursed him tonight. Let me—"

He paused on the steps, out of her reach. "I got a cow. He'll get plenty of milk. You do as I say, and you'll come up and sit outside once a week. But you don't, you don't."

She fell to her knees. "I'll do anything. Anything. Please don't take him from me."

"Babies grow to boys, boys to men. It's time he knew more of his daddy."

When the door shut, locked, she got shakily to her feet.

Something snapped inside her. She could hear it, like the *crack* of a dry twig inside her head.

She went to the chair, sat, folded her arms, rocked. "Hush now, baby. Hush now." And smiling, she sang a lullaby to her empty arms.

— *Present Day* —

More than ready to go home, Bodine stepped out into the lingering wild lights of sunset. She justified leaving earlier than usual — knowing she'd concentrate better on reports, spreadsheets, and schedules at home.

She just couldn't shoulder more grief on top of her own without breaking down.

Then she stepped out under a sky licked and laced by reds and purples and golds, and saw Callen standing with the horses, entertaining a young couple and their deliriously delighted toddler.

"Horsie, horsie, horsie!" He chanted, bouncing on his mother's hip, stretching out to bang his hands on Sundown's neck.

She noted Callen confabbing in low tones with the father, then the father whispering something in the mother's ear that had her shaking her head quickly, then biting her lip, then giving Callen a long look.

"Up to you," Callen said. "But I can promise this one's gentle as a lamb."

"Come on, Kasey. He'll be fine." The father, already grinning, pulled out his cell phone.

"Just sitting. Just sitting," Kasey insisted.

"You got it." Callen swung into the saddle—a move that had the toddler clapping as if he'd performed a magic trick. "Want to come up here, partner?"

When Callen held out his arms, the little boy would have leaped straight into them. Conflicted, the mother held him up, then pressed both hands to her heart at the sight of the toddler squealing with joy in front of her.

"Horsie! I ride horsie!"

"Smile at your daddy so he can get your picture."

"I ride horsie, Daddy!"

"You sure are, Ricky. You sure are."

"G'up!" Ricky shouted. Sundown turned his head and looked at Callen with what Bodine could only call a grin. "G'up, horsie!" Ricky craned around, looking pleadingly at Callen. "G'up."

"Oh God." Kasey blew out a breath. "Maybe, just walking a few steps. Is that okay?"

"Sure is."

"Kasey, get pictures. I'm switching to video. This is great."

"Put your hand right here." Callen guided the boy's right hand, laid it on top of his own on the reins. "Say, giddyup, Sundown."

"G'up, Thundow!"

When Sundown walked forward, the boy stopped squealing. For a moment, his sweet little face was awestruck, his eyes were filled with shocked joy. "Mama, Mama, Mama, I ride horsie!"

Callen walked Sundown in a couple slow circles while the boy bounced, grinned, and even hooted up at the sky. On the final return trip, Callen sent Bodine a quick wink.

"Gotta say adios, partner."

"More, more, more!" Ricky insisted when Callen started to lift him out of the saddle.

"That's enough for today, Ricky. The horsie has to go home." As Kasey reached up, Ricky leaned away.

"You're a real cowboy now, Ricky," Callen said. "Real cowboys always listen to their mas. It's the cowboy code."

"I a cowboy." And with some reluctance, Ricky went to his mother. "Kiss horsie."

"Sundown likes kisses."

Ricky planted wet kisses on Sundown's neck, then pointed to the patient Leo. "Kiss horsie."

"Leo likes kisses, too." Bodine stepped up. "Some horses are shy about kissing, but not these two."

Kasey shifted so Ricky could smack his lips on Leo's neck.

"Ride this horsie. Please. Now. Please."

"I have to take him home now and get him his dinner. But . . . Are y'all going to be here tomorrow?"

"Two more days," the father told her.

"If you bring Ricky down to the Activity Center tomorrow, we'll see what we can do."

"We'll do that. Hear that, Ricky? You're going to see more horses tomorrow. Say thank you to Mr. Skinner," his father instructed.

"Thank you! Thank you, cowboy. Thank you, horsie."

"Anytime, partner."

Bodine mounted, turned Leo around.

"Adios," Callen said, flicking the brim of his cap as they walked the horses away.

"Adios," Bodine echoed.

"Gotta play to the crowd."

"I'm not even going to mention insurance, waivers, liability."

"Good. Don't."

"Since I'm not, I'm going to say that's just what I'm looking for, that interest, in having the horses around Bodine Town now and then. And why doing a little show for kids and families is going to work. I didn't expect you to be here, with the horses."

"I called up. Guy at the desk said you were heading out 'round five."

"I'd arranged for transportation home. Canceled that while you were giving young Ricky the biggest moment of his life. I appreciate it. I appreciate it because it was an unexpected antidote to a horrible day."

He took a study of her. "You got through it."

"And I'll get through tomorrow. I'm going to warn you, Garrett Clintok's tried to lay some trouble at your door."

"I already know it."

"He twisted my words. I want you to know he twisted my words. I never said—"

"Bo." Callen cut off the building rant with quiet. "You don't have to explain to me."

"I need to say it. I never said things he said I did, and it pisses me off he'd try using me, and worse, so much worse, Billy Jean to cause you trouble. I straightened it out with Sheriff Tate, but if—"

"Tate knows what's what. I'm fine with Sheriff Tate."

Fire sparked in her eyes. "Because the sheriff's not an idiot, but it pisses me off. It pisses me off, and Clintok's getting an earful next time I see him."

"Just let it go."

"Let it go?" Shocked, outraged, she shifted in the saddle. "I don't let things go with liars and bullies. With people who say I said what I didn't. With people who ambush my brother and his friend, and have that friend held down so he can try to beat the shit out of him."

Callen pulled Sundown to a stop. "Where'd you hear about that?"

"Chase told us today, and he should've—"

"He broke a spit oath." With the look of a man disillusioned, Callen shook his head, walked on.

"I'll say he was riled to boiling at the time—as I know spit oaths are sacred. To twelve-year-old boys."

"Age doesn't have a thing to do with it. An oath's an oath. And the past is the past."

Men, Bodine thought. How could she have grown up surrounded by them and still have them irritate the living crap out of her?

"You can skin Chase for sticking up for you, for providing evidence of what a snake Garrett Clintok is, if that's your stand on it. But if the past was the damn past, Clintok wouldn't still be trying to ambush you."

"That'd be his issue, not mine."

"Oh, for—" Disgusted with anything approaching reason, Bodine kicked into a canter.

Callen paced her easily, and couldn't seem to leave reason behind. "I don't see why you're pissed at me."

"Oh, just shut the hell up. Men." Riding her own temper, Bodine urged Leo into a gallop.

"Women," Callen said under his breath, and let her take the distance she needed even as he kept her in sight all the way back to the ranch.

He hadn't meant to kill her. When he looked at it clear, thought long and hard, he understood she'd really killed herself.

She shouldn't've run like that. Shouldn't've tried yelling like that. If she hadn't tried kicking at him that way, he wouldn't have had to shove at her. She wouldn't have gone down so hard, hit her head so hard.

If she'd come along quiet, he'd have taken her on home, and she'd've been right as rain.

His mistake? Not smacking her down right off. Just smacking her down, loading her in the truck. He'd wanted a quick taste of her first, that was all. To make sure she'd do for him.

He needed a wife of childbearing age. A young, good-looking woman who'd give him a good ride, and strong sons.

Maybe he'd decided on her too quick, but he'd sure wanted that ride.

He'd done the rest right, he reminded himself. Siphoned the gas out of her tank, left her just enough to get good and away from the center of things. Followed her with his lights off, then gone to the rescue when he saw her car stop.

Got her out of the car just fine, kept it all nice and easy.

Then he'd gotten himself too excited—that's where he'd gone from right to mistake. Shouldn't've grabbed her, tried to get that taste of her. Should've waited on that.

He'd learned his lesson there.

Next time, he'd put her down, truss her up, and get her back to the cabin. Simple as that.

Plenty of good-looking women around to pick from. He'd take his time on it. The bartender one had been pretty enough, but he'd seen prettier. And thinking about it, maybe she'd been older than he should look for. Not so many years in her to bear children, which was a woman's purpose in life.

Younger, prettier—and it might've been that the one who killed herself had been a whore, seeing as she worked a bar. Could be she'd've carried some disease.

He was better off he hadn't taken that ride with her.

He'd find the right one. Young, plenty pretty—and clean.

Pick her out, bide his time, truss her up, and take her to the cabin. He had her room ready for her. He'd train her right, teach her what so many forgot. Women were created to serve men, to submit and obey, to bear sons.

He wouldn't mind punishing her. Punishment was his responsibility as well as his right.

And he'd plant his seed in her. And she would be fruitful and bear forth sons. Or he'd find one who would.

That might take some patience, some planning.

But that didn't mean he couldn't find one to give him a good ride in the meantime.

In the cabin, in his room, he brushed a hand over the Bible on the stand by the bed. Then reaching under the mattress, pulled out a skin magazine.

Women were mostly whores and trollops, he knew. Flaunting themselves, tempting men to sin. He licked a finger, turned a page, felt righteous as he hardened.

He didn't see any good reason not to take a woman up on her flaunting until he found the right wife.

CHAPTER NINE

Four days after Billy Jean's death—ruled a homicide—Bodine drove to Helena for the funeral.

The very next day she stood on the second floor of the Mill listening to Tim McGraw and Carrie Underwood and Keith Urban—Billy Jean's favorite—play in the background while people paid their respects.

She gave Jessica full credit for creating the right atmosphere. Photos of Billy Jean, some alone, some with friends, stood around the room in simple iron frames. Flowers, bursts of color, speared out of milk or Mason jars. Simple, casual food—cold cuts, fried chicken, mac and cheese, cornbread—ranged on a long table covered with an oilcloth.

Nothing fussy or fancy, and everything speaking of comfort.

People who came could step up to the mic on the stage, say a few words, or tell a story about Billy Jean. Some stories brought tears, but more brought laughter, that great leveler of grief.

A few people brought guitars or fiddles or banjos, played a song or two.

Bodine prepared to slip out, then stopped when she saw Chad Ammon come in, head right for the stage.

Conversation stopped, started up again in murmurs. Bodine stood where she was, scanning the room until she found Chase, met his eyes.

With that one look they agreed to let him speak, and to handle whatever trouble might come of it.

"I know a lot of you think I shouldn't have come." His voice cracked a little. "Anybody has anything to say to me, you can say it after I'm done saying my own. I didn't treat her right. She deserved better than me."

Somebody called out, "Damn right," which started up the murmurs again.

"I know it's damn right. She was . . . she was a good woman, a good friend. She was kind. Maybe she didn't take crap off of anybody, but anybody could count on her when they needed it. She couldn't count on me. I cheated on her. I lied to her. Maybe I didn't ever raise my hand to her or any other woman in this world, but I didn't treat her with respect. If I'd been a better man, maybe we'd have still been together. Maybe if we'd been together, she'd still be here. I don't know."

Tears slid down his cheeks.

"I just don't know, and I never will. All I know is someone kind and good, someone who knew how to laugh, who liked to dance and gave her trust to me is gone. There isn't a thing anybody here can say to me worse than what I say to myself every day. But you can say it. I won't blame you for it."

He stepped away from the mic. His legs seemed to shake as he walked off the stage.

Bodine saw she had two choices. Let those murmurs and hard looks turn to words, and maybe worse. Or start the healing.

She moved through the crowd, saw Chad stop, raise his tear-streaked face to hers. He broke into sobs when she slid an arm around him.

"All right now, Chad. You come with me now. You don't blame yourself for what happened. She wouldn't want you to. She wasn't like that."

She made sure her voice carried as she led him out of the memorial, and to the steps leading down.

In the heavy silence, Jessica walked quickly to the stage. From what she could see, Bodine had started turning the tide. She'd try to keep it moving.

"I didn't know Billy Jean very well. I haven't worked here as long as most of you. But I remember after my first week here, going into the Saloon. I was feeling good about the work, but a little out of place, maybe a little homesick."

She brushed her hair back from her face. She'd left it down so it waved its way to her shoulders. More casual, more friendly, she thought, than wearing it up and sleek.

"I wanted to fit in here," she continued, "so I went into the Saloon that evening. Billy Jean was working the bar. I asked her what she'd recommend, told her I'd just started working here.

"She told me she knew that already, that bartenders hear everything sooner or later, and usually sooner. She recommended a huckleberry margarita. I'm going to admit it didn't sound appealing."

On stage, Jessica smiled at the chuckles.

"A lot of customers were in there that night, and I noticed how easy she made her job look. How she had a smile for everybody, even if she was working with both hands. She put that drink in front of me. I looked at it thinking why in the hell did people around here put huckleberries in everything. Then I took a sip, and got the answer."

She smiled again at the quick laughter, waited a moment. "I drank my first huckleberry margarita. Then I drank a second one, sitting at the bar, watching Billy Jean work. When she put a third one in front of me, I told her I couldn't. I had to drive home. Only to the Village, but I couldn't get behind the wheel with three drinks in me. And she said: Honey, you go ahead and have that drink, and celebrate your first week here. That she was off in an hour, and she'd drive me home. So I did, and she did. It wasn't the huckleberries that made me feel like I was beginning to fit in. It was Billy Jean."

She stepped off the stage, took an emotional test of the air around her. And, deciding the tide had fully turned, moved to the background.

"That was a good thing."

She glanced over at Chase. She hadn't seen him move in her direction. "Your sister did the right thing. I just finished it off. And the story was God's truth."

"That was a good thing," he repeated. "Just like this memorial. I want to say you put it together just the right way, and maybe you knew her better than you think."

"I had a sense of her, and I talked to people who knew her well." She looked around the space, at the photographs, the flowers, the faces. "All this has taught me a couple of things. I wish I'd spent more time sitting at the bar when she was working it. And she was—we all are—part of a whole, not just employees of a good company. Bodine told me some who came here today are seasonals, and some of them drove a hundred miles and more to come. That's what family does. And that kind of sensibility comes from the top. Your family set that tone, and it rings true."

"I'm going to apologize."

She aimed those blue eyes straight into his, raised her eyebrows over them. "Are you?"

"I didn't mean to make you feel you don't belong."

"You just don't think I do?"

He shifted his feet. "I'm apologizing."

"And I should be gracious enough to accept it. So I will. Bygones." She held out a hand.

"All right." Though it felt awfully damn small in his, Chase shook her hand. "I need to get back, but—"

"Miss Fancy's sitting over there, and Rory's due any minute. It's fine if you go."

"Then I'll . . . ah . . ." Since he'd run out of words, he nodded, escaped.

As he made his way out, exchanging more words with some who sat at tables set up on the main floor, he saw Callen coming toward the Mill.

"Couldn't get away before now," Callen said.

"More than enough time. We had some drama when Chad came along, had a say."

"Is that so?"

On a sigh because he knew the tone, Chase settled his hat down further on his head. "You're still mad."

"You broke an oath."

"You weren't there. I'm sorry I let temper get in the way of it, but it did. And it's done. You want to even it up, I'll give you leave to break the oath we took about me pouring whisky into a Coke bottle and sneaking it out of the house, and the pair of us trying to drink it up at the campsite, and getting sick as dogs instead."

"You got sicker."

"Maybe. You puked your share. You can tell that one if it levels this."

Considering, Callen hooked his fingers in the front pockets of his jeans. "Picking what you say I can tell doesn't level it. I should be able to pick one."

Because he couldn't argue with the logic, Chase frowned out at the mountains. "Go ahead then. Pick one and let's put this away."

"Maybe I'll pick how you lost your virginity when Brenna Abbott lured you into the hayloft at your sister's thirteenth-birthday party."

Chase winced. It might not have been his proudest moment—considering his whole family and about fifty others had been within shouting distance—but it had been a seminal one.

"If that'll do it."

Callen stood hipshot, studying the mountains along with his friend, listening to the music and voices from inside the Mill.

"Hell, it'd just make me feel like an asshole, and stop you from feeling so much like one. I'd rather you feel like one awhile more. Whatever happened to Brenna Abbott?"

"Last I heard she was living in Seattle. Or maybe Portland."

"How quickly we forget. Well, bygones," Callen said, offering a hand.

Chase stared at it, then let out a laugh. "That's the second time in under ten minutes somebody said that to me. I must be making it a habit to mess things up."

"Nope, not a habit. Just a blip on the screen."

"I got something else. Clintok starts something, you come and get me before you finish it."

"I'm not worried about Clintok."

"You come and get me," Chase repeated, then spat on his palm, stuck out his hand.

"Jesus." Touched, amused, and struggling not to think of Bodine's comment about twelve-year-olds, Callen mirrored the gesture, clasped hands.

"All right then. I've got to get back." Chase sauntered away.

Rubbing his hand on his jeans, Callen walked inside to pay his respects to the dead.

Bodine wouldn't rank herself as a top cook. She might not rank herself in the top fifty percent of cooks. But on Thanksgiving, she did her duty.

She chopped, peeled, stirred, mixed. And following a tradition set years before, bitched that neither of her brothers served in the duty.

"It's not altogether fair." In her placid way, Maureen basted the turkey. "But you know as well as I do there's not a man in this house who's anything but a nuisance in the kitchen. Clementine and I both did our best to teach them, the same as we taught you, but Rory could burn water, and Chase turns into a bull in a china shop."

"It's on purpose," Bodine grumbled as she and Cora peeled a mountain of potatoes.

"Well, sweetie, I know that, too, but the results are the same. Grammy, can you take a look at this ham?"

Miss Fancy, wearing an apron that stated WOMEN AND WINE IMPROVE WITH AGE, peered into the lower oven, nodded. "I'd say it's about time for me to make the glaze. Don't fuss too much, Bodine. You got the men out there doing the beef on the grill. And they'll be hauling the second turkey and all the fixings over for the bunkhouse boys. I'd as soon not have them in here, crowding me.

"I like the smells and sounds of a Thanksgiving

kitchen," Cora added as she plucked up another potato. "Remember, Reenie, how I used to make extra pie dough and let you and Alice . . ." She trailed off, let out a sigh. "Ah, well."

"I remember, Ma."

Maureen spoke briskly, turning to stir something on the stove that didn't need stirring.

"I'm not going to get maudlin," Cora said. "I like to think Alice is smelling and hearing Thanksgiving today, too. That she found whatever she was looking for that we couldn't give her."

Miss Fancy opened her mouth, then firmly shut it. Bodine carefully said nothing. On the rare times her mother's sister's name came up, the grannies seemed to square off in separate corners. One heavy with sorrow, the other sharp with resentment—and her mother ranged on the resentment side.

"I think the whole kitchen staff deserves a glass of wine." Maureen walked to a cupboard, pulled out glasses. "You can bet your butt those men have cracked more than one beer by now. Bodine, wash off those potatoes and let's get them boiling. Ma, these sweet potatoes look about ready for your magic."

"Just a couple more white ones to skin."

Maureen set down the glasses, gave her grandmother's hand a quick squeeze. In response, Miss Fancy jerked her shoulders.

"You think I can't hear what you're both thinking?" Cora demanded. "Don't the pair of you start pandering to me."

Bodine popped up at the sound of the doorbell. "That's the door." Relieved, she dashed to answer.

She opened the door to Jessica, said, "Perfect."

"Well, thank you. And thank you for inviting me."

"Come on in. When did it start snowing? I wasn't paying attention due to kitchen duty and a family ghost." Gesturing Jessica in, she stepped back. "You can join in the first and help exorcise the second just by being here. You didn't have to bring anything," she added, nodding at the cake holder Jessica carried.

"*Have to* implies obligation. *Happy to* is appreciation."

"Thanks either way. Let me get your coat."

Shifting the cake holder from hand to hand, Jessica drew off her coat and scarf as she studied the entranceway.

"This is fabulous. I love the beamed ceilings, the wide-planked floor, and oh, that fireplace."

"I'd forgotten you haven't been here before. We'll have to give you a tour."

"I'd love it."

In her simple blue dress, Jessica wandered a few steps into the living area. "And the views!"

"We're all about them. They're pretty terrific from the kitchen, too. Come on back. Let's get you a drink."

The house rambled, charming her. Everything about it spoke of comfort, in a casual, family style. A lot of wood and leather, Jessica noted, a lot of Western art and artifacts interspersed with pieces of Irish crystal and Belleek. Windows framed with wide square trim and left uncurtained to bring in the fields, the sky, the mountains.

She stopped outside a room with a large antique desk, pointed to the wall. "Is that a . . . papoose?"

"A papoose would be what went into it," Bodine explained. "It's a cradleboard. My father's grandfather's cradleboard."

"It's wonderful, and enviable, to be able to trace your heritage back so far, on both sides, and have pieces like that, the tangible connection."

"We're a jigsaw puzzle of ethnicities." Bodine led the way back. "Look who I've got."

"Jessie. So good to see you." Maureen left her vigil at the stove to welcome Jessica with a hug. "You always look so pretty."

"It wouldn't hurt you to put a nice dress on every once in a while, Bodine," Miss Fancy said as she stirred the glaze for the ham.

"Thanks," Bodine muttered to Jessica. "What can I get you to drink?"

"Whatever you're having." Jessica put the cake holder on the counter. "How can I help?"

"Wine first," Maureen decreed. "What have you brought us?"

"It's *ptichye moloko*."

"Not sure I can pronounce that, so I'm going to take a peek."

Cora walked over, lifted the lid. "Oh, that's just gorgeous!"

"It's a Russian dessert—bird's milk cake, though you don't use milk from birds. My grandmother always made it for special occasions."

Bodine held out a glass of wine, studied the smooth chantilly frosting drizzled artistically with chocolate. "You made it?"

"I like to bake. It's not much fun baking for myself, so this was a treat."

"I'm getting out the fancy cake stand, putting this on the dessert buffet with the pies and Ma's trifle." Maureen rushed toward the dining room for the cake stand. "You sit down and drink that wine, Jessie."

"I will," she told Maureen, "if you put a kitchen tool in my hand."

"Put the girl to work," Miss Fancy ordered. "The

men'll be trooping in here before much longer and getting in the way of things."

For Jessica, taking part in a large family gathering fascinated. The interaction and dynamics of the four generations of women, with some roles loosely assigned— Bo, grab me that, Ma, will you taste this—and other roles fiercely guarded.

Miss Fancy baked the ham while Maureen took charge of the turkey. The gravy stood squarely in Cora's domain.

Whatever family ghost Bodine had referred to appeared to have departed, as the women worked in easy harmony, and with a great deal of affection. Though she couldn't imagine herself ever making a vat of gravy, she got tips on doing so from Cora. And thought of the hours she'd spent in the kitchen with her own grandmother.

"You look a little melancholy." Cora spoke quietly. "Missing your family?"

"I was thinking about my grandmother, how she taught me to cook, to appreciate the creativity of it."

"Is she back East? Maybe she can come out for a nice long visit."

"She died last winter."

"Oh, honey, I'm so sorry." Instinctively, Cora wrapped an arm around Jessica's shoulders as she whisked the gravy with her other hand. "Did she teach you to make that cake?"

"She did."

"Then she's here all the same, isn't she?" So saying, Cora pressed a kiss to Jessica's temple.

Chase stepped in, surprised to see Jessica a little teary-eyed and leaning against his grandmother's side.

He cleared his throat. "Ah, we're about ready to haul the turkey and such over to the bunkhouse."

The announcement caused a quick and ruthlessly

organized scramble for the sides and the desserts designated for the ranch crew.

One of the crew, a grizzled, barrel-chested man with his hat in his hands, stood behind Chase.

"We sure do appreciate all this fine food, Miss Fancy, Miss Cora, Miss Reenie, Bo, ah . . ."

"Jessica," she told him.

"Ma'am. It smells a treat in here. Now, don't you lift that big pot, Miss Cora. I got that."

"You and the boys enjoy what's in it, Hec, and be sure that pot comes back."

"I'll get it back to you, but you can be sure there won't be a scrap of these mashed potatoes left before I do. Mighty obliged. And happy Thanksgiving, ladies."

The minute the door shut behind him and Chase and a load of food, Bodine snorted. "He's still sweet on you, Nana."

"You stop that, Bodine Samantha Longbow."

"Calling me by my full name doesn't change the facts. Hector's been sweet on Nana as long as I can remember."

"You aren't old enough to remember all that long, are you?" Cora said tartly.

"Old enough to know you'd have a boyfriend if you gave him the opening."

"I'm too set in my ways for a man. And you're a fine one to talk about boyfriends. When's the last time you stepped out with a man on a Saturday night?"

Bodine bit into one of the eggs her great-grandmother had deviled. "Maybe I'm too set in my ways."

"I see one out there who'd change those ways." Miss Fancy grinned out the window. "That Callen Skinner sure fills out a pair of Levi's nice and fine."

"Grammy!"

Miss Fancy laughed, winking at Bodine. "I've got eyes,

and I don't even need the glasses since they fiddled with my lenses taking off the cataracts. Yes, sir, I see just fine. Hear fine, too, like hearing you ride into town with him most mornings now."

"There's nothing to that."

"Doesn't mean there couldn't be, or he couldn't make there be, if he sets his sights on you."

"I'm not a target," Bodine retorted.

Cora poked her shoulder. "Teach you to mind your mouth about who's sweet on who."

"You ought to ask Jessica why she's not stepping out on a Saturday night."

"Why is that, Jessie?" Maureen wanted to know.

"Right under the bus?" Jessica asked Bodine.

"Around here it'd be wagon, but it's all the same."

Jessica was spared finding an answer as the men trooped into the house and, as predicted, got in the way.

Outside of an event, Jessica had never seen so much food. In addition to the traditional turkey, they offered ham and beef, mashed and scalloped potatoes, an ocean of gravy, brandied yams, candied yams, stuffing, a bounty of vegetables and salads, fresh-made applesauce, cranberry sauce, biscuits and sourdough rolls warm from the oven.

Along with the food, the drink, conversation flowed. She noted the subject of Billy Jean remained off the Thanksgiving table, and could only be grateful.

Not a day passed at work without speculation, questions. She considered the holiday meal a reprieve.

Seated between Chase and Callen, Jessica sampled the ham.

"You be careful with those slivers of meat on your plate," Callen advised. "You won't have room for dessert."

"There's too much here for more than a sliver. Where are you going to find room?" She wagged a finger toward his more generously filled plate.

"Miss Maureen's apple pie is like nobody else's. I dreamed about that pie every Thanksgiving I wasn't at this table."

So this was tradition for him, Jessica thought, sharing Thanksgiving with this family rather than his own. She filed that away. "I guess you work it off. I couldn't make it to your show last Saturday, but I hear you and your horse were major hits."

"We had some fun with it."

"I want to get some pictures next time." Bodine leaned around from the other side of Callen, then shifted to gesture at Rory across from her. "We should put one or two up on the website. I caught part of it. Sundown had the people eating out of his hand. You weren't bad, either," she told Callen.

"He taught me all I know."

"Smartest horse I ever knew," Sam put in. "I wouldn't be surprised if he said, 'Howdy, Sam,' one day when I walk by his stall."

"We're working on it," Callen told him.

"I'll have to meet this wonder horse." Jessica tried a forkful of mashed potatoes.

"He'd be pleased. He likes pretty women. Especially ones who bring him a carrot."

Bodine shifted a little as Callen aimed a look at her. "I suppose you're going to claim he told you about that," she said.

"We have our ways. Sundown and me, we have our ways. You get much chance to ride, Jessie?"

"Me? Oh, I don't ride."

Conversation, all the little pockets of it around the table, emptied into silence. And once again Bodine leaned around Callen.

"At all?"

"There wasn't much opportunity in Lower Manhattan."

"But you've been on a horse. Like a trail ride." Surprised enough to ask, Chase shifted to face her.

"Actually, no. I've never been on a horse."

"How did we not know that?" Rory wondered. "How did we not know that?"

"Nobody asked." Feeling suddenly exposed, as if she'd inadvertently confessed to a crime, Jessica reached for her wine. "It wasn't in the job description."

"Well, we'll fix that." Sam snagged another biscuit. "Cora here's a fine teacher. The fact is, everybody around this table could teach you basic horsemanship in no time at all. We'll get her up on Maybelle, don't you think, Bo?"

"Maybelle's as gentle and patient as they come. Abe always put her in for the dead novice or the skittish."

"Really, you don't have to bother. I don't—"

"Are you afraid of horses?" Chase asked, gently enough that she felt heat rise up the back of her neck.

"No." Not in theory. "No, not at all," she said more firmly.

"We'll get you up in a saddle," Sam told her. "Don't you worry about it."

Stuck, Jessica smiled, drank more wine.

She hadn't been worried about it. Now she imagined she'd worry about little else.

The break between dinner and dessert included cleanup, and a choice of cards or watching football.

Since Jessica understood football better than cards, she opted for that. But she'd barely settled in when Chase brought in her coat and a pair of barn boots.

"Mom said I should take you over, get you used to the horses."

"Oh, really, that's not necessary."

"I don't argue with my mother. It's a waste of time because she always wins."

"That's a fact," Rory confirmed, then snarled at the game. "For God's sake, where's the defense? Are they taking the day off?"

"She said these ought to fit." Chase held out the boots. "You can't go walking across the yard in those high heels."

"Fine." She'd get it over with. Her hostess—and employer—had made a request. She'd walk over, look at horses, and be done.

She'd looked at plenty of horses since moving to Montana.

From a comfortable distance.

She put on the boots, which did fit well enough even if they looked ridiculous with her dress, then pulled on her coat.

Chase led her out the side door. The snow had stopped, but a fresh three inches glittered under the yard lights.

Making her grateful for the boots.

"It's not like I need to ride anywhere," she began.

"It's a good skill to have. Like swimming. Can you swim?"

"Of course I can swim."

"I've never been to Lower Manhattan. Didn't know if there were many opportunities for that there, either."

"It's an island," Jessica reminded him as a raucous cheer erupted from the bunkhouse.

"They're watching the game."

"You'd probably like to do the same," she realized. "We'll make this quick so you can get back to it."

"I like football well enough, but it's just a game."

He opened the door, hit the lights.

It was a soft smell, Jessica thought. Horses. Different, a little different from what it was when she walked by them in paddocks or rings.

He walked down the sloped concrete, stopped. "This is Maybelle. She's a good choice for the first time up on a horse."

As he spoke, the horse lifted her head, dark brown with a jagged white blaze, over the stall door.

"If she had wool, she'd be a lamb. Isn't that so, Maybelle?"

Her ears flicked forward as he rubbed her cheek. Her eyes looked deep into Jessica's.

"You can pet her. She likes it. Have you petted a horse before?"

"No."

"I'm not going to say some won't bite, because they will. But not this one. She's a good girl. Here you go."

Before Jessica realized he meant to, he'd taken her hand pressed it to the mare's cheek.

Soft—like the scent. Smooth. Warm.

Her heart stopped hammering so she could enjoy the experience.

"She has beautiful eyes."

"She does."

Chase waited until her confidence built enough for her to stroke her hand down Maybelle's neck.

"Have you ever been thrown?"

"Not what you'd call thrown. Slid off once and landed on the ground. But we were riding bareback, Cal and me, and half-drunk with it. A long while back," he added when Jessica looked at him.

"Your family really wants me to do this."

"Nobody's going to make you do something if you're afraid of it, or just plain don't want to."

"I should try it. Have the experience." She backed up. "I'll think about it anyway." She jolted a bit, turned, at the snort behind her. "Who's that one?"

"That's the famous Sundown."

"Sundown the wonder horse." She approached warily, but she approached. "He's beautiful. And big. He's big."

"Runs seventeen hands, so some bigger than most. Smart, like Dad said, and he can be sly. But he's got no mean in him."

To test her mettle, she moved closer. Her hand paused halfway up, hesitating. Could a horse look amused? she wondered, making herself lift her hand all the way to his cheek.

"Okay, two for two. You're really big, very impressive, and very, very handsome."

Sundown turned his head, angling it down, as if suddenly shy. Chase laughed.

"I swear I don't know how he does it. It's like he understands every word we say."

Smiling, Jessica turned around. "Maybe he does. I think—"

This time she didn't just jolt, she all but leaped and landed hard against Chase.

"He was just sniffing your hair." To steady her, Chase put his arms around her—or told himself that was why. "It's pretty, and it smells good. He didn't mean to scare you."

"I was startled. He just startled me." Still a little breathless, she looked up. His eyes were so green, she thought, so strongly green and flecked with gold.

"It's pretty," Chase said again. "Your hair's pretty."

And lowered his mouth to hers.

He smelled of the horses, she thought. Soft and warm. His mouth was the same, warm and soft against hers. A quiet kiss, one that might have been peaceful if not for the rapid drumming of her heart. Despite the drumming, leaning into him, into the moment, was the easiest thing she'd ever done.

He pulled back, stepped back. "I'm sorry. I shouldn't've . . . taken advantage like that."

The soft, shiny bubble popped. "Like what?"

"Well, I . . . It might seem like I lured you in here, and then I grabbed hold of you."

Now she lifted her eyebrows. "I think I did the initial grabbing."

"That was—" He broke off, pulled off his hat, raked his fingers through his hair. "I'm not sure what to . . . I'm not sure."

"I can see that. I guess you should let me know whenever you are. We should get back."

He shoved his hat back on, caught up with her. "It's just I don't want you to feel I'd take advantage, that you'd feel obligated—"

She stopped in her tracks, froze him with a look. "Don't insult me."

"I wasn't. I didn't mean . . . Christ almighty, I can talk to people better than this. Women. I'm not saying what I mean to say."

"If you think for one minute that I believe you did, or you would, pressure me into a physical or sexual relationship because you're a member of the family that employs me, you're insulting my intelligence and my character judgment. And I'm saying exactly what I mean to say."

"All right."

"If you think I'd encourage or allow the same, you're an idiot."

"I think I got your point, all the way through. I only wanted to apologize if I crossed a line. I didn't mean to cross it, right or wrong. You smell good."

"We established that last part, thank you. And I'll let you know if and when you cross a line."

"All right." Deciding it was safer all around to leave it at that, Chase opened the door for her.

He glanced back, saw Sundown watching the human drama with apparent delight.

Chase snapped off the lights, shut the door.

CHAPTER TEN

December rushed in with a flurry of events, parties, the madness of decorating, juggling schedules when a number of key staff were out with a twenty-four-hour virus, and for Bodine, the annual frustration of shopping.

She didn't mind shopping, especially the point-and-click style of online. But Christmas raised her gift-giving bar. She couldn't and wouldn't settle for adequate or good enough or even not bad at all when it came to Christmas.

When it came to selecting Christmas gifts, she demanded perfection.

She had her father's—two dozen Cohiba cigars and an antique humidor she'd battled for fiercely on eBay. She topped it off with a bottle of Three Ships single-malt whisky. She had her brothers' presents in the bag, and the grannies'. She'd ordered the managers' gifts and would shortly hand sign the cards that would hold Christmas bonuses for staff.

A couple more gifts for friends, and some gag gifts—a Longbow tradition for stocking stuffers—didn't worry her. But she'd yet to hit on the perfect gift for her mother.

That worry and weak spot left her vulnerable for Jessica's not-very-subtle push for a shopping trip to Missoula.

So on a rare day off—when she'd have preferred to sleep late, to take a long, solo ride on Leo—Bodine searched for an empty slot in a parking garage in town.

Since every mother's son and daughter seemed to have the same idea, it took some doing.

At least the morning held clear, she thought as she finally maneuvered her truck into a slot. Cold turned into bitter, but it was bright and cloudless.

After she climbed out, hung her purse cross-body over her coat, she eyed Jessica. "When I find my mother's perfect gift, and I will, we're going for pizza at Biga."

"All right."

"You've eaten there, haven't you?"

"No." Jessica pulled out a lipstick, and without benefit of a mirror, perfectly retouched her lips.

"How'd you do that?" Bodine demanded.

"Do what?"

"Put on that lipstick without looking?"

"Well, I know where my lips are."

Bodine knew where hers were, too, but she'd like to learn that particular trick. "Did you say you haven't eaten at Biga's? Ever?"

"If I end up eating in Missoula, I usually have a salad."

"That's just sad." Bodine took the stairs to street level. "You come in here a couple times a month, but haven't had the best pizza in Montana—and likely anywhere else."

Jessica answered with a pitying look. "I have to remind you I'm from New York. There's no better pizza than New York pizza."

"We'll see what you say after." On the sidewalk, Bodine put her hands on her hips, scanned the pretty town with its clever shops, restaurants, breweries. "I don't have a single good idea in my head for my mother."

"Something will click. I thought I was a discerning gift-giver, but compared to you, I'm a peasant. Honestly, Bo." Always a happy shopper, Jessica hooked an arm with Bodine's. "Those photographs you had enlarged and tinted for Cora, and that really lovely triple frame? It's so perfect, so thoughtful."

"I got the frame from Callen's sister's shop. They have great stuff. The Crafty Art."

"I love that shop! Cal's sister owns it?"

"She and her pretty adorable husband, yeah."

"I've burned up my credit card in there more than once. But the gift's really about the photographs."

"The wedding picture of her and my grandfather's a winner, and the one of the two of them with my mom is so sweet. Just the way he was holding both of them so close. It's the one of Nana and Mom, with Alice as a baby, that may stir things up a little."

When Jessica said nothing, Bodine added, "You can ask."

"I know there are some difficult feelings about Alice. That she ran away when she was young."

"The day of Mom's wedding. Just lit out, left a bratty little note from what I can gather, took off in one of the trucks. Going to California to be a movie star." Bodine rolled her eyes. "I know she sent a couple of postcards, then nothing. Not even one word to her widowed mother."

Since the door was opened, Jessica poked around a little more. "I imagine they tried to find her."

"Nobody talks about it very much, as it upsets Nana, puts her at odds with Grammy. I can't blame Grammy for her hard feelings there, watching her daughter grieve and suffer all this time. I guess I can't blame Nana for her feelings, either."

They passed a man who wore reindeer knee socks outside his jeans and sleigh bells around his neck.

"Alice is her daughter, the same as my mother. Which puts Mom solidly between them, and that's a hard place. So, not much talk, but kids know how to hear things, and we heard enough to know Nana hired a detective for a while, and they found the truck abandoned in Nevada, I think. And Alice just disappeared. It's not hard to do, I guess, if you want to."

"Brutal for Cora," Jessica comforted.

"Yeah. Grammy won't much like my gift to Nana, but I figure I'm offsetting that by digging out the christening gown her own grandmother made for her and having it restored and framed."

"It's such gorgeous work. And coming up with the little photos of all the babies who wore it was genius."

Bodine paused in front of a shop. "I have my moments. Now, since I've often thought if I ever came across Alice Bodine, I'd want to punch her straight off, that's enough about her. Let's try this place, see if something clicks."

Nothing did, but at Callen's sister's shop she hit gold.

"I should've known to come here first. I was hoping Savannah would be in today."

"I come in here every time I'm in Missoula. I must have met her."

"Really pregnant right now."

"Yes! She's wonderful. And now I have another Montana connection."

Bodine held up a fancy ladies ostrich-skin clutch. "This is Sal. Purple's her favorite, and this isn't something she'd buy for herself. Isn't practical."

"Maybe not, but it's beautiful."

"We go back, me and Sal. She does love girlie."

"Many of us do, and so does Chelsea. I'm getting her this scarf."

Bodine eyed it—it looked like a painting of a Montana sky at sunset. "It's more than pretty, but that's not going to keep her neck warm."

"It's not about that." Jessica swirled it around her neck, twisted this, flipped that, and had it looking like something out of a fashion magazine.

"How did you do that without looking? And don't say you know where your neck is."

"Mad scarf skills." But she walked over to a mirror now, brushed her fingers over the thin, soft silk. "I want it for my own, so it's a good gift."

"I'd never find anything for anybody if that was my yardstick. I just . . . Oh!"

"What is it? Oh, the painting. That's your house, isn't it?"

"It's the ranch house. There's snow on the mountains, on the high peaks, but the fall flowers are in the pots and the beds. And the ginkgo trees have gone gold."

The shopkeeper, sensing multiple sales, wandered over. "One of our local artists' work. I love the vibrant color of the ginkgos, and the wonderfully sprawling lines of the ranch house, and how the sky's showing red behind the mountains. It makes me want to sit on that old bench under the trees and watch the sun set."

"What did the artist call it?"

"*Serenity.* I think it suits. That's the Bodine Ranch. The family owns and runs the Bodine Resort, one of the finest places to vacation or just dine in the state. The family's lived there, about an hour's drive from Missoula, for generations."

"You can just see the near paddock in the corner there, and there's Chester sleeping on the front porch. Our dog," Bodine said to the shopkeeper. "I live there. Bodine Longbow." She offered her hand.

The shopkeeper flushed with embarrassed pleasure as she gripped Bodine's hand. "Oh, well for goodness' sake! Listen to me explaining it all to you. I'm so pleased to meet you, Miss Longbow. Stasha—the artist—she's going to be over the moon you admired her painting."

"I hope she's just as pleased I'm buying her painting. For my mother for Christmas. You can tell her I admire her work very much, but it's the ginkgos that sealed it."

Bodine turned to Jessica. "On a crisp fall evening, on that bench under those trees, my father first kissed my mother."

"Oh, for goodness' sake," the shopkeeper said again, waving a hand in front of her face as her eyes filled. "That is so romantic. And this, this is like kismet, isn't it? Oh, I have to call Stasha. Would you mind if I did?"

"Not a bit. You can tell her when my mother relates the story of that first kiss, she said it felt like her whole world had turned to gold, like the leaves overhead."

Now the shopkeeper dug in her pocket for a tissue.

"How long would it take her to paint them in?" Jessica wondered. Then caught herself. "Sorry. I was thinking out loud."

"Well, Jesus, Jessie, that's the best damn idea ever! Could she do that?" Bodine demanded. "It'd be more of an impression of people, wouldn't it, from the distance. I can get her photos of them from back then, but it wouldn't be like she'd have to paint portraits."

"I'm calling her right now. She lives right in town. I'm calling her. Oh my goodness."

"Jessica." Bodine draped her arm around Jessica's

shoulder. "I hit perfection on this, and you boosted me up a full rung over that. She's going to be thrilled. Just thrilled. I'm buying the pizza."

Over the years, Bodine had enjoyed shopping— occasionally—with her mother, with the grannies. Together or one at a time, even though it seemed her mother, on a hunt for a black purse, for instance, felt obligated to look at the universe of same before making a decision.

But she had to admit that an excursion with Jessica, and the exceptional success, topped all. She loaded up on gag gifts—she especially liked the boot socks with cowboys clad only in boots, hats, and tighty-whities.

Flushed with the fun of it, she was primed for Jessica's expert wheedling, and ended up buying herself a red leather vest—a color she usually bypassed—a white shirt with fancy cuffs to go under it, and a new lipstick she'd forget to put on more than half the time.

Plus, anytime she could down a couple slices of Biga pizza equaled a very good day.

Bodine bit into hers, watching Jessica. "Well?"

"It's good." Jessica took a second bite, considered, savored. "It's really good."

"Rest my case. Though I don't know why you'd want spinach all over your half."

"Healthy and delicious. And your case doesn't rest. It's really excellent pizza, but—".

Chewing, Bodine wagged a finger in the air. "That's just New York stubbornness."

"One of these days, we're going to do some shopping in New York, you and I."

Biting into her slice, Bodine snickered. "Yeah, that's going to happen."

"I'll find a way to see it does. And when it does, I'm taking you to Lombardi's. Although . . ." Jessica ate a little more. "I will admit, knowing this place is here makes me miss New York a lot less."

"You still do?"

"Off and on. I may never get used to the quiet. I still wake up in the middle of the night sometimes because it's so quiet. Or I'll glance out the window expecting to see buildings, traffic, and there's space and fields and mountains."

"Seems odd things to miss. Noise and traffic."

"And yet." On a laugh, Jessica sipped some wine. "Some days I miss the pace, the sheer force of energy—and the Thai place around the corner. But then I'm struck by those mountains, and the air, the work I really, really love, and the people I've gotten to know. And now I'm learning to ride a horse."

"How's that going? I wanted to come down, but I thought for now you might not want an audience."

"You've got that right. Your grandmother's amazing, and she's a very patient teacher. I've stopped feeling like I'm taking my life in my hands every time I get up on Maybelle. That right there isn't bad for three lessons."

"We'll have you out on a cattle drive in no time."

"Let me take a page from your book." Jessica toasted her. "Yeah, that's going to happen."

"You're going to surprise yourself. I don't want to get into business too much, but I want to say you've become, in a short time, a vital member of the resort family. I've come to depend on you, to know I can, and that makes me better at my job."

"That means a lot. I love working for you, for the family. God, I really love coordinating with Rory. He's so smart and creative, and he makes me laugh every single day."

"He's flirting with Chelsea, isn't he?"

Jessica tried to poker up, but her lips curved as she lifted her pizza. "Maybe. It's hard to blame him. She's adorable, on top of being bright and energetic. She shines on big-picture concepts, and knows how to handle details when I toss them at her. She's become another reason I love the work. I wasn't sure I would."

"It's hard to believe you were unsure of anything, moving across the country the way you did."

"I took this leap at a difficult time in my life, and told myself it was better to take the leap and make a mistake than to stand still and be unhappy. I'm glad I took the leap and learned it wasn't a mistake but exactly the right thing."

Studying Bodine, Jessica sipped more wine. "I think it's safe now for me to ask why you hired me. The woman from New York who'd never been west of the Mississippi."

"Well, your résumé made my eyes pop. Your résumé and your references made me do a butt jiggle in my chair. I didn't know if you'd stick. You were sad."

"I was."

"But you could say I decided to take a leap, too. I had a good feeling all along. The first phone interviews, the face-to-face when you flew out. I've got a lot of Irish in me, and Chippewa. It sort of negates the more practical French blood that's in there. I believe in feelings, and following them when you can."

"So here we are."

"And here's to us." Bodine tapped her glass to Jessica's.

The sun dipped toward the white peaks, giving them a gloss of pale gold, as Bodine drove toward home.

With her Christmas list complete—and the painting even now in the hands of the jubilant artist for that last, sentimental touch—she foresaw clear sailing in these last two weeks before the big day.

"I'm so glad you talked me into this. Even if I do think that red vest is a mistake."

"It looked amazing on you. You can pull off vivid colors. I don't know why you don't wear red and more jewel tones."

The absent tone had Bodine glancing over. With every mile Jessica had grown quieter, more subdued.

"You okay?"

"Hmm? Yes. Yes, I'm fine." But she lapsed into silence again, seemed content to stare out the window as the light went soft with dusk.

Then she straightened in her seat. "We're friends."

"Sure."

On a frustrated sound, Jessica shook her head. "I've been careful about making friends nearly all my life. I make exceptionally good acquaintances, interesting casual friends—the sort you have a drink with every couple months. I've had work friends, but I've been careful about making friends who don't have all those qualifications, those limitations."

"Why is that?"

"Child of divorce maybe. I barely remember my parents being together, and honestly didn't spend that much time with either one of them. My grandparents raised me. At first there was this illusion. You're staying with us because your mother's taking a trip or because your father's working. After a while the illusion was obvious even to a child. My parents didn't want me."

"I'm sorry. That's—" Bodine couldn't find words. "I'm just sorry."

"My grandparents did want me, loved me, and they showed me every day. But it's a hard thing to shake. Your own parents don't want you. Anyway, that's probably the foundation for being careful about making friends. But we're friends, and I really, really don't want to screw that up."

"Why would you?"

"I kissed Chase. Or he kissed me. I'd say we kissed each other by the time we were finished."

To give herself a moment to absorb, Bodine lifted a hand off the wheel, held it out in a stop gesture. "What?"

"It wasn't planned, on either side. The horse knocked me into him. Well, no, didn't knock me, but the horse— Cal's horse—sniffed at my hair, and it jolted me into Chase. Then it just happened."

"When? Thanksgiving?"

"Yes."

"I *knew* it." Bodine shook her fist in the air. "Not the kiss, but I knew something. Chase had that flustered and trying not to show it look he's always gotten when he's been up to something."

She put her hand back on the wheel, realized she'd punched the gas as well as the air, and eased off the speed a little. "A real kiss? On the mouth?"

"Yes, a real kiss. And it occurred to me he's your brother. I'm your friend, but I'm also your employee, so—"

"Oh, just bucket the employee business. Chase is a grown man and can kiss whoever he wants to kiss—if they want it. And he wouldn't kiss somebody who didn't because he's not made that way, so if the two of you were fine with it, why wouldn't I be?"

"I wouldn't say he was fine with it. He's the one who stopped, then started apologizing all over himself until I wanted to knock him down. I mean, what kind of idiot—" She broke off. "He's your brother."

"I can love and stick up for my brother and still know

he's an idiot in some areas. Apologized about kissing you?"

"Taking advantage of me." Realizing she had a sympathetic audience, Jessica let it fly. "Advantage of me? Do I look like someone who'd let anyone take advantage of her? I'm from New York! Does he think I haven't put down my share of men who pushed when I didn't want to be pushed? Then it's how he didn't want me to feel obligated—like I'd start something with him because I felt pressured as a resort employee. *That*'s what he gets out of me kissing him? Oh, I better go along with this if I want to keep my job! If I felt sexually harassed, he'd know it like that!"

She snapped her fingers. "I'm not some scared, weak little mouse who can be taken advantage of or pressured."

Bodine let her wind down. "I'm going to say this. Apologizing like that? It's just like him. And I'm going to guess he'd thought about kissing you for a while. Chase isn't one for impulses—unless he's running around with Skinner, who brings out that side of him. He . . . deliberates things, and he obviously hadn't finished deliberating about you before you ended up in this particular situation. Then he straight off feels responsible. I'm not saying don't be pissed a little at how he fumbled it, and his fumbling was downright insulting, but I hope you can give him a little leeway, seeing as he was only being Chase."

"I can try."

Reaching over, Bodine poked Jessica's arm. "I'm not sticking up for him, or only a little. I expect you let him know he'd insulted you."

"Oh, I did."

"Which would've confused and frustrated him, and

when it sank in, would've appalled him, as he's got a powerful respect for women. I'd never call him smooth."

Jessica let out a short laugh at the very idea.

"Not like Rory is, and just to digress a minute on that?
Rory's going to do more than flirt with the adorable
Chelsea sooner or later, if she'd like more than flirting.
He reads people as well as a scholar reads books, it's why
he's so good in sales. He wouldn't take advantage any
more than Chase, but he'll move a lot faster. Anyway."

She drove for another minute as she put her thoughts
together. "I wouldn't be surprised if he—Chase—worked
up an apology for the apology, so I'm going to ask you,
as a friend, do you like him?"

"Of course I do," Jessica began. "He's a very nice man."

"Rory's a nice man. Are you planning on kissing him?"

Jessica blew out a breath. "No." Friends, Jessica thought.
Not just work friends, not just acquaintances.

Friends. She could take that next leap.

"I'm attracted to Chase. I'm interested in him."

"Then if you want a repeat, or more, you're going to
have to make the next move. He won't, or it'll be a year
or so before he works up to it on his own."

"Just to be clear"—Jessica held up a finger—"are you
saying I should go after your brother?"

"I'm saying, as your friend, and as your employer, just
so we touch all the bases, you and Chase are both grown-
ups, both single, both with minds of your own. As his sister, who knows him inside and out, I'm advising you: If
you want to start something, you'll have to start it. And
nobody who knows either of you is going to be shocked
or worried if the two of you start sleeping together. I don't
know why people let sex be so damn complicated."

"I'm not talking about having sex with him."

"Of course you are."

Jessica let out a sigh. "Of course I am. I need to think about it. Not for a year or so. A day or two is enough for me. Bodine?"

"Mmm-hmm."

"I like having a friend."

Glancing over, Bodine grinned. "You got lucky with me. I'm a hell of a good friend."

She continued to grin as she punched the gas again. Nearly home now, she thought as she passed a blue compact heading in the opposite direction, and she really wanted to get there.

If Karyn Allison's tire had blown two minutes sooner, Bodine would've seen her on the side of the road and stopped rather than zipping by the car as Karyn drove toward Missoula.

Two minutes would have changed everything.

He cleaned blood from his hands with snow. He hadn't meant to do it. Why hadn't the girl just *behaved*? He had a right—God given—even an obligation to procreate, to continue his line.

To spread his seed into the world.

And hadn't God put her right in his path?

There she'd been, on the side of the road with a blown-out tire. A clearer sign of divine intervention he'd never seen.

Now, if she'd been too old—for childbearing—or uncomely, as a man had a right to take a comely woman for his wife, he'd have changed the tire for her, like a good Christian, and continued on his way.

On his hunt.

But she was young. Younger than the tavern whore and pretty as a lemon drop. Since she'd already set about jacking up the car, she showed she had some spirit, and a man wanted some spirit passed on to his sons.

And hadn't she thanked him, smiled pretty as you please when he stopped to do the job for her?

He appreciated good manners. How she'd stepped back to let him take over demonstrated she knew her place.

But then she'd gone and taken out her phone, said how she'd call the friends she was meeting, let them know what was going on.

He couldn't have that.

He told her so, and she'd given him a look he didn't much like. Disrespectful.

He hit her. Looking back now he could see he shouldn't have let what happened with the other one cause him to pull his punch. Should've put her down hard, considering how she'd yelled and hit back at him.

Caught him right in the balls, too, before he'd given her a good whack with the lug wrench.

But she'd been breathing, even moaned a little when he hauled her into the back of his truck, trussed her up, slapped some duct tape over her mouth in case she started that yelling again.

He'd gone back, too, picked up her phone and got her pocketbook out of her car. He'd heard about how the police found those things before.

He'd felt too damn good, knowing he'd done what he'd set out to do, what he was meant to do. She'd wake up in her room, and he'd teach her her place right quick. Her duty.

But when he'd gotten back to the cabin, gone to pull her out, there was a lot more blood than he'd expected. His first thought was that he'd have to clean it off.

His second was she'd gone and died on him right in the back of his damn truck. Just died on him.

It not only soured his righteous mood, it scared him some.

He'd covered her back up, driven straight off. He hadn't even gone in the cabin. Home wasn't the place for some damn dead girl who didn't know how to behave.

Especially with the ground too hard to dig a grave.

Bitter about his bad luck, he drove through the night, through a squall of snow toward the wilderness. It took some doing, some snowshoeing with a dead girl over his shoulder, but he didn't have to go far.

He buried her in snow, along with her phone, her pocketbook. But he took the money out of it first, took the blanket he'd wrapped her in. He wasn't stupid.

Nobody would find her until spring, most likely, and maybe not then. The animals would take her first anyway.

He considered saying a prayer over her. Decided she wasn't worthy of it, hadn't been worthy of him. So he cleaned her blood from his hands with snow, and left her in the dark stillness of wilderness.

CHAPTER ELEVEN

Bodine purely loved Christmas Eve. The resort closed midday after the last of the checkouts, and remained closed until the day after Christmas. Security would make their rounds, of course, taking shifts, and horses would be tended. But for all intents and purposes, everyone had a day and a half to spend with friends and family.

The grannies would come, spend the night, and the ranch hands and any employees who weren't with their own families were welcome to a feast of food and drink.

Bodine rode home with Callen—a habit at least three times a week now—through a steady Christmas snowfall.

"Are you going to see your mom and sister for Christmas?" she asked him.

"Tomorrow, yeah, for dinner."

"You give them my best. What did you do for Christmas back in California?"

"Mooched off friends. Like I'm doing at your place tonight."

"We've got enough food for an army. I only praise Jesus

the women in my family conceded years back to have the resort kitchen handle this do. Otherwise, I'd be stuck peeling and chopping the minute I walk in the door."

"You could come hide out at the shack, help me deal with the presents I'm hauling to my sister's tomorrow."

"You haven't got them wrapped yet?"

"I've got till tomorrow, don't I? And I don't wrap. That's what those fancy bags are for." He glanced over. She had her hair braided back, a long dark twist, and her face was flushed from cold and pleasure. "Are you all wrapped up?"

"Wrapped, bowed, tagged, and under the tree."

Didn't she look all smug about it? And pretty as a Christmas ribbon.

"Show-off."

Laughing, she angled her head, fluttered her lashes. "Being smart and organized isn't showing off. Plus, I'll admit I had Sal help me. She likes to fuss with wrapping, is a hell of a lot better at it even if it does take her half of forever. And it kept her distracted."

Her smile dimmed, dropped away. "She's missing Billy Jean. They always spent Christmas Eve together drinking champagne cocktails. And now that other girl's gone missing, and Sal's decided she was taken off by the same one who killed Billy Jean."

When he said nothing, Bodine looked over. "You think the same?"

"I think they were both women alone, both had breakdowns—out of gas for one, flat tire for the other. I leave the rest of the thinking to the sheriff."

"Car jacked up like she started to change the tire, but she didn't have a lug wrench—from what I read about it. It seems she'd have called somebody, as her mother said she had her cell phone when she left. But it could be the battery was dead. It could be, most likely, she hitched a ride, and then . . .

"I had to pass her," Bodine added. "Almost had to."

"What do you mean?"

"I read what time they said she'd left her mother's. She'd gone to see her mother, and was driving back to Missoula to meet some friends, some of her college friends. She goes to U of M. Jessie and I almost had to pass her, her going, us coming from town that evening. I went right by where they found her car. I have to wonder how much I missed her by."

She shook it off.

"But I think what happened to Billy Jean was some-body from outside did it. It could have even been a guest, though I hate to think it. I think somebody snatched that girl, and that's a terrible thing, but it's not the same. She was only eighteen—a lot younger—and Billy Jean drove home the way she did most every night. This Karyn Al-lison hadn't been home for a visit, I heard, for a couple weeks."

He understood why she needed to believe that—and maybe she had it right. But believing that wouldn't push her to take precautions. So he firmly stomped on her theory.

"It could be two different people went after two women having car trouble inside of a month within about twenty miles of each other."

Bodine hissed out a breath. "That's what I tell Sal when she gets worked up about it, and what I tell myself because I want to sleep at night."

Since that satisfied him, he nodded. "No harm in that, as long as you stay smart and keep your eyes open. I've never known you to do otherwise."

"I don't even know why I'm talking about it on my favorite night of the year. Except I was thinking how your mother must bc so happy to have you home for Christmas, and that other mother doesn't know where her girl is, or if she's all right."

To comfort herself, she leaned forward to stroke Leo, then straightened. "Wait. Keep my eyes open? Is that why either you or Rory ends up hitching a ride to and from with me if I'm not on Leo?"

Callen rode easy. "Just saving fuel."

Her sarcasm dripped like melting ice. "Just thinking about the environment'?"

"More should."

She couldn't argue that. And found, when she broke it all down, she couldn't be insulted, either. Very much. "I appreciate the concern. Though I can handle myself just fine, I appreciate the sly, manly lookout all the same."

She smiled, overbright, when Callen sent her a slow, careful look.

"Is that so?"

"It is. I don't appreciate the big, strong men not just coming out and saying so in order to spare my little female sensibilities, but I appreciate the concern."

"It wasn't about your female sensibilities. It was more about your stubborn streak and temper."

"Why is it men are called strong or tough, and women stubborn?"

"I'm not touching that." He clucked his tongue instead and took Sundown into a trot.

"Coward," Bodine accused, but she laughed as she came up beside him.

"About some areas."

They rode companionably into the ranch yard.

"I've got to get something from the shack."

When Callen veered off, Bodine shrugged and led Leo into the stables.

"That was a nice ride," she said as she unsaddled and unbridled him. "You deserve a good rubdown, and maybe a little something special after."

She grabbed a hoof pick, tended to his feet before giving him a good rub with a towel. As she picked up a soft brush, she heard Callen come in with Sundown.

Since she had a jump on him, she finished first, carted her saddle to the tack room, then came back for Callen's.

"I'll get that in a minute."

"I've got it now." But she paused outside the stall. "I've also got a jar of peppermint treats—"

As Callen said, "Don't!" Sundown let out a long, high whinny, gave Callen an enthusiastic butt with his head before sticking it over the door. The horse aimed a wildly bright-eyed look at Bodine.

"Next time spell it. I expect he'll figure that out before long, but for now don't say either of those words out loud. Out of the way, you."

Callen managed to nudge Sundown back, get out of the stall, before the horse stuck out his head again.

Testing—she couldn't help it—Bodine said, "Peppermint treats."

"Oh, for Christ's—" With a shake of his head, Callen hefted the saddle from Bodine as Sundown danced and whinnied.

"Is he . . . like . . . cheering?"

"You could say that's his version of *yippee*. Just hold on a minute."

Fascinated, Bodine went back into Leo's stall as Callen carried his tack away. She pulled the jar of peppermints from the stall box—she'd bought them especially, and sentimentally, for Leo for Christmas.

Digging in her pocket, she cut off the seal with her pocketknife.

She gave Leo two, which he gobbled with pleasure, then kissed his cheek. "Merry Christmas, Leo."

She took two more out of the jar, and stepped out of the stall. Spotting them, Sundown did an excellent mimic of smacking his lips.

"He beats all," she said as Callen came back. "Is it all right to give them to him?"

"Not until he says please."

In response, Sundown made a sound in his throat, and his eyes said *please* as clearly as the word.

She held them out, and he nibbled them off her palm. Seemed to sigh, then blew his lips against her cheek.

"You're welcome. Leo's pleased to share his Christmas— the word I'm not saying—with you. If I'd known he was that fond of them, I'd have picked up another jar."

"I keep one at the shack. If I kept one anywhere near him, he'd find a way to get to it, even if I put it in a damn vault. Speaking of Christmas."

Callen opened the stall again, lifted a gift bag from inside.

"Oh." Flustered, Bodine stared at it, then up at Callen. "I didn't— You didn't have to get me anything."

"Who says it's for you? Try to remember, the spirit of Christmas is about giving, not getting, Bodine. It's for Leo, from Sundown here."

"It's . . . Your horse got a present for my horse?"

"They've gotten to be good pals. Are you going to give it to him?"

"Of course. I think I'll need to take it out, if that's all right with Sundown."

"Is that a yes?" Callen asked his horse, and got a quick nod.

"Well, let's see what we've got here, Leo." She stepped across to Leo's stall, dug in the tissue, felt leather.

"Look here, Leo, you've got a new halter. A fancy one, too. Oh, it's got his name and the Bodine brand on it. Callen, this is so nice, so thoughtful. Thank you."

"Don't thank me." Leaning back against the stall door, Callen wagged his thumb behind him. "Sundown picked it out."

"Of course he did. Thank you, Sundown. It's the nicest head collar Leo's ever had. We're going to try it on right now. Let's try it," she murmured to the horse as she slipped it on. "It fits just right, and look how handsome."

She turned back to Callen. "I appreciate you helping Sundown out with the particulars."

"Well, he had his mind set on it."

Watching her with his horse and her own had Callen's mind set.

"See that up there?" He pointed to the ceiling.

She looked up, saw nothing but beams. "I don't see anything."

"That mistletoe hanging down."

She looked up again. "There's no mistletoe up there."

"You must not be looking in the right place."

But he was, he thought. He surely was.

He pulled her in.

No accidental lip bump this time. This time he meant it, and made sure she knew it. The hands on her shoulders slid down her sides to her waist, cinched there, while his mouth took hers the way he'd imagined. Slow, sure, strong.

And as he'd imagined, she didn't pull back, but met him head-on.

She'd grown prettier, he thought, and her lips were full and warm and far from shy. Her body pressed against his until he knew the shape of her would stay imprinted on his mind.

When her hand came up, gripped the back of his neck, he felt every cell in his body leap.

She'd known this was coming, sooner or later. Too much heat, too many sparks under those companionable rides not to lead to this. While she'd wondered how she'd react, wondered if she'd make the move or he would, she'd thought herself fully prepared.

She'd thought wrong.

It was bigger and bolder and brighter than anything she'd foreseen. Her body's reaction stunned her as she felt herself quiver, at least inside.

He tasted of heat and secrets, smelled of horses and leather and man, and his mouth showed skills she'd underestimated.

When he started to draw away, she pulled him back.

He'd started it. So she'd finish it.

When she was right on the edge of breathless, she pushed him back. "Mistletoe, my ass."

"I might've been mistaken about it." He glanced up again, seemed to consider, then met her eyes. More blue than gray now, she noted. Those hints of lightning through the storm. "But I wanted to give us both a preview of what's coming."

"And what's coming, Skinner?"

"You know as well as I do, but we'll go there after Abe's back this spring. I can wait."

She turned to take her coat off the hook outside the stall. "You sound pretty damn cocksure of yourself."

"I'm sure with more than that part."

Damn it, he made her laugh. "Maybe, but I've got something to say about it."

"You just did."

Eyeing him warily, she put on her coat. She wasn't certain if she wanted to fight or find an empty stall and really finish what he had started.

"Maybe I was just feeling a little Christmas spirit."

"We can test that out." He took a step toward her. She held up a hand.

"I think it's best we leave this where it is for right now."

He just slid his hands into his pockets. "Like I said. I can wait."

"April's a ways off. We can both change our minds before then."

"I don't think so. But we'll see come spring."

"All right." She'd consider it a kind of agenda. Come spring, they'd see. "Are you coming in?"

"I'm going to go clean up some first."

"Then I'll see you after you do." She strode down the concrete. "You know, Skinner," she said, without turning around, "I might sleep with you just because of your horse. Keep that in mind."

As the door closed behind her, Callen looked at Sundown. "You're not why."

Sundown proved a horse could guffaw.

Linda-Sue's wedding, even with the additional pomp and circumstance, proved a major success—and a big, fat feather in Jessica's cap. Or, at least, in the flat-brimmed Stetson Bodine had given her for Christmas.

She handled the bride and her party, assigned Will to the groom and his, and with Chelsea's help tackled the biggest issue.

The mother of the bride.

From arrivals to wardrobe emergencies, from flowers to decor to music—and a harpist—the wedding kept

Jessica and her team scrambling, adjusting, consoling, cheerleading, and coordinating for three solid days.

The wedding rolled right into the New Year's Eve package: the menu of activities, the entertainment, and the big, rowdy party.

She didn't argue when Bodine ordered her to take two full days off afterward, and slept through nearly half of them.

Once, popping awake at two A.M., foggy and disoriented, she got out of bed, glancing out the window on her way to her little kitchen for a bottle of water. She noticed an unfamiliar pickup on the road in front of the Village rather than in the designated parking area.

Idly, she wondered if Chelsea—her nearest neighbor— had an overnight guest, and why they had parked on the road.

But when she came back, the truck was gone. Without giving it another thought, she slid back into bed and sleep.

The early January lull drove straight into the writers conference—another feather in her cap—and that slammed straight into the Snow Sculpture Extravaganza.

Every time another booking came in, Rory bounced into Jessica's office to do a victory dance.

Local media interest didn't hurt a thing.

With the field behind her filled with people, horse-drawn sleighs jingling by holding even more, and younger kids taking pony rides in the near paddock, Bodine did an on-site interview for local TV.

"We're thrilled to host our first annual Snow Sculpture Extravaganza here at Bodine Resort. We have guests from all over the country, and from Canada. We have a couple honeymooning here from England who decided to participate today."

Out of the corner of her eye, she saw Callen hitch a kid

onto his back while the boy waited for his turn on a pony, and wondered where he'd gotten that smooth way with kids.

But she kept her attention on the reporter, answered questions.

"I want to say everybody associated with the Bodine Resort worked hard, really got into the spirit to make this event something special, to make it fun for everyone participating. And we're happy to see so many of our friends and neighbors joining in, either as contestants or just to watch the show. We're pleased to have Anna Langtree and the Mountain Men providing entertainment this afternoon from two to three-thirty and again this evening at nine, in the Mill."

When she wrapped it up, Bodine wandered over to Jessica.

"You're great at that," Jessica commented. "Getting the message and details across while looking and sounding relaxed at the same time."

"It's just talking. You know, some of these are starting to look pretty impressive. Looks like a whole snow family being built over there, a couple of castles going up. I think that may be a horse—a really big one. And . . . I don't know what that is, right out at twelve o'clock."

"It looks like a big snake."

"Not fond of snakes, but it takes all kinds." Smiling, she tapped the brim of Jessica's hat. "You know, that suits you."

"I really kind of love it. Who knew? Well, you. If anybody had suggested a year ago I'd be in Montana, wearing a Stetson and watching somebody build a snake out of snow, I'd've laughed until I broke a rib. And here I am."

"That suits you, too. Since it does, and so well, we're

changing your title to events director, and giving you a raise."

"Well." Jessica took off her sunglasses, narrowed her eyes against the bounce of light off the snow. "Wow. We were going to talk about that after I was here a year."

"We moved it up. You earned it."

"Thank you." On a laugh, Jessica pulled Bodine in for a hug. "Thank you, all of you. I—" She broke off as her phone signaled an incoming text. "Chelsea," she said, "right on time. They're setting up the buffet in the Mill. You can announce that in fifteen minutes. I'm going to go make sure everything's in order."

"That's why you're director."

At a burst of laughter, Bodine looked over at the paddock, saw Callen and Sundown doing an impromptu show. Currently Callen sat backward in the saddle while the horse hung his head, shook it sadly.

"You gotta turn around, mister!" one of the kids shouted.

"I gotta what?"

"Turn around," several chorused.

"Maybe he should turn around."

Obliging, Sundown reversed direction.

"That better?" Callen asked, and had the kids squealing with laughter as they shouted: *No!*

He listened, with apparent interest, as several kids explained he had to sit facing the front of the horse.

"All right, all right, I gotta figure out how to get from here to there."

He twisted one way, twisted the other while Sundown let out a snort that spoke of derision. He half slid out of the saddle left, overcompensated right while the kids laughed or covered their eyes.

"Okay, all right, I think I've puzzled this out."

He swung his legs over the side of the horse, sat facing three o'clock. Sundown turned his head, blew.

"I don't wanna hear anything out of you. I almost got this."

In answer the horse bucked his back legs—giving Bodine a little jolt. As if the movement had bounced him up, Callen swung into the saddle.

At the cheers, Sundown danced right, danced left, then took a bow.

Callen looked straight over at Bodine, and winked.

A good day, she thought as he rode Sundown in tight, fast circles. A good, fine day.

While people enjoyed barbecue, buffalo chili, and grilled beef, a photographer intent on getting shots of the pristine wilderness found what was left of Karyn Allison.

For her, all but stumbling over the mauled remains, it was anything but a good, fine day.

Twenty-four hours later, shortly after the sheriff sat in Karyn's mother's living room, telling her that her daughter wasn't coming home again, Garrett Clintok pulled into the lot at the BAC.

The way he saw it, nobody was going to tell him how to do his job. Not the sheriff, who'd already taken a strip off him, and not anybody.

He saw it, clear as day.

He'd been a deputy long enough to know a bad egg when he smelled it. He'd seen his share of them as an Army MP. He'd seen his share of bad eggs all his damn life.

Most trouble around these parts ran to brawls, drunkenness, the occasional domestic dispute—where, in his opinion, the woman likely deserved a little pop—spoiled college kids fucking off, maybe some drugs here and there.

You had your women crying rape, and he didn't believe half of them on that. Your accidents and so on.

But you sure as hell didn't have two women murdered inside two months' time.

Not until Callen Skinner came back.

In his book, you added two and two, you got four.

Maybe the sheriff would turn a blind eye given Skinner was tight with the Longbow clan.

He wouldn't.

He walked over to where Callen was unloading horses from a trailer.

"You're going to want your boy there to deal with the horses. You're coming with me."

Callen calmly led the horse he'd unloaded to the shelter. "Now, why would I do that?"

"Because I'm telling you."

"Easy, go on and rub her down. I'll get the other."

Clintok expanded his chest. A peacock preening. A bull readying the charge. "I said you're coming with me."

"Nope. Not unless you've got a warrant in your pocket." Callen guided the second horse down the ramp. "You got a warrant, Deputy?"

"I can get one."

"Then go do that." Callen glanced toward Easy, who stood wide-eyed and a little slack-jawed beside the mare. "Get her rubbed down, Easy." Then with a hand hooked loosely in the other horse's head collar, Callen turned back to Clintok.

"We've got things to do around here. If you want to book a ride, you do that inside."

"You want to do this the hard way?"

"Sure looks like it." When Callen smiled, no trace of

humor showed. "I'm going to tell you up front, and in front of this boy, who'll serve as a witness, you go at me without a warrant, I'll be going right back at you. Is that hard enough to suit you?"

He could see fury blaze over Clintok's face, like fire over sagebrush. And stood just as he was, eyes level, body deceptively relaxed.

"Where were you December twelve, starting at four in the afternoon, going to nine?"

"Well, let's see." With his free hand, Callen pulled out his phone, tapped open his calendar. "Looks like I started that day early. Took a before-school lesson. We had some sleigh rides. When I got here, Easy there took one, I took one myself, and Ben—he's still down at the center right now—took the others. Had feed delivered that day, and I've got here the paint we call Cochise was favoring his left foreleg. We had—"

"I don't want all that bullshit. Four o'clock."

"I'd've been heading out about then."

"Alone?"

Callen pocketed his phone. "It was more than a month ago, but since I don't believe you're showing a sudden interest in how I spend my time, I recall December twelfth is when that girl from college went missing. That being the case, I'd have been on my own, as Bodine was off in Missoula, and I came in too early for Rory and me to ride in together."

"You don't have the high-and-mighty Longbows lined up for your alibi?" Clintok took an exaggerated look around. "I don't see Bodine rushing up here so you can hide behind her."

"You're going to want to be careful there," Callen said softly.

"We'll see who has to be careful. Money doesn't buy sense, which the Longbows and Bodines proved by hiring you on. I wonder how they'll spin it around when you're behind bars where you belong."

Even as temper clawed its way through his gut, Callen spoke evenly. "You and me, Clintok, we both know your problem's not with the Longbows or Bodines, or not most of it. So why don't we stick with you and me?"

"Since you don't have them backing you this time around, did anybody see you December twelfth? Anybody who can verify where you were?"

Not a damn soul, Callen thought, as he'd loaded Sundown in a trailer, had taken him down to the center to work with him for a couple hours.

"That'd be hard to say."

Clintok leaned in. "What's hard about it?"

"Ah, boss?" Swallowing deeply enough to be audible, Easy stepped out a little. "Sorry, but I heard you trying to remember. The day Cochise needed his foreleg wrapped, wasn't that the same day we started working on the tack? Cleaning, repairing. You ended up staying, working with me on that till damn near six o'clock. We cracked open a beer after that, being done for the day. I don't think I headed out myself till close to seven, and you were still here. Wanted to check Cochise's leg before you went on home. I remember pretty clear on it."

Callen held Easy's eyes another moment. "Maybe it was."

"I'm pretty clear on it. Is that what you wanted to know, Deputy?"

Clintok angled toward him. "Are you lying to me? It's a serious offense to lie to a police officer."

"Why would I do that?" Easy backed off a step. "I'm

just saying what you asked about. How we were here till about seven—it was nice to sit and have a beer after a long day—and then I went on home."

"Go on back, Easy," Callen told him.

"Okay, boss, just trying to help."

"How come you don't have all that shit he just spread on your fucking phone, Skinner?"

"I've got my schedule, and I was off at four. Sometimes things need to be done, or I want to get them done, and I stay later. I don't note having a beer with one of my men down on my calendar. If that answers your questions, I've got horses to take care of."

"Two women dead, Skinner. Two since you came back here. Maybe I'll do some checking back in California, find more."

"You spend your time as you see fit, Deputy. I'll do the same."

Callen led the horse into the shelter, carefully removed its blanket, then rested his tightly fisted hands on the withers. Another ten seconds, he figured—likely no more than five—he'd have used those fists.

He wouldn't have been capable of holding back longer.

Now he forced himself to relax those fists as he heard Clintok's engine roar to life, heard him drive off, spitting gravel from his tires.

He had the boy to thank for sparing him what would've been an ugly brawl. But . . .

"You didn't have to do that, Easy."

"I was just giving my recollection. We had all that tack to get to."

"We started on the tack a couple days after that. You know that as well as I do."

"I don't know as I do." Easy looked over the horses' backs. The stubborn set to his jaw loosened under Callen's steady stare. "Maybe I do now that I think on it, but I didn't like the way he came at you, boss. I didn't like how he talked, or how he looked. I swear he wanted to pull out his sidearm, draw down on you. I swear. I didn't want to see him give you trouble, that's all."

"I appreciate it. I do. But next time—and with Clintok there's always a next time—don't. There's no point in you walking into his sights. He's had me there since we were boys, and it's never going to change."

"Some people get born with a mean streak, I reckon. Was he talking about that girl who went missing? Is he saying she's dead?"

"That's how it sounded to me."

"Holy hell, Cal." Easy let out a long breath as he ran a soft brush over the mare. "Holy hell. That's terrible. That ain't right. But he's got to be stupid thinking you'd do something like that."

"Like I said, I've been in his sights a long time. Sooner or later, he'd like to have an excuse to pull the trigger."

Sooner or later, Callen thought, he might get pushed into giving him one.

CHAPTER TWELVE

— 2012 —

Esther scrubbed the bathroom, top to bottom, as she did every other day.

Cleanliness was godliness.

Her hands, red, raw, and cracked from years of hot water and harsh soaps, burned some as she dunked the scrub brush in the bucket. Her knees ached; her back pinged and popped.

She barely noticed.

She took such pride in the white linoleum floor, in the shine she worked out of the faucets and knobs in the sink and the shower.

She sang while she worked, her voice as young and strong and pretty as she'd once been.

When she finished there, she'd sweep and scrub the rest of the house, and when Sir came, he'd be pleased with her.

He'd built it for her, hadn't he, even said how she'd earned it. And he warned her, as she was weak-minded and lazy, he could take it away again if she didn't show it—and him—the proper respect.

He'd even let her hang a flower-print curtain to separate the bathroom from the rest of the house.

The rest consisted of an eight-by-ten-foot space that held a twin bed, a rusted iron pole lamp with a torn shade, the chair he'd hauled from her room in the basement, a counter formed out of birch logs and plywood, a shower rod that served as her closet.

Unfinished drywall covered the walls; a brown braided rug, frayed at the edges, spread over the subflooring. She had two cupboards, one for the plastic dishes, one for foodstuffs, and a cold box for keeping perishables.

Best of all, she had a window. It was small, and high up at the ceiling, but she got light when the sun shined, could see the sky, and the night stars.

When she stood on the bed, she could see more. A few trees, the mountains—or a hint of them.

The space was smaller than the room in the basement, but she'd wept with gratitude when Sir had brought her to it, told her she would live there now.

She no longer wore the leg irons, though Sir had bolted them to the wall to remind her what he'd need to do if she angered him.

She tried hard not to anger him.

Here, in what was a palace to her, she could heat water on the hot plate and make her own tea, or open up a can and cook soup.

In the season, he'd even let her out to work the vegetable garden. Of course, he had to tether her, lest she wander off and get lost or mauled by a bear.

She had to work at first light or at night with the dog chained, as he was watching her, but she prized those hours in the air, with her hands in the dirt, planting or weeding.

Once or twice she thought she'd heard a child calling or crying, and another time—maybe more than another time—she was certain she heard somebody call for help. But Sir said it was birds, and to get about her work.

Sir provided for himself and his own, he liked to say, with chickens in the coop, the milk cow in the pen, the horse in the paddock.

The garden served an important role in providing, and a woman worked the earth and tended its fruit. Just as a woman was to be planted and bear fruit.

She'd had three more children, all girls, as well as two miscarriages and a boy, stillborn.

The girls he took away, and though she'd wept for each precious one, she let herself forget. Then the boy. She'd felt such joy, such hope, then such shock and grief.

Sir said it was God's wrath on her, a punishment for her evil ways, the curse of Eve.

Holding that still form, that lifeless child, like a pale blue doll, she knew Sir spoke truth.

God punished the wicked. She was the wicked. But every day, she repented her wicked ways, worked toward her redemption.

She pushed herself to her feet, wincing as her knees creaked. She wore her scrubbing dress—a cotton tent that hung to the middle of her calves—and thin-soled slippers. Her hair, well past her waist now, hung in a brittle, graying braid down her back.

She was not afforded a mirror, as vanity was a sin lodged dark in every woman's heart, but her fingers could feel the lines scoring her face.

She told herself to be grateful Sir still wanted her to do her marital duties, that he rewarded her by providing for her.

She pressed her hand to her belly, where she knew another child grew. She prayed it would be a boy. Every night, she knelt and prayed for a son, one her husband would allow her to keep with her. One she could love and feed at her breast, could tend and teach.

She emptied the bucket, filled it again. Time to scrub the cupboards, the counter, the cold box, and the little kitchen sink. Time to do her work.

But after she carried the bucket into her kitchen, she had to lean against the wall. It was the baby, of course. Growing inside her, needing to take from her, that made her so tired, and half-feverish with it.

She'd make some tea, sit for a little while until she felt stronger. Stronger for the baby, she thought as she got out the jar holding the dandelion greens Sir had been so kind to teach her, an ignorant woman, how to dry.

She put a cup of water in a pot to boil, and while it did, used the hot, soapy water in the bucket to scrub while she waited.

It wouldn't do to let it go cold. Waste not, want not.

By the time the water boiled she felt hot and dizzy. The tea would put her to rights, the tea and a little sit-down time.

She poured the boiling water over the plastic teaspoon of greens, carried it with her to the chair.

As she sat, she closed her eyes. "We're just going to rest a minute," she told the baby. "Just going to take a rest. We've got beans and tomatoes to harvest tonight. And maybe some summer squash. We've got—"

She broke off, gasping at the sudden, vicious cramp.

"No! No, please!"

The second doubled her over in the chair, dropped her onto her knees as the cup fell out of her hand, spilling dandelion tea on the old braided rug.

She felt it leave her, that life, felt it flood out of her in blood and pain.

God punished the wicked, she thought, and lay on the rug, wishing for her own death.

— *Present Day* —

Bodine managed to get home just before dark—and before another hit of February snow. As she stripped off her winter gear, she caught the scents of cooking from the kitchen.

"God, that smells good! We're in for another couple feet they're saying, Clementine. You might want to—" Spotting the sturdy, stoic cook wiping hastily at tears, Bodine broke off, rushed forward. "What's the matter? What happened? Is somebody hurt? Mom—"

Sniffling, trying to shoo Bodine aside, Clementine shook her head. "She and your dad are out on a date. It's nothing. I got something in my eye."

"Don't hand me that bull. You could have a splinter the size of my thumb in your eye and you'd pluck it out without shedding a tear. You sit down."

"Can't you see I've got this chicken to finish?"

With a flick, Bodine turned off the burner. "It'll keep. I said you sit down, and I mean it. Right now."

"I'd like to know when you started giving orders around here."

"I'm giving this one. Or do you want me to call Mom?"

"Don't you dare do any such thing!" Face set, cheeks still damp, Clementine sat. "There. Satisfied?"

Though she wanted to snap back, Bodine held her tongue. She thought to make tea, decided it would take too long and she might lose the advantage. She pulled out a bottle of whisky instead, poured two fingers.

After slapping it down in front of Clementine, Bodine sat. "Now, you tell me what's wrong. How many times have I told you when I got hurt or upset or just mad enough to cry?"

"It's nothing to do with you."

"You're everything to do with me."

Defeated by that, Clementine lifted the glass, downed half the whisky. "I don't know what came over me. I just heard . . . A friend of mine in my quilting club—you know Sarah Howard."

"Sure. I went to school with her younger son, Harry. I— Oh, Clem, did something happen to Mrs. Howard?"

"No, no, she's fine. I'm just—" Holding up a hand, Clementine composed herself. "Sarah's friends with Denise McNee—that's that poor child Karyn Allison's ma. She took her name back after the divorce some years back. Sarah's cousin Marjean married Denise's brother, and Sarah and Denise got friendly over the years."

"All right."

"We were meeting up tonight, the quilting club, at my house. Eight to ten. Sarah just called, said how she couldn't come—she was bringing her coffee cake."

The rambling road wasn't hard to follow. "What happened to Denise McNee, Clem?"

"She took a bunch of pills, Bodine. Just swallowed a bunch of pills the doctor gave her to help her get through this terrible time. I don't know what kind of damn pills."

"Oh, Clem."

"It was Sarah who found her, went over to take her a casserole, give her some company for a while. It was Sarah who found her and called an ambulance."

"She killed herself."

"Tried to. Might have done it yet. She's in the hospital, and Sarah said they just don't know yet. She was sobbing over the phone, Sarah was. Just beside herself. And I just started thinking how that poor woman wanted to die, how she lost her child in such an awful way, and it's the same as losing her heart."

"I'm so sorry, Clem. I'm just so sorry."

"She ain't never going to be the same, that mother." Chin quivering, Clementine used the hem of her apron to wipe at her red-rimmed eyes. "If she goes on living, she'll never be the same as she was. People look at me and think I've never had children, but that's not the truth."

"No, it's not." Tone gentle, grip firm, Bodine took Clementine's hand. "You've got me and Chase and Rory. I guess Callen, too, really."

"It just came over me so hard." Steadier, Clementine dashed away tears with her free hand. "A good friend of mine crying over the phone for a friend of hers. That poor girl dead for reasons we just don't know. And Cora, bearing up all these years, not knowing if a child of hers is dead or alive. It just came over me so hard, and had me thinking how would I bear up, how would I live through if something happened to one of mine?"

She rocked herself a little, sipped at the whisky. "There's just no love like the love of a mother for a child, no matter how that child comes into their life, and no loss or grief to match it."

"We're going to take care of ourselves, and look out for each other, I promise you. Don't I let Callen tag along with me half the time going to work, or Rory? So I can keep an eye out for them?"

Clementine smiled. "You're a good girl most of the time, Bodine."

"I am. Now, I want you to do what I know you're fret-
ting about, and what you'd tell me to do in your place. You
go, be with your friend at the hospital. She needs you."

"I haven't finished dinner."

"I can figure it out. You go now. We've got snow coming, so you drive careful, and I want you to text me when
you get home tonight. So I won't worry," Bodine said
quickly.

"I've been driving in Montana snow since before you
were born. I would feel better being there for Sarah."

"Then you go."

"I will." She rose. "Now, you put that chicken on a me-
dium heat, let it simmer for another twenty minutes.
Don't go running off and leaving it to burn."

"No, ma'am."

"I got carrots and potatoes roasting in the oven."

Bodine listened to the detailed—and repeated—
instructions as Clementine bundled up.

On her own, she turned the burner on again, checked
the oven, lifted the cloth on the bread dough Clementine
said needed another fifteen minutes to rise.

She poured her glass of wine, and thought about a
mother's despair, about a mother bearing up. One hadn't
been able to handle the loss. The other pushed through it.

But both needed shoulders to lean on, friends around
them. Family to fill the voids, friends who were the same
as family.

She looked out the window, saw the lights on in the
shack.

And going with impulse, texted Callen.

You had dinner yet?

It took a minute for his answer. *Nope.*

*Come on over and eat with us. I'll even buy you a
beer.*

This time the answer came in seconds. *Pop the top and grab me a plate.*

Done.

She went back, poked at the chicken, and thought all Clementine's chicks would eat together in the roost tonight.

A day passed, then another, and Bodine couldn't get the conversation with Clementine out of her mind. It didn't matter that Clementine bounced back to her steady, stoic self, bringing the normal again.

Maybe it lodged in her mind because Denise McNee had fallen into a coma, and seemed to hover in that misty place between life and death. Could it be a choice, which way she went? Was it always a choice?

She wasn't sure there were answers, but she decided to ask the questions.

She rode down to the Equestrian Center, Leo's hoof strikes bright as church bells on the hard road. Snowy fields spread all around her as winter kept a firm, frozen grip on everything.

Still, the sky rolled blue and hawks circled through it. Maybe as February made its turn into March there'd be signs of spring.

She saw her grandmother's truck, Jessica's SUV, steered Leo around them. Dismounting, she opened the doors, led him inside.

Cora's voice echoed. "Change leads and take her around the other way. You don't need to hold on to that pommel now, Jessie."

"It feels like I do."

"Keep your back straight. That's the way. Why don't you take her into a trot?"

"Okay. God, I'll be sitting on a pillow again tomorrow."

Amused, as Jessica had done so twice already, Bodine tethered Leo to a rail, loosened his cinches.

When she walked to the edge of the ring, she noted Jessica had the mare circling in a nice, steady trot.

"Back straight." Cora, on her favored Wrangler, watched with an eagle eye. "Move with her now, let her feel you're with her."

To Bodine's mind, her grandmother never looked better than when she sat a horse. Her checkered shirt tucked into jeans, her jeans tucked into bold red boots. Her pretty hair under a crisp turned-brim black hat.

"Keep it going and change leads. Don't think too hard, just do it."

"I did it!"

"Of course you did. Now take her down, let her walk awhile. Keep those elbows down." Cora turned her horse, caught sight of Bodine.

Bodine put a finger to her lips, got a grin in return.

"You feel how she responds?"

"I do." Jessica lifted a hand to adjust the riding helmet. "I honestly didn't understand what you meant the first couple times. But I do now. I can't believe I'm doing this. That I can start and stop her, walk and trot, go one way, then the other."

"And have fun with it?"

"It is fun. Even if my ass, my legs, pay for it later. It's such a feeling."

"You're going to get an even better one. You're going to take her from walk to trot to canter."

Even at a distance, Bodine saw Jessica's eyes go wide, go huge.

"Oh, Cora, I don't think I'm ready. Honestly, I'm fine just poking along."

"You're ready. You need to trust me, trust her, trust yourself. A little trot now. Keep those knees in, those heels down, elbows, too. Tell her what you want. That's right. She wants to please you. You just want to give her another little nudge now, keep your form, give her the signal, and she'll take it from there."

"What if I fall off?"

"You're not going to, but if you do, you'll get back up. A little nudge, Jessie."

The pure anxiety on Jessica's face had Bodine wondering if her grandmother pushed too far, too soon. But Jessica, lips pressed tight, rocked in the saddle, nudged with her heels, and moved smoothly into a pretty little canter.

The anxiety melted into a kind of shock. "Oh my God!"

"Move with her, that's it. Elbows down! Look at you. Take her around. That's beautiful, honey. Just fine. Bring her down again, easy."

Pulling Maybelle to a stop, Jessica pressed a hand to her heart. "Did that just happen?"

"Got it on video." Bodine stepped forward, holding up her phone. "The last few seconds anyway. You did great."

"She's a faster learner than she thinks she is," Cora said. "Take her around one more time. Walk, trot, canter."

"Why does that scare the crap out of me when I just did it?"

"Do it again, and next time it'll be easier."

"One more time," Jessica complied.

Bodine circled in place, following the novice rider and veteran mare round the ring with her phone.

"I'm going to send you this video," Bodine told her when Jessica led Maybelle back to the center of the ring.

Breathless now, face flushed, Jessica frowned at the

phone in Bodine's hand. "Am I going to be happy or embarrassed?"

"I think you'll be impressed."

When Bodine started to get a mounting block, Jessica shook her head. "I don't need one. Getting off is one of my top equestrian skills. But, oh, my aching butt."

"When you put more time in, ride more often, your butt won't ache." Cora dismounted smoothly. "Let's see if you remember how to unsaddle your horse."

"Actually, I'll do that." Bodine took Maybelle's reins. "I need to talk to Nana about something."

"Then I'll head home, and into a hot bath." Jessica gave the mare a rub. "Thanks, Maybelle. Thank you, Cora."

"You're more than welcome. You've reminded me how much fun it is to teach somebody from the ground up."

With Bodine, Cora led the horses back to the stall area. "I was going to unsaddle them here so Jessica got the practice, then rub them down at the BAC. But we can do that here if you need to talk to me. Want a Coke? We've got some in the tack room."

"I'll get us some." Bodine carried the saddle back, stowed it, grabbed the drinks.

Cora had the second saddle on the post, already toweling off Wrangler. "What's on your mind, darling?"

"I never asked you because I didn't want to make you sad." Bodine picked up a fresh towel, got to work. "If it makes you too sad and you don't want to talk about it, I'll stop."

"This sounds serious."

"It's about Alice. I think I understand why Grammy gets angry, and why Mom does. Grammy—you're her daughter, and it makes her angry somebody hurt you so much. And Mom, it's the same. And I think hurt of their own, too."

"I know that's true, and we don't talk about it much because it stirs up the hurt."

"I don't want to do that." As she brushed the mare, Bodine looked over at her grandmother. "I don't want to add to the hurt."

"But you wonder about it. You've got questions stored up, and you're somebody who wants answers." As she worked, she met Bodine's eyes. "You go on and ask."

"I guess it was Karyn Allison's mother who gave me the push on this, Nana. How she just wanted to die, and she might. And I talked to Billy Jean's mother myself, and know even though they weren't close the way you hear Karyn and her mother were, her grief was beyond measuring. It made me wonder what it's been like for you, all these years, not knowing for certain if Alice is . . ."

"Alive. If she's alive," Cora finished. "I feel in my heart she is. I need to believe she is."

"But why aren't you angry? I see Grammy and Mom angry, and understand it. I see you believing she's just alive, and I understand it. But why aren't you angry with it?"

That formed the core, Bodine realized. She'd never known Alice Bodine, and the name alone lit an anger in her.

"Alice just walked away, she cut all of you out of her life. What kind of person, Nana, doesn't even let you know she's alive and well somewhere? What kind doesn't understand the hurt and worry or care?"

"I was angry. Oh, *angry*'s a small word for it. I don't have a word big enough." And still she combed out Wrangler's mane with patient hands, steady strokes. "She lit out the day of her sister's wedding. Her sister's happiest day. The night of, really, as we pieced it together. Left a note how she wasn't going to settle like Reenie for the chains of marriage, the boredom of ranch life. Got some shots in there about how I never understood her, didn't love her the same as I did Reenie. Hurtful. Deliberately hurtful. Alice had a way of poking her thumb in your eye."

Though Bodine kept her thoughts to herself, she wondered if leaving hadn't been a favor to the rest of the family.

"I didn't want to tell Maureen and Sam, didn't want to spoil their honeymoon. But they stayed in a cabin that night, and when they came back to say good-bye to everybody before they left on their honeymoon, I had to. Then I had to make them go, had to tell them—and I honestly believed it right then—Alice was just stirring everybody up as she liked to do, and would be back in a few days."

"But she didn't come back."

"She didn't come back," Cora echoed. "Postcards here and there for a while. I hired a detective. I wasn't going to make her come back. She was eighteen, so I couldn't anyway, but it's no good trying to lock somebody in who wants to go. I just wanted to know she was all right, that she was safe . . . but we couldn't find her."

Drawing in a breath, Cora stroked a hand over Wrangler's neck. "I stopped being angry, Bodine, because being angry didn't change a thing. I'd ask myself: Had I been too hard on her, too easy on her? I was working to keep the ranch going, then the dude ranch, and the bare start of the resort. Had doing all that taken too much away from being a mother to her?"

Self-blame wouldn't do, Bodine thought. No, she wouldn't allow it.

"Nana, I see how you and Mom are with each other. I see that and I know what kind of mother you were, you are. I hate knowing you've doubted yourself."

"Mothers do, every day. It's funny, Bo, how a woman

can bring two children into the world, raise them up the same way—the same rules and values, indulgences and disciplines. And still two separate people come out of it all."

For a moment Cora rested her cheek against Wrangler's neck.

"My Alice, she was born with hard edges. She could be funny and sweet, and, God, charming. But where Maureen thrived on the ranch, Alice always felt limited by it. I know Alice felt I favored Reenie, but when one child is working hard to do well in school, and the other is skipping classes, well, one child's going to be praised and the other punished."

Cora let out a sigh, a half laugh. "Alice never seemed to understand how it all worked. When she was in a good place inside herself, she was a delight. Bold and questing and curious. Where Reenie could be too serious, too worried about all the details fitting just right, worried too much about pleasing everybody at once, Alice would pull her out of that some, tease her into some adventuring. A lot like Chase and Callen—but Callen . . . he didn't have those hard edges, never in his life resented Chase for being what he was, having what he had. There's the difference."

"And none of it mattered, or matters now," Bodine said quietly. "Hard edges, resentments, bold or curious, she was yours. You loved her. You love her."

"I did, and I do. The loss of her? The knowing she's chosen to forget me, forget all of us? It's as keen as it ever was."

"How do you stand it? How do you get through it?"

"I have to look at the whole picture, not just that dark, empty spot."

Digging peppermints out of her pocket, Cora fed them to the horses.

"When your granddaddy died, the one you never knew, my whole world broke. I loved him, Bodine, so much I didn't know how I'd take the next step in a world he wasn't in. But I had your ma, and she needed me. I had Alice inside me. I had to take the next step."

After running a hand down Bodine's braid, Cora picked up a hoof pick.

"Your grammy and grandpa . . . I know Ma and I squabble now and then. Two women living in the same house are bound to. But there's nothing in this world will ever brush away a speck of my love and gratitude for her and my father. They sold their own place to come here because I needed them. I couldn't have gotten through without them. I might've lost the ranch, even with your uncles helping me."

"You could've let it go, sold it. No one would've blamed you."

Cora looked up, under the brim of her hat as she cleaned Wrangler's right rear hoof. "My Rory loved the ranch. Risked everything he had to build it. I could never let it go, but without that help, I might have lost it. Instead, it thrived, and I know my Rory would be proud of what we've done."

Smiling now, she leaned against Wrangler's foreleg, checked his hoof when he lifted it.

"I have a daughter who's a light in my life, a son-in-law who's the best man I know. And three beautiful grandchildren who make me proud every single, solitary day. I have a full life, Bodine, because I chose to live it. I have sorrows. No life is full without them. I miss my husband. It doesn't matter how many years have passed since I've seen his face, heard his voice. I still see him, I still hear him, and it comforts me. I miss my daughter—the sweet and the sour of her. I can wish for another chance to be her mother without making all I have, all my blessings, less for that wish."

"You have a full life because you chose to live it, and you worked to make it."

"I did, but don't think less of that poor girl's mother, Bodine, because her grief overwhelmed her. Despair is a powerful, living thing."

"I won't. I don't think less of her. But I can think more of you, Nana, for being stronger than despair and braver than grief."

"My sweet girl," Cora murmured.

"I see how strong you are, Nana. Strong and smart, and loving with it. I see those things in Grammy, and in Mom. It's not taking anything away from the men in our family for me to say I'm proud to be the next one holding the Riley, Bateau, Bodine, Longbow line. And for you, I'll hope that wherever Alice is, she's made a good life for herself."

"You're a treasure to me, Bodine. A shining bright, rich treasure."

When Cora came around the horses to hug her, Bodine squeezed tight.

But, she thought, while she could hope, for her grandmother's sake, she couldn't believe anyone could make a good life by ignoring her own line, and all who'd loved her.

CHAPTER THIRTEEN

Information, straight gossip, sly innuendo, and wild speculation all bore fruit on the grapevine that extended from ranch to resort. How plump the fruit might depend, but you could always squeeze out a little juice.

As Bodine wasn't sure of the size and ripeness of the fruit she'd come across that day, she felt it her job to find out.

She had a two-pronged reason for knocking on the door of the shack after the evening meal. The timing took it out of the business day—something she thought important, just as she felt it fair and just to hold this discussion on what was, essentially, more Callen's turf than her own.

He called out a "Come in."

She found him on the couch, his laptop in his lap as he slouched with a beer on the table beside him, and a basketball game on TV.

He'd gotten some winter sun along the way, she noted, as the lamp caught some lighter tones in that deer-hide mop of hair. "Hey." He continued to tap his keyboard—not the two-finger style both her father and Chase employed, but as competently as anyone in her offices.

Where had he learned that?

"Grab a beer and a chair," he invited.

"I'll pass on the beer." But she took a seat.

"Give me one second, I just need to . . . Okay, that should work."

She waited while he saved the file, put the computer aside. He looked comfortable, relaxed, she thought, and a little scruffy, which always struck her as oddly appealing on him.

She could understand the appealing, even the comfortable if the juice squeezed true and clear, but damned if she could balance in the relaxed.

He stretched out his legs, boosted his boots onto the coffee table. "How's it going?"

"Actually, that's something I want to ask you."

He nodded, picked up his beer. "Can't complain. Got the advance bookings for the next couple weeks laid out, and the schedule done. Worked out the rotation on the horses. Got your spreadsheet and numbers on expenses. Projecting that to go up some as bookings increase in the spring. And I'm going to want to talk to you about replacing some tack. We're inventorying now whenever we've got the chance."

He'd learned a lot more, she realized, than how to type with all ten digits.

"Send me a memo on that when you're done. I meant, how's it going on a more personal level."

He raised his eyebrows and his beer. "Again, can't complain."

"I'm puzzled why you can't complain about Garrett Clintok coming back on you. And coming back on you, additionally, while you were standing on resort property working for us. I think that warrants a complaint."

Though he shrugged, sipped his beer, Bodine saw annoyance flick in and out of his eyes. "Maybe because Clintok doesn't worry me."

As intrigued as she was frustrated, Bodine crossed an ankle over her knee. "You've become an awfully mellow bastard, Skinner, if that's the truth. He came to the BAC while you were working and accused you of murder."

"Not in so many words."

Whether or not the mellow ran all the way through, *she* had become a woman who knew how to hold back her own frustrations to get to the meat.

"Why don't you give me the words so I don't have to hear the variety of them that trickle down to me from other sources?"

"First place, Easy shouldn't have said anything to you."

"I completely disagree, but he, in fact, didn't. He said something to Ben. If I have the chain of speculation right, Ben saw Clintok drive up, saw you in what he viewed as an altercation, saw Clintok drive away, spitting gravel. Then *Ben* asked Easy about it, got some details, related those details to others, and so on, until a damn convoluted version of those details came to me."

She had to take a breath—found herself annoyed Callen continued to stretch out, say nothing, and damn near *radiate* relaxed. "I don't like getting trickle downs, Skinner. And especially on something as incendiary as this. You should have come to me."

He gave her a thoughtful nod, an easy shrug as if considering her point of view.

"I don't see it that way. It was personal, and I handled

it. It didn't have anything to do with the work or you or the resort."

"It happened—again—on resort property." She held up a hand before he could argue that one. "I have an absolute right to complain to the sheriff when one of his deputies harasses one of our people on our property. I don't care if you don't see it that way because that's the way it damn well is. And if you're going to sit there and tell me he didn't bring the Bodine or the Longbow names into it, at least by insinuation, I'm going to have to call you something you've never been. That would be a liar."

Now, at last, the mellow dropped away. He shoved up, paced around the limited space. This time she cocked an eyebrow, waited. Apparently it took more to rile him than it once had, but she recognized the impressive temper cooking up.

So she'd wait and see.

"You know damn well, Bo, you know good and damn well this business with Clintok goes back way before any of this. He's just using this as an excuse to start something with me. I'm not going to accommodate him, and I'm damn well not going to go running to you when he gets in my face. Fuck that, and fuck him. *That's* the way it damn well is."

She smiled, put all the sweetness of a strawberry parfait into it. "Well, golly, Callen, you don't appear so awfully mellow about it after all."

"See how mellow you are when some asshole accuses you of murdering two women."

"That's part of my point. Exactly my point, so we agree there. Sheriff Tate warned him off you, specifically and justifiably. He didn't listen and, from all I can see, took it on himself to come at you at work, and in front of another employee, one you're charged to supervise. I think the sheriff wouldn't be happy to hear it."

"That's not for you." He rounded on her, eyes a fired-up blue. "It's not for you to go running to Tate, and it's not for me to come running to you."

"That's hard and hotheaded under the mellow. I won't go to the sheriff on it. That comes from growing up around men, working with them, living with them, and understanding—maybe even appreciating—how doing that translates in the male brain as an insult to your mighty balls, but—"

"It's got nothing to do with . . . Okay." She had him there, and he wasn't one for lying. "Okay, that's one part of the whole of it. The rest is just what I said. This is, always has been, between me and Clintok."

"Which also comes back to the massive and mighty balls, which is not said as an insult to your kind, Skinner, just a statement of fact. So I won't go to Tate, but I will say what I know and what I think should the sheriff hear about it and ask me."

Maybe it irritated the crap out of him—and made his balls itch—but he couldn't rationally argue with any of it. So he dropped back on the couch. "That's fair enough."

"And I'm asking you as the manager of the resort, as your friend, to tell me if Clintok comes back at you again. I need to know what happens on my place, and I know under the mad, you understand that."

Callen took another pull on the beer. "You're pretty goddamn good at this."

"I'm exceptionally goddamn good at this. I'm asking you to trust me, and to stop being so bound up in stupid macho pride you can see telling me about his threatening bullshit isn't running to some female. You do that, you keep me informed so I don't have to hear bits and pieces as it travels around the resort or the ranch, I'll let you handle it your own way."

"Exceptionally is probably understating." He hissed out a breath. "You're so all-fired reasonable, I can't hold my own line without looking like a fool."

"You're nobody's fool, Skinner, and never have been." Leaning over far enough, she gave his leg a light punch. "And from what I've seen, you've gotten exceptionally goddamn good about how you handle assholes. Now, have we got a deal?"

"Yeah, yeah, yeah." And with it struck, he felt free to cut some of the anger loose. "Christ, he pissed me off. Pushing at me, insulting me—and the rest of you, you were right about that—doing what he could to provoke me into taking a swing at him."

"There was a time you would have, with less provocation. When did you learn to coat that renowned temper of yours with mellow?"

He thought now of how close he'd come—five seconds—to taking more than a swing. But . . .

"If a man doesn't learn a few things along the way, he's wasting his time. Which is a pretty good description of Garrett Clintok. The son of a bitch hasn't learned a damn thing. He's just acquired a badge so he can bully from behind it."

Callen shifted his gaze to hers. "I want another part to the deal."

"We already struck the deal."

"We didn't shake on it."

Bodine only rolled her eyes. "What would the other part be?"

"If he goes at you or your family about me, you tell me."

Leaning over again, Bodine held out her hand. "No problem at all."

They shook. Callen flopped back.

"I'm going to admit something. I've been stewing about it ever since. Just couldn't pull the damn thorn clean out of my side. Because whatever Clintok is, I get the feeling he believes I could've done this. He actually believes it."

Bodine started to disagree, thought better of it. "You might be right on that. He hates you, and always has. It's irrational and genuine so he'd need to believe the very worst when it comes to you. And he's never known you. Anyone who knows you wouldn't believe it."

"Maybe not, but he was so wound up about it Easy felt obliged to step in and cover for me on the timing, and not altogether truthfully. That doesn't sit well, either."

"I expect Ben would have done exactly the same."

"Maybe." He scowled into his beer. "Yeah, hell, he would've. That doesn't set very well, either."

He studied her as she studied him. She'd taken her hair out of the braid so it lay loose and a little wavy from the twining, ink black over her shoulders.

The tone, mirrored in her lashes, deepened, enriched the green of her eyes. In those eyes he read understanding, some sympathy rather than the hard-line, no-bullshit he'd seen in them when they'd started this round.

"I'm going to admit, having this out with you? I don't much feel like stewing about it anymore."

"You're family, Callen."

"Maybe, but I don't think about you like my sister anymore."

She snorted. "You never thought about me like your sister."

"I thought about you like my best friend's baby sister. It comes to the same. Now I look at you, and can't leave it at that. There was this wrangler I knew back in California. I've never known anybody as attuned with horses. I used to say he'd likely been one in a past life. He loved horses, a good whisky, and the company of men. But now and again, he'd say to me: 'Skinner, I've got a hankering for a woman.'"

Bodine snorted again, and Callen grinned. "His words. So, he'd find one, and take care of the hankering until the next time it gave him an itch."

She saw, appreciated, the simple logic and organization of the method. "Is that how you handled an itch?"

"A man has to consider his massive, mighty balls."

She had to laugh. "You turned that one around on me. Point for you."

"The thing is, since I'm in the admitting mode, since I've been back I've had a hankering for a woman."

He watched her eyebrows cock up, that little smirk move on her pretty lips.

"But the only hankering has been for you." And watched the smirk vanish. "And reminding myself you're the sister of the best friend I've had, ever will have, hasn't dulled it one damn bit."

All manner of things stirred up inside her. Stirred hard and hot enough she wished she'd taken that beer. "That's a bold admission."

"Well, you said yourself, I'm no liar. I want my hands on you, Bodine. I'm going to get them there before much longer."

"I got over my crush, Callen."

"I think we both know we're past teenage crushes on this. You're no liar, either."

"You've got a point, and I might like having your hands on me just to see what it was like. Sex is simple enough if you're honest about it."

He laughed. "If you think that, you've never had the right kind of sex. I can look forward to changing that."

"You're raising the bar awful high for yourself, but . . . I had another reason for coming over to talk to you tonight."

"You want to fire me, and I can show you how I vault over that bar?"

"No. No, it's contrary to that. I heard from Abe today."

"How's Edda doing?"

"She's doing well. She's taken up . . . it's not Kung Fu, it's . . ." Searching for the name, Bodine did a slow, surfing wave with her hands.

"Tai Chi?"

"That's it! And yoga, and according to Abe is half a vegetarian. I can't picture it."

"Whatever works," Callen decided.

"And it seems to be. But she—the two of them had a scare, and have done a lot of talking, evaluating. They're going to move closer to their daughter, to Bozeman. They're not coming back, Callen."

"Hell. I need another beer." Slowly, he stood up. "You sure you don't want one?"

"Not right now. He said he'd come back and give me more time, help train a replacement if we needed it. But he figured if we had you in there, we wouldn't need it. The job's yours if you want it. And if you don't, I'd ask if you'd stay on as manager long enough for us to find somebody else. As one of the owners and the manager of Bodine Resort, I'd rather you took the job."

He walked back, set the beer down. She wasn't surprised when he pulled her out of the chair.

She wondered if she surprised him by gripping his hair in both fists and assaulting his mouth with hers.

Hankering be damned, she thought. This was hunger,

deep, grinding hunger, and the perpetual ache of it had kept her entire system on edge from the moment she'd walked into the kitchen months back to see him charming Clementine.

It didn't have to make sense, it didn't have to be smart. It just had to be.

She blew through him, a perfect storm of lust and power, lightning strikes that flashed and burned, leaving erotic afterimages of tangled, frantic bodies. And she took, beyond what his frustration and impulse had prepared for. Stirred up the currents, threatened the flood, and all with only a single, urgent kiss.

Though he cursed her, himself, the altogether sticky situation, he backed off. Now she grabbed his shirt front, and the molten look in her eyes told him clearly she wasn't done.

Me, either, he thought, but carefully, eyes level with hers, pried open her grip.

She dropped her hand quickly, and he couldn't quite read the mix on her face now. Shock, insult, disappointment seemed to come and go.

"You—" She broke off, took a long breath. Now he read disdain, and plenty of haughty with it. "You can't possibly believe I'd use sex to persuade you to stay on as horse manager."

"You know, Bodine, as good a rider as you are, you're going to bust your ass falling off a horse that high. Now just—" He held a hand up, palm out, to signal her back. And took a step back himself.

Her eyes narrowed for a moment, then lit up. Oh so sly, he noted. Her lips curved.

"That's right." He couldn't say why that sheer smugness on her face made him want her more. "I've got my limits, and right now I've got one foot over the edge of them. So we're just gonna—" He broke off again, waving her back. "Keep our separate spaces for right now."

"You're the one who started it."

"Maybe, and maybe I didn't factor in . . . certain eventualities. I need to think all this over, and while I'm thinking all this over, I need to talk to Chase, as he's the one who hired me on."

"All right. And will your talk with Chase include those certain eventualities?"

Talk about sticky situations. But a man didn't bullshit his best friend. "Most likely."

"Well, that would be up to you. But I'll remind you—and him, if it comes to it—I don't need his permission regarding who I take to bed."

Another time, he'd have valued the frankness, but at the moment it only made the thin ledge he balanced on all the shakier.

"It's not about permission. Now I need you to . . ." He gestured toward the door. When she angled her head, lifted her eyebrows, he shoved his hands in his pockets. Hands that really wanted to take hold of her and wipe that smug satisfaction off her face. "Go on, Bo, out, before both my feet are over that edge."

"All right. I'd appreciate it if you let me know about the job in the next couple of days." She opened the door, then stood with the cold swirling in around her and awash in the yard lights that added mystery.

"I'm going to tell you: Whether or not you take the job, I'm going to have you. I've made up my mind about it."

The damn ledge started to crumble under his feet. "Keep walking, Bodine."

She left him with a laugh he already knew would keep

him up half the night. He sat, picked up his beer. He wasn't sure if he felt like a righteous man or a fool.

At the moment he didn't see much daylight between the two.

Stringing out a yes or no struck Callen as cowardly, and since the yes or no would depend, for him, on what Chase had to say, he'd hit that straight on.

Before sunrise, he found Chase, along with a couple of hands, moving horses from stall to paddock. "Morning, Cal." Chase gave the sorrel gelding an easy slap on the flank to send him through the open gate. "Getting your rotation up, but I'm holding Beans back today. Looks like an infection in his right eye, so I want the vet to take a look. You all right with Cochise instead?"

"Sure. Have you got a minute?"

"Got a couple of them," Sensing Callen wanted more privacy, Chase walked away from the horse paddock. "We're castrating calves today."

"Can't say I mind missing it."

When Chase figured they'd gone far enough from perked-up ears, he stopped. "Supposed to climb up to the forties today. At least the rest of us won't freeze our balls off while we turn little bulls into steers."

"I could use a shirtsleeves day."

"Wouldn't hurt my feelings. I heard Abe might not be coming back."

"Bodine said that's definite." Callen's breath whooshed out in a cloud. "I'd say a heart attack—and a minor one's not minor to the one having it—is a wake-up call. I guess it shouldn't surprise anyone they decided to retire."

"They'll be missed. Both've been with the resort since before it was one. I'm not going to be surprised if Bodine offered you Abe's job permanent."

"She did."

"Are you taking it?"

"I'm not saying yes or no until I hear what you have to say."

"It's not up to me, Cal."

"Oh, horse shit. Where did I go when I knew it was time to come back?" Callen demanded. "You took me on, even fixed up the shack."

Accustomed to the flare, Chase met it as he usually did. With equanimity.

"I'd've done that out of friendship, all of us would've. But we didn't need to. You're an asset, Cal, the best all-around horseman I know, and that includes my own father. He'd say the same. We all know you could've gone anywhere."

"I didn't want to go just anywhere. I've been there."

"So here you are." Sensing dawn was close, Chase looked up at the sky, watched a few stars gutter out. "I might fight Bo for you, might even win, though God knows she's a fierce and dirty fighter. Remember that time we had to haul her off Bud Panger? Bud had a year on her, ten pounds, too, easy, and she had him down in the dirt crying for his ma."

"I remember. She caught me one on the shin while we were hauling her off Bud. I limped for two days. I'm not going to be a cause of upset between you and Bo."

"You wouldn't be. I might fight her, but the resort's part of the whole, so it's all, well, of a piece, isn't it? Besides all that, it's what you want here, Cal. As dirty as Bo can fight, she'd say just the same. And I expect she has."

"I came here to work for you, Chase."

"You came to work for the Bodine Ranch, and the resort's part of it."

The long night shifted toward day, a lessening of dark,

a slight rise of wind. Horses whickering, the low of cattle, the boot steps of men already about the day's work.

"I love this place." Callen breathed it in. "I love it nearly as much as you. Leaving it was one of the hardest things I've ever done. Had to do it or I'd never have made anything of myself."

Knowing his friend, Chase kept his silence, waited for Callen to work through the rest.

"I admire the resort. I admire the hell out of what you all have built there. That Bodine/Longbow vision, it's an awesome, admirable thing. I know I could be an asset to you here on the ranch, I know you could depend on me to pull my weight here, and maybe take some weight off you and Sam. At the resort . . ."

He took another minute, gathered his thoughts. "I think I might be able to add to the vision. I can see ways to do that, to contribute to that."

"Then that's what you ought to do. To my ear that's what you want, and what's holding you off is feeling obligation here. There's no need for that. If we need you for something over here, we'll work that out, too. And don't feel bad we're likely going to have to hire two in the next month to replace you."

Most of the stress lodged at the back of Callen's neck loosened. "Three'd be better."

"You're not that damn good. Work it out with Bo, give me a few hours here like you have been until we start hiring on, and we're square."

"Yeah." The stress punched right back again. "About Bodine." Callen shifted, looked east, waiting for the sun to rise. "I—we—" he corrected, as last night cemented the mutual. "We have a thing going on." He rubbed the chin he hadn't bothered to shave that morning. "An intense sort of thing."

"What thing?"

Callen glanced over, saw the mild and puzzled interest. "You've always been obtuse when it comes to the romantic and sexual dynamics of people, Longbow. A block of wood buried in cement obtuse."

"I've got more to think about than the . . ."

And it struck him, Callen saw, like that block of wood—right between the eyes.

"What?"

"We've got a mutual interest and attraction going on, me and Bo."

"What?" Chase repeated, taking a step back as if his body had just reacted to that strike. "You—you've—with my sister?"

"Not yet, but only due to my heroic restraint so far, and hearing, in my head, you say 'my sister' in just that way."

"You never looked twice at her," Chase began, then reevaluated. "Did you?"

"Christ almighty, Chase, she was still a kid when I left. Mostly a kid." An itch worked into the stress. "Maybe I looked twice, a couple times. But only because, hell, she's always been pretty, and I guess she was starting to blossom some right about the time I left. I never did anything about it. Never thought of doing anything about it. But she's not a kid now. And she's . . ."

Brother to brother, Callen reminded himself. Even if a sister stood between them. "She's smart. Always was, but, man, she's honed that to a sharp edge. The way she runs that place? She's smart and crafty, and she has a way of seeing to it that everybody who works there does good work, and stays happy doing it. That's some talent there. I admire that."

"So you've got this *thing* due to her brain and her managerial skills."

It wasn't often Chase laid on sarcasm, but when he did it had some serious weight.

"They're part of the package. She's beautiful." Callen let out a sigh. "I don't know when she went from really pretty to beautiful, and maybe if I'd been around the whole time it wouldn't have hit me like a lightning bolt. I've got feelings for her—I'm not altogether sure where they're going, but it's clear enough we're going to find out. I couldn't do that behind your back, or without telling you right out."

"You're standing here, telling me right out, you're planning to have sex with my sister."

"I'm going to put it this way. It's not a small embarrassment to me to admit, due to not going behind your back and the job offer, I had to tell her to get out of the shack last night. She packs a punch."

"She hit you?"

Callen laughed, laughed until he had to bend over to brace his hands on his thighs. "There's that obtuse again. How do you ever manage to get laid?"

"Kiss my ass, Mister Hollywood. And be careful talking about getting laid and my sister in the same conversation."

Heaving out a breath, Callen pushed up again. "She left, telling me whether I took the job or not, she intended to follow-through on . . . the personal area. I guess I can fight her off if you feel strongly against it. I think she'd probably take me down, but I could put up a fight."

Chase stared hard at the hills, the mountains, just coming into silhouette relief as day waited to bloom. "This isn't a conversation I expected to have when I got up this morning."

"I've got the advantage, as I spent most of the night thinking about this conversation. When I wasn't thinking about her. She knew I would, too. Crafty. Didn't I say that? She's a crafty sort of woman. I like it."

Chase stood, mulling, weighing, struggling a little as the first shimmers of red rose up over the eastern peaks. "She's a grown woman who makes her own choices. If that choice is . . . I'd just as soon not go into that detail inside my head. I'm going to say I love you like a brother, and there are times when Rory devils me enough I like you more than the brother my parents gave me. I trust you with my life, not one instant's hesitation on that. I'm telling you: If you hurt her, I'll kick your ass. And I'll kick it harder than Bo kicked Bud's."

"That's fair."

Understanding each other, they stood a moment longer, and as the cock began to crow, watched the sun rise red into a purple sky.

CHAPTER FOURTEEN

Not to avoid Bodine so much as the temptation of her, Callen rode to work well before her. On his own, in the quiet, he finished doing the tack inventory, drafted up a memo of what he felt needed replacing, what he believed could be repaired.

By mid-morning he'd sent Easy down to the center with a pair of horses for Maddie and a lesson. Along with Ben, he'd saddled up four more mounts for a trail ride, ordered supplies—with a copy for the boss—and confirmed more bookings.

A fine, bright day for riding, he thought, as the forties might even nudge at fifty degrees by afternoon. He imagined the snow sculptures that had held up well so far would show some sags by the end of the day.

"Hey there, cowboy."

He straightened up from checking a hoof, smiled at Cora. "Ma'am. Good morning, Miss Fancy."

"I heard you're helping Abe out," Miss Fancy said, tipping up the bold bright green brim of her pinch front Stetson to study him.

"I'm always glad to help."

"He's a good man. You were a half-bad boy, Callen. I always had a weakness for half-bad boys. From my vantage point you need a few more miles on you to make a man, but I think you'll do."

"Ma's feeling feisty this morning. We haven't had a day like this since November, and the pair of us want to take advantage. Can you spare us a couple horses for an hour or two?"

"As long as you want. Miss Fancy, do you still favor that bay mare? The one you named Della."

"How in the world did you remember such a thing?"

"I never forget a beautiful woman or a good horse."

She gave him a smile that struck a perfect balance between flirtation and indulgence. Hardly a wonder he was crazy about her.

"It happens she's in the paddock here today. If you want her, I'll bring her in, saddle her."

"I'd be glad to have Della, and I can still saddle my own horse."

"I'm sure of it, but I'd appreciate you letting me do that for you. You've been using Wrangler in the ring, Nana, but that's where he is right now, doing a lesson."

"Let's see who else you have."

They walked over, and when Cora made her choice, Callen led the bay mare and a chestnut gelding from one paddock to another.

A hand on her hip, her denim jacket—with its emblazoned peace sign—unbuttoned, Miss Fancy eyed him while he saddled the mare.

"You've got good hands, boy. I set considerable store in a man's hands. I'm surprised I haven't heard about you using them on a two-legged female."

"Ma." Cora rolled her eyes as she saddled the gelding.

"If I can't devil a boy whose backside I swatted when he was three, who can I devil? You've got good hands and a handsome face," Miss Fancy added. "You ought to have your eyes on a woman."

"As they keep roaming your way, are you offering, Miss Fancy?"

She let out a hoot. "It's a damn shame you were born fifty—oh, hell, sixty years too late."

"But I'm an old soul."

She laughed again, patted his cheek. "I always did have that soft spot for you."

"Miss Fancy." He took her hand, kissed it. "I've been in love with you all my life."

"A safe thing for a man to say to a woman pushing toward ninety." But this time she kissed his cheek. "Don't you go insulting me by getting a mounting block. You just give me a boost up."

He basketed his hands, and marveled how smoothly she swung into the saddle. If he lived to pushing toward ninety, he hoped he could do the same.

"Come on, Della, let's see how we feel today."

While Cora checked the cinches on her saddle, Miss Fancy turned Della, turned a walk to a trot, a trot to a canter in the paddock.

"She was raring to get out today." Cora adjusted her hat over her short crop of salt-and-pepper hair. "The winters are getting longer for her. A day like today is a gift. No, I've got it," she said when he formed another basket. "We'll have them back in a couple hours. I'm raring myself. It's been a while since we rode around the property."

"You enjoy it. Ah, I hope you don't take this wrong, but do you have a phone on you?"

Little silver dangles glinted in her ears as she smiled

down at him. "Both of us do, and I appreciate you worrying about us. Are you and Della ready, Ma?"

"Born ready in every life I've led."

"I got the gate." Callen crossed the sandy soil of the paddock, held it open.

The women rode through, a sedate walk. Then Miss Fancy looked back, sent him a wink. And leaped into a gallop.

"That's all right," he mumbled. "I didn't need that year of my life."

He watched them, admired them, then went back to work.

When it was close enough to quitting time, he left Ben and Carol covering and rode over to Bodine Town, leading Leo.

He tethered both horses before striding into the building, giving the front desk a wave, continuing back to Bodine's office.

She sat at her desk, phone to her ear, scrolling through something on her computer. "Yes, I have that. Of course you can, Cheryl. We do have our own gardens, greenhouses, and . . . It's absolutely up to you. Yes, we're thrilled to have you. We're already billing it on our website and our brochures, and will highlight you and the event beginning the first of the month."

When she just sat back, closed her eyes, made *mmm-hmm* sounds, Callen poked into her cooler, took out a couple of Cokes. He opened one, put it on her desk, opened the other, sat down with it.

"I can promise you'll find our kitchen and our staff worthy of our five-star rating. I'm afraid we can't pay for that. If you feel you need your own sous chef, you're welcome to bring one, at your own expense. Yes, yes, that's firm, and is so stated in your contract. As I said, we're delighted to have you as our guest chef for the event. I expect it to be sold-out. Please let us know your travel arrangements when you have them. We'll have you picked up from the airport."

As she listened again, her gaze narrowed, went just a little fierce.

"I'm sorry, Cheryl, let me just pull your contract up, see if it says anything about providing a limo. Uh-huh. Why don't you send me an e-mail on all that, and I'll run it right by legal. Anything else I can do, personally, to make your visit with us more enjoyable, you be sure to let me know. Bye now."

Bodine hung up very carefully, drew a breath. "Arrogant, snootified bitch."

"I admire that. I admire how your tone stayed absolutely polite and reasonable, even when you covered it with enough frost to crack a tree branch."

"Cheryl's contracted as our guest chef for next month's Spring Bounty Banquet. She's head chef at this swank place in Seattle, and when we invited her, did the contract, she was thrilled and cooperative. Since then she had an appearance on *America's Top Chefs*, and now she's a prima donna, wants her own people—and for us to pay for them—wants to bring her own herbs, went on about her own tit soy—"

"Tatsoi, more likely. California," he said, and she stared holes in him. "You pick things up."

"Tit or damn tat, I don't care. She's being a pain in my ass, and is suddenly insulted we aren't providing a limo for her during her stay."

"Tell her to kiss off."

More fire flamed into her eyes—he admired that, too.

"I'm not breaking the contract and giving her an excuse to sue. If she breaks it, I'll deal with it. She and her tats and tits can be replaced. So . . ." She lifted the Coke, drank. "What can I do for you?"

"I think about that a considerable lot, but right now, it's me for you. I'd like to take you up on the job."

"I'm glad to hear it. Really glad, Callen."

"I'm glad about that. Especially since I've got some asks of my own."

"All right." She picked up her pen, nudged a tablet in front of her as if prepared to note those asks down. "It never hurts to ask, unless you're an asshole chef from Seattle."

"Happy I'm not. I'm assuming there's a contract involved here, too, though."

"There is. We do yearly contracts for managers, with reasonable outs for either party should the relationship not work satisfactorily. I can have one printed out for you, so you can look it over."

"I'd like you to add in if Chase or your father needs me at the ranch, and I've got things covered here, it's not a problem."

Sitting back again, she sipped the Coke. "I can do that, Callen, but that doesn't have to be written and signed. It just is. I hope my word's enough on that."

"It is."

"So you talked to Chase about this?"

"First thing this morning."

"And the . . . other factors?"

"Yeah. He took a little more time coming around there." Callen smiled at her. "Anytime you want my ass kicked, you just have to tell him I screwed up with you, and he'll take care of that."

"I expect no less from my brother," she said sweetly. "But I can do my own ass-kicking. Still, nice to know he cares."

"He does. I'd like to look over the evaluations of the seasonal hands you plan on bringing back. I'm not saying I'd try to outthink you on them, as you've already worked with them. I'd just like to know who I'll be dealing with."

Sitting up again, she noted it down. "I'll have that sent to you."

"Last, I've got a couple ideas for add-ons we could offer."

"Such as?"

"Some people just want to get on a horse, ride around a little, get off again, and go have a drink. Others might like to learn something, and take more active parts. Saddling, grooming."

"We offer equine education for the kids' club in the summer."

"It's not just kids might want to learn something, or groom a horse. You do a whole thing for cooking, right? Shopping, teaching, tasting. I'm saying sort of do that for horsemanship. Learning, feeding, watering, grooming. Not just the ride, the full . . . cowboy experience."

"Write it up," Bodine invited as she made a note. "Once you do, run it by Jessie. It'll go through Rory and Mom and me, but Jessie's the one who'll put a shine on it before it gets to us."

"All right, I'll do that."

"We're not only open to fresh ideas around here, Skinner, we like them. Got any more?"

"A couple I'm still formulating."

"Okay. Meanwhile, I'll have that contract printed out for you."

"Good enough." He rose. "I brought Leo up."

"Oh, I'm not . . ." She trailed off as she checked her watch, saw she might not have been ready to leave, but she should've been. "I need about fifteen minutes."

"I'll wait. I said I'd take you dancing come May."

"I recall that."

"The way things panned out, there's no point in waiting. How about Saturday night?"

She started to smile, then angled her head. "Are you talking about actual dancing?"

"What else? You got sex on the brain, Bodine. It's hard to fault you for it, but I'm thinking the Roundup still has dancing on Saturday nights. I can pick you up at eight, but we could make it seven, have some dinner first."

"Dinner and dancing at the Roundup? All right."

"Good. I'm going to check on the horses."

Dinner and dancing, she thought when he left her. Who knew Callen Skinner would turn into such a traditionalist?

Though she faced a busy Saturday, Bodine calculated she could wrap up her workday by about three. Four latest.

Not that she needed a lot of fussing time to put herself together for a night at the Roundup. Though she might wear a dress, she considered, just to keep Callen off-balance. She liked dancing, and hadn't taken the time to go, either with a date or with girlfriends, in . . . Lord, she couldn't even remember.

But as much as she liked dancing, she wanted that extra time to fuss and polish up for after. She intended to do some of her own rounding up once the band packed it in.

She'd already tucked the key to the Half-Moon Cabin in her pocket, and had a list of what she wanted to stock it with in her briefcase. All things being equal, she could take care of that, freshen up the linens, and be home to groom and dress with time to spare.

She had her maybe-I-will underwear tucked in her dresser. If things continued with Callen, she'd need to invest in more, but what she had would do. She'd already checked to be sure, as it had been thirteen full months since the last time she'd had cause to put it on.

While a busy year played a part in that, it didn't play the main role. Sex didn't have to be complicated, but a woman had her standards. She had to feel a spark and have a real liking for a man before he rated the maybe-I-will underwear.

Before most of the staff arrived for the day, she selected a bottle of wine from the wine cellar, a couple of beers and Cokes from the Saloon—making a note on inventory, and adding them to her personal tab.

She'd pick up coffee at the Longbow General Store, and though she doubted they'd need them, a few snacks.

She tucked what she had in a burlap tote, stored it in her office, and had just settled in to work when Jessica came in.

"I didn't expect you in so early."

"I'm hoping to leave the same way today. I have a date."

"Well." Taking that as an invitation, Jessica stepped up, leaned a hip on the desk. "Who, where, what?"

"Callen Skinner, dinner and dancing at the Roundup."

"If there'd been an office pool, I'd have put money on Cal. What are you wearing?"

"Haven't decided. I might shock his sensibilities and break out a dress. I do have a few."

"Is this a first date?"

"I guess you could call it that."

"Definitely a dress. The Roundup's on my list to

recommend to guests who want to venture out. It's casual, right?"

"It's good for a burger, a cold beer, and dancing on the weekends. You haven't been?"

"No."

"Well, you should. It's good to know the places you have on the list, and this is a fun one."

"Oh, Jess, there you are. Sorry, should I catch you later?" Chelsea hovered in the doorway.

"Now's fine."

"I was just telling Jessie she should go to the Roundup some weekend."

"You haven't been?"

"Apparently I have a hole in my personal activities list."

"You should go," Chelsea told her. "It's fun. The food's pretty good. Not like you get here, but it's good. And the music's always local. It's a great spot for a night out if you don't want to go all the way into Missoula."

"What is?" Rory wondered as he wandered in.

"What are you doing here?" Bodine asked him. "You're off today."

"Carlou's wedding. Carlou Pritchett. I'm invited, so I figured I'd come in, give a hand with setting up the event. What's a good spot?"

"We were talking about the Roundup." Chelsea executed a slow, subtle hair flip. "Jess hasn't been."

"Well, you gotta. Bitterroots are playing tonight."

"Oh, I love the Bitterroots!" Chelsea added a quick, flirty eye bat to the hair flip. "I dance my feet off when they're playing."

Now Rory executed a quick, charming smile. "Let's go. It's a small, afternoon wedding, right? We'll be done in plenty of time."

"Oh, well, I'd like to . . ."

Leaning back in her chair, Bodine watched her clever brother seal the deal. "We'll all go. Blow off some steam. Hell, let's get Cal and Chase in on it. Come on, Jessie, you can't go better than the Roundup and the Bitterroots on a Saturday night."

"I'm not sure I—"

"Oh, come, Jess," Chelsea insisted. "We'll have a party without having to plan it or work it."

"We'll teach her to line dance." Rory gave Chelsea a little shoulder bump, making her laugh.

While Rory and Chelsea wandered out again, making plans, Jessica sent Bodine a panicked look.

"Don't think twice," Bodine assured her. "It will be fun."

"But now you're going to have a bunch of people crowding in on your date."

Bodine only shrugged. "We'll get a bigger table. She forgot what she came in for. That's Rory Longbow magic."

"I'll find out. Honestly, Bo, I can explain to them about you and Cal having a date."

"No." Appalled, Bodine held both hands up, palms out. "Big Montana no. It makes it too important, which is something I'd like to avoid with the family, and around here. And, the fact is, I haven't hit the Roundup with Chase and Rory for months. We're due. Get yourself ready for a genuine Montana night."

Once she'd shooed Jessica out, Bodine sent Callen a text.

Word got out on the Roundup. Dinner and dancing for two just expanded to six. More dance partners. But don't make any plans for after closing. I've already made them.

Minutes later, he texted back.

I'm good with a crowd. Before closing time.

"Good enough," Bodine said aloud, then made a note to contact the manager of the Roundup when it opened for lunch and sweet-talk him into reserving a table that could hold six.

Callen got home later than he'd planned, but with plenty of time to shower off the horses and change into something clean. Maybe he had planned for a one-on-one night of dinner, conversation, dancing—and whatever happened next—but he'd grown up learning how to adjust both plans and expectations.

Besides, the way he looked at it, the party atmosphere might take some of the pressure off what happens next.

She said she had plans. He was pretty sure, the way they'd left things, what those plans would focus on.

He'd taken time that morning to rotate his sheets—stripping off the one set, putting on the second. One thing he knew for absolute certain: If their plans aligned, he wouldn't spend his first night with Bodine in her bedroom in her family home.

That was just disrespectful to her family.

He stepped into the shack, took a quick glance around. Other than the sheets, already seen to, he didn't have any picking up to do before entertaining a lady. He knew how to keep a small space neat enough: washing up dishes as he went, hanging up clothes.

He skipped his post-work beer. He'd have a couple at the Roundup, but since he was driving, he'd hold it to that. Heading toward the shower, he pulled his ringing phone out of his pocket, noted the display.

"Hi, Ma. Sure I got a minute. Plenty of them."

He listened as he shrugged out of his coat, tugged off the bandanna around his neck. He tossed his hat on the chair, scraped his hand through his hair.

She didn't ask for much, and never had. A son couldn't say no even when it put a shadow over him.

"I've got time on Monday. I could come for you about four, if that works, drive you to the cemetery. How about I take you out for dinner after? Now, why would it be a bother to me to take my ma out to dinner? If Savannah and Justin want, I'll take you all. The rug rat, too."

He flipped open the buttons of his shirt as she talked.

"No, that's fine then. Just you and me. How's she doing? Not much cooking time left on the new one."

He sat, pulled off his boots while his mother chattered on about his pregnant sister. When she'd wound down, thanked him one more time, he set the phone aside.

She didn't ask for much, and never had, he thought again. So he'd take her to visit her husband's grave. He would never understand her love and devotion to the man who'd gambled away his life, and the lives of his family, but he'd take her to lay her flowers, to say her prayers—and keep his thoughts on it to himself.

He reconsidered the beer, then shook his head. Grabbing one now was weakness not want. He stripped off his jeans, headed in to shower in the tiny bathroom.

And reminded himself that tonight and Bodine were a lot closer than Monday and graves.

About the time Callen stepped out of the shower and Bodine stood in front of the mirror doing a testing turn in the dress she'd decided on, Esther, who'd forgotten Alice, laid a cloth, as cold as she could get it, on her bruised jaw.

She'd already wept a little, knew she might weep again, but the cold helped ease the throbbing.

Sir had been so angry. She'd heard him shouting, and someone shouting back before he'd stormed in on her. She hadn't finished her scrubbing, and that made him only madder. He hadn't hurt her in a long time, but he'd hurt her then, dragging her to her feet by her hair, hitting her face, punching her stomach, taking his husbandly rights in a hard, mean way—harder and meaner than usual.

Someone had made him mad—a part of her knew that, but the other parts, long since indoctrinated, blamed herself.

She hadn't finished the scrubbing. Though her internal clock and the slant of the sun through her tiny window told her it was hours before his usual visit to her. Her house hadn't been in order. The house he'd provided her.

She'd deserved his punishment.

Now he'd gone off; she'd heard his truck leave, just as she'd heard someone—the one who'd shouted back— leave minutes before Sir had come in.

His face red with temper, his eyes dark and mean with it. His hands hard and cruel.

And it was her day of the week for sitting out for an hour, of sitting out in the air and not working. Just being allowed to sit and watch the sunset.

She looked mournfully at the door, the door he'd slammed as he'd gone out, cursing her for being a lazy whore. Though her face, her belly, and where he'd taken her so hard all hurt, she'd finished the scrubbing, using the water, gone cold, that had spilled all over the floor.

He'd knocked the bucket over. Or she had. Probably she had, as she was the clumsy one, the lazy one, the ungrateful one.

She told herself to make tea, to read the Bible, to repent her evil ways, but tears gathered in her eyes again as she stared at the door.

It was selfish of her to wish for that hour outside, to wish for the sitting and seeing the sky fill with color, maybe even seeing a star or two come out. Selfish because she hadn't earned it.

Still, she shuffled to the door, stroked her fingers over it, laid her hot cheek against it. She could just hear the birds if she listened hard enough, but not the air through the trees as she would if she could stand on the other side of the door.

The air that would cool her aching jaw and settle her heart again.

She didn't realize she'd touched the handle until it moved.

Shocked, terrified, she jumped back from it. It never moved. Not even when she scrubbed it clean.

Slowly, she reached out, touched it again, just a little pressure. It moved again, made the clicking sound it made when Sir used it.

With her breath coming fast, she gave it a little tug.

The door opened.

For one blind moment she saw Sir standing there, his fists raised to punish her for taking such a liberty. She actually cringed back, lifting her hands to cover her face.

But the blow didn't come. When she lowered her hands again, looked out, she saw no one, not even Sir.

The air waved around her, all but tugged her out.

She jumped when the door shut behind her, shoved at it, then pulled, raced back in. Heart hammering, she fell to her knees, murmuring prayers.

But the pull was so strong, the air so sweet, she crawled back, opened the door again.

She got up slowly. Had Sir left it open on purpose? A reward? A test?

She looked toward the snow-covered ground where, come spring, she'd work the garden. Nearby, the dog slept under his crooked lean-to.

She took two steps, waited.

A couple of scrawny hens pecked around in the coop, the old cow chewed her cud. The swaybacked horse dozed on its feet.

She saw not another living thing. But she heard birds, and the air through the trees, and took another step along the roughly cleared path leading from her house to Sir's.

She walked on, simply dazzled, forgetting the attack, the hurts in the sheer joy of being outside, without a tether, to be able to walk in any direction.

Bending down, she picked up snow in her bare hand, rubbed it against her face. Oh, it felt so good!

She picked up another handful, licked at it. The sound that came out of her was so foreign, she didn't know she'd made it. Didn't know she laughed.

But the dog heard, and woke with a ferocious bark, a lunge toward her. Fear of him had her rushing away in a limping run. She ran until her lungs turned to fire, until that awful barking fell away. The exertion winded her, and she stumbled, her body spilling into the snow.

Gasping for air, she rolled over, staring up at the sky through the trees, lying still, caught in wonder at the shape of clouds, how the branches cut through them.

Something tickled some part of her brain, some deep memory that had her moving her arms, her legs, laughing again at the sensation.

When she crawled up, looked down, she saw an angel in the snow. It seemed to point west. Yes, west where the sun would set.

Sir would want her to obey the angel.

In her long cotton dress and slippers, she limped west.

As she searched for angels, the sky began to burn in red, to billow in purples, to glimmer in golds. Enthralled, she trudged on. It seemed to her the sound of snow dripping from branches was music. Angel music, guiding her path. She came out to a place where little stones—*gravel* her memory bank told her—ran through the snow.

She didn't notice when the gravel went to dirt, when the road forked. She'd seen a bird and, mesmerized, followed its direction for a time.

Birds flew, angels flew.

The air grew cold, very cold when the sun dropped away. But the moon sailed overhead, so she shuffled on, smiling up at it.

Deer, a small herd, bounded in front of her, leaping across the track. She stumbled back, heart hammering again as their eyes—yellow in the dark—gleamed at her.

Devils? Devils' eyes gleamed yellow.

With a twisting jolt she realized she didn't know where she was, she didn't know which way her house would be.

She had to get back to it, get back and close the door she should never have opened.

Sir would be so angry with her. Angry enough to take the belt to her back as he'd done to teach her to obey.

In full panic—she could feel the bite of the belt on her back—she ran. Ran on a leg that dragged behind the other, on feet gone numb. When she slipped and fell, her knees burned, the heels of her hands bled.

She had to return to her house, repent, repent her great sin.

Tears poured down her cheeks; her breath tore from her lungs until, dizzy and weak, she had to stop, wait for her head to stop swimming.

She ran again, walked, ran, limped, lost in her mind, lost in despair, fell again on the gravel. On her knees she saw the gravel gave way to smooth. A road. She remembered a road. You traveled on a road. A road would take her back home again.

With a flutter of hope in her chest, she limped along with blood trickling down her calves from her scored knees. The road would take her home. She'd make tea and read the Bible and wait for Sir to come back.

She wouldn't tell him he'd left the door unlocked. It wasn't a sin not to tell him. Telling him was disrespectful, she reasoned. It would be saying he'd made a mistake.

She'd make her tea and be warmed by it; and she would forget the angel in the snow and the bird and the sky. Her house, the house Sir provided, was all she needed.

But she walked and walked and couldn't find it. Walked and walked until her legs buckled, until her head swam again. She could rest once more, for just a minute. She'd rest, and then she'd find her way home.

Before she could, the moon circled and circled above her. It spiraled down, and it fell away, leaving her in the black.

PART THREE

A Sunset

There are sunsets who dance good-by.
They fling scarves half to the arc,
To the arc then and over the arc.
Ribbons at the ears, sashes at the hips,
Dancing, dancing good-by. And here sleep
Tosses a little with dreams.
—Carl Sandburg

CHAPTER FIFTEEN

The Roundup, a big barn of a dance bar, kept things simple. Music on Saturday nights—with the occasional Friday added in—from November through the first of May. May to November featured the addition of Open Mic on Wednesdays.

Otherwise, the head bartender played tunes for whoever warmed a barstool or chowed down on nachos or a burger at one of the tables.

Music ran from country to western, and the occasional crossover. Rock was not king here, though it could be tolerated in brief doses.

Callen had grown up on that country-western beat, its laments, its story-songs. But his musical tastes had expanded considerably during his travels.

Regardless, he didn't much care if the band played disco on this particular evening, as he'd gotten a good look at Bodine's legs.

They were every bit as excellent as he'd imagined.

She wore a dress that scooped down just enough over

her breasts, narrowed in nicely at her waist, then flared out again to float just above very pretty knees.

He'd always favored pretty knees on a woman, though he couldn't say just why.

It had taken him a while to register the color over what was inside the dress, but he liked the happy blue with those little swirls of pink and green over it. And the way she'd paired it with boots that picked up the tone of the green swirls.

She'd left her hair down, long and straight over her shoulders.

He didn't mind they'd gotten there first, could clink beers together before the others piled in. Not when he could take the time for some lazy flirting.

"I don't think I've seen you in a dress since you were about fourteen. A wedding, it seems to me. One of your cousins."

"It must've been Corey's if you have my age right— and you probably do. After that Mom couldn't veto my wardrobe choices."

"You fill this one out better than you did that one."

"Puberty took its time with me, but it got there. You filled out well yourself."

He wore jeans and a chambray shirt that edged his eyes toward blue. He didn't smell of horses tonight, but of the forest, which was almost as good.

"I want to say before Rory and the rest of them get here, I appreciate you not being annoyed—at least not that it shows—that they will be here. It just sort of happened."

"I'm not annoyed. I like everybody who's coming. I don't know Chelsea very well, but she seems fine."

"Rory's got his eye on her, and she's got hers right back on him."

"I've had a look at her. It doesn't surprise me Rory'd have an eye."

"As I believe Jessica and Chase are circling around having an eye on each other, this could be considered a kind of triple date."

"Given it's Chase, the circling could go on, oh, another five or ten years."

"I think Jessie'll cut that down some, if she stays interested."

"I'll wish her luck," Callen decided. "You and me, Bo, we're done circling."

"Well, hey there, Bo! Haven't seen you in weeks." A waitress settled by the table, gave Bodine's shoulder a quick squeeze. "Y'all having dinner? You got more coming, right? How about I leave some menus so . . ." She angled toward Callen, got a good look. Her eyes popped. "Callen Skinner! I heard you were back, but I haven't seen a trace of you."

She leaned right down, kissed him full on the mouth. "Welcome home!"

"Thanks. It's good to be back." His brain did a desperate search through old files for a name to go with the face.

"One of these days I want to hear all about you working in the movies. That must've been so exciting. Why, who'd've thought, when we were riding around in your old truck, you'd be off rubbing shoulders with movie stars? You ever meet Brad Pitt?"

"I can't say I did."

"I bet you don't know Darlie's married, do you, Callen? She's not Darlie Jenner now, but Darlie Utz," Bo chimed in.

"Just like the potato chip," Darlie said with a laugh.

"Though if we had a share of that I wouldn't be working at the Roundup. All right, Lester, God's sake's! I see you. I'm having a minute with an old friend, so just hold your water."

She turned back from berating an impatient regular, beamed at Callen.

"Married three years now, and we've got a little girl."

"Congratulations, Darlie. How's your brother? Is Andy still in the Army?"

"He is. He made sergeant. We're really proud of him."

"You tell him thanks for his service when you talk to him next."

"You bet I will. I gotta get Lester off my back. You take your time with the menus. You want another round when I come back?"

"We'll wait for the others, thanks, Darlie."

"And thanks for the save," Callen said when the waitress stalked over to Lester. "I couldn't place her. I took her out a couple times, but I couldn't place her."

"She's gone from coloring her hair blond to coloring it red, and she's curling it till it springs around like a rabbit. I don't mean that in a hard way, just to say she doesn't look like she did when she was sixteen or seventeen. Her husband's a Zulie."

Callen thought of the smoke jumpers who trained just down the road, and fought wildfires all through the season. "I should've thanked him for his service, too." He tapped the menu. "Are you hungry?"

She rested her chin on the palm of her hand, smiled dead into his eyes. "I've been working up an appetite."

"You're killing me, Bodine."

"Skinner, I haven't gotten started. Oh!" She straightened, waved before Callen could pull her in, get started himself. "It's Rory. Looks like he's got Jessica and Chelsea. Don't tell me Chase backed out."

Callen stood up as Rory guided the women to the table.

"You guys good there?" Rory gestured to the beers as he pulled off his coat. "I've got drink orders, taking it to the bar."

"We're good, right?"

Callen nodded at Bodine. "All good."

"Give me a minute," Rory added.

"I'll go with you." Tossing her coat aside, Chelsea went with Rory.

"I didn't realize this place was so big." Jessica looked around as Callen helped her with her coat. "That's about the longest bar I've ever seen."

"Plenty of beer," Bodine told her. "Lots of local brews. The wine?" She wagged her hand in the air to signal it was only so-so.

"Good thing I went with a huckleberry margarita. I've developed a taste for them. You know, we could think about working out some sort of package with this place."

"Not tonight." Bodine tapped her arm. "No work in the Roundup."

"Right."

"How about Chase?"

"Oh, Rory—who insisted on picking me up—said . . . Oh yeah. Chase said he had a couple things to finish up, and to order him a Green Flash and the Saturday Special Burger if we got started before he made it. What are those?"

"That's a local beer, and a buffalo burger with bacon, pepper jack cheese, and jalapeño sauce," Bodine told her. "Chase has a fondness. How are you going to dance in those shoes?"

Jessica glanced down at her hot red stilettos. "Very gracefully."

"I like 'em." Callen gave them a leer and a wink. "How'd the wedding go?"

"Without a hitch. The bride wore a lace off-the-shoulder gown with a fringed hem, white boots, and a white Stetson with a crystal hatband. The decorations were, well, obsessively Western—silver horseshoes, wildflowers in cowboy boots and hat vases. More boots in table favor shot glasses, bandannas for napkins, burlap table runners. The cake had fondant to replicate cowhide, and the topper— the happy couple on horseback. It actually worked."

"I wouldn't mind having a boot shot glass," Callen said.

"Well, I'll see if any got left behind." She glanced at the menu as she spoke. "What are Screaming Nachos?"

"Melt your face off," Bodine told her. "Sounds good. We ought to get some for the table."

"I don't see any salads."

For a second or two Bodine just blinked, then she threw back her head and howled. "Jessie, you come here for the red meat, the hot sauce, the beer, and the music. Rabbit might find its way onto the menu, but rabbit food won't."

She grinned as Rory and Chelsea came back with the drinks. "Have a drink, or two. It'll all go down easier." So saying, Bodine hailed Darlie and ordered a large platter of Screaming Nachos.

By the time Chase got there, the nachos were a memory—one Jessica feared would live in her stomach lining for years—and dinner was ordered.

"Sorry, had a couple things."

"You missed the nachos—and they're just as potent as I remember." Callen lifted the beer he continued to nurse. "Dinner's coming."

"I'm ready for it. Place is filling up."

Most stools at the bar had already been claimed. A few tables remained open, but at others people ate, drank, and talked so the noise pushed against the bartender's playlist.

The band wouldn't take the stage for nearly an hour, but dancers already circled the dance floor. The big square of plywood held stains from countless spilled beers, and infamously, nearly dead center, a faded bloodstain from a fight—over a woman, so the story went—nearly a decade before.

Dancers twirled under three enormous wagon wheel lights. When the band came on, the head bartender—the captain of the ship—would dim those lights from their current high-noon glare.

Callen might have imagined the evening differently, but he couldn't find a single flaw sitting around a crowded table, elbow-to-elbow with friends—close enough to Bodine to smell her hair every time she turned her head.

He'd frequented places not dissimilar to the Roundup in his years away, drinking with friends, flirting with women with sweet-smelling hair.

But he knew without a doubt, for him, there was nothing like home.

It didn't matter what they talked about, and with Rory at the table you'd never have a conversational lag, but eventually it turned toward Callen and his Hollywood experience.

"It had its moments," he said when Chelsea, a little wide-eyed, asked if it had been exciting, glamorous.

"Mostly it was horses, but it had its moments."

"Not too many," Bodine put in, "as he never met Brad Pitt."

"Never did."

Rory pointed a finger at him. "Best female meet—movie-star division."

"Well, that's not even close. Charlize Theron."

Now Rory went wide-eyed. "Kiss my ass. You met Charlize Theron?"

"I did. *A Million Ways to Die in the West.* Seth Mac-Farlane movie. Funny guy."

"Screw MacFarlane. You met Charlize Theron. What's she like? Did you get close enough to touch?"

"She's beautiful, smart, interesting. I might've touched her in the general course of things. Mostly we talked horses. She's good with them."

"Before Rory lapses into a coma." Bodine swallowed the last of her burger. "Best male meet, same division."

"Pretty much as easy. Sam Elliott. I'm not going to say beautiful, but smart and interesting. And I never knew an actor to sit a horse better."

"'I still got one good arm to hold you with.'"

Jessica turned toward Chase, and the iconic gravelly voice. "That sounded just like him. What's that from?"

"*Tombstone.* Virgil Earp."

"He's got a million of him," Rory claimed. "Do Val Kilmer, Chase. Do Doc Holliday."

Half smiling, Chase shrugged. "'I'm your huckle-berry,'" he said in a lazy Southern drawl.

"What does that mean?"

Chase looked at her. "It means, mostly, I'm your man." He looked away again, picked up his beer.

"So it's a romantic idiom."

Even as Rory snorted, Chase turned back to her. "Ah, I don't expect Doc had romantic feelings for Wyatt Earp. You never saw *Tombstone*?"

"No." Now Jessica's gaze circled the table and the looks of amusement or shock. "Uh-oh, am I about to be tossed out of here?"

"Ought to see the movie" was all Chase could say.

When the table as a whole began to grill her on what Westerns she had seen, or hadn't, she was treated to Chase's mimic quotes from John Wayne through to Alan Rickman.

As entertaining as it was, she was relieved when the band took the stage—to cheers and applause—ending the inquisition.

They busted right out with a song she didn't recognize any more than she had the quotes from *Quigley Down Under.*

"We're up." Rory grabbed Chelsea's hand, spun her out onto the dance floor.

"Said I'd take you dancing." Callen stood, held out a hand for Bodine's.

"We'll see how good you are at it."

He was pretty damn good. He had a way of holding her right in, moving with her and against her in a prelude to what they both knew was coming. She laughed, twirling easily when he spun her out, then gave him a taste of her own by shifting on the way in so her back pressed to him. Undulating.

"You learned some new moves," he said in her ear.

She tipped her head back so their lips almost touched. "I've got more."

She twirled again, let him draw her in, and hooked an arm around his neck as she matched her steps to his.

"You sure as hell do. What have you been up to while I've been away, Bodine?"

"Practicing."

At the table, Jessica watched the dancers. A lot of stomping, spinning, and what she thought of as scooting. While Bodine and Callen did all of that, they coated it with a layer of sex.

She'd never thought of country western dancing as sexy.

When the second number picked right up after the first, Chase cleared his throat. "I'm not much of a dancer."

She angled toward him. "That would make us about even here, as I've never done this kind of dancing in my life. Why don't you teach me a little?"

"Ah . . . I can try." Rising, he took her hand. "You're probably going to need another drink after we're done."

"I'll risk it." After she reached the plywood, she turned, put a hand on his shoulder. "Right?"

"Yeah, and . . ." He put an arm around her waist. "We'll just sort of . . . Can you walk backward in those shoes?"

"I can run backward in them. And—" She took it on herself, raised their joined hands, executed a twirl out, then back to him. "No worries."

"You're already better than I am."

She smiled. They seemed to be moving around the floor just fine. "I can teach you if I have to."

About the time the women took to the floor to "Save a Horse (Ride a Cowboy)," and Jessica learned—or tried to learn—her first line dance, Jolene and Vance Lubbock headed home.

They'd taken what they called their Escape from the Kids Night—a once in a blue moon event. The intention had been a quiet dinner—something dimly recalled from before the advent of three kids under six—and a movie that didn't have any sort of animation or talking animals.

Along the way, Jolene realized what she really wanted to do with the four precious hours they'd roped in a baby-sitter. She directed Vance to get on and off Interstate 90, and check into a Quality Inn.

He didn't put up a fight.

For the first time in more than a year they had energetic, wide-awake, uninterrupted sex. Twice.

Then a third time after Vance ran out to get food from the eatery next door.

While they couldn't quite pull off a fourth, they indulged in a long, hot shower where no one called out for Mommy or Daddy.

They drove home again in the dreamy afterglow, vowing to make Motel Sex Night a regular event.

"We'll make more of an effort." So relaxed she wondered she didn't slide out of the seat, Jolene smiled at the father of her children, remembering why she'd married him in the first place.

"Next time, we add a bottle of wine." Vance kissed her hand.

"And some sexy lingerie."

"Oh, baby!"

She laughed, sighed. "I love our babies, Vance. I couldn't imagine life without them. But oh my God, having a few hours not being Mommy first? Once a month. We can do once a month."

"It's a date."

He kissed her hand again, absolutely and blindingly in love with his wife. He saw the gray lump on the side of the road, took it as roadkill. Had already passed it when his brain registered what his eyes told him.

"Vance!"

"I know, I know. Hold on." He hit the brakes, backed up.

"It's a woman. I swear it's a woman."

"I see her. I see." He edged the car to the shoulder. "You stay here."

"I will not!" Jolene pushed out even as he hit the flashers. "God, Vance, she's half-frozen. Get the blanket out of the truck."

"I'm calling nine-one-one."

"Get the blanket first. She's got a pulse. She's alive, honey, but she's freezing out here. I can't tell if she's hurt anywhere. She's got some scrapes, some nasty scrapes, and she's hit her head or someone hit it for her."

He tossed his wife the blanket, pulled out the flares.

"I'm calling for an ambulance."

Jolene tried to warm the cold hands with her own, looked at her husband in the red light of a flare. "Tell them to send the police, too."

A little after midnight the Lubbocks gave their statement to the responding officer while EMTs loaded the unconscious woman into an ambulance.

Chase drove Jessica home. Rory's idea, she thought, not because he wanted to link up the two of them, but because—clearly—he'd wanted the chance to linger with Chelsea.

"I imagine they'll shut the place down. Your brother and Chelsea."

"Rory's not one for leaving a party until he's dragged out."

"I appreciate you taking me home. I couldn't keep up with them."

"Oh, it's no trouble." He shot her a glance. "Seems like you had a good time."

"I had a great time. I learned two line dances, danced with a man named Spunky, and ate Screaming Nachos."

"A lot different from back East."

"Worlds."

"What would you do on a night out like this back home?"

"You mean in New York?" Closing her eyes, she thought it out. "I'd probably have dinner—probably Asian—with some work friends, then go to a club—probably techno—where a martini cost as much as two full rounds tonight. I'd dance with complete strangers, pretend I was interested in what they did for a living or their issues with their exes, then I'd take a cab home."

"What's techno?"

Absolutely charmed, just charmed down to her now-aching toes, she smiled at him. "Electronic music. What do you do on a night out if it's not the Roundup?"

"Oh, I don't go out a lot, I guess. I like the movies though."

"Westerns."

"Not just Westerns. I just like movies. I went out to visit with Cal once a couple years back, and got to go on a set. A location sort of thing. Not a Western, but this period piece about this woman trying to keep her farm going after her husband dies. *Fourteen Acres*, it was called."

"I saw that movie. That was a good movie."

"You like the movies?" he asked as he pulled up in front of her building in the Village.

"Despite the dearth of Westerns on my list, I love movies."

"You ought to see *Tombstone*."

"I'll do that."

He charmed her again by getting out, rounding to her side of his truck, opening the door for her. She considered telling him he didn't have to walk her to her door, but she wanted him to.

They'd spent the evening dancing, talking, and, unless she read him wrong, flirting.

She might have been a woman with a hard-and-fast rule about cabbing home from a club night alone. But the Roundup was no club. And Chase Longbow was no stranger.

"Have you settled into your place here?"

"Chase, I've been here for over six months. I've been settled in."

She unlocked the door, turned back to him. Decided. "Why don't you come in and see for yourself?"

"Oh, I don't want to bother you."

She rose on those aching toes, brushed her lips over his. Sometimes a woman has to take charge, she thought. And grabbing the front of his shirt, she yanked him forward.

It only took him about ten seconds to stop being shy.

On the drive home, Bodine stretched her arms, rolled her shoulders. "You had a fine idea, Skinner. Dinner and dancing was just right."

"I've got other ideas."

"I bet they're fine, too. I need you to turn up here, into the resort."

"That's the long way around."

"Depends on where you're going."

He knew where he wanted to go. Onto those nice, fresh sheets with her under him, but he made the turn.

"There's something so pretty about the dark and the quiet. Take the left road here. I don't know how people sleep in the city, with all that light and noise."

"It has its moments."

Curious, she glanced toward him. "Would you ever go back to it?"

"I hate saying never, but there's no pull for me. I guess I missed the dark and the quiet."

"We got plenty of it. Slow down, make this next left right there."

"That's not a road, Bo."

"No, it's not a road. But it's a cabin. And look here." She drew out a key, held it up. "What I just happen to have."

He looked at the key, looked at her. "You are a smart and interesting woman."

"I couldn't agree more."

He might have come around to get her door, but she didn't give him the chance. So he took her hand as they walked across the gravel and up the steps to the porch. "I was smart enough to get some food and beverages in case we want some, and coffee for the morning if we stay awhile."

"More interesting by the minute."

She unlocked the door, turned on the light in the living area. "Why don't I give you a tour?" She tossed the key aside, then her coat. "We can start with the bedroom."

He walked with her.

"We here at Bodine Resort offer rustic luxury. Hot tub on the back deck, big soaking tub, rain shower with jets, premium linens."

Those linens spread over a bed already turned down for the night, one framed in thick posts and facing a window he imagined offered beautiful views in the daylight.

He was more interested in the view right in front of him.

"Full kitchen, which we'll happily stock upon guest request, wood-burning fireplace, flat-screen TVs, and, well, whatever we can do to make the guest's stay memorable.

"Why don't we see if we can make your stay memorable. You can start by getting me out of this dress."

"It's a nice dress. I've been thinking about getting you out of it all night."

"Nothing stopping you."

He stepped to her, took her face in his hands, laid his lips on hers. Soft at first, then a little deeper when her hands gripped his hips.

As he'd done on the dance floor, he twirled her around, made her laugh. Pressing his lips to her shoulder, he drew down the zipper at the back of the dress.

A long, smooth back, bisected by a thin line of midnight blue.

She toed off her boots as the dress slid down.

Long again, and lean, subtle curves, more midnight blue riding low over narrow hips.

"Well, look at you."

"Is looking all you want?"

"Not nearly, but it'll do for a minute." He traced a fingertip over the tops of her breasts, felt her shiver. "Yeah, you sure got prettier."

"I ought to get to look some myself."

She unbuttoned his shirt, ran her fingertip over the line of exposed flesh. "You keep in shape."

"I do what I can."

To see for herself, she shoved the shirt aside. "Well." She used her palms now, pressing them to a hard chest, a tight stomach. "Look at you. Used to be you could count your ribs at a quarter-mile distance."

She looked up at him from under her lashes, that sly smile, and unbuckled his belt.

"Bodine."

As she flipped open the button of his jeans, he yanked her to him, crushed his mouth to hers, felt his body all but implode when she chained her arms around his neck, her legs around his waist.

He fell onto the bed with her.

Hot body and cool sheets under him. Her hands digging into his back, then dragging at his jeans.

He kicked off his boots, sent them tumbling to the floor with a *thud*. Helped her strip off his jeans.

She lifted her hips, pressed against him until the need all but blinded him.

He struggled to catch his breath, his control. "It's been a long night of foreplay."

Impatient hands yanked at his boxers. "Main event, Skinner. Now. Oh God, right now."

His hands weren't altogether steady as he stripped her panties away, flipped the hook of her bra so he could taste those lovely, lovely breasts. He wanted to know she ached as he did, just another minute to make her ache.

Then he was inside her, and he swore the world quaked.

She cried out, not in shock but with a kind of triumph. Her hands vised at his hips, digging in, urging speed as hers pumped under him.

He had to clamp her hands over his head, press down, or it would have been over before it really began.

"Just a minute," he managed. "Just a minute."

"If you stop, I'll have to kill you."

"Not stopping. Couldn't. Jesus, Bodine." His mouth ran over her throat, her breasts. "Where's this been?"

"I can't." She felt it build, beyond her control, that rising storm of deep, dark pleasure, that instant where she clung. "I can't."

It ripped through her, gorgeous, glorious, the rush of heat, the pound of pulse, and the slow, staggering fall.

"God. God. Can't breathe."

"You're breathing," he whispered, taking them both up again.

He gave her that speed now, the power with it. Dazed,

nearly delirious, she heard the rhythmic slap of his flesh
against hers, saw his eyes were like tornado clouds—
deep, deep gray with green undertones.

He was the storm inside her.

When it broke, broke for both of them, she let it sweep
her away.

CHAPTER SIXTEEN

They never opened the wine or cracked a beer. By the time exhaustion trumped lust, Bodine fell asleep sprawled on top of him with his hand still tangled in her hair.

Still, Bodine's body clock woke her before dawn. Clock aside, her body felt loose, warm, and thoroughly used. They'd shifted in the few hours of night they hadn't been active, and Bodine, who'd never considered herself much of a snuggler, realized she'd snuggled right up against Callen.

As his arm lay over her waist and one of his legs hooked over hers, she didn't imagine he minded.

She closed her eyes and, cozy as a kitten, hoped sleep would slip her away for another hour.

But she could feel his heartbeat, slow and steady. She could smell his skin. And she could remember exactly how his hands—rough, hard, and skilled—learned and fulfilled every secret she owned.

Sleep wasn't happening, and since she wasn't entirely

sure she could handle another round of sex, she eased away and rose to start her day.

Callen dreamed of her, of lying naked with her in a field of meadow grass. Starry little white flowers scattered through her hair. They moved together slowly, as need, greed, impatience hadn't allowed through the night. But in the meadow, sweet overcame urgency.

He could watch her face, the way those green eyes deepened as they held on his, the way her breath sighed out. The way her hand lifted to lay against his cheek.

Rain fell so the grass shined with it, as green as her eyes.

Wet grass, wet hair, wet woman.

He woke reaching for her.

Baffled, he lay where he was, assessing the tone of light that told him sunrise was still a ways off.

And the rain in the dream? The sound of the shower in the adjoining bathroom.

The dream, the tenor of it, amazed him, and embarrassed him even more. Erotic was one thing, but meadows and flowers and rain showers? That was downright romantic.

He'd just nudge that over in a corner for now.

He heard the shower shut off and, before long, the door opening.

"It's Sunday," he said.

"Oh, you're awake. Yeah, Sunday all day."

He heard her milling around the room, saw the shadow of her in the dark. "Why are you out of bed?"

"I've got this alarm in me. Sometimes I can shut it back off again, sometimes I can't. I gotta have coffee. Go ahead and go back to sleep awhile. I know you're working today, but you've got a couple hours. I'm just going to borrow your shirt here until I get some coffee in me."

When she walked out, he stared up at the ceiling. How was a man supposed to sleep after some romantic dream—even if it sat in a corner? Especially when a woman stepped out of a shower making the air smell of honey?

When he imagined her wearing nothing but his shirt?

The weaker sex, his ass. Women had all the damn power just being women.

He got up, walked naked into the bathroom to grab a shower of his own, and found a boxed toothbrush and a travel-size tube of toothpaste on the counter.

She didn't miss a trick.

By the time he came out, coffee scented the air. She'd lit a fire, and stood by the big front window, drinking her coffee.

Wearing nothing but his shirt.

"The elk are calling," she said. "Coming down to graze. Sunrise is close. We'll see it from here, and it's a hell of a show."

She turned back, long legs bare, his shirt hanging on her, just a couple of the middle buttons fastened. Her hair hung wet, sleek, dark as midnight.

All the power, he thought again.

"We've got some Greek yogurt and granola, if you want some."

"Why would anybody?"

"I know." Laughing, she walked back to the open kitchen, opened the fridge. "I tell myself I'll learn to like it, but I'm losing faith in that. I got some chips there. Picked them up in case we got hungry last night."

He glanced at them, thought what the hell, and opened the bag. He just needed a few minutes for his system to settle again. Leaning back on the counter, he watched her mix a blob of yogurt with a scoop of granola.

"I just need to change up the sheets and towels, give the bathroom a cleaning, wash up the dishes."

"I'll give you a hand with that."

"It won't take long. I can ride into the BAC with you, then walk to the office. I'm not getting in my workout otherwise." She ate a spoonful, winced. "It never gets any better."

Callen held out the bag of chips.

She struggled, lost. "Just this once." She reached into the bag. "Why is everything that tastes so good bad for you?" She frowned at the yogurt. "Maybe if I crumbled up chips in it."

Callen took the bowl from her, set it aside. "I've got something to say."

Her eyes went from amused to wary. "All right."

"I don't know where this is heading, where we're heading, but as long as we're on the road— Are we still on the road?"

"We're standing here after rolling around naked half the night, having coffee and barbecue potato chips. It looks like the road to me."

"Okay then. As long as we are, it's just us. We don't have any other traveling companions."

Studying his face, she ate another chip. "I'm taking that to mean neither of us sleeps with anyone else."

"That's the meaning."

Still studying him, she drank some coffee. "I think you're probably aware at this point that I like sex just fine."

"Yeah, I got that. You're good at it, too."

"I like to think so." Enjoying the casual sin of it, she crunched into another chip. "But liking sex doesn't mean I play fast and loose."

"I never thought you did, and I'm not just talking about you. There are two of us here."

She pursed her lips, nodded. "All right. So, a reasonable bargain. No hitchhikers, for either of us."

After setting her mug down, she dusted the salt off her fingers. "Do you want a spit oath?"

It was that damn sly smile again. "Nope."

He tossed aside the bag of chips, shoved her back against the refrigerator. "I've got something else in mind."

He took her then and there, more fiercely than he'd intended, while the rising sun burned red against the windows.

While Bodine didn't absolutely have to go into the office, she'd already scheduled it into her Sunday. Just an hour or ninety minutes, to clear up some paperwork. She considered pulling out her gym bag—always packed—and taking another hour in the fitness center.

But she figured she'd had plenty of exercise during the last twenty-four hours. Enough that she hadn't balked when Callen insisted on dropping her off right at the door rather than letting her walk from the BAC.

She left him the tote of wine, beer, and coffee—told him to keep it on hand, then surprised herself, and him, by leaning over and giving him a memorable see-you-later kiss.

To her mind, if you slept with a man and intended to keep right on doing it, you shouldn't be ashamed if people knew it.

She strolled into her office, humming a little, and decided to continue the screw-it state of mind that had started the day with potato chips.

She grabbed a Coke rather than the water she'd been trying to drink more of.

She'd barely settled at her desk when Jessica clipped by, backtracked. "I didn't know you were coming in today."

"Just for an hour or so," Bodine told her. "You're on the post-wedding brunch."

"I gave Chelsea lead, but I'm standing by. So far, so good. The theme continues with Western omelettes, breakfast burritos, biscuits and gravy, huckleberry mimosas, and so on."

Brows lifted, Jessica angled her head. "You must really like the dress."

"I do, and I consider it a sign that I'm doing the Walk of I'm Not a Bit Shamed."

"Good. He's pretty terrific. I really enjoyed having the time to get to know him, and everyone, better. God." She stepped in, shut the door, leaned back on it. "I slept with your brother."

"Rory or Chase? Joking," Bodine said with a laugh as Jessica's mouth dropped open. "He's also pretty terrific."

"I initiated it."

"I've known him all my life." Bodine tapped her own cheek. "This is not my surprised face."

"You're okay with it." On a kind of *whew*, Jessica ran a hand over her smooth twist of hair. "I know we'd talked about it in the theoretical sense, but now it's reality. I'm relieved you're okay with it."

"I'm assuming you're okay with it, too."

"I . . . I'm exhausted," Jessica said with her own laugh. "I don't want this to be weird, so I'll just say: Once Chase gets off the mark, he has a lot of stamina. And that is weird to say to his sister."

"On the contrary, it makes me proud. I love him, Jessie. There's nothing weird about knowing he's interested in someone I like and respect, and she's interested right back."

"You make friends easily." A touch of wistfulness ghosted around the smile. "I've seen it. You make them, and you keep them. I've made acquaintances easily, and they come and go. I want to tell you how much I value you as a friend. Now I'm going to let you get to work, go hover around Chelsea for an hour or so, then I'm going home. I need a nap."

"Do a friend a favor?"

"Of course."

"Come back so you can drive me home before you take a nap."

"You got it."

Alone, Bodine took another moment to consider something else interesting. If Jessica wasn't halfway in love with Chase, she was one step away.

"Sweet," she said aloud, then turned to her computer.

Sheriff Tate stood outside the hospital room where he'd assigned one of his female deputies. He'd checked first thing that morning with the nurse on duty, and knew the Jane Doe had been sedated because when she'd finally come to, she'd been hysterical, nearly violent.

Terrified was the word the nurse had used.

He'd read the report from the responding officer, the statements from the nine-one-one callers, and now wanted a rundown from the doctor before he took a look for himself.

"I wasn't on when they brought her in." Dr. Grove, a stern-faced man with gentle hands, continued to study the chart as he spoke. "I did consult with the ER resident who examined and treated her. He did a rape kit, and we'll have that for you. She exhibited signs of forced and violent sex. She's been treated for frostbite on her feet. The air temperature wasn't cold enough for hypothermia, but her clothes were wet. Severe abrasions, the heels and palms of her hands, her knees, elbows. Gravel in the cuts and scrapes. Severe contusions and lacerations on her right temple and forehead, most likely from striking the ground. She's concussed."

He looked up now, met Tate's eyes. "There's scar tissue around her left ankle, and scars on her back."

"Would that be ligature scars, from being bound?"

"I would give you a most likely on that. And another most likely on the scars on her back resulting from repeated beatings. A belt or a strap. Some are years old, some not."

Tate blew out a breath. "I need to talk to her."

"I understand that. You need to understand that when I attempted to do so this morning, she was incoherent, hysterical. We've sedated her to prevent her from injuring herself further."

"She didn't tell you her name?"

"She did not. As the sedative took hold, she begged us to let her go, that she had to get back. She spoke of someone she called Sir. He'd be very angry."

"When's she going to be awake enough to talk?"

"Soon. I'm going to advise you to go slowly. Whoever she is, whatever happened to her, she's suffered long-term abuse. Our staff psychiatrist will speak with her as well."

"Have you got a woman for that? If she's been raped and abused by a man, a woman might do better with her."

"We're on the same page there."

"All right then. I want to take a look at her. We got her prints, and we're going to see if she's in the system somewhere. May take a couple more days, seeing it's Sunday, and the red tape's always a tangle anyway. I'd like to try to get her name, at least."

"I'll go in with you. I can treat her more successfully if she begins to see me as a familiar face, and not a threat."

They went in together.

The woman on the bed lay still, seemed to barely breathe. But the monitors beeped. The IV tube in the back of her hand led to a bag hanging on a stand.

In the dim light she looked pale as a corpse, the long, gray-streaked hair witch-wild.

"Can we bring up the lights some?" Tate asked.

He moved closer to the bed as Dr. Grove turned the lights up. "My deputy has her as early sixties, but he's young. She's lived hard, but I'd go more like fifty."

"I agree."

Tate studied the bandaged head and hand wounds, the bruising on her jaw. "She didn't get that jaw from falling on the road."

"No, sorry, I neglected to say. I'd speculate she was struck. A fist."

"Yeah, I've seen enough of it to say the same." He judged his deputy had been more accurate judging the height, the weight.

"She's given birth more than once," Grove told him.

A hard life, Tate thought again, a brutal one to have driven those lines so deep in her face, to have given her what he thought of as a prison pallor. And even so, he could see she'd been pretty once—good bones, a well-shaped mouth, a delicate jaw, despite, or maybe in contrast to, the bruise.

Something struck him, gave him a slow burn in the belly. "Can I?"

Grove nodded when Tate held a hand over the sheet, over the right ankle. Tate lifted it, studied the thick scar tissue. "How old do you figure this is?"

"As I said, some of the scarring's newer, but the widest area, ten years, at least."

"So it could be older. She could've been bound longer?"

"Yes."

"What color are her eyes? The deputy missed it. He's young, like I said."

"I'm not sure myself." Grove moved over and, with a gentle hand, lifted an eyelid. "Green."

The burn intensified. "Does she have a birthmark? I need you to look at the back of her knee. Left knee, right in the crease. See if there's a birthmark."

Grove moved down the bed, but kept his eyes on Tate. "You think you know who she is."

"Check. Just check."

Grove lifted the sheet, bent to check. "A small, oval birthmark, in the crease behind the left knee. You know her."

"I do. Jesus God Almighty, I do. It's Alice. It's Alice Bodine."

As he spoke she stirred, and her lashes fluttered.

"Alice." He spoke as quietly as he would to a fretful baby. "Alice, it's Bob Tate. It's Bobby. You're all right now. You're safe now."

But when her eyes opened, terror lived in them. She screamed, a high wailing, shoved her hands at him.

"It's Bob Tate. Alice, Alice Bodine, it's Bobby Tate. I'm not going to let anybody hurt you." Tate gestured Grove back. "You're safe. You're home."

"No. No. No." She looked around wildly. "Not home! Sir! I have to get home."

"You got banged up some, Alice," Tate continued in that same calm, quiet tone. "You're in the hospital so you can get fixed up."

"No. I have to go home." She wailed again while tears flooded her cheeks. "I disobeyed. I have to be punished. Sir will drive the devil out."

"Who is Sir? I can try to find him for you. What's his whole name, Alice?"

"Sir. He's Sir. I'm Esther. I'm Esther."

"He called you Esther. He named you that, but your ma and pa named you Alice. We went skinny-dipping together one summer, Alice. You were the first girl I ever kissed. It's Bobby Tate, Alice." Say her name, say her name, over and over again, soft and clear. "It's your old friend Bobby Tate."

"No."

But he saw something come into her eyes—or try to. "Don't you worry about it. You'll remember later. What I want you to know . . . Can you look at me, Alice?"

"E—Esther?"

"Look at me, honey. What I want you to know is you're safe here. Nobody's going to hurt you."

Those eyes, those green eyes he remembered well, rolled in her head, flicked from point to point like a frightened animal's. "I have to be punished."

"You have been, more than enough. You're just going to rest awhile, and get strong again. I bet you're hungry."

"I—I— Sir provides. I eat what Sir provides."

"The doctor here is going to tell them to bring you what you can eat. It's going to make you feel better."

"I need to go back home. I don't know how to get home. I got lost under the moon, in the snow. Can you tell me how to get back to my house?"

"We'll talk about that, maybe after you eat some. The doctor here, he's been taking good care of you. He's working on getting you better. He's going to talk to the nurse about bringing you some food. Are you hungry?"

She started to shake her head, fiercely, but her swimming eyes stayed on his. She gnawed her bottom lip, then nodded. "I can have tea whenever I want. From the herbs."

"I bet we can rustle up some herbal tea. Maybe some soup. I'm going to sit here with you and help you eat. I'll

sit right here. I'm just going to step over there for a minute, and talk to your doctor."

"I shouldn't be here, I shouldn't be here, I shouldn't—"

"Alice." He interrupted her with that same quiet tone.
He didn't touch her, though he wanted to take her hand.
"You're safe."

As he stepped back, she clasped her wounded hands
together, closed her eyes, and muttered what he took as
prayers.

"Alice Bodine?" the doctor asked. "The Bodine family—
who is she to them?"

"She's Cora Bodine's daughter. Maureen Longbow's
younger sister. She's been missing for twenty-five years
or more. I need you to keep that information right here in
this room. I don't want word getting out on this." The burn
in his gut heaved up to scorch his throat. "God, my sweet
God, what's been done to her? Can she eat?"

"I'll have tea and broth sent in. We'll go slow there.
You did very well with her, Sheriff. You knew what to say,
how to say it."

"I've been a cop almost as long as she's been gone. You
learn." Out of his pocket, Tate pulled a bandanna, used it
to wipe his face, wipe away the sweat. "I have to call her
mother."

"Yes. But I need to speak with her, with any family
members before I can let them see her. She's fragile, on
every level. It may take time."

Tate nodded, watched Alice pray as he took out his
phone.

Cora primped for Sunday dinner. She dearly loved these
family meals at the ranch, appreciated so much the way
Maureen made certain they happened once a month no
matter what. She appreciated, too, the way her girl fussed

a bit over these monthly Sundays in her own easygoing way.

Nothing much rattled her Reenie. Cora could remember like it was yesterday the Sunday dinner where Cora served a pretty summer picnic with potato salad and fresh-from-the-garden green beans and tomatoes with Sam and Cora's own father grilling steaks and chicken.

Little Chase running around with the dogs like his pants were on fire, and Bodine trying so hard to keep up on her toddling legs.

How they'd sat and talked and laughed at the big picnic table right through the strawberry shortcake and huckleberry parfaits before Maureen announced, calm as you please, they'd better call the midwife because the baby was coming.

That girl, Cora thought as she tried out a new rosy lipstick. Downright determined to have her third baby at home. Timing her contractions for more than three hours without telling a soul—or batting an eye.

And hadn't she brought Rory into the world barely two hours later, in the big old bed, with the whole family right there?

Easygoing determination, Cora thought, approving the new lip color with a smile. That was her Maureen down to the ground.

When she counted her blessings there, there was no cup could hold them. Maybe there were moments she missed living on the ranch, even moments still she waked in the morning telling herself to get going, get to work, stock needed tending.

But she never regretted, not for an instant, turning the ranch over to Maureen and Sam and moving into Bodine House with her parents.

Torches should be passed while they still burned bright.

Her girl and her girl's man, they carried that torch in strong, steady hands.

She glanced down at the pictures Bodine had had fancied up and framed for her. How handsome her Rory had been, how proud he'd be of what they'd made together. Their two girls.

She touched a finger to her lips, then to the face of the love of her life, then to her first baby girl, then to her last.

If she had a wish to spare, it would be for her oldest daughter to understand that her mother had enough love for her, enough pride in her to light the world—and could still long so deeply for a lost child.

Cora put the wish away, as blessings always outweighed wishes. She still needed to box up the pound cake she and her mother had made.

She took a last look at herself in the mirror.

"Still holding the line, Cora. It's a tougher battle, God only knows, but you're still holding the line."

Laughing at herself, she grabbed her purse, jolting a little as her phone rang at the same instant. An odd little shiver ran down her spine, had her rolling her eyes at her own reaction.

She answered the phone.

Miss Fancy sat on the side of the bed studying her boots. She liked their style just fine with the red lightning bolts flashing down the sides. She'd always been one for pretty footwear. But, Lord, she missed wearing a sexy pair of high heels.

"Those days are over," she said with a sigh, then repeated it when she heard Cora's footsteps. "I'm just reminding myself my days of prancing about in high heels are done and gone."

"Ma."

"Was a time I could dance all night and into the morning in a pair of high red shoes. I had this pair—red, with peep-out toes—I saved up nearly six months to—"

"Ma. Ma. Mama."

The tone got through, had Miss Fancy looking up. The pale, stricken expression on her daughter's face shot an arrow into her heart.

"My baby, what's wrong? What happened?"

"It's Alice," Cora managed as her mother pushed to her feet. "It's Alice. They found Alice."

She broke, crumbling to her knees as her mother rushed to her.

As Jessica pulled up to the ranch, Bodine turned to her. "You really ought to change your mind about Sunday dinner. It's epic around here. And you'd have a chance to flirt some with Chase."

"Tempting, believe me. But I need a nap," Jessica insisted. "And I think I shouldn't push the flirting too hard right this minute."

"Strategic game." Approving, Bodine tapped a fingertip on Jessica's shoulder. "Next move's Chase's."

"You could say that."

"Well, thanks for the ride."

"Anytime. Say hi to everybody."

"I will."

Since Jessica had pulled up to the front of the house, Bodine went in the same way. She'd just run upstairs, she thought, change her dress, then see what help her mother might need for dinner.

She stepped in, stopping short as she saw her mother crying in her father's arms. Not just crying, Bodine thought in that flash of an instant, but shaking with it.

"What happened?" A fist squeezed around her heart so hard, she went light-headed. "The grannies—"

Sam shook his head, stroking Maureen's hair as he met Bodine's eyes over his wife's head. "Everyone's all right."

"I'm all right. I'm all right." Swiping at her face, Maureen pulled back. "Did I turn everything off? I need to check if—"

"Everything's off," Sam assured her. "We need to go now, Reenie."

"Go where? What's happening?" Bodine demanded.

"Alice." When her voice cracked, Maureen took a deep breath, let it come out slow. "They found Alice. She's in the hospital. In Hamilton."

"They— *Alice*? But where—"

"Not now, honey." Sam kept his arm firm around Maureen's shoulders. "We've got to go get your grannies. We can't let Cora drive with the state she's in."

"I—I—left everything in the kitchen," Maureen began.

"I'll take care of it, Mom."

"Chase, Rory, I was going to leave a note. I forgot. I need—"

"I'll tell them. I'll tell them." Bodine moved in, hugged Maureen hard, felt the tremors. "We'll be right behind you. We'll be there." She framed her mother's face with her hands. "Take care of the grannies."

It was, she saw, exactly the right thing to say. Her mother's eyes cleared. "We will. We'll take care. Chase and Rory."

"I'll find them. Go now."

The minute her mother was out the door, Bodine dashed toward the back of the house, dragging out her phone. She didn't stop when she hit the kitchen with its scents of Sunday roast and fresh bread, but punched Chase's number as she streaked outside again.

"Where are you?" she demanded the second he answered.

"Checking some fences. We're riding in now. We're not late."

"You need to get home right now. Right now, Chase. They found Alice—Mom's sister, Alice. Is Rory with you?"

"Right here. We're coming."

Relieved, she ran back in, up the back stairs. She tore off her dress, grabbed jeans and a shirt. Her mind flashed back to her mother, crying and shaking.

Her mother didn't have her purse, Bodine realized and, half dressed, dashed into her parents' room to grab it. She tried to think of what else her mother might need, thought of the state of the kitchen and the meal.

She dragged on the rest of her clothes, called Clementine. Then ran down to meet her brothers.

CHAPTER SEVENTEEN

It felt like a dream. Nothing seemed quite real.

Maureen sat close beside her, gripping her hand, and that was real. That was real. So was her mother holding her other hand.

Cora wondered if they kept her from floating away.

She heard the doctor, but the words he spoke just kept circling in her head, couldn't seem to take root.

The grandchildren came in. Did she smile at them? They always made her smile, just by being.

Bob Tate was there, standing by. Bob had called her, told her . . .

Alice.

"I'm sorry." She struggled through the fog, tried to concentrate on the doctor's words. "I can't seem to make my mind work. You're saying she doesn't remember who she is?"

"She's experienced considerable trauma, Mrs. Bodine. Long-term trauma, physical, mental, emotional."

"Long-term," Cora repeated, blankly.

"She'd do better with straight talk." Tate stepped

forward, crouched down so his eyes and Cora's were on level. "It's looking like somebody held Alice against her will, likely for years. He hurt her, Cora. She's got scars from him hurting her. Scars on her back from beatings, on her ankle from what I'm going to say looks like a shackle. She was raped, and not long before she was found. She's had children, honey."

The shudder, like sharp fingers clawing, ripped right through her. "Children."

"The doctor said she's given birth more than once."

Yes, straight talk, she thought. Better.

Horrible.

"Someone took her, and chained her up, and beat her, raped her. My Alice."

"Some of the scars are old, and some aren't so old. He hurt her mind, too. They've got a doctor here who's going to help her with that, just like Dr. Grove's going to help her."

Years. She'd lived years and knew how they flew, even when some patches of them crawled like snails.

But *years*? Her Alice, her child, her baby, held and hurt for years?

"Who did it?" she demanded, the fog burned to cinders by rage. "Who did this to her?"

"I don't know yet." Before she could speak again, his hands tightened his grip on hers. "But I can and do promise you, on my life, Cora, I'll do everything there is to find out, to find him, to make him pay for it. I swear that to you."

Rage could wait, Cora told herself. The weeping and wailing already churning inside her could wait. Because . . .

"I need to see my girl."

"Mrs. Bodine." Dr. Grove moved in again. "You need

to understand she might not recognize you. You need to prepare yourself for that. You need to prepare yourself for her appearance and emotional state."

"I'm her mother."

"Yes, but she may not know who you are. You need to be very calm when you go in to her. Your instincts will be to hold her, to ask questions, to expect a response. She may become agitated. If so, you'll need to leave her alone, give it more time. Can you do that?"

"I can and will do whatever's best for her, but I need to see her, with my own eyes."

"She doesn't look the same," Tate told her. "You prepare for that, Cora. She doesn't look or sound like you remember her."

"I'm going with you." Maureen got to her feet. "I'll stay outside the room, but you're not going by yourself."

Cora gave her own mother's hand a squeeze, then rose and took her daughter's. "I'll do better knowing you're there with me."

"I'll take you in. Mrs. Bodine," Grove continued as he led the way, "you need to resist asking her questions about what happened to her, reacting to the signs you'll see of what's happened to her. Stay calm. She may not want to be touched, she may not want to talk. Use her name. She's calling herself Esther."

"'Esther'?"

"Yes, but the sheriff continued to call her Alice, and she calmed when he talked to her."

"Did she know him?"

"I don't believe so, at least not on a conscious level, but he was able to connect." Grove paused outside the door. "Sheriff Tate says you're a strong woman."

"He'd be right."

With a nod, Grove opened the door.

In her mind, Alice had stayed the pretty, wild-natured young girl who'd run off to be a movie star. That pretty young girl, and all the stages of that girl before that day.

The little girl in frilly dresses and cowboy boots. The fretful baby she'd rocked late at night. The defiant teenager, the child who'd crawled into bed with her seeking comfort from a bad dream.

The woman in the bed with the bruised face, the dull and graying hair, the hard lines dug in around her mouth and eyes bore little resemblance to those precious images.

Still, Cora thought, she recognized her daughter.

Her heart twisted in her chest, a rag wrung hard, and her legs went weak under her.

Then Maureen tightened her grip on her hand. "I'm right here, Ma. I'll be right here, right outside."

Cora straightened her backbone, walked toward the bed.

The woman in the bed cringed back. Her eyes, green as her father's had been, darted around the room with terror chasing behind them.

Some nightmares couldn't be soothed away with cuddles.

"It's all right now, Alice. Nobody's going to hurt you. I won't let anyone hurt you again."

"Where's the man? Where's the . . ."

"Bob Tate? He's right outside. He called me to tell me you were here. I'm so happy to see you again, Alice. My Alice."

"Esther." Alice hunched in on herself. "I don't want any more shots. Sir will be very angry. I can't stay here."

"I had a teacher named Esther," Cora made up on the spot. "Esther Tanner. She was so nice. But I named you Alice, for your daddy's ma. Alice Ann Bodine. My frisky Alley Cat."

Was it her own blind hope, her own desperate need, or did she see something flicker in those frightened eyes. Carefully, so carefully her bones hurt, she eased onto the side of the bed.

"I used to call you that when you were just a baby, fighting sleep. Oh, you'd fight sleep like it was your fiercest enemy. My Alice never wanted to miss a minute of life."

"No. Alice was a whore and a trollop. God punished her for wickedness."

Her heart twisted again, this time with that churning rage, but Cora dammed it up. For later.

"Alice is, and was, and always will be high-spirited, stubborn, but never wicked. Oh, you could drive me to distraction and back again, my Alley Cat, but couldn't you make me laugh, too? And make me proud. Like that time you stood up for little Emma Winthrop when the other girls were making fun of her for having a stutter. You pushed a couple of them right on their asses, got in trouble for it. And made me proud."

Alice shook her head, and Cora took a chance.

Gently, so gently, she laid her hands on Alice's cheeks. "I love you, Alice. Your ma always loves you."

When Alice shook her head again, Cora only smiled, lowered her hands to her lap. "You know who else is here, whenever you want to see them? Reenie and Grammy. We're all so happy you're home."

Eyes darting again, Alice rubbed her lips together. "Sir provides. I have to go back. I have a house Sir built for me. I keep it clean. I have to clean the house."

"I'd just love to see your house." Cora kept her smile easy and thought dark, bitter, vengeful thoughts. "Where is it?"

"I don't know, I don't know." Now the darting eyes flew

back to Cora's. They held such fear, such confusion. "I got lost. I was wicked, and fell into temptation."

"We're not going to worry about that. Not a bit. You look tired now, so I'm going to let you rest. I'm just going to leave something with you, one of my favorite things."

Rising, Cora reached in her pocket. She'd taken the wallet snapshot out of her purse on the drive in. Gently again, she took Alice's hand, pressed the photo into it.

In it, Cora stood flanked by her two teenage daughters, their cheeks pressed to hers as they smiled for the camera.

"Your grandpa took that on Christmas morning when you were sixteen. You hold on to that. If you get afraid, you look at that. Now you rest, my Alice. I love you."

She got as far as the door and Maureen before the tears started.

"It's all right, Ma. You did everything right."

"She looks so sick and scared. Her hair, oh, Reenie, her pretty hair."

"We're going to take care of her now. We're all going to take care of her. Come on now. Come on and sit back down. Chase," Maureen said as soon as they reached the waiting area. "Go get your nana some tea, and for Grammy, too. Sit down, Ma."

Miss Fancy wrapped her arms around Cora, rocked, soothed.

"Dr. Grove," Maureen said. "I'd like to speak with you a moment."

She walked out, scanned the area for something approaching a private spot.

"First," she began, "you said someone would be evaluating her mental and emotional state. I'm assuming you mean a psychiatrist."

"That's correct."

"I'll need the name and the qualifications of that doctor. Understand me," she continued before he could speak. "My mother is, as advertised, a strong woman. But she needs an advocate, and my sister certainly does. That will be me. I need to know everything there is to know about her condition, every part of her condition, and her treatments."

She drew out her phone. "I'm going to record this, if you don't mind, so there's no chance I'll misunderstand or mix something up later. Before I do that I want to thank you for the care you've given my sister so far, and the compassion you showed my mother."

"I'll be as thorough as I can. I think it would benefit my patient if you and I and Dr. Minnow had a conversation before she evaluates Alice."

"Is that Celia Minnow?"

"Yes. Do you know her?"

"I do, so we can skip going into her qualifications. I can meet with both of you whenever you can set it up. Now." She turned on her phone recorder. "Let's start with Alice's physical condition."

Bodine took a page out of her mother's book. She waited until Tate stepped out to make a call, slipped out behind him.

"I have questions."

"I understand that, Bodine, but—"

She simply took his arm, steered him past the nurses' station. "You said she'd been raped—before she was brought here. You did a rape kit?"

"That's right."

"Is there DNA, his DNA? I've watched my share of *CSI* shows."

"And you should know it doesn't work just as it does on TV. It's going to take time to get results from the kit. And if there's DNA, we'll need a suspect to match it up against."

"She could identify this man."

In a gesture as weary as he looked, Tate scrubbed at the back of his neck. "She can't identify herself right now."

"I understand that. And I understand most of my family is focusing on Alice, how she is more than how she got there. So I'm going to start with how she got there. Where was she, exactly? Who found her?"

"A couple driving home from a night out found her on the side of Route 12. We can't say where she'd come from, how far she'd walked before she just collapsed there. She was wearing a housedress, house slippers. She didn't have any identification. She didn't have a damn thing."

"How far could she walk dressed like that?" She paced away, paced back. "A few miles maybe."

"In any direction," Tate pointed out. "We sent her clothes off to State. Their forensic people will go over them, look for something that might tell us more. But that's not going to be quick as a whistle, either, Bodine, as all of this takes time. You need to trust me on this. There's not a stone I won't turn over to find who did this to her."

"I'm not doubting that, not one bit. I just need a sense. I need to have something I can work through my own head. The idea she might've been snatched up and held since she left home—"

"I don't think that's the case. The truck she took back then was found in Nevada. She sent postcards from California."

"That's right, that's right. Nobody much talked about Alice, but I knew that. She must've been back around here. She must have been taken around here, Sheriff. She couldn't have traveled from California or Nevada in a housedress and slippers."

So that gave her a sense, at least.

"All right." She nodded, decisively. "That's something to think about."

She turned back to him. "You said she'd had children. Where are her children? God, they'd be cousins to me." As it struck home, she pressed her fingers to her eyes. "She's my aunt. I never thought about her that way."

Bodine looked back down the hallway. "I hardly ever thought of her at all."

She would now, Bodine told herself.

Bodine convinced her mother to go home with her and Rory, used Grammy as the lever. Grammy couldn't stay sitting in a hospital waiting room all night. Grammy should come stay at the ranch, and needed a little tending.

Cora wouldn't budge, so Sam and Chase stayed with her.

They'd take shifts.

Since no one had eaten at the hospital, Bodine warmed up the meal the loyal Clementine had finished cooking and stored away. When two of the women she loved poked at the food on their plates, Bodine put her foot down.

"Looks like Rory's the only one who'll get a shot of whisky after this late dinner. I happen to think we could all use one, but I'm damned if you're putting that whisky on empty stomachs."

"That's an incentive." Miss Fancy managed a half smile, ate a bite of beef. "I've held such anger in my heart for that girl."

"So have I," Maureen agreed. "Anger, resentment, and all the hard words I'd say to her if I ever got the chance."

"Oh, stop it, both of you."

More than a little shocked, Rory sat up straight. "Just hold on, Bodine."

"The hell I will. The anger and resentment and hard words came from what she did. She took off, and this doesn't change that careless act. The anger and all the rest was because you were thinking of Nana. You were thinking of your daughter's hurt, and you your mother's. Alice did what she did and deserved a good kick in the ass for it."

"Jesus, Bodine," Rory began, but Bodine shut him down with one scorching look.

"But that careless act doesn't mean she deserved what happened to her. Nobody deserves that. And nobody at this table is responsible for what did happen. So stop it, and eat."

"I don't care for that tone," Maureen said stiffly.

"I don't care for sitting here while my mother takes on guilt that isn't hers to take, and taking it tosses a share on my grammy. I don't care for my grammy doing the self-same thing to my mother."

"I don't like the tone, either." Miss Fancy ate another bite. "Just like I don't much like that the girl has a point."

"One that could be made more respectfully." But Maureen picked up her fork again.

"If she's getting away with it . . ." Rory glanced around the table. "Feeling bad about how you felt doesn't do a thing to help, Nana. What's going to help is the family standing together, doing what needs to be done, together. Guilt's not a uniter, and we're going to be united on this."

He added a smirk for his sister. "That's how you make the point respectfully."

"I plowed the field," she reminded him.

Miss Fancy waved that away. "Every now and again

the boy makes sense." She reached over, rubbed the back of his hand. "She's going to need us, Reenie. They're both going to need us."

Maureen ate carefully. "The doctor says physically she'd be able to leave the hospital in a few days. But it might take longer for her to be emotionally ready. They'll transfer her to the psychiatric unit until . . . But I . . ."

"What, honey?"

"I talked a little with Celia Minnow. She's going to be treating her. She needs to evaluate and talk with Alice, and decide what's best. It may be we could bring her here. She grew up here. Her family's here. We'll get a nurse if we need to. And Celia will either come out here for her sessions or we can take Alice to her. I need to talk it over with Sam, and with all of you because it's a lot to ask, a lot to expect."

"Of course she'll come here." Bodine looked at Rory, got his nod. "Bodine House is too small when you add in nurses and doctors. There's plenty of room here, and it's somewhere she knows."

"That lightens my burden," Miss Fancy stated. "Bodine, I can't eat any more this late at night, but I think I earned one scant finger of whisky to help me sleep. I dearly want that and my bed."

Bodine rose, got glasses, poured one for Miss Fancy, cocked an eyebrow at her mother. Maureen held up two fingers. She poured that, the same for Rory and herself.

"Well." Maureen lifted her glass. "However hard a road it's been for her, however hard a road's still to go, let's drink to Alice. To the prodigal's return."

Using Grammy again, Bodine convinced her mother to go upstairs, settle Grammy in, get some rest herself while she and Rory dealt with the kitchen.

"She can't be left alone. Alice," Rory said. "Do we call her 'Aunt Alice'? Jesus, Bo."

"I think Alice will do. We'll have to take shifts there, too, if and when she comes here. Probably hire nurses with psychiatric experience. Mom will handle that part, and having something tangible to handle is going to help her deal with the rest. It may be Nana and Grammy end up staying here for a while, too."

"We've got room. I wonder how long she's been back here. Back in the area."

As she wiped the counter, Bodine sent him a look of approval. "We're tugging the same line on that."

"You'd have to figure . . . I always figured she was dead."

"I did, too. I couldn't understand how she could be alive and not even write a letter or call now and then. Nothing for years. Knowing now somebody held her like a prisoner, and was so cruel to her—and all the time close by. Close enough by here. Rory, we could have driven or ridden within a mile of where she's been."

"Has to be isolated, don't you think?"

"I don't know. I just don't. Those women in—was it Ohio where that bastard held them for years? That wasn't so isolated, and nobody knew."

"I can't figure it. Can't figure why any man would want a woman he'd have to keep locked up. It makes me sick." Filled with disgust, he tossed down his dishcloth. "I'm going to go on up. I can drive in early tomorrow, give Chase and Dad time to come home."

"Mom's going to want to go with you, and maybe she can talk Nana into coming back, even just for a change of clothes. If she can, I'll bring Nana back."

"We'll make it work." He turned to her, drew her in for

a hug. "No matter how many times you annoyed the sheer hell out of me, I'd've been mighty pissed if you'd ever just taken off."

"I feel exactly the same."

"You get some rest, too." He kissed the top of her head, proceeded upstairs.

She knew she wouldn't settle, not yet. She told herself she needed a walk, and even though she knew exactly where she intended to walk, she didn't admit it until she knocked on Callen's door.

He answered so quickly she knew he'd been waiting.

"You heard."

"Clementine." He pulled her inside. "I went over hoping to mooch Sunday dinner. Are you okay?"

"I don't know what I am, but that's the least of it."

"It's on my list." His hands rubbed up and down her arms as he drew her back to take a good look at her. "I didn't call or text because I didn't want to get in the way. Didn't go over when I saw the lights come on in the kitchen for the same reason."

But he'd waited for her, she thought. He'd waited. "Do you think you could just hold on to me a minute?"

"I can do that. Is Cora holding up?"

"She's still at the hospital. Won't leave yet. Callen, can we lie down—I don't mean sex. Can we just lie down so I can tell you all of it? I'm too tired to stand and don't want to sit."

He hooked an arm around her waist, led her to the bedroom.

"Let's get those boots off."

She let him tug them away as she stretched out on the bed. "Thanks. I've been going at it all in sections, and in bits. I want to run through it altogether. Maybe it'll finally make some sort of sense."

He stretched out beside her. "Go ahead."

"When I got home from work, Mom was crying."

She took him through it all, step-by-step. He interrupted rarely, simply let her tell him what she'd seen, heard, felt, as it came to her.

"Mom's going to bring her home to the ranch," she concluded. "It may be soon, it may be months from now, but she's made up her mind on it."

"That worries you?"

"I worry how much stress it'll add to Mom's life, but she'd have the stress anyway. I worry they won't catch the son of a bitch who did this, and it'll just hang over us like a storm ready to break. I worry that somewhere close to home—close enough to home—there's somebody who'd do this. Children, Callen. She had children. She could have one my age or Rory's or have young ones. Are they being held and hurt like she was, or are they part of it? Like, I don't know, a cult."

He smoothed her hair back from her face. "That's a lot of worry."

"It's like the bad shoved in. Two women dead, Alice. It's like the bad shoved in and changed the world on me. Could you hold on again? I need to shut my eyes for a minute."

"Sure."

He held on, felt her fall away into sleep almost as soon as her eyes closed.

He understood her worries, every one of them. But there was one she hadn't come to yet that leaped straight to the top of his pile.

Alice Bodine wasn't dead. A live woman could, once her mind settled in again, identify whoever had kept her a prisoner, beaten her, raped her.

He worried a man who would do those things wouldn't

hesitate to kill the woman who knew his face, and anyone who stood in his way.

She woke with her head pillowed on his shoulder, and him still holding on. The comfort of that? She didn't know how to express her gratitude for the simple comfort of that.

When she started to ease away, he held tighter.

"Get some more sleep," he told her.

"I didn't mean to sleep at all. I need to get back, in case they need me." She sat up, shoved her hair back.

He sat up with her, stroked his hand down its length. She wanted to lean into him, lean on him, just another minute. But . . .

"Is that clock right?"

He glanced at it, read three-thirty-five. "Yeah."

"It's a late hour to bring this up, but we may need you to shuffle some between resort and ranch until we figure all this out. At least a couple of us need to be at the hospital. We'll be taking shifts."

"It's not a problem."

"Not tomorrow—or today, I should say." She located her boots, pulled them on. "You're visiting with your mother."

"I can put that off."

"No, don't. I need to figure out some sort of schedule anyway, and your mother, she'll be counting on it." She leaned into him a moment. "Thanks for being a friend when I needed one."

"I'm a friend even when you don't. But next time I'm going to want sex."

He made her laugh, as intended. "Me, too." She cupped his face, kissed him. "Me, too."

"Keep in touch about this, Bodine."

"I will." She pushed up. "I'm going to head to the

hospital, since I got some sleep in me, relieve Dad and Chase whether they want me to or not. Chase is going to need a friend, too."

"I'm his friend, needed or not. But I'm not having sex with him."

Laughing again, she started out. "You and Alice both left, but you sure came back different ways. Get some more sleep, Skinner."

Still fully dressed, he lay back when he heard the door close. But he didn't sleep again.

CHAPTER EIGHTEEN

Callen added to his already-packed day by pitching in with the stable horses. Hell, he was up anyway, he thought as he mucked out a stall.

He'd chosen that particular duty because he knew Chase's habits as well as he knew his own.

Twenty minutes after he'd begun, Chase came in.

Looked tired, Callen thought, and worn around the edges.

"Are you on our roll today?" Chase asked him.

"Nope, just killing some time."

"Because you love shoveling horse shit?"

"It's my life's work." Pausing, Callen leaned on the shovel. "What can I do?"

"I haven't figured out what anybody can do. We're all just waiting. Not even sure for what right yet. I know one of us has to be there to catch Nana if she falls."

His nana, too, Callen thought, and she had been as far back as his memory ran. "How's she holding up?"

"She's got steel in the spine. I guess I always knew it, but I never saw it so true as now. She pushed to stay the night in Alice's room. I looked in a couple of times, Dad, too. It looked like they were both sleeping. Then Bodine walks in, about five-thirty this morning. She'd gone over to the grannies' house, got Nana a change of clothes and whatever she figured was needed, and told me and Dad to go home. Wouldn't take no."

"Apple, tree. Short drop."

"I know it. I don't know Alice," Chase said abruptly. "I don't have feelings about her, for her. Except feeling sick and sorry finding out she's been through the worst kind of hell, and likely years of it. But I don't know her, I don't have that kind of connection with her. I've got to think about the women I do know, I do have that tie with."

Running out of words for a moment, Chase rubbed his hands over his face. "Grammy's damn near ninety. How am I supposed to stop her from spending hours in a hospital waiting room?"

"Give her a distraction. Give her a task."

Chase threw up his hands, a dead giveaway of frustration in a man of economic words and gestures. "Like what?"

"Well, Jesus, I don't know. A grandmother thing. She's Alice's grandmother, so she's got that tie you don't— and you sure as hell shouldn't be feeling guilty over that, son."

"She's my mother's sister."

"So the fuck what, Chase? You never met her in your life. Clothes." It struck Callen as inspired.

"What about clothes?"

"Bodine said Alice only had the clothes on her back— and they took those, sent them off to be analyzed. She's going to need clothes, isn't she?"

"I expect, but—"

"Think about it. You go back in there and over breakfast you mention how Alice doesn't have anything but
those hospital gowns, I'll bet you a week's pay your ma
and Miss Fancy jump all over that like they've got springs
in their feet."

"I . . . They would, too. I never thought of it."

"Likely they haven't yet, either." Callen pitched more
soiled hay into the barrow. "They're reeling from all this,
but it won't be long before they think of the practical. You
think of it first, get them going on it."

"That's a damn good idea."

"I solve world issues while shoveling horse shit."

Chase's smile came fast, but faded just as quickly. "Cal,
there's a man somewhere, somewhere too damn close,
who'd do what was done to Alice. Any way to solve that
one?"

"I'll work on it, as there's plenty of horse shit. Take
care of your family, and remember I can warm a seat in a
waiting room. I'm going to be in Missoula this afternoon,
so I can head to the hospital after I'm done there."

"I wouldn't mind if you did."

Callen nodded. "Then I will," he said, and went back
to his mucking out.

That afternoon, after readjusting the schedule, tapping
Maddie to come in for a last-minute lesson, and putting
Ben in charge, Callen knocked on the bright blue door of
his sister's pretty house. The windows flanking the door
held chili-pepper-red window boxes he knew his brother-
in-law had built. Pansies, with the purple and yellow
faces he always thought a little too human, spilled out of
them.

His sister would have planted them.

He knew a greenhouse stood in the backyard that—along with a clever swing set that mimicked a spaceship—they'd built together.

Just as they'd built a life together, a family, their clever arts and crafts shop. The backyard also held a kiln house, so some of the pottery on the store's shelves carried his sister's mark.

She'd always been clever, he thought now. Able to make something interesting out of something most would take as cast-off trash.

They'd fought as siblings do, and he'd preferred Chase's company and the ranch to hers and home. But he'd always had an admiration for Savannah's creativity. Even her near-to-unflappable calm—though when his own blood boiled inside him, her cool attitude frustrated the shit out of him.

But when Savannah opened the door, her brown hair in braids, her face as pretty as a frosted cupcake, and her belly outright huge under a checkered shirt, he felt only a warm shot of love.

"How do you get out of bed hauling that around?" He gave the belly a gentle poke.

"Justin rigged up a pulley system."

"I wouldn't put it past him. Where's the big guy?"

"Nap time—though that precious hour is nearly up. Come in quick, while there's some actual quiet."

She pulled him inside, bumping her belly—just a little weird—against him in a hug. "He's got the puppy in bed with him, too. He thinks he's pulling one over on me."

She walked into the living room—a big, deep cushioned sofa with happy red poppies on a blue background, wing chairs in red with blue stripes—all of which they'd found at flea markets and reupholstered. Like the tables they'd refinished, the lamps Savannah had saved from some junk pile, painted up and made new again.

All the pieces all around, he thought, bits and pieces, nothing perfect, nothing exact. And everything that made a home.

She plopped down in a chair, rubbed her belly.

"Ma's getting dressed. You're early. You want coffee? I've already had my one allowed cup for the day—I just can't quit it—but I can make you some."

"Just sit."

"How about some sassafras tea, cowboy?"

He grinned. "Not in this life, you weird-ass hippie. Why aren't you at the shop?"

"I needed a day off. I had some things to finish up in the workshop, and Justin starts getting overprotective about this stage of the bake-off." She patted her belly again. "I could've taken Ma today, Cal. I know how you feel about it."

"It's no problem."

"I can get a sitter easy, if you want me along."

"Don't worry about it, Vanna."

"She's really looking forward to it—mostly it's spending time with you." She looked up at the ceiling as she heard a *thump*, a series of yips, and boy-size gut laughter. "Time's up."

"I'll go get him."

Savannah waved Callen back down. "No need for that. Believe me, he knows the way. And I made the mistake of telling him you were coming by. So brace yourself."

"I like him. He's got your what-can-I-do-with-this way and Justin's look-at-the-funny-side attitude. You made an entertaining kid."

"Working on another. Want to know which kind?"

"Which kind of what? Oh, boy or girl? I thought you weren't finding out."

"We weren't—we didn't with Brody, and he was the best surprise ever. So we weren't, and we didn't, then we were talking one night about how the nursery, which was gender neutral, evolved into boy. Did we leave it, do it neutral again, or what now that we've got Brody in his big guy room, and are about to fill the crib again. So we decided, just find out. And we did."

"Okay, what flavor's in there?"

"Strawberry ice cream."

"Pink? A girl." He stretched out his foot to give hers a nudge. "You'll have one of each. Nice work." He watched her belly ripple. "Talk about weird."

"She knows we're talking about her. Aubra or Lilah. We've got it down to those two. Whoever wins gets first name, the other middle. Which one do you like?"

"I'm not going there, between Ma and Pa."

"I'm not saying which one's mine, which is Justin's. Just asking which strikes you."

"I guess 'Aubra' then."

"Yes!" She shook a fist in the air. "Another vote for me. Now, if I talk him into Aubra Rose, and saving Lilah for if we have another girl—"

"You're already thinking of another?"

The puppy, a wildly affectionate Lab, streaked down the steps and straight into Callen's lap, forelegs braced on Callen's chest as he lapped Callen's face. Brody, hair in mad sleep tufts, face rosy, eyes as manic as the pup's, navigated the steps with a plastic bucket.

"Cal, Cal, Cal!" Whatever else he babbled was too fast for Callen's limited toddler-speak, but when the boy dumped the bucket, flung himself into Cal's lap like the puppy, Callen understood unfiltered love.

He couldn't say how he'd come to deserve it, but it sure as hell brightened a day.

Brody wiggled down again to retrieve the bucket, dig in for an action figure.

"'Ronman."

"I can see that. I thought you were a Power Ranger man."

"Red Ranger. Hulk. Cap'n 'Merca. Sliver Ranger."

"Silver," his mother corrected. "Sil-ver."

"Sil-ver."

He named his collection as he pushed them at Callen.

"I can't stop Ma from buying them for him."

"Why should she stop?" Katie Skinner came down the stairs. She wore a dark gray dress, short, sensible black boots.

More, Callen thought, she wore happy. To his mind, that hadn't been a staple of her wardrobe for far too many years.

It suited her, that happy, like the hair she'd let go stone gray, and the laugh she let loose when Brody raced over to hug her legs.

"Cal!" he told her.

"I can see that."

"Cal play."

"Go ahead," Katie told Callen. "Give him some time, we've got plenty. I'm going to make Savannah some tea."

"Ma, I would really love some, thanks."

"She wants sassafras," Callen said as he slid down to sit on the floor, thrilling both boy and puppy.

"I actually do."

"Two shakes."

Callen chose some men for battle. "You put a light back in her, Vanna. You and Justin and this boy."

"I think we got it going again. You lit another when

you came back home. It's amped up a little bit more still at the idea of you and Bodine Longbow."

When his head shot up, his eyes narrowed, Savannah hugged her belly and laughed. "You might've been away, Cal, but you shouldn't have forgotten how much overlap there is in people we all know. We heard all about you and Bodine dancing sexy at the Roundup this past Saturday night."

"'Dancing sexy.'" Callen held his hands over Brody's ears. "Is that any way to talk around a child?"

"His daddy and I have been known to do some sexy dancing right in front of him."

"I might have to cover my own ears."

Smirking, Savannah ran a hand down one of her braids. "So, about you and Bodine."

"Don't get ahead of yourself."

"I've always liked her—all of them, but Bodine especially. You don't know how she'd ride over two or three times a year with a bag of clothes for me. She'd say how I was so handy with a needle, maybe I could fix them up and use them. There wasn't a thing wrong with them— maybe a button missing or a little tear in a seam. She said that to spare my feelings. And when Justin and I opened the shop, she was one of the first in the door. She has a kind heart, and class. I'm not sure you deserve her."

She smiled when she said it.

"Women, Brody? They are contrary creatures. It's best you learn that now."

"W'men." Brody held up Pink Ranger and hooted.

An hour with his sister and entertaining nephew, another hour or so taking his mother to dinner—Callen considered them nice bookends. What stacked between them was duty.

He stopped as she asked so she could buy flowers,

waited patiently as she selected what she wanted—and kept his thoughts about the yellow tulips not lasting the night to himself.

He'd have paid for them, but she wouldn't have it.

He drove to the cemetery, let her lead the way after he'd parked. He hadn't been since the funeral, hadn't intended to come again. Now he realized he'd make this sojourn with her whenever she asked.

He could be grateful they maintained the place, he supposed, cleared most of the snow. What was left made hard-packed paths easy enough for her to walk.

He kept a hand on her arm in any case as she navigated through the stones to the small, simple one marked with his father's name.

Jack William Skinner
Husband and Father

True enough, Callen thought. He'd been both. The stone didn't need to take into account the degrees of success on either.

"I know it's hard for you to come here," Katie began. "I know it's not altogether fair for me to ask you to come."

"It's not a matter of fair."

"He had weaknesses," she continued as the wind blew through her hair. "He broke promises to you."

To all of us, Callen thought, but kept silent.

"He made life harder for you because of those weaknesses and broken promises. He knew that. Oh, Callen, he knew it, and he did try. I could've left, taken you and Savannah and left him."

"Why didn't you?"

"I loved him, and love's a powerful thing." While the

wind blew through her hair, she stroked a hand along the top of the gravestone. "It can take hard knocks, again and again. He loved us. That's why when he gave in to those weaknesses it hurt him more than it ever hurt me. He'd work hard to make up for it, but then . . ."

Then, Callen thought. He remembered a whole lot of *then*s. "There were times you could barely put food on the table, when the bills piled up like cordwood."

"I know it. I know." Still, she continued to run a gloved hand over the top of the gravestone, as if soothing a mournful ghost. "Just as I know gambling was a sickness for him, one he struggled with. He never blamed anybody but himself, Callen, and that's an important thing to remember. Some do, they cast the blame around for their addictions. Liquor or drugs or gambling. Casting blame is cruel, violent. Your father was never cruel, never laid a hand on me or either of our children. He didn't have a mean bone in him."

With a sigh, she stopped stroking the stone, took her son's hand. "But he let you down."

"What about you?" God, it infuriated him she never blamed her husband for the losses, the scrimping, the humiliations.

"Oh, Cal, he let me down. And the down was harder, so much harder when he'd go so long without falling. A part of you blames me for not making him stop."

"Used to," he admitted. "I used to blame you for that. I know better now. I don't blame you for anything, Ma. That's God's truth."

She stared hard at him, eyes seeking, then closing. "That lifts a weight. I can't tell you the weight that lifts, knowing that's the truth."

His father, Callen thought, hadn't been the only one to

make mistakes, to let people down. "I can be sorry I didn't lift it sooner. I am sorry."

"I made mistakes. I made mistakes when I made excuses for him, when I made them to you and Vanna." She squeezed his hand. "I can be sorry for that, and I am. He'd tell himself he had it licked. He'd know better, but he'd tell himself that. He'd just sit in on a friendly poker game, or put a small bet on a horse race, anything really. He knew he'd slide back, but he'd tell himself he wouldn't. He'd stop going to his meetings."

"What meetings?"

"Gamblers Anonymous. He didn't tell you or Savannah about going to them. The truth is, part of him was ashamed for going, for needing to go. He wouldn't tell me when he stopped going, though I'd start seeing signs. The only thing he ever lied to me about in our lives together were those meetings—skipping them to gamble. I could forgive him for that, because the lies and the gambling were the same.

"He was proud of you, you and Savannah. Maybe you'll never feel the truth of that—and that's his blame not yours. Maybe you're not going to remember the good times, and we had them. Or how he put you up on a horse the first time, brought home your first dog, taught you how to hammer a nail and mend a fence. But he did those things, Callen, and had a father's pride in you. And your father never forgave himself for costing you and Savannah your birthright, for gambling away the ranch acre by acre."

"It was your home."

"I'll tell you a secret." She laid a hand on his arm, rubbed. "The ranch was nothing but work for me. Means to an end. I'd have liked a house like Vanna's. Neighbors close by, a yard, a little garden. Horses and cattle and fields to plow and plant—just endless work. Your daddy loved it. You love it. I never did."

"But you . . ." He trailed off, shook his head. Maybe a man could never understand women, and the strength that ran through them. Or how they could love.

"I learned well enough how to be a ranch wife, but the truth is, it was never natural for me. I love living with Savannah and Justin and that baby boy. And I'm useful to them—that's natural to me. I can help make their lives easier, and every day I'm blessed to see how happy they are together. How my girl's made a good life for herself. I've never figured out what to do to make your life easier, to make up for having what was yours gambled away."

"You don't need to. I can make my own. I don't need what was."

"I know you can. Didn't you send money to me every single month? Don't you still—and there's no need for you to—"

"I need to," he said, cutting her off.

"You can make your own, Callen, and I know you'll build your own happy life, but the land was yours, and I couldn't keep it for you."

"I don't want you to carry that, Ma. I don't want to think I've left that weight on you. If it was only the land, I could've bought it back, or enough of it. I left to make my own, to prove I could—to myself. I came back because I had, and I missed home. Home wasn't that plot of land."

"I wanted you to bring me today so I could say these things, and maybe put them aside for us. He never forgave himself for losing what should've been yours. And when he finally accepted he'd never get it back, it was in that despair that he took his own life. I couldn't forgive him for that."

Katie looked back at the stone, at the name carved there. "For all the rest, I'd forgiven him. The day we buried him here, I had no forgiveness in my heart. Anger and blame. I couldn't feel anything else. Friends and neighbors came, I said the words back to them you're supposed to say. I said words to you and your sister you're supposed to say. But the words I said to him in my private thoughts were angry and unforgiving."

"But you come here, to put flowers on his grave."

"I'd have done that whether or not I'd forgiven him. And I have. I have forgiven him. He lost so much more than some acres of ground, some buildings, some animals, Callen. He lost the respect if not the love of his daughter, he lost his son. He lost the years he might have had with his grandchildren. So I forgave him. I come here, and put the flowers on his grave and remember there were good times, and there was love between us. We made you and Savannah between us, and that's my miracle. So I can do that, and let the rest go."

She bent down, laid the flowers. "I don't ask you to forgive him, Cal. But I needed you to try to understand, and try to put this aside between us. I want to watch my boy build his own good life."

For too long, for too many times, he'd thought her weak. He saw now that Cora Bodine wasn't the only woman in his life with steel in her.

"There's nothing hard between us, Ma. I'm sorry if I let you feel there was. I just couldn't stay."

"Oh, no, Cal, you were right to go." She dug a tissue out of her pocket. "I missed you something awful, but I was glad you left to make your own."

They weren't words he said easily or often, but he saw she needed them, would never ask, but needed. "I love you, Ma."

Her eyes already swimming, spilled out tears. "Callen. Cal." She leaned against him, pressed her face to his chest. "I love you so much. My boy, I love you so much."

He felt her release a breath as if she'd held it for years. "Now I know you're really home again."

"I left because I needed to. I came back because I wanted to. I missed my ma," he said and heard her muffled sob against his heart. "Stop worrying now. You're getting cold. Come on, let's get you in the truck with the heater going."

Katie looked down at the stone, the flowers. "Yes, it's time to go."

"Good, because I've got a date with a pretty woman." He slipped an arm around her. "I'm going to buy her a fancy dinner."

She dashed the lingering tears away. "Would that run to a glass of wine?"

"You've got a taste for wine, do you?"

"I do tonight."

"Then we'll get ourselves a bottle."

When he got back to the cabin, he'd seen the tracks in the snow right off. The rage that he'd nearly choked down spewed back up as he strode to the shed, found the door unlocked.

He roared inside sure, still sure, he'd find her. She wouldn't dare, wouldn't *dare* disobey.

But the place he'd provided for her was empty, not even fully put to rights.

She'd pay for it, pay dear.

He rushed back out, squinting as he surveyed. The moon gave him enough light to see those tracks, though the clouds were coming in.

She wouldn't get far. Ungrateful whore. And when he

caught up with her, he'd break both her legs. Walk off, would she? It would be the last time she walked at all.

He marched to the cabin, unlocked the door.

He had stores set by to last a year. Sacks of beans and rice, flour and salt. Cans stacked floor to ceiling.

He had cordwood inside and outside under a tarp.

But he kept his armory in his bedroom.

Three rifles, two shotguns, a half dozen handguns, and an AR-15 that had cost him dearly. He had the tools for making his own shotgun shells, and enough other ammunition to wage a small war.

The day would come, he knew, when there would be one to fight. He'd be ready. Ready when the sovereign citizens of this once-great country rose up to overthrow the corrupt government and take back the country, the land, the rights denied them and given to immigrants and blacks and homosexuals and women.

A government that pissed on the Constitution and the Bible in equal measure.

The war was coming, and he prayed nightly it came soon. But tonight, this night, he had a woman to hunt down, a woman he'd taken as his wife and provided for, a woman to punish.

He chose a good, hefty Colt revolver—made in the U. S. of A. and already fully loaded. Stripped off his coat to don an ammo vest, filling it with bullets and shotgun shells. He strapped a knife and sheath on his belt, hung night-vision goggles around his neck, and slung a shotgun over his shoulder.

He'd been tracking and hunting these woods most of his life, he thought as he headed out again. No ignorant whore of an ungrateful woman would get far once he was on her trail.

A trail pitifully easy to follow, even when some thin snow blew in. Wandering around without any sense at all, he concluded, quickening his pace.

It worried him a little when he saw she'd changed directions and if she'd kept on would come to a ranch road. He had no truck with the people who lived there, and their fancy house was a good mile back. But if she'd taken that road, walked that way . . .

She hadn't. Too stupid for that, he thought with grim satisfaction when he saw her tracks heading away from the direction of the ranch house.

He lost them for a while, decided she'd walked on the road some, picked them back up again when she'd either walked or stumbled off into the snow.

With the cloud cover, he put on the goggles, picked his way along. He could follow her on the gravel, too, the way she dragged that one leg.

Stupid bitch, stupid bitch. He used the words like a prayer as he followed the tracks, as his legs began to ache. How had she walked so damn far?

He spotted some blood, crouched down, studied it. Hard to judge with the wet snow, but it was fresh enough, so it was likely hers.

He walked on. A little blood trail, just a drop here, a drop there, but he picked up his pace until he grew winded.

His head began to throb as he realized where those tracks would have taken her. Though his lungs burned, he forced himself into a hard jog, the shotgun slapping against his back, the revolver a weight at his thigh.

He would kill her, and it would be a righteous kill.

Hadn't he told himself to lock her up, snap those irons back on her, and take another wife? Younger, childbearing

age. A wife who'd carry sons instead of useless girls he
sold off rather than keep.

He wouldn't bother to chain her and feed her now. Not
after she showed her deceitful heart. He'd gut her like a
deer, leave her for the animals to take.

He'd be more discriminating with his next wife. He
wouldn't show the next one such kindness.

But when he reached the road, he knew he'd missed his
chance. He could see a quarter mile in either direction,
and didn't see Esther.

He told himself she'd die of exposure or exhaustion,
and good riddance. He told himself even if she lived, she'd
never lead anybody back to his cabin. He told himself the
corruption of local law enforcement would never follow
her trail as he had.

But he'd make sure of it, wiping it, backtracking, leaving false tracks.

When the thin snow turned to rain, he smiled. God
provided, he thought and said a silent prayer. The rain
would wash away the blood trail, help with her tracks
through the snow. Still, he worked through the wet, laying other tracks, carefully backtracking, pleased when the
rain came down heavy for an hour of the work.

By the time he got back to his own land, his legs trembled with fatigue, and the jeans over them were soaked
through wet.

He still found the rage and energy to kick the dog, viciously.

"Why didn't you stop her? You let her walk off."

As the dog whimpered, tried to crawl back to its
shelter, he yanked the Colt free. Had his finger on the
trigger, and in his mind the bullet already in the dog's
brain.

Then he thought better of it. He'd take the useless dog out on a rope in the morning. Let it run through and across any tracks near the cabin. Saddle up the fleabag of a horse, ride around some. A man on his horse, taking his dog out for a run.

That's what he'd do.

He went back into the cabin, built up the fire. He stripped down to the skin, dragged on some winter underwear to warm his bones.

Hunger gnawed at him, but the cold and exhaustion was worse. With his head throbbing again, he crawled into bed.

In the morning, he told himself, he'd ride out, make sure he'd covered all that needed covering.

Falling into sleep, he wished Esther all the wrath God aimed at the wicked and profane.

While he cursed her, Alice spent her first night of freedom in more than twenty-five years in a drug-cushioned sleep.

In the morning, his skin hot to the touch, his chest tight, his throat raw, he pushed himself to dress, to eat, to saddle the broken-down horse. The dog limped and wheezed, but crossed the faded tracks.

Though the rain had done most of the work, he reminded himself God helped those who helped themselves. He rode more than an hour before bone-rattling chills turned him toward the cabin again.

He didn't bother to chain the dog—where would it go?—barely managed to unsaddle the horse. Inside he downed cold medicine straight from the bottle. He needed to go out, put an ear to the ground, see if anybody was talking about finding some stupid old woman, see if that deceitful bitch had anything to say.

But that would wait, would have to wait until he'd slept off the cold she'd caused him to catch.

He crawled back into bed, slept fitful between chills and fever.

He didn't wake enough to take more medicine until about the time Callen ordered his mother a bottle of wine.

CHAPTER NINETEEN

By the third day, Bodine became so familiar with the hospital rhythm she could identify which nurse walked by the waiting room by the sound of the stride.

She worked remotely via laptop and smartphone during what she thought of as her on-duty time. Her mother, her partner-in-waiting this morning, did the same. The waiting room served as their de facto offices, living room, and limbo.

In the afternoon, as the afternoon before, either Sam or Rory would arrive with Miss Fancy, and Bodine and Maureen would drive back to chip away at work. They'd try to convince Cora to come with them, take a break until the night shift. But so far, no one could budge her.

Bodine knew Callen had sat through the night on that same reasonably comfortable couch with Chase. He wouldn't want her gratitude for it, but he had it.

When she'd arrived with her mother, shortly after sunup, she'd poured coffee for all of them from a thermos she'd filled at home. She'd unwrapped bacon and egg biscuits, passed them out.

That's when Callen had kissed her, enthusiastically.

"Mom made them," she'd told him, and he'd turned straight to Maureen and kissed her, enthusiastically.

It was the first time in three days she'd heard her mother laugh.

Yes, he had her gratitude.

The fabric of their lives woven over the past twenty-five years had been torn. Their routines of home and work and family shattered.

Their world became the hospital, the being there, the going to and from, the constant juggling on snatches of sleep and rushed meals between. The demands of work, the people and animals depending on them, the low simmer of worry for Cora.

If Alice's return created such tears and breakage, Bodine thought, how much had her careless departure caused so long ago?

"Is it harder?" Bodine asked.

Maureen stopped frowning at an e-mail, looked up over her cheaters. "Is what harder, honey?"

"Having her come back like this, than it was having her leave. I'm not asking that the right way."

"No, it's right enough. It's right enough. I've asked myself the same." To answer them both, Maureen set her tablet aside, folded her cheaters on top of it. "I was so mad, wasn't worried a bit at first. Here I was about to go on my honeymoon, and Alice pulls a stunt to get attention. We didn't want to leave Ma in the middle of that mess, but she wouldn't have us staying. She said it would upset her a lot more. I so wanted to go, too. Here I was, a married woman, flying off to Hawaii with my husband. So exotic, so romantic, so exciting. It wasn't just the sex part. I didn't save myself for marriage."

"Why, I'm just shocked. I'm just shocked to hear that."

Maureen laughed a little, leaned back. "I was just so smug—the married part—so crazy in love, so excited to be going off with my husband to what was the same as a foreign country for me back then. And Alice had one of her famous snits, put a cloud over it all."

Reaching down, Bodine gave her mother's hand a squeeze. "I'd've been mad, too."

"I was spitting mad," Maureen replied. "I wasn't really worried until toward the end of our honeymoon week. Every day I was sure she'd come back. And every day, I heard a little more strain in Ma's voice when we called. So we came back a day early, and then I could see that strain. In Ma, in Grammy and Grandpa.

"We were going to build a house."

As she'd been imagining the strain, the stress, the face, Bodine missed the postscript. "Sorry, what?"

"Your dad and I, we were going to build a house of our own. Had the land picked out for it. Close enough he could ride over to work, and I could do the same. We were just doing the first expansions on the dude ranch, just starting to make real plans for what we have now. And we'd build our own house. We never did."

This time, Bodine took her mother's hand and held it. "Because Alice left."

"I couldn't leave my mother. At first we thought we'd just put it off until Alice got back and everything settled again. The first year was the worst, every day of that first year. When they found the truck—the battery dead. She'd just left it—that was Alice. Don't fix it, just walk away. The postcards, all bright and braggy. The detective Ma hired following some lead and losing it again. It was Grammy who made Ma stop throwing money there, and breaking her heart over it. And I was pregnant and having Chase, all in that first year. So, it was the happiest and the hardest year of my life. Of our lives. Alice wasn't there, but she was everywhere."

Maureen reached over, rubbed Bodine's leg. "And now here we are, with our world spinning around her again. Now it's my children spinning, too, and I don't like knowing it. I don't like when we can get my mother out of that room for ten minutes, how tired she looks, how worn. She's pale, Bodine."

"I know it," Bodine agreed.

"I don't like the ugly resentment I have inside me. It's there even though I know terrible things happened to her, things she couldn't stop, things she didn't deserve. Somebody hurt my sister, stole her life from her, and I want to make him pay for it. But I still resent that selfish girl who couldn't celebrate my happiness, who didn't think of her mother and only thought of herself."

Bodine set her laptop aside, draped an arm around Maureen's shoulders.

"I have to forgive her." Giving in, Maureen pressed her face into the curve of her daughter's throat. "I have to find a way to forgive her. Not just for her sake, but for Ma's, for my own."

"Not once have I heard you or Dad say you'd planned to build a house. Part of you must have forgiven part of her a long time ago."

Straightening again, Maureen tried to brush it off. "Well, I was going to be a country-western singing sensation at one time, too."

"You've got such a good voice."

"I don't regret not heading off to Nashville, and I sure don't regret raising my children in the house where I was raised. Things fall into place, Bodine, if you work at it and make your choices with some care."

Bodine heard footsteps—heels not crepe soles—and

when they turned into the waiting room, her mother's body shifted.

"Celia."

"Maureen. And this must be your Bodine." The woman, sharp-looking with glossy brown hair waving to her shoulders, stepped up, offered Bodine a hand. "I'm Celia Minnow."

"It's nice to meet you. You're one of Alice's doctors."

"I am." She looked back at Maureen. "Could we talk?"

"I'll take a walk," Bodine began, but Celia waved her down.

"You're welcome to stay. Your grandmother speaks so highly of you." Celia sat, smoothed her dark skirt. "I've had three sessions with Alice, in addition to my initial evaluation. I can give you the broad strokes."

"Please."

"I know you've spoken extensively with Dr. Grove on her physical condition, and you're aware of his evaluation of her mental and emotional state."

"Celia, I hope you know me well enough not to feel obliged to dance and cushion."

"I do." And crossing her legs, Celia stopped dancing. "Alice has suffered extreme physical, mental, and emotional trauma over a period of years. We can't yet determine how long. She doesn't remember, and may, in fact, have no true gauge of how long. It may be her memory will come back, it may not. More likely it will come in pieces and patches. It's my opinion that over this undetermined period of years she was indoctrinated by methods of force, physical assaults, praise, and punishment. Your mother tells me Alice was never particularly religious."

"No."

"She quotes scripture—Old Testament—some verbatim, some bastardized. Vengeful God, a man's superiority and dominion over women. The sin of Eve. Again, it's my opinion these views were part of her indoctrination. Physical assaults, religious fanaticism, imprisonment, and as she speaks of no one but the man she calls Sir, probably isolation."

"Torture," Maureen said.

"Yes, extended until she submitted, until her will broke and she began to accept the will of her torturer. He is a sexual sadist, a religious fanatic, a psychopath, and a misogynist. And he was her provider. He provided her with shelter, with food, with, however horrid, companionship. He beat her, but he also fed her. He raped her, but he put a roof of some kind over her head. He imprisoned her, but given her condition when she was found, allowed her basic hygiene. She was completely dependent on him. While she fears him, she feels loyalty to him. She believes him to be her husband, and the husband, however cruel, is designed by God to rule."

"No one ruled Alice. And boys . . . she liked boys," Maureen said. "She liked using her appeal. Not in a mean way, she wasn't mean like that. Careless, maybe even callous. She didn't think much of marriage back then, made noises about how it was just a trap for women. She pushed that on me off and on while we were planning my wedding. Some of it was just Alice-talk, and some was her idea of being a free, desirable, and famous woman one day. She was always so sure of herself, Celia, impulsive and headstrong and confident."

"She wanted to scrub her hospital room."

"She what?"

"She's supposed to scrub her house every other day. She became agitated about cleaning her hospital room."

"Alice would rather have gone without eating than wash a dish. Making her own bed in the morning was a daily bitch fest." Sliding a hand under a wing of her chestnut-brown hair, Maureen rubbed at her temple. "Can somebody really change somebody else like that? Make them all but the opposite."

"If you were punched or slapped every morning before making your bed—"

"I'd make it faster," Maureen finished.

"Can I ask a question?"

Celia turned her deep brown eyes on Bodine. "Of course."

"She had children. Has she said anything about them? I can't get them out of my head."

"She said Sir took them away, their father took them away. She became despondent and withdrawn when we approached the subject. I won't probe there again until we've built up more of a relationship. She has accepted your mother—not as her mother, but as a companion and an authority figure. She also looks to Sheriff Tate, and seems to trust him as far as she trusts anyone."

"She and Bob were friendly," Maureen told her. "Might've been a bit more than friendly for a while."

"Yes, he told me. She's accepted Dr. Grove, though she continues to become agitated during exams, and can be jittery with the nurses. But she's obedient. She eats when she'd brought food, sleeps when she's told to rest, showers when she's told to. Who thought of bringing her mother's crocheting in?"

"Bo did."

"Well, it's excellent therapy for both of them. Cora's teaching Alice to crochet, and they're spending time quietly that way. It's good for both of them. It's going to take time, Maureen. I wish I could tell you how much time."

"She can't stay in that room forever. Neither can my mother."

"No, you're right. Physically she's recovered enough to be released. Dr. Grove and I have discussed a rehabilitation center."

"Celia, she needs to come home. My mother will end up sleeping in her room at another kind of hospital just as she is here. We can take care of Alice at home."

"Home care, considering her condition, is a complicated and demanding enterprise. You need to understand just what that would mean, for Alice, and for all of you."

"You could recommend nurses or aides as long as she needs them. You could continue to treat her. We'd bring her to you every day if you say she needs it. I've thought it through. It might spark something in her. Her home, her views, Clementine and Hec—they work for us, and did when Alice and I were teenagers. Wouldn't what's familiar help her, and the normal of it?"

"She couldn't be left unattended in her current state of mind. She could wander off, Maureen. There's medication to administer, and there's, most importantly, a need not to press her, not to overwhelm her."

On a nod, Maureen rubbed at her temple again. "I've been reading as much as I can find, and I think I have those broad strokes. You and Dr. Grove tell me what needs to be done, and not to be done. We'll abide by it. I know I can take her home without your permission, but I don't want to do that. And I don't want to put my sister in a psychiatric hospital—because that's what you mean by 'rehabilitation center'—until I've tried to bring her home."

"She needs to agree. She needs to feel she has some control."

"All right."

"Driving her back and forth for sessions is far too much stimulation, too overwhelming. If she and Dr. Grove agree, I'll agree to a week trial. I need to come to her, talk to her every day. You'll need round-the-clock psychiatric nurses until I'm convinced she's adjusting and won't harm herself."

"Harm herself?"

"She's not suicidal," Celia said. "But she could inadvertently harm herself. Your mother should be close by."

"She and my grandmother will both move to the ranch for as long as they need to."

"Let's start here." Celia rose. "Come down with me and see her, talk to her."

"I—I thought I wasn't allowed to yet."

"Now you are."

"Oh, I— Give me a second." Maureen held up a hand, palm out. "You threw that one at me too quick."

"She'll throw more."

"I know it. That one just knocked the wind out of me for a minute." But she rose. "Bodine."

"I'll be right here. I'm going to call Clementine, and have her fix up the room for Alice. It'll be ready for her when we bring her home."

"Bodine, you're my rock. All right, Celia."

The walk down the hospital corridor seemed endless, and far too quick. "I'm nervous."

"That's natural."

"I want to ask if I look all right, and I know just how foolish that sounds."

"You do, and that's natural, too. You're going to be shocked at how she looks, Maureen. Try not to show it."

"I've been told already."

"Being told and seeing for yourself are different. Keep your voice calm, call her Alice, tell her who you are. She probably won't remember you, at least not consciously. It's a deep block, Maureen."

"And it'll take time, I heard that." Taking a deep breath, Maureen waited for Celia to open the door, lead the way in.

They could have told her a hundred times, and nothing would have prepared her for her sister's transformation. The shock hit her belly like a fist, but she held back the gasp.

Because her hands trembled, she slipped them into her pockets, hoping it looked casual.

The Alice who'd come back sat up in the bed, long graying hair neatly braided, her bottom lip caught between her teeth as she carefully worked with a crochet hook and green yarn.

Their mother sat in a chair, working a more complex pattern with variegated blues.

They worked in comfortable silence.

"Alice, Cora."

Alice's fingers stopped, curled tight at Celia's voice. And her eyes latched on Maureen's face.

Her shoulders hunched, her chin dipped.

"I've brought you a visitor."

"I'm making a scarf. I'm making a green scarf. Visitors aren't allowed."

"They're allowed now."

"I like the green." Maureen heard her own words, swallowed the tremor in her voice before she took a few steps forward. "I like to crochet, too. Ma taught me." Maureen bent down, kissed Cora's cheek, and with her hand on Cora's shoulder smiled at the woman staring at her. "It's so good to see you, Alice. I'm your sister, Maureen. I look different than I did before."

"I need to make the scarf."

"You go ahead. Ma braided your hair, didn't she? It looks nice."

"Women are vain creatures, painting false faces to seduce men with lustful thoughts."

"We're made in God's image," Cora said calmly as she continued to work. "I'd think God wants us to present a pleasing image when we can. And he said to go forth and propagate, so a little lust helps that along, doesn't it? Those stitches are nice and even, Alice."

Alice looked down at them, and Maureen saw her lips try to curve. "It's good?"

"It's very good. You learn quick, always did. I never could get you to sit still long enough to learn needlework when you were little."

"I was bad. Spare the rod, spoil the child."

"Don't be silly. You were just rambunctious. You did like planting flowers, had a creative hand with that. I loved when you and Reenie would plant your sister garden."

"Impatiens and geraniums," Maureen began.

"Reenie, Reenie, Reenie," Alice muttered. "Always bossing, always better."

"Alice, Alice, Alice," Maureen echoed over her hammering heart. "Always pushy, always bitchy."

Eyes narrowed, Alice looked up. And though her throat went dry, Maureen held the stare, and smiled. "I'm still glad to see you, Alice."

"Reenie never liked Alice."

"I wouldn't say never. There were times I didn't like you, but you were always my sister. I still plant the garden, the sister garden in the spring. Impatiens and geraniums, sweet alyssum and sweet peas."

"Snapdragons. I like red ones."

Now her eyes burned, seemed to throb with the tears pushing behind them. "I still plant the red ones."

"I have to finish this, I have to do a good job. Flowers

don't feed anybody. No point in planting flowers. Vain as women, and as useless."

"Bees need them. Birds, too." Cora reached out, squeezed Maureen's hand. "They're God's creatures."

"Sir said no flowers!" She snapped out the words. "You plant beans and carrots, potatoes in the barrels, cabbage and tomatoes. And you hoe and you weed, and you water if you know what's good for you. It's almost planting time. I have to get back. I have to finish this scarf."

Celia touched Maureen's arm, but Maureen wasn't finished. Not quite yet. "I could use help with the planting. The kitchen garden and the flowers."

"Sir said no flowers." A tear slipped down Alice's cheek as she worked fiercely with the hook. "If you say please, he has to hit you to show you what no means."

"We have them on the ranch. Would you like to come home, Alice, and plant with me where no one will hit you?"

"Back to my house?"

"Back to the ranch, back to your home. Plant the sister garden with me again."

"God punishes the wicked."

Maureen fervently hoped so. "But not sisters, Alice. Not sisters who plant flowers together and tend them, who watch them grow. Come home, Alice. Nobody'll hit you again."

"You hit me."

"You usually hit me first, and you're not supposed to tell Ma."

More tears spilled, but through them some of Alice showed through. "I don't know what's real."

"That's okay. I know you are. You go ahead and work on that scarf. I'll come back later and see how it looks."

Maureen stepped back.

"You cut your hair."

It took all her will to keep her hand from shaking as she brushed it over her own hair. "Do you like it?"

"I . . . Women aren't supposed to cut their hair."

"That's all right, Alley Cat," Cora said. "Not all rules are real, that's for certain. Some are just made-up. Reenie, would you see if they'll bring us some tea? We like our mid-morning tea, don't we, Alice?"

Alice nodded, went back to her scarf.

The minute Maureen stepped back, she pressed her hands to her face. Expecting the reaction, Celia put arms around her. "You did great. You did better than I expected. She remembered you."

"She remembered I was bossy. I guess I was."

"She remembered her sister, a dynamic. She remembered red snapdragons. She'll remember more. This was a good thing, Maureen."

"He twisted the life out of her, Celia."

"He tried, but it's still there, and coming back. You just held a therapy session, Maureen, with really positive results."

"She can come home?"

"Let me talk to Dr. Grove. We need to work out the rules of the road, and you need that professional in-home help for right now. But I think if you're careful, if you're patient, continuing her recovery at home might be a good step.

"I'll tell her nurse about the tea. Go get your daughter, take a walk."

"I could use one, and I'm about to lean on Bo pretty hard."

"She strikes me as someone who can handle that."

Maureen nodded. "She's in there, Celia. Alice is in there."

The next twenty-four hours spun around Alice again, this time for her homecoming.

In the ring, Bodine held the mare's bridle.

"I know you don't have time for this." Jessica strapped on her riding helmet. "You've got a backlog of work you're catching up on, and if you have a free hour—which you don't—you should take a nap."

"I don't argue with Nana, and she pinned me down hard about giving you a lesson. She says you're not to miss another one. Our world's upside down, Jessie. This is normal. I could use an hour of normal more than a nap."

"I wish I could do more to help."

"You've taken on more of Rory's work, and Mom's, just like Sal's taken on more of mine. Callen's spent damn near as much time at the hospital as any of the rest of us. We've had plenty of help."

Bodine leaned her cheek against the mare's. "I don't know if it's going to be easier or harder after today. Mom and the grannies are determined she comes home today, and they're probably right. The doctors say it may help trigger her memory. And God knows we all want her to remember enough so Sheriff Tate can find this bastard.

"I haven't even met her yet. I don't know how I'm supposed to act around her."

"You'll know what to do."

"I feel like I don't have the first clue. But I do know what to do here. Mount up."

Chase came in while Jessica rode at a pretty canter around the ring. It lightened up his heart. Just looking at her did that—it seemed like years since he had—but seeing her ride, smiling with it, added an extra glow.

The past week had been like dragging through molasses.

Everything dark and syrupy, just push through one step to the next, grab some sleep, start again.

Now the light was back for him.

Jessica slowed to a walk at Bodine's instruction.

"You've got an audience," Bodine said, grinning at Chase.

"I don't want to get in the way."

"If you were in the way, I'd boot you out. As it is, you can take over the lesson. It's time the greenhorn here rode outside the ring."

"Oh, but—"

"Nana said the second half of the hour to take you out. You can ride with her, can't you, Chase?"

"Yeah, I can. I've got an hour."

"Great. I'm going to ride back to the office then, hit that backlog."

She rode straight out before anyone could stop her.

"She dumped me on you."

Chase walked over, took the bridle. Took a moment to just look at her, with her sunny hair down and loose under her helmet, her eyes blue and clear. "It's sure good to see you."

"How are you?"

"I'm going to say a little tired, and more than a little mixed-up. Taking a ride with you, it'll be good, help on both those fronts."

"Then we'll ride. I'm a little nervous about not having the ring, the walls."

"I think you're going to like being out in the air." Still holding the bridle, he walked her horse over to his. "I'm sorry I haven't—since we . . . I don't want you to think—"

"That I took advantage of you, and you ran off?"

His head jerked up, his face stunned and not a little horrified.

"Chase, I know what your family's going through. I didn't think anything like that."

"I'd hate if you did." When he swung into the saddle, she noticed the purple irises poking out of his saddlebag.

"Are those flowers for me or my horse?"

He fumbled a little as he pulled them out. "I just wanted you to know . . . to make sure you know . . . I'm bad at this."

"Not from where I'm sitting. They're beautiful, and thank you. If you don't mind, could you keep them for me while we ride? I don't think I'm good enough to hold flowers and reins at the same time."

"Sure."

After he stuck them back in his saddlebag, she reached over, gripped his shirt. "I guess I have to take care of this myself again."

She pulled him to her, felt a lift everywhere when his mouth met hers. When the mare shifted, she grabbed the saddle horn and laughed. "That's the first time I've kissed anyone on horseback. Not bad for a novice."

"Hold on a minute." He took her reins to keep both horses steady, and pulled her in.

Reminding her, once she started his engine, he ran hot and smooth.

"That was even better," she told him.

"I've missed you. It's been a crazy few days, and it feels like weeks. I really missed you, Jessie. Maybe I could take you out tonight. Just out for dinner or something."

"Don't you have to be home? Your aunt."

"They're saying it's best to take all that slow, not to throw everybody at her at once. I was going to make myself mostly scarce. We could have a date if you're not busy with something."

"We could. But here's another better. You come over tonight, to my place. I'll cook you dinner."

"You'll cook?"

"I like to cook. I'd like to cook for you. I'd like you to come to my place. I'd like you to spend some time in my bed."

He smiled like he did everything. Slow. It always hit his eyes first. "I'd like all of that."

"I'll make something we can eat anytime, so you can get there when you can get there."

"I've never known anybody like you."

"That makes us even." She glanced around, laughed. "I've been riding. I've been riding and didn't even realize it."

"It happens when you're good and comfortable on a horse. You've got good form."

She slanted him a look. "Do I?"

"In lots of ways. You want to try a trot?"

"All right." She lifted her face first, looked at the sky, the mountains, felt the air that held just teases of spring. "I do like riding outside. All right, cowboy, show me the ropes."

CHAPTER TWENTY

A lice trembled throughout the drive from the hospital—
the room with the bed that moved up and down, the
red Jell-O, the door that opened and closed without locks—
to the ranch.

Vague pictures jumped in and out of her mind of a
house with many, many windows instead of only one. Of
a dog that didn't growl and bite, of a room with bright pink
walls and white curtains.

Far-off sounds in her ears. Voices calling—Alice, Alley
Cat—*Stop being such a brat! Eat some of those peas if
you want ice cream.*

The smell of . . . horses and cooking. A bathtub filled
with bubbles.

It frightened her, all of it, made her heart beat too hard
and fast even when the mother held her hand.

But more, everything went too fast. Everything. The
car the sister drove while the grandmother . . . (*Grammy,
Grammy, such pretty red hair. I want red hair, too,* a little girl's voice said in her head, and laughter followed.)

The grandmother with the red hair sat in the front of

the car. Alice sat in the back with the mother, holding tight to the mother's hand because the car went so fast, and the world kept changing.

She longed for her quiet house, her still, quiet house. She wondered if this was just one of her dreams, the dreams she kept secret from Sir.

Sir. Would he be at this home place? Would he be there waiting for her, waiting to take her back to her quiet house?

Locks, locks on the door, the tiny window. Hard hands hitting, the belt whipping.

She lowered her head and shuddered.

"We'll be there soon, baby."

The woman doctor had said it was all right to be nervous, to even be scared. She hadn't ridden in a car in a very long time, and everything would look new and different. When she got too nervous and scared, she could just close her eyes and think of something that made her happy.

Sitting outside her quiet house and watching the sunset made her happy. So she closed her eyes and pictured it.

But when the road went from smooth to bumpy, she cried out.

"It's okay. We're on the ranch road now."

She didn't want to look, didn't want to see, but she couldn't help it. She saw fields and trees, snow melting away under the sun. Cows—not rib-racked, but . . . *cattle*— she remembered the word. Big, healthy, cropping through the snowmelt to eat.

The road would turn in a minute, to the right. Was that a dream?

When it did, her breathing came fast. She saw in her head, a pretty young girl—oh, so pretty!—with bright red streaks in her hair, driving a truck and singing along with the radio.

"'I see you driving by just like a Phantom jet.'"

She heard the voice, not just in her head, but coming out of her mouth now. It jolted her, and the mother's hand tightened on hers.

The sister looked at her through the mirror, and sang back at her.

"'With your arm around some little brunette.'"

A laugh, small and strange and rusty with it, broke out of her. The fields, the sky—oh God, so big—the mountains that didn't look the same as from her little house stopped scaring her so much as she sang the next words. As the sister sang the ones after that.

And they sang the chorus together.

Beside her, the mother made a little sound, and Alice looked, saw her crying.

She trembled again. "I did bad. I was bad. I'm bad."

"No, no, no." The mother kissed Alice's hand, her cheek. "These are from happiness. I always loved hearing my girls sing together. My girls have such beautiful voices."

"I'm not a girl. And a woman is—"

"You're always my girl, Alice. Just like Reenie."

The road rose and she saw the house. She made a garbled sound as her mind slammed between memories and a quarter century of enforced denial.

"It's a little different than it was," the mother said. "We've added on some rooms, and opened up a couple of them on the inside. Different paints," she continued as the sister stopped the car. "Some new furniture. Kitchen's changed most I'd say. But it has the same bones." As she spoke, the mother put an arm around her, rubbed at the chill. "Still the barn in the back, and the stables, the paddocks. The chickens, and we added pigs some time back."

Dogs raced up to the car, and Alice cringed.

"Dogs! They growl, they bite."

"Not these two. They're Chester and Clyde, and they won't bite."

"Tail-waggers, both of them." To Alice's shock, the grandmother hopped right out. The dogs circled her, but didn't growl, didn't bite. They wagged all over as the grandmother touched them.

"Tail-waggers," Alice repeated.

"Do you want to pet them?" the mother asked. Alice could only hunch her shoulders. "You don't have to, but they won't bite, and they won't growl at you."

The mother opened the door of the car, slipped out. Panic spewed into Alice's throat, but the mother held out a hand. "Come on, Alice, I'm right here."

Taking the mother's hand, she inched her way across the seat. Cringed back when one of the dogs poked his nose in and sniffed at her.

"Sit down, Chester," the sister ordered. And to Alice's surprise—and something she didn't recognize as delight— the dog plopped his hind end down. It seemed like his eyes smiled. His eyes weren't mean. They looked happy. He had happy eyes.

She inched out a little more, and the dog's butt wriggled, but stayed down.

She put a foot on the ground. It wore a pink tennis shoe with white laces. For a minute she stared at it, transfixed, moved her foot to assure herself it was hers.

She put the other pink tennis shoe on the ground, breathed in, stood up.

The world wanted to spin, but the mother held her hand.

Clinging to it, she put one foot in front of the other.

She wore a denim skirt—she hadn't been able to put on any of the pants or jeans the women bought for her. But the skirt covered most of her legs, as modesty decreed.

And the white blouse could be buttoned to the neck. The coat provided warmth that the old shawl she'd worn at her house hadn't. Everything on her felt so soft, smelled so clean. And still she trembled as she stepped up on the porch.

She stared at a pair of rocking chairs, shook her head.

"We painted those just last year," the sister told her. "I like the blue. Like the summer sky."

Now Alice stared at the open door, took a step back.

The grandmother slid an arm around her waist. "I know you're afraid, Alice. But we're all here with you. Just us girls for now."

"Two cookies after chores," Alice mumbled.

"That's right, my lamb. I always had two cookies for my girls after chores. No chores today," the grandmother added. "But we'll have some cookies. How about some tea and cookies?"

"Is Sir inside?"

"No." Now the grandmother's voice had anger in it. "He'll never be inside this house."

"Ma—"

"You hush a minute, Cora." The grandmother turned to face Alice. "This is your home, and we're your family. Standing here, we're three generations of women who can take anything that's dished out. You're strong, Alice, and we're here to stand with you until you remember how strong you are. Now, let's go inside."

"Will you stay with me, too? Will you stay in the home like the mother?"

"You're damn right I will."

Alice thought of stepping out of the door left unlocked, and stepped through the open one.

There were flowers in a vase, and tables, and there were chairs and couches and pictures. A fire—not a campfire, not a stove. A fire . . . place. A fireplace where flames simmered.

Windows.

Compelled, she walked, on her own, from window to window to window, marveling. Everything was so big, so far, so near. And not as frightening from inside. Inside seemed safe again.

"Do you want to see the rest?" the sister asked.

How could there be more? So much, so big, so far, so near.

But.

"A room with bright pink walls and white curtains."

"Your room? It's upstairs." The sister walked toward a staircase—so many steps, so much space. "Grammy remembered how you'd wanted pink walls, so I had my boys paint them like they were. As close as we could remember. Come up, see what you think."

"Let's take your coat off first."

Alice hunched inside it. "Can I keep it?"

"Of course you can keep it, honey." Gently, Cora slipped the coat away. "It's yours, but you don't need your coat inside. It's nice and warm in here, isn't it?"

"It's cold in my house. Tea keeps you warm."

"We'll have some tea in a bit." Cora guided Alice to the stairs. "I remember the first time I saw inside this house. I was sixteen, and your daddy was courting me. I'd never seen stairs so grand. The way they go up, then split off in both directions. It was your great-grandfather built them. The story is he wanted to build the finest house in Montana to convince your great-grandmother to marry him and live in it."

"Sir built me a house. The man provides."

Cora let it go, led Alice down a wide hall, and into a room with pink walls and white curtains.

"I know it's not exactly the same," she began. "I'm sorry I didn't keep all your posters and . . ."

She trailed off as Alice stepped away from her, her face astonished as she wandered the room, touched the dresser, the bed, the lamps, the cushions on the window seat.

"It faces west for the sunset," Alice murmured. "I sit outside once a week if I've been good. One hour, once a week, and watch the sunset."

"Did you have a window in your house?" the sister asked.

"It's a little window, high up at the ceiling. I can't see the sunset, but I can see the sky. It's blue and it's gray and it's white when the snow falls. Not like the room with no windows."

"You can watch the sunset every night," the mother said. "From inside the house or from outside."

"Every night," Alice repeated.

Overwhelmed at the idea, she turned. Then jumped in shock when she faced a mirror. The woman wore a long skirt and a white blouse, and pink shoes. Her hair, gray like an angry sky, was braided back from a pale face with scoring lines.

"Who is that? Who is that? I don't know her."

"You will." The mother put arms around Alice, around the woman. "Do you want to rest now? I bet Reenie would bring you those cookies and some tea."

Alice stumbled to the bed, dropped down to sit. The bed felt so thick, so soft, she began to cry again. "It's soft. It's mine? It's pretty. I can keep the coat?"

"Yes. See? You can cry when you're happy, too." The mother sat beside her, then the grandmother on the other side.

The sister sat on the floor.

In that moment, for that moment at least, Alice felt safe.

Though her feelings about bringing Alice home remained mixed and murky, Bodine put on a cheerful face as she walked into the kitchen.

She found her mother and Miss Fancy at the counter, peeling potatoes. "I expected to see Clementine."

"I sent her home. We decided to keep new—or half-remembered—faces to a minimum this first day. And the nurse is already up there with Alice and your nana."

"How'd it go?"

"Better, I think, than anyone expected." Miss Fancy set a peeled potato aside, picked up another. "She had some bad moments, and she'll have more, but by God, she had some good ones, too. We were right to bring her, Reenie."

"We were, and Ma seems easier already. I think she'll get her first good night's sleep tonight. Clementine got a chicken in the roaster before she left. We're having it with mashed potatoes, gravy, your grammy's candied carrots, and buttered broccoli. It's a meal Alice favored once, so . . ."

"I'll give you a hand."

"No." Setting down the peeler, Maureen wiped her hands on a dishcloth. "I want you to come up and meet her."

"But—"

"We decided we'll hold off on the boys, or having Sam go up. Keep it to women today. We're going to take a tray up to her room for dinner, ease her in there, too. But she should meet you."

"Okay."

"You two go on. I'll get these potatoes peeled and on the boil."

They went up the back stairs. "We all talked about keeping things calm and as natural as possible."

"I know, Mom."

"I know this is hard on you, Bodine."

"It's not."

"It is. On you, on all of us. So I'm telling you like I'm going to tell everyone else: When you need a break from it, you take one."

"What about you?"

"Your father's already made it clear I'll be taking one from time to time." She lowered her voice as they reached the second floor. "The nurses are going to use the sitting room off Alice's bedroom when they're not in with her, and the bathroom across the hall we've designated for them and for Alice. Celia's coming about eleven tomorrow. Our house is going to be full of people for some time to come."

"Mom." Bodine drew her mother to a halt. "Weren't we all there, all of us, when Grandpa got sick? Didn't we bring him back here from Bodine House, and sit with him, read to him, do everything we could—even with the nurses—so he could die at home, at the home he'd chosen?

"Alice isn't dying," Bodine continued, "but it's the same. We're just going to do everything we can to help her start living again."

"I love you so much, my baby."

"I love you right back. Now introduce me to your sister."

They crocheted together, mother and daughter, in the two chairs Maureen had chosen hoping for just that.

Though Bodine had been prepared for Alice's appearance, if she didn't know the woman was a couple years her mother's junior, she'd have sworn Alice was ten years older.

"Alice."

Alice's head shot up at Maureen's voice; her eyes glimmered with distress as she saw Bodine.

"Is she a doctor? Is she a nurse? Is she police?"

"No, this is my daughter. This is your niece, Bodine."

"Bodine. Alice Bodine. The mother says Alice Ann Bodine."

"I named her Bodine to honor that part of us."

"She has green eyes. You have green eyes."

"Like my mother's, and yours." Trying for casual, Bodine stepped closer. "I like your shoes."

"They're pink. They don't hurt my feet. I ruined my slippers and the socks, too. That was bad and wasteful."

"Sometimes things just wear out. Is that a scarf you're making?"

"It's green." Almost lovingly, Alice smoothed the length of the wool. "I like green."

"Me, too. I never could get the hang of crocheting."

Lips pressed tight, Alice applied herself to it.

"The sister has a daughter," she muttered to herself. "I had daughters. The sister gets to keep the daughter. I don't keep the daughters. A man needs sons."

Bodine opened her mouth, saw her grandmother shake her head.

"This is a pretty room. It's cheerful, this pink. Do you like it?"

"It's not cold. I don't need a shawl. The bed is soft. It faces west for the sunset."

"That's my favorite part of it. It's a beautiful sunset tonight."

Confused, Alice looked over.

Her crocheting fell out of her hands into her lap. A

long, long gasp escaped as her face transformed. Cora
plucked up the hook and yarn as Alice pushed to her feet.

Outside the window, the sky seemed to fill the world,
mad rich colors, undertones of gold etching billowing
clouds, streaks of light shooting out of them and painting
the white mountains.

"Do you want to go outside to see it?" Maureen asked
her.

"Outside." Wonder filled her voice, her face, then she
scanned down, rapidly shook her head. "People, people
are outside. You can't talk to the people. If people see you,
hear you, God will strike you down. Strike you down as
they die."

"That's not true here." Cora rose, joined her daughter.
"But we'll watch from here tonight. It's beautiful, isn't it,
Alice?"

"Every night? Not once a week?"

"Yes, every night. I think a God who gives us something so beautiful as that sunset is too loving, too kind,
too wise to strike anyone down."

Whether she believed it or not, the words and the
beauty soothed, and Alice rested her head on her mother's
shoulder.

In the shack, Callen washed up his dishes. He'd been waiting for a knock on his door, but since it hadn't come, he
thought he might take himself over to the bunkhouse. Seek
the company of men. Maybe sit down for a poker game.
He didn't gamble often or much, but since he didn't have
his father's problem, he enjoyed the occasional game.

One thing he knew: He didn't want to spend the evening
in his own company. Too much thinking and worrying
about what might be going on at the main house, too much

thinking and wishing for Bodine. Too much thinking about the things his mother had told him.

Just too much thinking.

So maybe a beer with the men, a few hands of cards—which might add some change to his pockets. He didn't have his father's problem, and generally a lot better luck.

He'd talk to Bodine in the morning when they rode into work. He could settle for just talking until her life smoothed out some.

Then the knock came. He stayed at the sink, annoyed with himself for the instant flash of pleasure. He'd be better off, he knew he'd be better off, not being so damn tied up in her. But he just couldn't cut the rope.

"It's open," he called out.

When she stepped in, the stress and fatigue on her face made him ashamed of the annoyance.

"I really need to get away for a while."

"You've come to the right place. Want a beer?"

"No."

"Wine. I still have that bottle from the cabin."

She started to shake her head, then let out some air. "Yeah. Yeah, that'd be just fine. I haven't had my glass of wine tonight."

"Have a seat. I've got huckleberry shortcake, too."

"Where'd you get that?"

"Yolanda, dessert chef? I let her boy ride Sundown. He's been giving me the pleading eye after school every day for a week. I gave in, and I got huckleberry shortcake out of it."

"With whipped cream?"

"It ain't huckleberry shortcake without it."

"Good deal. I'm in for that." She tossed off her coat, sat.

He took out his multitool for its corkscrew. It wasn't until he'd pulled the cork that he saw tears swimming in her eyes.

"Ah, hell."

"I'm not going to cry, don't worry. I may teeter on the edge of it for a couple minutes, but I won't fall off."

"Was it that bad?"

"Yes. No. I don't know. I don't know, that's the truth." Breathing, just breathing for a moment, she pressed her fingers to her eyes as if to shove back the tears. "She looks a decade older than my mother, soft and kind of doughy in the body, with a face that's lined deep, like a woman who lived hard. God, I hear how that sounds out loud. I'm not saying it to be judgmental."

"I know it." He poured her wine, and though a beer would've suited him better, poured himself a glass of wine in solidarity.

"Her hair's frizzed up and dry as straw, and has to be down to her ass. Like it hasn't been conditioned or trimmed in years—and I guess it hasn't been. She's got spooked eyes—you see animals with eyes like that who expect the boot or the crop because they've felt it too often. Then she saw the sunset, saw it through the window of that room I know you helped paint."

"I came in on the tail end."

"You helped paint," Bodine repeated, a tear slipping through after all. "And there was such joy on her face, Callen. Such wonder—like a child's. She wouldn't go out because some of the men were still working outside, but she watched every minute of the sunset like it was fireworks on the Fourth of July and Christmas morning and a circus parade all rolled out in one shiny package."

"Nobody does sunsets like Montana." He set a plate of cake in front of her.

"God, Yolanda knows her cake. You know, Sal and I, and a couple of other girls, went up to the Oregon coast the summer after graduation. They've got some impressive sunsets, but they don't beat Montana, not for me. And for Alice . . . Callen, she said she was allowed to sit out for an hour once a week, at sunset. If she was good."

"She's going to remember enough so they find him, Bo."

"She's remembering some—some of the grannies and of Mom, maybe the house. She said she'd had daughters, but she didn't get to keep them like Mom could keep me. It ripped my heart."

When her voice broke, she stuffed cake in her mouth. "Ripped it in pieces."

Her breath tore. She bore down, made herself eat more cake.

Callen said nothing, gave her the comfort of listening silence so she could finish it out.

"We took up trays for her and Nana and the nurse. A good home meal on one of Mom's pretty plates, with a cloth napkin. You'd've thought we'd set a banquet in front of her. The rest of us—well, except Chase—ate downstairs. But all I could think was how she'd looked at a plate of chicken and potatoes like it was the finest French cuisine, and she didn't know quite what to do about it."

She sighed, ate some cake. "So I had to get away for a while."

"I'm not saying it's going to be easy, but I think it's bound to get easier. I was hoping you'd come by."

She worked up a smile for him. "Well, you did say you wanted sex."

"I was hoping for that, too, but wine and cake aren't bad."

"It's really good cake. Chase went over to Jessica's for dinner."

"I heard."

"He took his *Tombstone* DVD."

Callen laughed, pleased to see that laughter mirrored in her eyes. "The man can't help himself."

"They might actually watch some of it. I'm pretty sure he's hoping to stay overnight. He brought her flowers today."

Callen just grunted, ate more cake.

"He's in love with her."

"Because he brought her flowers?"

"You tell me—I know you've been gone some years, but you know him as inside out as I do—so you tell me if you ever recall him bringing a woman—or a girl back a ways—flowers."

Callen drank some wine, thought it over. "He got Missy Crispen one of those . . ." He circled a finger over his wrist. "For the spring formal."

"You've got to do that. This is midweek, not even a date involved, flowers. I saw them sticking out of his saddlebag. Irises, so he went out and bought them deliberately."

Callen wagged his fork at her. "Has every man who brought you flowers been in love with you?"

"I'd sure as hell know he was seriously sweet on me if he bothered. And Chase has shy ways with women. Flowers for him are a statement of intent."

"Intent of—"

"She won't know that," Bodine breezed on. "But I know that. He's in love with her, and he's never been more than halfway sweet on anybody before. You know what else?"

"I might, but you're going to tell me anyway."

"I can't say if she's in love with him—I haven't known

her long enough to be sure of that. But I do know she's seriously sweet on him. It's not halfway sweet."

She pushed the plate aside. "God, I feel better. I think Rory was going out with Chelsea."

"He in love, too?"

"No, but he's in substantial like and definite lust. I think that's absolutely mutual. Dad's going to make sure Mom gets some rest, and the grannies are better for being at the ranch right now. So . . . Have you got a spare toothbrush?"

"No."

"Oh, well."

"You want to brush your teeth?"

"Not right this minute, but I will in the morning." She polished off her wine, stood. "I'd like to try your bed out."

"It's not as big as the one we tried out before, but it's got good springs."

"Well, let's give them a good bounce. Do you mind if I lock the front door? I'd just as soon nobody wanders in while I'm naked on top of you."

"Who says you'll be on top?"

"I guess we'll see."

"Lock the door."

The springs held up just fine. And once they had, Bodine lay in a limp, sweaty daze.

"Oh yeah, I do feel better."

"Glad I could help. But I think it's time for you to feel a lot more than better."

He rolled back on top of her.

The daze ran sugary enough that she tangled her fingers in his hair and just smiled. "That would be a heroic recovery, Skinner."

"Not really, because we're going to do something we haven't managed before."

"I can't think of anything we missed."

"We missed taking our time." He brushed his lips to hers, skimmed them over her jaw.

"The fast and furious works pretty well."

"Let's see how we do with the slow and thorough. I like how you're put together, Bodine."

His fingers glided up and down the side of her right breast. "You've got long limbs, long and pretty ripped with it."

"I work out," she managed.

"Firm, pretty breasts." He brushed the nipple with his thumb. "All that hair, straight as a ruler, dark as midnight. I like how it smells so I always want to get a little closer. I like how you taste."

He took his mouth to her throat.

"And those eyes, the color of leaves in the shadows. The way your skin feels under my hands, just silk smooth. The way your mouth fits on mine."

He took his back to hers, let the kiss spin on and on, soft and lazy as a spring shower.

"I do like how you're put together."

"You're going to turn my head." But she couldn't quite manage a laugh. Not when her head had started to spin, and those licks of heat ran under her skin.

"The more I touch you, the more I want to. This time, you'll just have to tolerate it."

Her pulse beat under his lips, slow and thick, just as he wanted it. Her body stretched, undulating under his hands, then quivered, then softened. He'd wanted her like this, wanted not just the excitement, the release, but all. What would all with Bodine be?

Sighs and sumptuous kisses, quiet moans and moonlight in a narrow bed. Response in an easy, unhurried rhythm. Pretty green eyes, heavy with what he could give her.

He worked his way down her body. And this time when she sighed, she sighed his name.

Her head no longer spun. Instead it seemed she moved, they moved, through a warm, lovely mist where everything shimmered. His hands, hard, callused, only made those lazy strokes all the more erotic. The stubble brushing over her skin as he ran his tongue down her belly made her quiver.

Then his tongue slid down, slid over, slid in, and had her rolling, rolling, rolling slowly, dreamily, helplessly over a velvet-covered peak.

Still he didn't rush. Still those hard-palmed hands drew her down, further down into dazed pleasure so the shimmering mists thickened. When his mouth took hers again, she'd already surrendered.

He slipped into her, heard her breath catch, saw her eyes blur.

"This part, too," he whispered, toying with her lips. "Slow. Nice and slow."

Long, slow, deep, and her so hot, so wet around him. She broke again on a moan, but he held on, moving in her, drawing out every moment, every ounce of pleasure. Up again, up again, slowly, relentlessly until he felt her give, just one more time, and gave with her.

CHAPTER TWENTY-ONE

Bodine overslept—something she never did. Maybe a half hour didn't rank high on the scale, but it put a dent in her rigid morning schedule.

She hopped out of bed so fast, Callen missed his chance to catch her.

"What's your hurry?"

"I'm running behind before I get started. I can cut back on my workout, prioritize e-mails." While she threw on her clothes, she calculated. "Take the truck instead of Leo."

"I can get Leo fed and saddled up for you. I was hoping to use him today."

She glanced back at the bed, at the shadowy outline of the man she'd slept with. "That'll add to your own time."

"Looks like I'm up anyway."

Not complaining, she thought, amused, more resigned.

"Do you want to come over for breakfast?"

"I'd get better than a fried egg on toast."

"Then I'll see you in an hour." She hesitated, then

stepped back, leaned down, and kissed him. "If I'd known this was going to happen, I'd have pushed to get you a bigger bed."

"This one worked out all right."

"I'll say it did. I have to go."

She dashed out. Seconds later he heard his door slam behind her.

The woman sure did move fast, he thought, dragging himself up to put the coffee on.

In under that hour, Bodine finished an abbreviated workout, grabbed a shower, dressed, answered a handful of e-mails. The rest could wait. Coffee just couldn't.

Since she still ran ten minutes behind, she'd sacrificed that first solo cup. Clementine would be in the kitchen by now.

As expected when she jogged down the back steps, coffee scented the air. Clementine had biscuit dough in a bowl and stood grating potatoes. It wasn't altogether unexpected to see Maureen chatting with Clementine and frying up bacon and sausage.

But seeing Alice sitting at the kitchen table, head bent over her crocheting, put a hitch in Bodine's stride.

"Running late for you." Maureen laid sizzling bacon on a paper towel, sent her daughter a silent signal.

"Just a bit. Morning, Clem. Morning, Alice."

"I'm making a scarf."

"It's coming right along, too."

"Like you, Alice is an early riser. Grammy's still sleeping, but Nana's getting a shower. I told Cathy, that's the night nurse, to take her time, and Alice could have her tea down here while we got breakfast going."

"Cathy is the nurse. She came to the hospital. Clementine makes biscuits. I like the biscuits."

"Got some cayenne pepper in them," Clementine said

easily. "You always liked when I put a little cayenne in them. Coffee's fresh."

"Yeah." Bodine poured herself a mug.

"Coffee's not allowed for childbearing women. It can stop the seed from planting."

"I never heard that." Bodine leaned back, sipped. "That'd make it the easiest form of birth control ever."

"Bodine," Maureen said under her breath.

Bodine kept the smile on her face, wandered over to sit with Alice. "I don't think coffee's going to manage that, but I'm not ready for babies yet."

"You're of childbearing age."

"I am."

"Bearing sons is a woman's duty to her husband. You should have a husband, a husband to provide for you."

"I provide for me. I might like a husband one of these days, but he's going to have to meet my standards. They're pretty high, as I have my dad as my first yardstick. So that one-of-these-days husband has to be handsome and strong and smart and kind and funny. He has to respect me for being who I am, the way Dad respects Mom. It's likely, given my personal bent, he's going to have to be a good horseman, too. And he's going to have to love me like I was a queen and a warrior and a genius and about the sexiest woman ever born."

"The man chooses."

"No, Alice, people choose each other. I'm so sorry, I'm so sorry, Alice, somebody took your choice away."

She caught movement, saw the woman standing in the kitchen doorway. About her mother's age with short, ash-blond hair, a little stern around the mouth.

The nurse, Bodine thought, worried she'd crossed some line. But the woman nodded.

"I think you're really brave," Bodine finished, watching

Alice's eyes twitch as they seemed to do when she struggled to process.

"Women are weak."

"Some people are weak. You're not. I think you might be the bravest person I know."

Alice ducked her head, hunched her shoulders, but Bodine caught the faintest smile. "I'm making a scarf. Clementine's making breakfast biscuits. The sister is—"

She broke off, let out a muffled cry as Callen came in the mudroom door.

Shit! Bodine thought. She should've run back and told Callen to hold off.

"Morning." Callen stood where he was. "I'm here to mooch breakfast. Are those your buttermilk biscuits, Clementine?"

"They are. Are your hands clean?"

"They will be. You must be Miss Alice." He spoke easy, in a tone Bodine had heard him use with a nervous horse countless times. "It nice to meet you, ma'am."

"One of the sons, one of the sister's sons."

"An honorary one." Maureen's voice might have been a few shades overbright, but it stilled Alice's fretful hands. "This is Callen. Cal's same as family. He's a good boy, Alice."

"Man. He's not a boy." Alice patted her cheeks.

In response Callen rubbed his own. "Didn't think to shave this morning. Slipped my mind. That's pretty work you're doing there. My sister does needlework. I wouldn't be surprised if she knitted up a house next."

"You can't knit a house. I'm crocheting. I'm making a scarf."

"If you want anything in this kitchen, you get over here and wash the horse off your hands," Clementine ordered as she cut out biscuits. "This breakfast'll be ready soon."

"Yes, ma'am."

"She tells the man what to do," Alice whispered to Bodine.

"She tells us all what to do."

"I washed my hands."

Though her eyes went damp, Clementine nodded at Alice. "Then you'll get your breakfast."

At the clatter on the stairs, Alice jolted again. Bodine laid a hand over hers.

Rory bounded in, cheerful as a puppy, hair still damp, face freshly shaved. "Overslept. Smells damn good in here. I could use—"

He spotted the woman at the table with Bodine. Like the rest of the family, he'd been schooled. And Rory was, at the core, a salesman. He shot out a megawatt smile.

"Good morning, Alice. I didn't have a chance to meet you yet. I'm Rory."

Alice's face went slack. Bodine heard the two rapid gasps before that face transformed into something beyond joy. Something too bright even for joy.

"Rory. Rory." Tears spilled even as she laughed. And as she laughed, she pushed up from the table, flew at him. Her arms wrapped around him. "My baby. My Rory."

Awkwardly patting Alice's back, he stared at his mother in baffled shock.

"This is my youngest, Alice," Maureen said carefully. "This is my son, Rory."

"My Rory." Alice eased back enough to look at his face, to stroke her hands over his cheeks. "Look how handsome. You were such a pretty baby, such a pretty boy. Now you're handsome. So big! So tall! Ma can't rock you anymore, my baby."

"Ah—"

"Alice," the nurse spoke, tone even, matter-of-fact. "This is your sister's son. This is your nephew."

"No. No." Alice clutched at him again. "My baby. He's Rory. You can't take him away. I won't let anybody take him away again."

"I'm not going anywhere," Rory told her. "It's all right."

"I prayed for my babies. For Cora and Fancy and Rory and Lily and Maureen and Sarah and for Benjamin even though he went right to heaven. Do you know where they are, Rory, the other babies? My baby girls?"

"No, I'm sorry. Let's sit down, okay?"

"I'm making you a scarf. It's green. My Rory has green in his eyes."

"It's nice. It's really nice." And as Rory looked at his mother again, Bodine stood up.

She moved to the back stairs to hug and hold Cora as she wept.

He was dog-sick for a solid week. He could barely crawl out of bed to do his business much less to down more medicine or open a can to eat.

The fever burned, the chills racked, but the hacking, tearing cough was worse. It left him weak, breathless, his chest fist-tight, his throat raw from the thick, yellow mucus that spewed from his lungs.

He blamed Esther, cursed her as he lay on sweat-stained sheets.

He'd track her down when he got back on his feet. He'd track her down and beat her bloody, choke the life out of her. She didn't rate a bullet.

Even when he managed to stand for more than a few minutes, the cough could bring him to his knees.

By the time he felt able to drag himself outside, he saw

the dog was half-dead—maybe more than half. He tossed some food in a bucket. Pumping water into another brought on a violent coughing fit. He spat out blood-tinged mucus, wheezed breathlessly as he took a look at the cow.

Hadn't been milked in a couple days, he judged, and like the horse had made due with snow and the spare grass under it. The chickens fared little better. It all showed him, clearly, bitterly, the boy had barely been around. And when he had been he'd done his work halfway.

Boy was useless, just like his cursed mother.

When he got his strength back, he'd take that boy to task good and proper. And he'd go out, get a young wife, get a young one who'd bring forth sons who'd honor their father instead of one who came and went as he damn well pleased.

Made a mistake with Esther, and he could admit it. Wasted too many years on her. Made a mistake or two trying to take on a second wife, but he wouldn't make another.

He just had to get his strength back, even enough to get himself some medicine, some supplies.

Dizzy from the effort of tending to the animals, he stumbled back inside. He wanted to check the Internet, gain some solace from the words of men who knew what he knew, believed as he believed.

He'd paid good money for the Wi-Fi antenna, for the hot spot devices and repeaters. And he'd learned how to use them and stay off the grid.

Goddamn government, spying on everybody, stealing land, shoving their gays and blacks and Mexicans down the throats of real Americans.

He was a sovereign citizen, he thought, a man prepared, even eager, to shed blood to protect his rights.

He'd shed Esther's, he thought. He'd thrash some

respect into the whelp she'd foisted on him. And he'd find a wife who'd give him the sons he deserved.

But all he could do was crawl back in bed, shiver with chills, wheezing out breath from lungs thick with fluid.

Callen's gut knotted when he saw Sheriff Tate pull up.

"Let me know if you need anything," he said to the farrier, walking over to meet Tate. "Has there been another one?"

"No. No, that's one blessing. Got a little May weather in March."

"It'll turn on us, but I'll take it."

Tate scanned the paddocks, the shelter. "You on your own?"

"We got two trail rides out, another two this afternoon, and a pair of lessons down at the center. May weather means May bookings."

Tate nodded. "Is that Spike over there?"

"Yeah. Hell of a name for a farrier."

"You don't often see a farrier wearing a spiked dog collar and sporting half a dozen tattoos. But he knows his work. Can you take a break?"

"It appears I'm already taking one."

"Let's walk over this way." Tate aimed for the big paddock. "Some fine-looking horses."

"We brought more in today. We're going to take them out to pasture tomorrow if this weather holds like it's supposed to. It's been some time since I herded horses to pasture at dawn, rounded them back up for the night."

"It sounds like you're looking forward to it."

"I guess I am. I like the work here, even though there's a lot of computer and paper involved." He reached out, rubbed a curious bay down the nose. "I know you didn't ride over here to see how I was taking to the job."

"No. I'm heading over to the Bodine Ranch to talk to Alice. She'd be having her talk with the psychiatrist now. I'm going to hope she remembers a little more."

"I can tell you she's had more to say. I heard her myself when I went over at breakfast. She thought Rory was hers. She named off seven children. All girls but for one named Rory and another. The way she put that one he either died in the birthing or right after."

"Ah, my Christ."

"I don't figure I'm telling you anything I shouldn't when I say she latched onto Rory. She talked about how she'd rock him, sing to him, play peek-a-boo, how he'd learned to walk on his own. It about broke your heart. Have you got anything on this son of a bitch, Sheriff?"

"I wish I could say we did. We're working with the Staties. We put up her picture, gave it to the media, in case anybody'd seen her. We had dogs out, trying to pick up her trail, but with the rain, and not having a damn clue how far she'd walked up or down the road before she collapsed, we don't have so much as a starting point."

"You need her to tell you, and you can't push at her."

"You're right on both counts." When the curious bay nudged at his shoulder, Tate gave him an absent pat. "But any little thing she can say is one more thing to work with. But that's not why I came by. I heard Garrett came out here in an official vehicle, wearing his official uniform, and went at you again."

"Clintok doesn't worry me."

"I suspended him."

Callen turned now, shoved at his hat. "There's no cause for you to do that on my account."

"I didn't do it on your account." Temper ruddied Tate's cheeks. "He disobeyed a direct order. He harassed and threatened a private citizen. I suspended him rather than

firing his arrogant ass, as he's got some good qualities under the bullshit, and . . . I've got two manhunts on my
hands. I got two women dead, and a cold trail on whoever killed them. I got a man who kept a woman I have a
fondness for locked up we don't know how many years.
And right now, that trail's cold, too. But if Garrett crosses
the line again, he loses his job, and that's for me to say."

Tate tapped a finger on Callen's chest. "Are you in
charge around here?"

"I guess I am."

"Would you tolerate one of the people out leading a
trail ride, giving a lesson, tending the stock doing the opposite of what you told them? Getting up in the face of
one of the guests here? Disrespecting your authority?"

Wedged firmly in a corner, Callen heaved out a breath.
"All right, you made the point."

"And my next is this. He's as pissed off as it gets. If he
comes at you, Cal, I hear about it. I don't want any bullshit
from you here about handling him fine, about him not
worrying you. He's one of mine, and if he comes at you
again, I need to hear about it. I can't have a man who'd
do that holding a badge and a weapon and working under
me. You got that clear?"

"Yeah, yeah, I do."

"You don't have to like it."

"Well, I don't. But I understand it."

"Your word on it." Tate held out a hand.

"Hell." Boxed in yet again, Callen shook hands. "My
word on it."

"Then we're good. I'm going to go talk to Alice." But
Tate stared out at the horses another moment. "Seven children."

"She named them off. She named them."

"Merciful God," Tate muttered and walked away.

When he pulled up to the ranch house, he hoped he'd timed it well. He recognized Dr. Minnow's car, so that was good. He wanted to hear what she had to say, too.

When he knocked, Cora came to the door.

"I hope I'm not intruding, Mrs. Bodine."

"Of course not. You went with 'Cora' at the hospital, Bob. You stay with 'Cora'. Ah, Alice is talking with the doctor. With Dr. Minnow. I think they should be almost done. You come right in."

He took off his hat as he stepped in. "How's Alice doing, ma'am, since you brought her home?"

"I really think better. I do. Ma, look who's here."

"Why, Bobby Tate." Setting aside some knitting, Miss Fancy patted the cushion on the couch beside her. "You come sit down and give me all the local news and gossip."

"I wish I could, Miss Fancy."

"Well, I'm going to get you a cup of coffee."

"Please, don't trouble, Miss Fancy."

"The day I can't get a cup of coffee for a good-looking man when he comes calling is the day I meet my Maker."

The shirt she wore said:

WOMEN BELONG IN THE HOUSE
AND THE SENATE

Miss Fancy believed both statements with equal fervor.

"You're going to have to wait a few minutes anyway," she added. "Alice is talking to the head doctor upstairs. You sit down, and I'll get that coffee."

"We're looking for things to do," Cora said when her mother left the room. "Trying to keep busy. I guess you'd have told me right off if you had anything to tell me."

"I'm sorry, Mrs. Bodine—Cora. We're doing everything we can."

"I don't doubt it. Oh, Dr. Minnow. You're finished?"

"We had a good talk. Sheriff."

"Dr. Minnow. Is she up for more talking?"

"Give her a few minutes. She's doing very well, Mrs. Bodine. I think your instincts, Maureen's instincts, about bringing her here were right. It's just the start, but she's calm."

"Can you tell me if she remembers anything about her abductor, her captivity?"

"She avoids it, and that's natural, Sheriff. She's struggling with what he indoctrinated in her, and this reality. This reality she remembers in some part of her mind, and this reality is where she feels safer, even happier. She did talk about the house, and when I asked her if it was bigger than her bedroom—the one upstairs—she said it was about the same, but now she has windows and pretty walls."

Celia turned another smile to Cora. "Painting it the way it had been makes her feel comfortable, gives her a sense of ownership, though she doesn't recognize it as such."

And now Celia turned toward Tate. "Her captor didn't live in the house with her. I'd say it was more the size of a shed than a house. She wasn't ready to talk about what she could see when she went outside. She mentioned a dog, a mean one, but she closed off on any other details."

"An outbuilding and a dog's more than I had."

"Here you go, Bob. Oh, Dr. Minnow." Miss Fancy carried the coffee to Tate. "Can I get you some coffee?"

"Thanks, but I have to get back. I'll be here the same time tomorrow. For now, don't push her about Rory. We'll give her some time there."

"I'll get your coat, walk you out."

Tate stood with his hat in one hand, the coffee in the

other. "Miss Fancy, I'm going to go up and see her, if that's all right."

"The nurse up there is . . ." Miss Fancy rubbed her temple. "Hell, her name's slipped my mind."

"Don't worry about that. I'll see you before I go."

He assumed they'd used her old room, and knew where to find it. For a few months long ago he'd pined outside her bedroom window. And sometimes she'd climb out of it to meet him.

Now, with the years between sitting heavy on her, she sat by the window, working yarn with a hook.

The woman in the second chair read a book, but rose when he came in. "You have company, Alice."

Alice looked up and smiled shyly. "I know you. You came to the hospital. You were very nice and came to visit me. You . . ." Her eyes twitched. "You can walk on your hands."

"I could once." His heart knocked a little as he remembered making her laugh when he'd walked over the grass on his hands. They'd been sixteen, he thought, and he'd been wildly in love with her.

"Not so sure I could do it now."

"I'll leave you to talk. I'm in the next room," the nurse told Tate quietly.

"You're drinking coffee. I'm not supposed to drink coffee, but Bodine does. She's the sister's daughter. She's nice, too."

"I know Bodine. She's a fine young woman. Can I sit with you?"

"The man doesn't have to ask. The man does."

"A polite man asks. Could I sit with you, Alice?"

She actually flushed a little. "You can sit. I'm making a scarf. It's for Rory. It's for my son. He has green eyes. He's so handsome. He grew so tall."

"How long's it been since you've seen him?"

"We had breakfast. Clementine made biscuits. I . . . I like her biscuits."

"I mean before breakfast. How long since you'd seen him?"

"Oh, he was just a year old. Just one year. Such a sweet baby. I could keep him and nurse him and bathe him, and teach him to clap his hands. I taught him to walk and say 'Mama'. Because he's the son."

"You had daughters."

"Baby girls. Cora and Fancy and Lily and Maureen and Sarah."

"Did you teach them to clap their hands?"

"I couldn't. Sir had to take them. He has no use for girls and they can fetch a good price. Maybe you can find them."

"I can try."

"But not Benjamin. God took him to heaven before he came out of me. And not Rory. I found Rory right here. I'm happy I came here."

"Did you have your children in your house? I mean to say were they born in your house?"

"Only Lily and Maureen and Sarah and Benjamin. Sir provided the house because I gave him a son, as a woman is meant to do."

"Where did you have Cora and Fancy and Rory?"

"In the room downstairs." Her lips pressed together. "I didn't like the room downstairs. I didn't like it. I liked the house better."

"It's all right." He touched her trembling hand. "You won't ever go back to that room."

"I can stay here with Rory. With the mother and the sister and Grammy . . . Grammy. Grandpa has M&M's. He smells like cherries, and he has a beard."

"That's right." It occurred to Tate she wouldn't know her grandfather had died, so he trod carefully. "Does Sir have a beard?"

"All over, all over." She rubbed a hand over her cheeks and chin.

"Does he smell like cherries?"

"No, no. Like the soap that stings at first. And sometimes not. Sometimes like whisky. Sometimes like whisky and sweat. I don't like it. I like making the scarf, I like making the scarf, I like making it, and the window and the biscuits. I like the pink walls."

"They sure are happy walls. What color were the walls in your house?"

"Gray with white spots and lines. I like these better. I'm ungrateful, I'm ungrateful for what Sir provided."

"No, you're not. You're grateful to be home with your family. Can you tell me something, Alice?"

"I don't know."

"Can you tell me where you were when you met Sir, the very first time?"

"I don't know. I have to finish the scarf, finish it for Rory."

"That's all right. I have to go now, but I'll come back, if that's all right."

"It's all right. I wanted to come home," she said as he rose.

"You're home now."

"I should've called Grandpa from Missoula when I got there. He'd've come to get me. He wouldn't be mad."

"You were coming home from Missoula?"

"From . . . otherwise. I don't know. I'm awfully tired now."

"I'll get the nurse for you. You can rest awhile."

"They roast turkey for Thanksgiving, but I like

Grammy's ham better. Grammy makes ham for Thanksgiving, and we all make pies. I'm going to sleep."

"All right, Alice. Here, I'll help you." He helped her to the bed, tucked a throw around her.

"It's soft. Everything is soft here. Is the mother here?"

"I'll go get her for you. You rest."

He went out, signaled to the nurse before he started down for Cora.

An outbuilding, a dog, somewhere on the road from Missoula to the ranch, sometime around Thanksgiving—though God knew how long ago.

It was more than he'd had.

CHAPTER TWENTY-TWO

Time moved. While most of home life centered around Alice—what to say, what not to say, what to do, what not to do—spring glided in with all its sweetness and all its demands. The sun came earlier, stayed later, and those daylight hours increased the work.

Bodine often thought of that work as an escape from the stress and worry of the eggshell-walking required at home. Then felt guilty for thinking it.

She thought of the nights she spent with Callen in his narrow bed or at an empty cabin as another kind of escape. And didn't feel the slightest twinge of guilt. If she analyzed it, as she sometimes did, she concluded he gave her balance, companionship, a good ear for listening, a steadier hand than she'd ever given him credit for.

And really good sex.

She liked to think she gave him just the same.

Most days she saddled up and rode to work with him, then home again. If she could juggle the time, she rode home again midday to give her grannies a little break from Alice.

"I like her." Though she had an agenda in mind, Bodine rode easily beside Callen. "Every once in a while something—someone—peeks out from the trauma. And I know I'd like that someone. And the dogs like her, which is a good gauge."

"The dogs like Alice?"

"And it's mutual. A lot of the time they sprawl and snore at her feet when she crochets. The sheriff came by while I was there this afternoon. He's got a good way with her, too."

"Did he get anything more?"

"It came out she was twenty-one—just turned twenty-one when she started hitchhiking home. So that gives him a closer when. I don't know what he can do to close up twenty-six years and find something, but I could see it mattered knowing. She wanted me to stay while he talked to her. She was happy starting out, like we were all having a little visit. She's making another scarf—for me. She finished Rory's."

Lifting her face to the sky, Bodine shook her head. "I'm all over the place."

"Not so much. She likes you, trusts you. She likes Tate. She's shy with me if I'm around, but I don't scare her."

"It's the same with Dad and Chase—the shy but not scared. And still she won't step outside. People are outside, and that's that."

"She needs more time."

"I know, and it hasn't been much time yet. But . . . We all have to be so careful, and it wears, Callen. It's helping, but it wears. Some days she knows Rory's not her son. Others she digs in there like a mama bear. It's hard on Rory. He's dealing better than anyone could expect. You forget to give him credit sometimes for his heart. He has such a good heart."

"You want to know what I think?"

"I'm blabbering about it, again, so I must."

"You've always been tight. God, I admired and envied that all my life. Your family pulls together, and this situation's made you pull harder. I figure Alice is peeking out from what that fucker made her because she's got that in her. I know what it's like to be eighteen and pissed at the world. More than you," he added.

"I've been pretty lucky in my world."

"It's more than luck, but yeah. I know what it's like to want to come home, to need to. Nobody stopped me from doing that, nobody stole more than half my life. And it was hard enough to come back."

"I never thought of that," she said quietly. "I never thought it was hard for you coming back." As they rode, slow and easy, she studied his profile. "I should've."

"You never know what's changed, what's the same, and if you'll fit back again. It's the chance you take going and coming back. I'd say the fact she's able to make her scarves and talk to Tate—to anyone without screaming—to get up in the morning and go to bed at night means whoever she was at eighteen, whatever that son of a bitch tried to turn her into, there's a hell of a lot of Bodine in there. It'll do more than peek through."

It took her a moment before she could speak. "Do you want to know what I think?"

"I'm listening to you blabbering, so I must."

"I think I might go a little crazy if I didn't have you to talk to. The things we say, and God knows the things we don't, at the ranch are always careful now. They have to be. Mom and Grammy are worried about Nana, Dad's worried about all of them. Chase takes Rory off more than he needs to just to give him some breathing room."

"You do the same."

"I do, we just don't say much about any of it. Really can't. And I bet I'm not the only one leaning on you."

"I've got good balance."

"I was thinking just that."

Shifting in the saddle, he gave her a long study. "So you don't have to think you need to change directions and not keep on the way you were going. We're already on land that might have been mine if things had been different. They weren't different. It isn't mine."

"I'm sorry." She stopped her horse, realized she shouldn't have been surprised he caught her turning away from his old house. "It seemed like a good idea. Now it doesn't."

He knew the land the same way he knew his own hands. For the moment he was content enough to sit his horse and look at it. "We signed the papers, and it's yours. Your family's. I don't regret it."

"It would break my heart if we had to sell our land."

Oddly, he thought it would break his own if that ever happened.

"It's not like that for me, not this land. I don't know if it ever was. One of these days I'll want my own, and I'll get it." With a shrug he smiled at her. "I did all right in California. You're not too polite to ask about that, but you haven't."

"There's not too polite and there's downright rude. I can be downright rude," she decided. "What's 'all right' for yourself, more or less?"

"Enough I didn't have to sell. I could've kept the land, given my mother and sister their shares. Bought some stock, got a decent ranch going."

Maybe that was more all right than she'd imagined,

and maybe that added another aspect to him she hadn't considered. She appreciated a good head for business and financial security.

"But you didn't."

"Nope. Because it's not what I wanted. I didn't mind running my own business, and wasn't bad at it."

"What do you mean your own business?"

Since he knew where she'd been heading, he rode forward. "I hooked up with a partner in California, and we had our wrangling enterprise, such as it was. And it did all right. When I was ready to come back, he bought me out. I don't mind working for somebody else, either. So I'm fine where things stand."

Yet another aspect she hadn't considered. "I didn't know you started a business—I thought you just worked for one."

"I wanted to try it out." As simple as that really, he thought now. He'd wanted to try things, get a feel for things. "It fit well enough, for a while. It fits you better from what I see. I've gotten real fond of women who know how to run things, and have to think a lot of one who juggles it all to get home for an hour in the middle of the day to put family ahead of everything."

"Why, Callen Skinner." Eyes wide, she pressed a hand to her heart. "You're going to bring a blush to my cheeks."

"That'll be the day."

He could see the house up ahead now, the single story with its slightly crooked L. The empty paddocks, the overgrown yard, the scrabble of a chicken coop. The empty barn gone to a faded, red-streaked gray where his father had hanged himself.

Some wildflowers were trying to bloom. In the distance, the mountains held some blue, some green under the frosting of snow.

"What was the idea?" he asked her. "Coming here?"

"We're still deciding what to do. We have some options. The first is whether to incorporate it into the ranch or the resort. I lean, big surprise, toward resort."

"That's a shocker," he replied.

"Chase is on the fence—another shocker. Though I think part of the fence-sitting is waiting until he knows what you'd rather."

"It's not my land."

"Shut up. Rory's with me. Mom's just too distracted to think clearly either way, and Dad leans ranch, but he's open. We haven't brought the grannies into it, but we will."

"Okay."

"Either way leads to other options, but right now the leans are swaying heavier toward resort's more likely, so I'll give you those. We could fix up the house, the outbuildings, rent this out as a mini-ranch experience. Families, groups, corporate events. We could raze the house, the outbuildings, and build new ones. Either toward that mini-ranch experience or a group of high-end cabins, with a central kitchen and community area like we do for the glamping. Bring in some stock, make it an educational experience for youth groups. How to tend horses, cattle, chickens. Lots of options."

"You've got your preference. Which is it?"

She shook her head. "They're all workable, all good, and can all be fluffed up and marketed. I'm asking you how *you* feel about it."

"I told you, I'm fine with it. It's not mine to say anyway."

She hissed, dismounted. "Oh, get off your horse, Skinner. I mean that literally and metaphorically." She walked Leo to the paddock, looped his reins over the fence. "You grew up in that house. You worked the land here, raised horses and cattle. You have a damn opinion. You have feelings."

He got off his horse, and distinctly felt the edges of the corner she had pushed him into. "I don't care as much as it seems you want me to."

"Bullshit. Just bullshit. I'm asking you to tell me right when we're standing here. Take it down, the house, the barn, all of it, or fix it up and make it new again. Just that. Tell me."

Angrier than she wanted to be, she knocked a fist on his heart. "Tell me what you feel, what you'd want."

She left her hand on his heart. He swore it burned right into it, like the sun burning across the sky on its slow descent. Like her eyes into his.

"Take it down. All of it. I—"

"Done."

"Bodine—"

"Done," she repeated. "That's all I needed."

He grabbed her wrist before she could pull away. The temper they both felt evaporated when she laid her other hand on his cheek.

"It matters, Callen, what you feel. Not just to me, but it sure as hell matters to me. They're options, and all of them good. Why shouldn't what you want count?"

"It's not mine."

"It was."

"It might've been, but it wasn't. If my only choice in coming back was to come here, to this land, to this house, I wouldn't be here. This isn't where I'm rooted, and whatever roots there were, were so shallow ripping them out didn't change a thing."

He pulled her close so they could look at the front of the house together. "I've got mixed memories, good and bad. I don't know that one outweighs the other so much. I remember when my father got it into his head to build that addition there. He didn't know what he was doing, and I was about twelve, so I didn't know, either. But he tried."

He heard his mother's voice as they stood in the wind over his father's grave.

He tried.

"He tried," Callen repeated, maybe finally accepting just that. "And it made my mother happy. It's lopsided and the floor inside slopes, but he tried and it made her happy. It's mixed that way."

Saying nothing, Bodine leaned into him a little. An offer of comfort.

"But my mother's never going to walk on that floor again. And she's never going to stand here and look over at that barn and remember how he looked hanging. I don't want you to take it down for me."

"I said it's done." Turning to him, she laid her hand back on his heart. "Maybe she'll come back here one day and see what we've built. Maybe it'll make her happy. Maybe it'll make you happy."

She gestured, waited until he stopped looking into her eyes, followed her direction. "You've got a couple of rose-bushes over there. You should dig them up. Make sure you get good root balls, cover them with burlap, and take them to your mother. I bet your sister would know how to get them going again. It would mean something to your mother."

In his throat, emotion lodged with gratitude. "There are times I don't know what to say to you. Times you just blow a hole through me."

He drew her in, held on. "I'll dig them up," he told her. "She'll like that, and I wouldn't have thought of it."

"You might have."

"I'd throw it all out," he stated, looking over her head at what might've been his. "That's the wrong way. There's some of those daffodils trying to come up on the side of the house. I could dig them up, too. Savannah always liked those when we were kids. And—"

"What?"

"Maybe I'll pry up a couple floorboards before you tear it down. Between Justin and Savannah, they could make something. She'd like that."

"There you go." Bodine leaned back enough to kiss him. "Why don't we walk around for a minute. See if there's anything else?"

Before he could answer his phone signaled. "Text from my mother." He frowned at the readout. "She never texts. She just— Christ, my sister's in labor."

"Well, you've got to go!" Grabbing his hand, Bodine dragged him back to the horses. "You have to get there."

"She's having it at home. Why would anyone do that? There ought to be a law or something. Why is she—"

"Mount up, Skinner." She said it with a laugh, for a moment seriously adoring him and his pure male fluster. "You can get to your truck in less than ten minutes, and drive there and ask her yourself."

He swung onto his horse. "Maybe Vanna doesn't want me in the middle of things."

"Men are idiots." Bodine sent Leo into a gallop, knowing Sundown would follow her lead.

Her mood high, Bodine strode into the house. She found Clementine at the counter with Alice, peeling potatoes.

"I'm making mashed potatoes. Clementine's showing me how. I can watch her fry the chicken."

"And I can eat it," Bodine said, making Alice duck her head and smile. "Something already smells good."

"We baked a chocolate cake. I like cooking with Clementine. My house doesn't have an oven. I couldn't bake chocolate cake."

"You're making me hungry for it." Bodine poured a glass of wine as her mother came in. "I brought home news," she announced. "Callen's sister's having her baby."

"That's happy news," Maureen said. "You can pour me a glass, and we'll drink to a healthy baby."

"I had babies." Alice continued to peel as she spoke, but her shoulders hunched. "It hurts, and there's blood, and it hurts more and more. If they're girls you can't keep them because they fetch a good price. The sister keeps her girl, but I can't keep mine."

She aimed a furious look at Maureen. "My girls would be as pretty as yours. *Prettier!* It's not fair."

"No, it's not," Maureen began. "I'm sorry—"

"I don't want your sorry. I don't want your sorry. I want my babies. I want my Rory. Why is he yours, too? Why do you get everything?"

"Let's sit down, Alice." Bodine moved toward her. "You can show me the scarf you're making me."

"No!" For the first time Alice slapped out at Bodine, then rounded on her. "You're the daughter. I'm the daughter, too! I'm the daughter. Why does she always get everything?"

"That's enough." Her own temper fraying, Maureen stepped between them. "That's enough, Alice."

"Just shut up. Shut up, shut up! You're not my boss. Reenie, Reenie, Reenie. Always the good one, always the winner, always, always." Alice shoved her.

To Bodine's shock, Maureen shoved Alice right back. "Maybe you should start acting your age. Maybe you should stop whining about everything just like you always did. Maybe you should stop blaming everyone but yourself."

"I *hate* you."

"Yeah, what else is new?"

"Girls!" Cora quick-stepped into the kitchen, Miss Fancy on her heels. "Stop it right now."

"She started it." Alice poked a finger at Maureen. "She can't boss me around, Ma. You always take her side. It's not fair. How come I have to wash the dishes for a *week* and she doesn't? Just because she gets straight As? The teacher doesn't like me, okay? And I was going to clean my room, Ma, I was! I just forgot. Reenie, Reenie, Reenie's such a beautiful bride. Well, I'm going to be a movie star. Just you wait and see. Why does she keep her babies? Why?"

Tears flowing, Alice pressed her hands to both sides of her head. "Why, why, why? I don't understand. Who am I? Who am I? Not the woman in the mirror. No, no, no! The old woman, who is the old woman in the mirror? Who am I?"

"Alice. My Alice." Cora stepped forward. "Alice Ann Bodine. There now." With her fingertips, Cora wiped at the tears. "Who am I?"

Bodine felt her own throat close as she watched Alice struggle. "Ma. Ma. I . . . I was coming home."

"I know. I know. You're home now."

"I don't feel right. I don't feel right anywhere in me. Can I go back? Just go back?"

"We're going to start from here, and it's going to be all right."

"Reenie's mad at me."

"No, I'm not." Maureen ran a hand down Alice's braid. "I'm not mad. I'm glad you're home, Alice."

"I was mad. I was mad. I was mad. I can't remember why. My head hurts."

"You can lie down awhile," Cora said. "I'll sit with you."

"No. No, I'm making mashed potatoes. Clementine's teaching me. Clementine . . . If complaints were a dollar, you'd be a billionaire."

"That's right." Though her eyes shined, Clementine tapped a half-peeled potato. "They won't peel themselves, girl."

"I'm going to sit down right beside you, make sure you do a good job." Miss Fancy walked over, sat on a stool.

"Grammy." Alice tipped her head to Miss Fancy's shoulder. "Grammy always smells so good. Where's Grandpa?"

"He's up in heaven, darling, taking care of your little Benjamin."

"Grandpa's with Benjamin. I don't have to worry." As she picked up the peeler, she looked at Maureen, her eyes full of grief. "He's not my Rory. He's yours."

"We're sisters. We share."

"I hate to share."

Now Maureen laughed. "Don't I know it."

Behind them, Bodine slid an arm around Cora, spoke softly. "Come on and sit down. You're shaking. I'll make you tea."

"I'd rather have that wine."

"Sit first."

Bodine dashed back for the wine, waited until her grandmother wrapped both hands around the bowl of the glass, took a sip.

"She called me 'Ma.'"

"I know."

"It's the first time. She called me 'Ma,' and when she

looked at me, she remembered. I could see it in her eyes. She's coming back. Alice is coming back."

Exhausted, confused, and overwhelmed, Callen stepped back into the shack. He tossed his hat and jacket in the vicinity of a chair. Though he deeply wanted a beer, he wanted sleep more. He headed into the bedroom and, dropping down on the bed to pull off his boots, sat on Bodine.

He said "Jesus Christ" inside the few seconds it took him to identify woman rather than God knew what. She rolled upright with a grunt.

"You're supposed to look before you sit."

"That's leap." He fumbled for the light, which had her slapping a hand over her eyes.

"What are you doing sleeping on top of my bed with all your clothes on?"

"I couldn't sleep."

"You were doing a damn good impression."

"At home. I thought I'd wait for you, and I fell asleep. Savannah? The baby?"

"Great and really pretty. I think. She's my first straight out of the oven. Here." He pulled out his phone. "See for yourself."

Bodine blinked her bleary eyes, focusing on the image of a tiny bundle swaddled in a pink-and-white blanket and wearing a pink cap. "She's not really pretty. She's gorgeous. What did they name her?"

"Aubra. Aubra Rose."

"Did you hold her?"

"I'm going to admit I didn't want to. Rather handle sweating dynamite, but I got roped into it. And it was a moment. There were lots of moments." He swiped through to show Bodine other pictures of the baby—in her mother's arms, her father's, her grandmother's. And finally his.

Bodine's thought, studying him with his niece, was: besotted.

"Mostly I have to wonder why any woman would go through that. I'm not ashamed to say I got out of the room as much as I could, but they kept pulling me back in. Yeah, lots of moments."

He finally pulled off his boots, then stretched out beside her, both of them still dressed. "I didn't do any of the work, and I feel like I climbed a couple mountains."

He shut his eyes. "And in the moment, I said I'd take the boy for a few hours a couple days this week, give them some rest time. I'll figure out what to do with him. Pony rides, let him scoop up some horse manure. Nothing a boy likes better at that age."

"Miranda—the kids activities coordinator—can help you out."

"Yeah?"

"Sure."

"Might save my sanity." He let his mind start to drift. "So, how was your evening?"

"Intense. Mom and Alice got into a big fight before dinner. yelling, shoving."

"What?" His brain fired up again. "What?"

"Actually, it started with Aubra Rose. I mentioned the baby coming, and Alice got going, then she and Mom got into it. It's a revelation to see your mother fight with a sibling the way you might do yourself. And Nana started to break it up, and Alice went off."

She turned a little more so they were stretched out face-to-face.

"She remembered things, Callen. Mixed-up things, silly, petty, kid-stuff things, but she remembered. She called Nana 'Ma.' Not 'the mother' the way she has been. She called my mother 'Reenie.' It was a lot. Really a lot. Maybe a breakthrough. I don't know. Nana's sure it is, and it worries me she's got her hopes up, because Alice could get up tomorrow and not remember any of it."

"There's nothing wrong with having your hopes up. You ought to do the same."

"Maybe. Chase, Rory, and I had a little meeting later, in the barn. We figured Dad's got Mom—and during the day Rory and I will keep an eye out there. Chase is taking Grammy, Rory Nana, and I get Alice. She could lean too hard on Rory, and she's still easier with me than Chase. All I have to do is figure out how to take the lead there. Today was the first day without the nurse rotation, and *boom*, intense."

"You'll handle it. We should get undressed and actually get in the bed."

"Yeah. In a minute."

In a minute they'd both fallen asleep just as they were.

The man known as Sir fashioned a rough cane out of a sturdy branch. It helped him when his legs got too shaky to finish his ranch work.

The dog died on him, but dogs were easy to come by. He'd get another when he felt up to it.

He considered shooting the horse—more trouble than it was worth—but felt while a man could do without a dog for a bit of time, a man without a horse was hamstrung.

So he fed it sparingly, rationing out the grain.

He took more time with the cow. The cow still produced milk, even if milking the thing exhausted him.

He wheezed as he walked, but he could walk. At least until the coughing struck. When it did he had to stop, sit, suffer through it.

In a few days, when he felt better, he'd go for more medicine, shell out the money for feed, for hay.

Start hunting for a new, young wife. One strong enough to plow the plot and plant it. One vital enough to give him sons. One comely enough to give him pleasure.

This was his waiting time.

He told himself every night when he crawled into bed that by morning he'd be strong again. Strong enough to start that hunt.

He'd readied the basement, and there she would stay. And as she plowed the field so he would plow her. As the field produced its bounty, so would she produce hers. From his secd.

Every night he slept with a revolver under his pillow, and a bullet ready to dispatch anyone who tried to stop him from defending his God-given rights.

PART FOUR

A Return

You're searching, Joe,
For things that don't exist; I mean beginnings.
Ends and beginnings—there are no such things.
There are only middles.
—Robert Frost

CHAPTER TWENTY-THREE

If Jessica had to run her feet off half the day, she'd do it in great shoes. According to the app on her phone, she'd logged more than seven thousand steps, and it was still shy of noon.

Even better, her big weekend event would absolutely rock.

As a nod to the bright sun—and Montana—she paired her great shoes with her Stetson over a low, smooth ponytail.

She thought of it as an East-meets-West fashion statement.

On her hot pink stilettos—think spring!—she strode back from the Mill yet again, intending to swing through the Saloon and the Feed Bag, but stopped when Bodine pulled up in one of the resort cars.

"Tell me this weather's going to hold for the weekend," Jessica said.

As she stepped out of the car, Bodine looked up at the big, blue sky. "It looks good for it. We might get a quick flurry tonight, but it's sun and sixties tomorrow. And a good thing," she added. "We're getting the camps set up."

"I've got event guests in Riverside Camp and the Eagle's Nest tonight. Will they be ready by check-in?"

"Riverside's ready now, and the crew's setting up Eagle's Nest. Your guests will be glamping tonight, no problem." She tapped Jessica on the shoulder. "So, no need for you to go out there and nag the crew."

"Nagging the camp crew, off my list. I really want this one to run smooth."

"The Cumberland family reunion, right?"

"Family reunion–slash–birthday party. The matriarch will be a hundred and two tomorrow. I'm fascinated and terrified. A hundred and two. Have you seen the cake?"

"Not yet."

"It's nearly finished, and rather than nag that crew I've looked on in awe. It's huge and gorgeous and clever. Towering really, with symbols and decorations marking milestones in her life. I'm taking pictures for the website. It's truly one of a kind. And big enough to feed the seventy-eight people attending, whose ages range from seven months to that hundred and two."

"You're practically bouncing."

"I know!" With a laugh, Jessica gestured toward the Mill. "There's something about it. The continuity, longevity, the big, spread-out family coming together. They've been sending pictures and mementoes for weeks. They've booked the Mill for the whole weekend, and we've arranged everything they've sent, like a fun museum of their family's history. It's like another world for somebody with hardly any family history and no close relatives."

"You're Bodine-Longbow family now."

Touched, Jessica bumped her shoulder to Bodine's. "And as such, I'm determined to make this event another highlight of Bertie Cumberland's life. Speaking of families, how's it going for you?"

"It's up and down, but maintaining for longer periods." Hooking a thumb in the front pocket of her jeans, Bodine took a long look around. "Since things are under control here, I'm actually going to head home pretty much now, work from there the rest of the day. It took some arm-twisting, but I talked Nana and Grammy into going out, getting their hair done, taking a few hours. Clementine will be there, and between her and me, we can look after Alice."

"It's a lot."

"It's miles of a lot. And it's family."

"I get bits and pieces from Chase—but you know how he is."

"I do. I also know he's happy. And while he doesn't say much, he does. Yesterday he saddled up Mom and Dad's horses and pushed them, in that way he has of pushing, into taking a ride together. They like their date nights, and haven't taken one since Alice came back. That's how he fixed it."

Bodine let out a sigh as they began to walk. "And Chase and Callen dragged Rory over to the bunkhouse for poker last week when he was overwhelmed with Alice."

"Chase said she has accepted Rory's not hers."

Nodding, Bodine watched a couple of guests playing horseshoes. So normal, she thought, so everyday.

"She seems to have settled there, but even a week ago, she thought—or needed to think—he was hers. They got him away from it for a few hours."

"What gets you away from it?"

"This." Bodine gestured to expand the resort. "And Callen's a good listener. So are you."

"Anytime."

"We should go dancing again. The six of us." That one

night at the Roundup seemed like a lifetime ago. "Rory's still seeing Chelsea off and on."

"I'm there, anytime. Except this weekend," Jessica qualified. "This event is going to—" She glanced at her watch. "Oh God! I need to check on the welcome buffet, and airport pickups."

"I'll confirm the airport pickups on my way through. Any problem, consider it fixed before I head home."

"Thanks. Bo, if you need any help. A hair day, a shopping day, just a bitch day, I'm your girl." Jessica took off at a trot on her pink pumps. "But not this weekend!" she called back.

When she got home, loaded with paperwork, Bodine put it aside. She needed both hands and all her will to shove the grannies out of the house.

Once she had—and she watched until they'd driven out of sight—she swung through the dining room, where Clementine polished the big table.

"Are you sure they're not doubling back?"

Blowing out a breath, Bodine dropped into a chair. "Pretty sure. I'm giving it a couple minutes before I go up, get into the work I brought home. Nana said Alice was resting, that her morning session seemed to go well."

"As far as I can tell. I'll tell you this. Getting your grannies out for the afternoon's the best thing all around. Alice needs a little distance, too, if you ask me."

Satisfied with the table, Clementine started on the big sideboard.

"Did they fight like that a lot?" Bodine asked. "Alice and Mom, like the other night? When they were kids?"

"They had their spats and their blowups, too. Likely as not, Alice got it going, but your ma got her licks in.

Your ma liked being the oldest, I can tell you that. Lorded it some."

Fascinated, amused, Bodine propped her chin on her fist. "Really?"

"Oh, she wasn't above some *I was here first*ing. But she'd fall back on Alice getting away with something because she was the baby, just like Alice whined her head off about your ma getting away with stuff because she was older. I've heard the same from you and your brothers over the years."

Clementine paused to point a long finger at Bodine. "You weren't above pulling those middle-child or only-girl cards when it suited you."

"Sometimes it worked." Bodine lifted her shoulders, let them fall. "Sometimes it didn't. But did they like each other, Clem? Love's different. I love Chase and Rory, but I like them, too. I can get mad at them, slap and snap, but I like them."

"I think they did. They could be tight as a pair of tangled-up springs one minute and at each other the next. Laughing together and telling secrets five minutes after they were shouting and shoving. Cora had the patience of Job keeping up with two moody girls."

Clementine polished, turning the air into an orange grove. "Once when your ma was pregnant with Chase, I found her sitting upstairs alone, crying. Crying and rubbing that little bump she had going. She said she wanted her sister, wanted Alice. You know they picked the names of their first babies?"

"What? How?"

"When they were girls, they let each other pick the name of their first son, first daughter. Charles after your great-grandfather, and Maureen was to call him Chase.

And Maureen picked Rory for Alice after their daddy. Bodine for Maureen if she had a girl. Cora for Alice."

Carefully Clementine set the big pewter candle stands back on the server. "I'd say they meant a lot to each other, as they both stuck by that, even when the other wasn't around to know."

"No one ever told me that."

"I don't know who knew besides them and me. They told me so it was official." Turning back, Clementine smiled. "I guess they were around twelve and fourteen."

"I'm glad you told me. It helps me see them." She pushed up. "I'm going to haul my briefcase up and get started. I'll check on Alice before I do."

"You're a good girl, Bodine, at least half the time."

"That'll have to do."

As she got her things, started upstairs, Bodine thought of her mother at fourteen making a pact with her sister, a pact that would become a family. And of Alice at twelve dreaming of babies the way a young girl might. Of Alice having those babies alone in some maniac's basement. Of having those babies, who might have given her some comfort, taken from her.

She was now determined to be more patient, more kind for Alice's sake alone. Not just from worry for her grannies, for her mother, but for Alice, who'd once been twelve.

Then she saw Alice, gray-streaked hair hanging limp, eyes wild and angry. And the scissors snapping and shining in her hand.

"Alice." She had to firmly slide the word over the lump of panic in her throat. "Is something wrong?"

"It's all wrong. All of it. I don't like it. I don't like it. I don't want it."

"Okay. What don't you like? What don't you want? I

can try to help." Hoping her tone sounded easy and un-forced, Bodine tried a step forward.

"I can say it's wrong!" Alice jabbed the air with the scissors, stopped Bodine in her tracks. "I can say I hate it. The doctor said. She said, she said."

"Sure you can. You can tell me if you want to."

"Ma and Grammy went out." Alice snapped the scissors, again and again. *Click, click, click.* "Ma and Grammy went out to get their hair done."

"But they're coming back soon. And I'm here. Clementine's right downstairs. Maybe you could show me the scarf you're making for me."

"It's finished. It's done." Teeth clamped, Alice jabbed the air with the scissors. "I can make one for Chase. All of Reenie's. All hers, hers, all hers."

"I'd love to see it. Could I try it on?" With her eyes on Alice's, Bodine tried another step forward. Just a few more and she'd be close enough to grab Alice's wrist. She was stronger, quicker, could take the scissors.

"Yes, yes, yes! But I don't want it." Alice grabbed her hair with her free hand, pulled viciously.

"Okay, that's okay. You can . . ." And she understood. "Your hair? You want to get your hair done like your ma, like Grammy?"

"I don't want it." Squeezing her eyes tight, Alice pulled again. "Sir said it's a sin for a woman to cut her hair, but the doctor said *I can* say. I can say I don't want or I do. Which is right? I don't know!"

"You can say." Bodine agreed, moving another step forward. "That's your right. You can say because it's your hair, Alice."

"I *hate* it."

"Then we can change it so you don't. We can go get your hair cut, Alice. I'll take you."

"Not out there. No, no, not out there." As she looked at the walls, the doors, her breath came fast. "No, not out there. I can cut it off. I want to cut it off. He can't stop me if I'm in here, in the home."

"Oh, the hell with him." Bodine's words had Alice's eyes going wide. "The hell with him, Alice. It's your hair, isn't it? Nobody's going to stop you. But how about I cut it for you?"

"You . . ." Alice lowered the scissors, stared. "You can do it? You can?"

"Well, you'll be my first, but I can sure try." Maybe Bodine's heart still skipped, but she smiled as Alice meekly held out the scissors.

"How about we set up our salon in the bathroom there? You can sit on the stool. Do you know how short you want it?"

"I don't like it. I don't want it. You can cut it."

Bodine guided Alice to the stool. "I was just thinking, I know this girl and she grew her hair really long, almost as long as you. She grew it long, then cut it because she was donating it to this place that made wigs for women who got sick and lost their hair. If you want to do that, I can look up how it's done."

"You send it to a sick girl. Send the hair?"

"Yeah. Would you want to do that?"

"But it's ugly. Old and ugly." Tears swam. "Who would want it?"

Hoping to soothe, Bodine ran a hand down the impossible length. "I bet they'd fix it up, make it look nice. I'll look it up on my phone while you brush out your hair."

Bodine got a brush, watched Alice frown into the mirror. Following the instructions, Bodine braided the long, long hair. "I bet there are at least two sick girls who'll be grateful to you. I'm going to turn you a little now, so you can see from the side. Do you want it this short?" Bodine held a hand to Alice's mid-back.

"More."

Bodine climbed up inch by inch until she held the flat of her hand above Alice shoulders, and got a hard nod.

"Okay, let's see." She bound both ends with a band, blew out a breath. "I'm nervous. You're sure about this?"

"I don't want it."

"All right then, here we go." Praying the result wouldn't send Alice into a rage or into tears, Bodine cut. She clutched the heavy braid as it fell away, held her breath.

Alice just stared at the mirror, eyebrows lowered.

"I can fix it up some, I think. Maybe get Nana's smaller scissors or . . ."

Slowly, Alice lifted her hand, pulled her fingers through. "It's still ugly, but better. It's cut away, and he can't stop me. You cut it away, and he can't stop you. But I don't know who that is." She pointed at the reflection in the mirror. "I don't know."

Bodine laid the hair aside, set her hands on Alice's shoulders. "That's my aunt Alice, who named me."

Alice's gaze met hers in the glass, and she smiled a little. "You're Bodine, because we promised."

"That's right. I've got this other idea. You know Grammy has some hair dye in her room. How about we color your hair now?"

"Red like Grammy's? I love Grammy's hair."

"Me, too. Let's color your hair, Alice."

Now Alice smiled, lips and eyes. "I want that. I want red hair like Grammy's. You have a red vest. It's pretty."

"You like it?" Bodine ran a hand over the red leather vest Jessica had talked her into buying. "You can borrow it sometime if you want."

"Reenie hates me to borrow her clothes."

"I don't mind so much, and I'm offering. Let me go get the dye."

As a precaution, she took the scissors with her.

She didn't get much work done, but she'd make up the time. As a hair and makeup consultant, Bodine figured she was in the lower tenth percentile, but she did her best.

Flushed with success, she talked Alice into jeans—a first since her return—a pretty shirt, and her own red vest. She even dug out some earrings.

When Alice stood in front of the full-length mirror, studying herself, Bodine ranked it as one of the best moments of her life.

"I can see me," Alice said with wonder. "I got old, but I can see me. I can see Alice. Alice Ann Bodine."

"You look really pretty, too."

"I was pretty." Alice lifted a hand to her cheek. "I was really pretty. He took my pretty away. I have some back. I have a little back. I like my hair. I like the red vest to wear, to borrow. Thank you."

"You're welcome. Let's go show off to Clementine."

Bodine held out a hand, and though she ducked her head, Alice put hers in it.

Halfway down the stairs, Bodine heard her mother's voice. So did Alice, as Alice's hand tightened into a vise on hers.

"I'm going to take this tea up, and have a nap," Maureen said. "I may go back after dinner, just to help Jessie with this event, but . . ."

Still pouring the tea, Maureen froze as Bodine led Alice into the kitchen. The hot water spilled over the rim of the cup before Clementine caught it, took the pot.

"Alice." Tears springing to her eyes, Maureen pressed both hands to her mouth. "Alice. Alice."

She rushed forward, and though Alice jerked back,

went stiff, kept coming until she'd caught Alice in her arms. "Oh, Alice."

"I didn't want it. Bodine cut it. A sick girl can have it."

"Oh, Alice." Drawing back, Maureen fluffed her fingers through the red hair Bodine had managed to style into an uneven, amateur bob. "I love it. Absolutely love it. I love you."

She clutched Alice to her again, held out a hand for Bodine's. She kissed her daughter's hand, closed her eyes. And rocked her sister where they stood.

As Jessica's event included trail rides, pony rides, cattle drives, and lessons, Callen put in some overtime. He'd need to be back at it by sunrise, but for now he could enjoy an easy ride home.

He hoped he'd find Bodine on the other end of the ride, maybe get her to sit out with him, have a beer, watch the sunset.

And maybe if their schedules meshed up over the next few days, he could take her out to a fancy dinner.

He couldn't figure why he wanted to. He'd never been one for fancy dinners. But he wanted to try one with her, see how it set.

He wanted her back in his bed again, and for more than sleep.

He just wanted her, and it was time to admit it.

Everything about her fit, so why make it less than it was?

He hadn't come back for a woman, but he'd found the one he wanted, the one he could see building a life with.

Maybe she wasn't there yet, but he didn't think she lagged far behind him. The puzzle of the moment was: Did he wait for her to catch up, or did he give her a push?

Something to consider.

"Doesn't get much better than this." Leaning forward, he rubbed Sundown's neck. "Does it, boy? Cool evening coming in after a warm day. Wildflowers popping. Deer over there, see 'em? Yeah, you see them. Losing their winter coats. Fields are greening up some. We'll be bringing some of the horses down to that pasture there at sunup. Still snow on the peaks there, but that just makes the sky bluer."

He pulled his horse up to enjoy the moment, watched the white tails of the deer bob across the near field. When he actively thought of dismounting, picking some of the wildflowers for Bodine, he embarrassed himself.

A man could take things too far.

He walked the horse around a slight curve. "Let's stretch those legs out."

He'd no more than given the signal and Sundown was bounding forward. He felt the sting low on his calf, heard the sharp *snap* of a bullet. Sundown let out a cry of pain, stumbled.

Instinct took over. "Go!"

He felt his horse labor, but they were in the open, so he pushed until he could pull up again where the ground rose, where a cabin sat, where trees provided some cover.

He leaped off, didn't spare a curse for the shock of pain in his leg. Not when he saw the blood seeping low on Sundown's belly.

"Easy, easy, easy." Dragging off his bandanna, he pressed it to the wound. "It's okay, you're okay."

He heard the sound of an engine, the echo and roar, yanked out his phone as he scanned the trees, the ridge. As he vowed vengeance on whoever hurt his horse.

Bodine stepped outside hoping Callen had gotten back. She imagined what a kick he'd get out of her cutting Alice's hair, giving her a makeover. She'd like to sit out in the cool, watch the sunset, and tell him about her day, hear about his.

She liked the idea of knowing she could, knowing they might wander in sometime after dusk and make good use of his bed.

Thinking about that, smiling about that, she turned sharply when she heard Chase give a shout and bolt out of the house.

Her first thought was Alice, but her father ran out, too, and Rory. And every damn body.

"What is it? What happened?"

"Somebody took a shot at Callen, hit his horse. He's a mile down on Black Angus Road."

Chase kept running toward the horse trailer. Rory streaked into the stables. Equine first-aid kit, Bodine thought as she charged after him. She grabbed a bridle, had Leo in it within seconds.

"What're you doing?" Rory demanded.

"I'm going. I can get there faster on Leo, cutting through."

"Stay here. Whoever did it might still be out there."

"Then you stay here," she snapped back. Swinging onto Leo's bare back, she rode out at a gallop.

She'd heard the shot, she thought now. Heard the echo of it when she'd stepped outside, and hadn't thought a thing of it. Now the idea that the shot had been aimed at Callen, had struck that gorgeous horse, filled her with fury.

Bent low, she took Leo into the trees, cutting off the longer length of the road, pushed him thundering down the narrow, uneven track, slowing him only to navigate down the slope.

She saw Callen, felt a dizzying wave of relief when she

saw him standing, saw Sundown standing. And another dizzying wave of fear at the blood soaking the ground.

He glanced up, his face carved with rage. It didn't fade off when he spotted her. "What the hell are you doing?"

"How bad is it?" she called out, picking her way down. "They're on their way. How bad?"

"I don't know. Goddamn it, Bodine, you've got no business—"

He cut himself off. She'd come, and he couldn't change that. "Take his head, will you? Talk to him. He's hurt, he's shaken up."

Quivering, Bodine thought as she jumped off Leo, went to Sundown's head to soothe. "It's all right. It's all right. We're going to get you home and all fixed up. His belly?"

"I think it's a graze. It's long, carved a damn groove. It's bleeding heavy." He'd yanked out the spare shirt from his saddlebag once the bandanna had soaked through. "Did someone call the vet?"

She said, "Yes," because someone would have, and Callen needed as much soothing as the horse. "Don't worry. He's going to be fine. Here they come."

She held both horses steady as her father maneuvered the truck and trailer. Rory jumped out while it was still moving.

"Vet's on her way, so's the sheriff. Can he walk? We've got the hoist."

"He'll walk. He'll load in."

"Let's have a look, son." Sam squeezed a hand on Callen's shoulder, hunkered down. "Don't think it went in him or through him. Looks like a bad graze. You're going to be just fine."

Checking as he went, Sam moved back to Sundown's head, studied his eyes. "You're going to be just fine. We're going to get you home." He glanced down as Callen limped forward. "You hit?" he said, remarkably casual.

"Maybe."

"For Christ's sake! You're shot." Bodine grabbed Callen's arm, got shaken off.

"I'm seeing to my horse."

Slowly, painfully for both of them, Callen guided Sundown into the trailer.

"Let him be right now." Sam patted Bodine's arm. "He's hurt and he's mad. Just let him be right now. Let's go home, tend to both of them."

Though she was hurt and mad herself, Bodine clamped her mouth shut, swung back onto Leo, and rode home.

She let him be. She hung back as the vet worked, as Callen continued to soothe the wounded horse. It broke her heart to see the horse rest his head on Callen's shoulder, to see him close his eyes when the vet gave Sundown something to ease the pain.

The whole time Callen stroked, murmured, and watched every move the vet made.

"I'm going to say he's lucky." The vet stripped off her bloody gloves, tossed them in a plastic bag. "Even though getting shot's never lucky. The bullet grazed over the meat. There's no penetration. He's lost some blood, and he's going to hurt. I'm giving you pills against infection, and I'm going to check on him tomorrow morning. He'll want rest and pampering. You're going to keep that wound clean."

"But he's going to be all right?"

"He's a strong, healthy boy. I'm going to write out instructions for you to follow, and we'll keep an eye on him. No vigorous exercise for a few days. No riding for at least a week. We'll see after that. He'll heal up, Cal. He'll have a battle scar."

"We won't worry about that."

The vet adjusted her little square-framed glasses, peered at Callen through them. "You'll be sleeping in here tonight?"

"What do you think?"

"I think I'm going to write out what to look out for, what you can call and wake me up in the middle of the night for. Otherwise, I'll see you both tomorrow."

"I'm grateful. Sundown, thank the doc."

He might've reacted a bit sluggishly, but Sundown bowed his head.

Now Bodine stepped forward. "Would you mind taking a look at Callen before you head out, Doc Bickers?"

When she gestured at Callen's leg, Bickers rolled her eyes to the ceiling. "God's sake. Get off that leg, boy. You there, Chase Longbow, help this idiot into the kitchen so I can see if he needs the damn hospital."

"I'm not leaving my horse."

"Well, get the idiot something to sit on so I can see what's what."

Chase hauled over a stool, then simply shoved Callen down on it. "Shut up about it," Chase warned, "or I'll stick one of those needles into you myself."

"I'd rather a beer."

Bickers shook her head, shoved up her glasses. "Not until I've seen what we have here."

She pried off the boot, and the movement, the friction drained the blood out of Callen's face.

At her sides, Bodine's hands went to tight fists. About two inches above his anklebone, the skin bloomed purple and red around a bloody gash.

"Well." Bickers sniffed, pulling on fresh gloves. "Your boot took the worst of it."

"I liked those boots."

Still beyond pissed, Bodine forced her hands to relax,

stepped over and took Callen's. "Don't be a baby. You can afford new boots."

"Took a little bite out of you, but not enough to do more than hurt like the living fires of hell for a day or so. You want something for pain, you go see a people doctor. I can treat this topically, and you're going to have your own battle scar. You want it stitched up, you get the people doctor for that. I can do it, but there's no reason. Now suck it up. I'm going to clean and disinfect this, and it's going to add some flames to that hellfire."

"Want something to bite on?"

Callen rolled a sour look up at Bodine. "Yeah." He pulled her head down, clamped his mouth on hers. When the fire hit, he lost his breath for a minute, but she gripped his jaw in her hand, pressed her lips harder to his.

"Almost done here," Bickers told him. "You stay off this as much as you can. Don't see you needing a crutch, but find yourself a pair of tennis shoes, a couple days of that before you try pulling boots over this. It's not near as bad as that sweet horse. Mostly a nick, is all."

"Right now it feels like you jabbed down to the bone with a hot poker."

"Yeah, that'll ease up. You're a strong, healthy boy." Bickers slapped his knee. "And nearly as good-looking as your horse. You can take something over the counter for the pain. You got anything tucked away that's stronger, you tell me beforehand."

"I don't."

"All right. I'll write all this down for you, leave it, and see you both in the morning."

"Thanks."

Bickers nodded, tossed away the gloves. "I'd like to know what kind of sick son of a bitch takes a shot at a sweet horse. I guess he was most likely shooting at you, but he hurt the horse more." She gathered her bag, nodded at Tate. "Your turn."

The sheriff stepped forward. "You up to talking to me, Cal?"

"Yeah, but I'd sure like a beer first."

Rory held one out. "Grabbed one for you. I'm supposed to go back, let the others know you and Sundown are okay."

"Thanks."

Callen took a long, slow pull. "I'll tell you what I know. Worked a little late, rode home slow. Pretty evening. I figured to give Sundown a run when we came around that first bend on Black Angus. He'd just changed gaits. I felt it hit me, then I heard it, then he stumbled. I had to keep him going. It hurt him, but we were in the open there, and I didn't know if we were going to get shot again. So I pushed him until we had some cover. I heard an ATV start up and take off."

"You sure about that? A truck, a bike?"

"I know the difference. An ATV. Probably up on the high trail. He had to wait until we came around that bend for a good shot, so he'd be up there, or why not take the shot when we were just standing there or walking? Going into a gallop's probably what threw the shot off. He had to compensate, change angles fast. Likely not much of a shot."

Callen took another long pull on his beer. "As memory serves, Garrett Clintok's not much of a shot. I'd like to know if he owns an ATV."

"You leave that to me."

Callen pushed the beer at Bodine, got to his feet. Fury turned his eyes into a storm cloud of fiery blue. "You see that horse? I love him like a brother. Some asshole hides up in the trees, tries to ambush me, and shoots my horse? I don't leave that up to anybody."

"If you go after Garrett, I'll end up having to arrest you for assault, and that'd be after he kicks your ass because you can't put all your weight on that leg. Do you think if he did this, I'll let it go?"

"I don't. Do you think if he did this, I will?"

Tate sighed, rubbed his face. "I'm going to deal with this. Don't do anything stupid."

Because his leg throbbed like a bad tooth, Callen sat again when Tate left.

"I'll take care of Clintok for you," Chase said.

He looked at Chase, shook his head. "I know you would, but I have to deal with this myself. Tate's right about getting my ass kicked right now. So I'll just heal up for a couple days."

"Tate'll have him in jail by then. He's got an ATV."

Callen nodded. "He'll get out sooner or later. I can wait."

"Well. I'll get you a bedroll."

"Get two," Bodine told her brother before he walked away.

Callen looked up at her as Chase walked away. "Are you sleeping out here?"

"What do you think?"

He pushed himself up again, pulled her to him. "I don't have it in me to shake you stupid for riding out there that way."

"Good. I'd hate to kick your ass under the circumstances. What I will do is go get you the plate I expect Clementine has warming in the oven, and get you another beer. A couple of Motrin."

"Four."

"Four," she agreed.

"Bodine." As his horse had with him, Callen lowered his head to her shoulder. "Scared the shit out of me."

"I know." Just as she knew he didn't mean getting shot. He meant coming close to losing his horse. "I'm going to go get your supper."

He let her go, limped back to his horse.

He thought how he'd nearly stopped to pick Bodine wildflowers.

He wished he had.

CHAPTER TWENTY-FOUR

Bodine woke snuggled up against Callen. That in itself had become pretty usual. But the fact that they both were pillowed on Sundown's chest added a brand-new element.

They'd slept better than she'd anticipated, especially since they'd left the lights on in case they'd needed to deal with any medical issues in a hurry. Right now the stall smelled of hay and horse and antiseptic.

And the horse snored.

She took that as a good sign as she eased herself away and sat up. She used her phone to check the time—five-fifteen. No, not bad at all, but her stable companions could use a couple more hours.

If it wasn't inside the bedroll, she'd have checked Callen's leg. Instead, she picked her way around, staying hunkered down to carefully examine Sundown's wound.

Nasty, she thought, and there'd be some pain when he woke. But the wound looked clean. She laid a careful hand on Sundown's belly. Warm, not hot.

After she crabwalked back, she stood, studied them.

Unable to resist, she lifted her phone again, took a couple of pictures. She'd print one out, frame it for Callen. Hell, she might even toss one on the website.

Thinking of that, and Callen's fancy riding show, she hunkered down again for another angle. A nice companion shot to the one of Callen, arm thrown up, and Sundown's forelegs pawing the air.

"Morning?" Callen mumbled. "Seriously?"

"Barely. Go back to sleep. He's fine," she said as Callen sat up. "I checked the wound. No heat, looks clean. Let me take a look at yours before I go grab a shower."

"It's fine."

"Then let's see."

He grumbled about it, but worked himself out of the bedroll.

The bruising, Bodine noted, bloomed glorious, but when she unwrapped the bandages, like Sundown's, the wound looked clean. No streaks of red, no troubling heat.

"Got some swelling, but no more than expected. Looks like you're both on the mend. And you've both got the day off to keep mending."

"I'm fine. We've got a full plate today."

"Which the rest of us will handle. Getting shot equals a sick day, horse and rider." She tapped her finger against Callen's chest. "I'm the boss of you. You're not going to want to leave him anyway."

She sat back on her heels. "I was so pissed off at you."

"For getting shot?" His fingers raked at his hair. "Doesn't seem quite equitable."

"For not saying you'd been shot. And for shoving me away once I realized you had."

"I can apologize for that part."

"No need. After I stopped being pissed, which was mostly from being scared brainless, I thought about it. I'd have done exactly the same. We've got that in common, I guess."

"Enough that I'd've been pretty pissed at you if the situation'd been reversed."

"So we're good there. Try for some more sleep. I'll bring some coffee out after I get that shower. Then you can grab one of your own and some breakfast. Dad, Chase, Rory, Mom, any of the hands will stay with him while you get cleaned up and fed."

"I know it."

She started to stand, but he tugged her into a kiss.

"I value a woman who'd sleep in a stall with a hurt horse."

"It wouldn't be the first time for me, unlikely it's the last."

"I value it."

She patted his knee, rose, pulled on her boots. "Stay off that leg."

Listening to her boot steps recede, Callen gave Sundown—he knew the horse had waked—a rub. "Looks like I've crossed into new territory. She puts an ache in me I don't know what to do with."

He glanced down, met Sundown's eyes. "Hurts some, doesn't it? Well, let's get up easy, you and me, and see how we stand."

Seconds after Bodine shut her door, Alice opened hers. She walked quiet and had a quick flash of the girl she'd been sneaking into the house—or trying to—after curfew.

She knew about the hurt horse. Everyone had jumped up, and there'd been shouting and running. It had scared her at first, scared her that Sir had come to take her back. That he'd hurt her because she'd cut her hair and made it red like Grammy's.

But it hadn't been Sir. Somebody had been mean to a

horse, and she wanted to see it. She liked horses. She could remember riding them and brushing them. She even remembered helping one get born once.

She wanted to see the hurt horse, but everybody said she shouldn't worry. Everything was fine.

But she wanted to see the hurt horse, so she *would*. *Hardheaded. Mile-wide stubborn streak.*

For some reason hearing those words in her head made her giggle. She had to slap a hand over her mouth to muffle the sound as she crept down the back stairs.

And she knew, she remembered where the creaky ones were. Oh my gosh, she remembered! Tears swam into her eyes as she navigated around them.

She hadn't been outside yet, not once. She hadn't even gone into the mudroom because she knew a door there led to outside.

Her stomach hurt, her bad leg hurt, her head hurt.

She should make tea instead. Some nice tea, and go work on her scarf.

"No, no, no. Don't be a scaredy-cat. Don't be a scaredy-cat. Don't be a scaredy-cat."

She couldn't stop saying the words, over and over, even when she put her hand over her mouth again. They just kept running out of her.

When she pushed open the door, she flashed straight back to pushing open the door in the house Sir provided. Now her head swam so she had to brace a hand on the doorjamb. The air blew over her face. Cool, sweet.

As she had weeks before, she stepped out.

Stars, so many stars. A world full of stars! She circled under them, arms held high. She remembered dancing—had she danced under a world of stars?

There was the big barn and there the bunkhouse and there the stables and there the chicken coop. Oh, and there's where Ma planted her kitchen garden. There was the sister garden.

She remembered, she remembered.

But when the dogs Bodine had let out came running, she froze.

They didn't bite. They didn't growl and lunge. They wagged and pranced and rubbed up against her legs. They liked to sleep at her feet while she made scarves. Being outside didn't mean they'd bite.

"You're good dogs," she whispered. "Not mean. I know you. You're Chester and you're Clyde. You come in the house and sleep when I work on my scarf. We're going to go see the horse."

She walked to the stables under a world of stars with the good dogs running in happy circles.

She tried to open the door quiet—mouse-quiet. She knew the smells here! Nothing scary, nothing mean.

Horses and hay and manure, saddle soap and linseed oil. Grain and apples.

She walked mouse-quiet, too, on her house slippers, creeping along in the flannel pajamas she liked so much. So soft.

A voice made her stop again, push a hand to her heart when it beat hard.

"You're going to take your medicine, and no whining. No use giving me that sad look, either. I'm going to take mine. You see me whining and looking pitiful? Fine. I'll take mine first."

She crept down a little more, saw the man. The man who came to the house sometimes to Sunday dinner, to breakfast. Sometimes.

She'd seen him kiss Bodine, and Bodine didn't seem to mind at all.

But if the man made her a little afraid, the horse . . .

Oh the horse was so beautiful. And the beautiful horse propped his beautiful head on the man's shoulder.

"I know it hurts."

The man's voice said kindness, said love, said the opposite of anything mean.

"You didn't hurt the horse."

The man turned around, one hand still stroking the horse's neck. He had a scruffed-up face and tired eyes, and his hair was all tousled.

"No, ma'am. I'd never hurt him."

"Who did?"

"I don't know for sure. Are you cold, Miss Alice? You want my jacket?"

He shrugged it off, stepped forward. She'd started to step back, step away, but saw he limped a little.

"I limp, too. Did somebody chain you up?"

"No. I got a little hurt when Sundown did. This is Sundown. Sundown, this is Miss Alice Bodine."

To Alice's delight, and to Callen's ridiculous pride, Sundown bent his forelegs into a bow.

"He's so pretty!"

"He sure thinks so. You can pet him. He really likes being petted by a pretty woman."

"I used to be pretty. I got old. Bodine cut my hair and made it nice again."

"Did she?" More pride. "It looks real fine. A lot like Miss Fancy's." He kept talking as she edged closer, lifted a hand to stroke Sundown's cheek. "You know I'm pretty sweet on Miss Fancy."

Alice laughed—a little high, a little rusty. "She's even older than me!"

"It doesn't matter a bit."

"Sundown," Alice murmured. "Your name is Sundown. I like to watch the sun go down. It makes the sky so beautiful. Like magic. I like horses. I remember. Things get so mixed-up in my head, but I remember I like horses. I like riding them, riding fast. I'd be a movie star and have a ranch in the Hollywood Hills. I'd shop on Rodeo Drive."

"Here, let's put this on." She didn't jerk away when he helped her into his jacket. "Maybe when he's better, you'd like to ride Sundown."

She pressed her hand to her lips, her eyes wide and full of wonder. "I could?"

"When he's better. The doctor needs to tell us when. But you could ride him when she says he can."

"I—I might not remember how."

"That's okay. I teach people how. Me and Sundown here. You can think about it."

"I can think about it. Nobody can stop me. I can think about it. Where did he get hurt?"

"Right along his belly. See here?"

She let out a gasp—and whether or not she remembered how to ride, showed Callen she remembered how to move and act around horses.

She crouched, one hand soothing Sundown's flank as she studied the wound. "That's mean. It's mean. I know about mean. About mean that chains you up and hits with fists and whips with belts. This is mean that way. He'll have a scar. I have scars.

"I'm sorry." She crooned it as she straightened, moved back to Sundown's head, stroked. "I'm so sorry somebody hurt you. Somebody mean."

When Sundown rested his chin on her shoulder, she closed her eyes a moment. Opening them, she looked directly into Callen's. "You're not mean. I know mean. I know there's meaner than you ever think. But I don't remember you."

"I wasn't around when you were."

"I went away."

"I did that, too, when I was about the same age you were when you did."

Tilting her head, she gave him a longer stare, and kept stroking Sundown. "Where did you go?"

"You know, it's funny. I went to California, just like you did. I ended up in Hollywood."

She gasped again, and something lit up in her eyes. "Were you a movie star? You're handsome."

"No, ma'am, but I worked in the movies some. I worked with the horses in movies."

There was something young and wondering in her sigh. "Was it wonderful?"

"I liked it."

"But you came back."

"I missed this place. The ranch, the people. I've got a mother and a sister, and they needed me around more than I wanted to think when I left."

"I missed the ranch, my family. I was coming back. Nobody stopped you when you came back."

"No. I'm real sorry somebody stopped you."

"I got old there," she told him. "Old and weak and crazy."

"Miss Alice? That's not what I see when I look at you. Not what I'm hearing having this conversation with you."

"Conversation," she said slowly. "We're having a conversation."

"What I see, what I hear, is somebody hurt, but strong over that. Just like Sundown. Strong and smart and good, just hurt some."

"I'm not scared of you."

He tried a grin on her. "I'm not scared of you, either."

She laughed a little, pleasing him. "I feel more like

Alice with my hair cut and red like Grammy's. I feel more like Alice with Sundown. If, when he's better, I can ride Sundown, but I can't remember how, will you help me?"

"That's a promise. Maybe you could do me a favor back?"

"I can't do much yet. I can make you a scarf. Your eyes are gray and they're blue. Gray and blue all at once. Maybe Ma has yarn like that, and I can make you a scarf."

"That'd be nice, but I was wondering if you'd help me with Sundown for a minute here. He needs to take some medicine, and he doesn't want to. He needs it to get better and stop hurting. Maybe you could talk to him for me."

He caught the look Sundown gave him, one that clearly accused Callen of being sneaky. Callen just smiled back. If anyone claimed that horse didn't understand every damn word said, Callen would call them unimaginative at best, a liar at worst.

Dressed for the day, Bodine carried a thermos of black coffee toward the stables.

She'd already addressed Callen's schedule, texted Easy, who'd had the day off, to ask him to fill in. Done. Texted Maddie to take one of Callen's lessons. She'd have to cancel Sundown's show when she got in—and was working on something fun to replace it—but everything else, she'd covered.

The ranch hands would be stirring in the bunkhouse, as her father and brothers were in the main house. Clementine, she imagined, would drive up any minute.

Another day would begin.

She hoped Garrett Clintok's day—because she joined

with Callen there on who'd taken that shot—began behind bars.

She nearly tripped over her own feet when she saw Alice walking toward her in the pearly dawn light.

"Alice? Alice, what are you doing out here?" Wearing Callen's jacket, she noted.

"I went to see the horse. He's hurt. And the man—the man—I can't remember his name."

"Callen?"

"Callen! Cal. 'I'm Cal,' he said. He got hurt, too. I helped him give Sundown his medicine and we had a conversation. He's going to help me ride Sundown when Sundown's better. Somebody was so mean. Mean, mean. I *hate* mean. You can get used to it. I got used to it, but now I hate it. There were stars. They're gone now."

"The sun's coming up." Bodine gestured east. "See?"

"The sun's coming up. I like it. The men are coming out."

Recognizing the jolt of panic, Bodine put a hand on Alice's arm. "They're not mean."

"How do you know?" Alice hissed. "Sir didn't look mean when I got in the truck. How do you know?"

"Because I know them. Every one of them. I know they'd all protect you from the mean. You remember Hec, don't you? He'd never be mean."

"I . . . think."

"It's all right. It's already a lot before sunrise."

"I'm going to make Cal a scarf. I like his eyes. Are they blue, are they gray? Are they blue, are they gray? It's fun. I'm going to tell Dr. Minnow I went outside. She'll be surprised."

"Maybe when I get home from work today, you can walk over and visit Sundown and Callen with me. You can meet my horse, too. He's Leo."

"I want to. If I don't feel crazy again."

"Fair enough."

Bodine continued toward the stables and decided she owed Callen more than a day off.

Word spread. While she hadn't expected otherwise, Bodine hoped to eke out the information rather than tamp out firestorms everywhere the minute she got to work.

Sal leaped at her literally the second she stepped into the lobby.

"Is it true? Nobody's here but me," she said quickly. "I heard it from Tess at Zen Town. Zeke texted her about it last night."

Zeke, ranch hand, brother to Tess, massage provider. God.

"It's true. Callen and Sundown were both grazed by a bullet. We don't know if it was intentional. Sheriff Tate's looking into it."

Sal fisted both hands on her hips. "It's me, Bo, and I know when you're hedging."

"I'd like to keep it to that, officially—and away from the guests. So please say that if and when you're asked."

"What's going on around here, Bo? Billy Jean's killed, and that other girl. Now this? Oh my God, is it connected? Is it all—"

"No. I can't see that. That's not hedging."

"But your aunt—"

"Sal, God's truth, I don't see how one thing links to another."

"They still don't know who killed Billy Jean." Just saying it had Sal's eyes going damp. "Nobody even talks about it anymore, hardly at all."

"We haven't forgotten her. You know that. What

happened yesterday, it was something else. Just mean stupidity."

"You know who."

"I think who, and that's different."

"I didn't even ask if Cal's all right." Sal rubbed her eyes. "And that horse. Everybody loves that horse."

"They're healing up."

"Good. Okay. How about if I do a pool, come up with some silly get-well gift from everybody?"

"I think that would be a great idea." ·

She'd barely settled behind her desk, trying to formulate a replacement for Sundown's performance, when Chelsea and Jessica came in together.

"I swear men talk more than women. Rory told you, Chase told you."

Jessica had enough presence of mind to shut the door. "They got shot!"

"They did, but it's the classic flesh wound. I'm not going to minimize it," she added quickly. "It scared the crap out of all of us, and a few inches different, it'd be more than scared. But they're both going to be okay. I'm not sure I can block Callen from coming to work tomorrow the way I did today."

"Rory said Garrett Clintok did it."

Bodine raised her eyebrows at Chelsea. "Rory needs to be careful accusing anybody."

"Then so does Chase," Jessica put in. "I've never seen him like that. So angry, so cold, hard angry. And he had plenty to say about Clintok going after Cal now, and back when they were boys."

"Let's keep that opinion, which I completely share, from running all over the resort."

"Is Sundown really okay? I mean Cal, too," Chelsea qualified. "It's just . . ."

"I know. And he is. He's hurt, but he's healing. It's going to be a little while before he can come back to work here. Which is another problem. I need to come up with something to replace his show. I know that's part of the weekend agenda."

"Hell." Jessica tapped a finger to her temple. "Went straight out of my head. We can just say the horse isn't well. I can come up with something. Let me think about replacing that program."

"Actually, I was thinking."

Jessica put an arm around Chelsea's waist. "Didn't I tell you, this girl's always thinking? Let's hear it."

"Well, Carol does barrel racing. Easy and Ben have both done rodeoing. It'd be a scramble for today, but I bet they can put something together."

"That's good. Chase does some fancy rope work."

"He does?"

Bodine smiled at Jessica. "I'm surprised he hasn't lassoed you yet. He'll make excuses, but I'll have Mom put the pressure on there. If the others agree—and we've got Thad at the ranch who's done the rodeo—we can put together an hour to fill the gap, keep your family reunion happy."

"I'll head down to the BAC, lay out the plan."

"You've got a meeting in five minutes," Chelsea reminded Jessica. "And you wanted to talk to the kitchen about today's lunch. I'll run down. I can have the program written up in about an hour."

"Don't ever leave me," Jessica told her.

Jessica's faith in her always gave Chelsea a boost. She loved the work, the people, the place. And really loved having someone she admired give her opportunities to create, even take charge.

Still formulating how to pitch the alternate program, she drove to the BAC. If time wasn't so tight, she'd have loved the walk. To her mind, nothing beat spring in Montana.

Halfway there, one of the maintenance trucks hailed her. The driver leaned out.

"I heard somebody shot Cal Skinner's horse right out from under him!"

Chelsea repeated the basic line Bodine had given her before she'd left the office. "They're okay. Somebody was shooting, and they were both grazed, but they're okay."

"I heard that horse had to be put down."

"Oh, no. The vet already fixed him up. He just needs a couple days off."

The guy—what was his name? . . . Vance!—gave her a beady eye. "You sure about that, girl?"

"I talked to Rory, and to Bodine just a minute ago. We're even doing a donation pool to get Sundown a get-well gift."

"Who's got that going? Sal?"

"That's right."

"I'll put my money in that. Damn good horse. People oughtn't to go around shooting unless they know what the hell they're aiming at. Buncha greenhorn dentists from back East. Bet that's what it was. You have a good one, girl."

"You, too."

She drove on wishing it had been some greenhorn. But Rory, spitting mad, had been sure about Clintok. And sure it had been deliberate.

As upsetting as it was, she didn't see Rory being that wrong.

She pulled up, saw Easy leading a couple of horses to the near paddock.

"Hey, Easy."

"Hey there, Chelsea."

"Is Ben around?"

"Just went in to get us a couple Cokes."

"How about Carol?"

"Early trail ride. She'll be back in . . ." He looked up, squinted, gauged the angle of the sun. "Oh, about a half hour maybe. Something I can do for you?"

"Yeah, actually. You, Ben, Carol. We need to replace Sundown and Cal's program this afternoon."

"Cal take sick? Got a text from the big boss asking if I'd come in today. Just figured we were extra busy."

"You haven't heard?"

He tethered the horses, turned. "Heard what?"

"Well, you're going to hear, and the story's getting bigger so it's better to hear it straight. Somebody was up in the woods above Black Angus Road yesterday, and took a shot. Cal and Sundown were both hit."

"What?" He grabbed her arm. "Shot?"

"Wait. I should've said 'grazed.' Both of them were grazed and they're going to be fine."

"Jesus H. Christ. How bad? Cal's a damn good boss, and that horse is something special."

"Grazed Cal's leg, Sundown's belly."

Easy's face hardened. "It was that damn deputy."

He'd released her arm, and now Chelsea took his. "Why do you say that?"

"I was right here when he came after Cal the one time. Went at him hard, too. And I saw him riding around on an ATV yesterday when I was bringing in a trail ride. Out of uniform, like, but I knew who he was. Didn't see he had any business on resort property, but I had guests in line and couldn't go after him to say so."

"You saw him," Chelsea repeated, "on property, on an ATV?"

"I did. About four, I'd say. Right around then."

"You might need to tell the sheriff."

"I sure as hell will if it means anything."

"And maybe nobody else right now? Bodine wants to keep it from getting, well, too hot."

"I'm feeling pretty hot. That's bushwhacking. Shooting a horse," Easy muttered, stroking the bay mare. "What kind of son of a bitch does that?"

"A heartless one, I think."

He looked back at her. "Me, too."

"I've got to get back, but we could really use your help this afternoon."

"You got it. I'm mad enough to spit."

"The program," she began, explaining what they had in mind.

"It'll be fun. We'll put that together, you bet. I'll talk to Ben and Carol. I don't know Chase so much, or this other one."

"We've got that. If you could figure out what you'd do, who goes when, that kind of thing. And if there's anything you'd need. If you could do that by noon, I think we could pull this off."

"Then that's what we'll do. I'm right pleased to be part of it."

"Great. I've got to get back and start working on it."

He looked over as Ben came running, shouting as he did.

"Holy shit! Holy shit, somebody shot Cal and Sundown!"

Easy tipped his hat back. "Go on ahead. I'll tell him."

"Not about Clintok, okay? Not yet."

Easy winked, put a finger to his lips. He admired the way she looked walking away, then shifted to the breathless Ben.

"Hold on, Ben. I've got the full story."

CHAPTER TWENTY-FIVE

Easy puzzled on what to do. He'd never had so much on his plate at one time and, along with Ben, was almost, sort of, in charge of things.

He had to load up the horses for the lesson down at the center, cull out more for another trail ride, and figure out how to put on a show.

He liked the show part of things, the fun of it, the being back in front of people like during his rodeo time.

And he had to think about Cal. He sure liked Cal—there was a man who knew horses and men and how to keep things running smooth. Somebody had shot at his boss, and that was bad enough. But that somebody had shot at a damn fine horse, too, and that couldn't be borne.

The fact he'd likely seen that somebody, knew that somebody made him proud. And made him plenty nervous along with it.

That pretty Chelsea said he needed to talk to the sheriff about it, and Ben said just the same. So he guessed he had to do that. He just didn't know how to go about it, especially with all the work and the show.

He sure didn't know how to go about being in charge.

He didn't know whether to feel relief or worry when Chase Longbow rode up, leading a second horse. Ben took the lead there, rushing right up before Chase had so much as dismounted.

"Have you seen Cal? Cal's really okay? How's Sundown?"

"They're both doing fine. Doc Bickers was giving them both another look when I left. Word is you boys have your hands full here, and my sister's signed us up for some damn show later today. I can give you a hand for now, and Thad and Zeke'll be along later."

"You going to do some fancy rope tricks?"

Chase patted the rope coiled over his saddlebag. "Looks like. When's the next trail ride?"

"Carol's out now," Easy told him. "She'll be back any minute. I'm signed for the next one. Ten o'clock. Ah, Maddie's giving a lesson down at the center, so we need to load up two horses for that."

"Well, let's get to it."

"Wait. Wait. Tell him, Easy," Ben insisted. "You gotta tell Chase about Clintok."

Chase's eyes went from friendly to hard—like an ice-ball hard—and had Easy gulping down spit. "What about Clintok?"

"Um . . ."

"Easy saw him, Chase, saw him riding on his ATV yesterday."

Chase walked the horses over to loop reins around a post, turned. "When? Where?"

"It was—"

"Let him tell me."

Clamping his lips, Ben gave Easy an elbow poke.

"Well, you see, I had a group out on the trail, and I saw

him—that deputy—over on the Bear Paw Road. I was leading the group down the Elk Trail when he went by below."

"When?"

"Had to be about four."

"You're sure it was him? Sure it was Clintok?"

"Yeah, I'm sure on it. He had goggles on, but wasn't wearing a helmet. He came around here once going hard at Cal, so I recognized him right off."

"How about the group you were with? Did any of them see him?"

"Well, yeah, they hadta." Easy paused, scratched at the back of his neck, adjusted his hat. "The lady right behind me even said something about riding the ATV and not wearing a helmet. Asked weren't they required 'cause her sons signed up to ride on the ghost town trip tomorrow. Well, today that would be now, as this was yesterday we were talking."

"Do you remember her name?"

"No, not right off. But they were all with that big group that's here. That big family group that's keeping us all hopping."

"Okay. Hold on a minute."

"Here comes Carol and her group," Ben said.

"You go on give her a hand with them, Ben. You hold on here, Easy."

Chase pulled out his phone. "Bodine, I need you to see who Easy had out on the trail yesterday about four. Just look it up, tell me if that group's still here. Do I sound like I care how busy you are?"

Easy shifted his feet, cleared his throat, looked longingly at Ben and Carol.

"All right," Chase said after a minute. "We're going to have to shift around Easy's schedule some. Shut up a damn minute," he snapped. "He saw Clintok on an ATV yesterday afternoon, riding on Bear Paw. That's what I said. You track down that group of people, just get a handle on where they might be. I'll take care of this. Well, Jesus, Bo, of course we're calling Tate. I'll let you know."

"We sure got a lot to do around here," Easy began when Chase lowered his phone.

"That's right. And now you're calling Sheriff Tate. If he can't come here and talk to you, you're going to go to him. We'll cover you."

"Holy cow," Easy said under his breath. "Do I call the nine-one-one?"

"No need." Chase scrolled through his phone for Tate's contact number he'd added in after Billy Jean's murder. "Use mine."

"I don't know what to say or how to say it right. I never did this before."

"Tell him who you are, and what you told me."

"Okay." Easy let out a breath, tapped the contact. "Ah, Sheriff Tate? This is Easy—that is Esau LaFoy. I work with the horses at the Bodine Resort? Chase—ah, Mr. Longbow said I needed to call you up, tell you what I told him just now."

Before he'd finished, Bodine drove up in one of the little cars. Easy's palms were damp by the time he handed the phone back to Chase.

"You're sure?" Bodine asked without preamble.

"Yes, ma'am, I surely am. The sheriff's coming to talk to me, says I should stay put here until he does, but I've got a trail ride, and—"

"We'll cover you. The group with you saw him, too?"

"Had to. I held them up for a minute—well, not half a minute, I guess, while he rode by below."

She nodded, looked at her brother. Her eyes weren't

ice-ball hard, Easy noted. They were fireball hot. "They're all part of the weekend event. Two are headed to Garnet on the ATV ride, one's on the cattle drive, and two are booked into Zen Town. If Tate needs more than Easy's word, he can talk to them."

She checked the time, drew a breath. "All right. Easy, you see to the horses that just came back from the trail. Carol can transport the horses down to the center for the lesson coming up. Ben can take your guided ride."

"We got another going out just about the time that one gets back."

"I'll take it," Chase said, without much enthusiasm. "If you're not finished with Tate, I'll take the ride."

"You want that show about three o'clock, so—"

Bodine shoved a hand through her hair, realized she'd forgotten her hat. "Here's what we do about that."

She laid it out fast, complete, in a way that left Easy breathless and impressed. He couldn't for the life of him figure how anybody thought so quick.

"And the pony rides," she continued, ticking down the list. "I can call in the grannies if we need more hands. I can clear my load, if we need, take one of the afternoon rides. You do whatever the sheriff says you need to do."

Easy scratched the side of his neck. "Yes, ma'am."

"We're grateful, Easy." She gave his arm a pat. "This is important."

She debated whether to contact Callen, considered it while she helped saddle the next group of horses. Decided if she'd been left hobbling around and tending to a beloved horse and he didn't tell her right away, she'd skin his ass.

Before she could, Tate pulled up. She made her way back as he headed to Easy.

"Bodine, Easy."

"You got here quick," Bodine commented.

"I was down on Black Angus Road with Curtis. You know Curtis Bowie?"

"Sure."

"He's down there now, taking some pictures. So, Easy, let's just start here. How about you tell me what this ATV you saw looked like?"

"Okay, sure. Wasn't one of ours anyways. It was smaller, one of them sporty ones like. Done up in camo paint. I didn't pay much more mind than that."

Tate nodded. Though he wore dark glasses that shielded his eyes, Bodine read resignation in his body language.

"Bodine, you got a private place nearby where Easy and I can talk?"

"I'll take you down to the back office in the BAC."

"That'll do." As they walked he glanced over at her. "The group Easy here was leading, they're all here?"

"Yes. Two are in Zen Town, and should be finished there in about a half hour. The others won't be back until afternoon, but I can give you their basic locations if you need."

"I'll let you know. How about you text me their names to start?"

"I'll do that right away."

She led the way in, skirted around the desk, the staff, the guests, and into the little office. "Anything I can get you?"

While Tate shook his head, Bodine studied Easy. He looked like a kid called to the principal's office. "You want a Coke, Easy?"

"I sure wouldn't mind one. Throat's feeling pretty dry right now."

"I'm going to get you a couple of Cokes, then get out of your way."

She gave Matt at the desk a look that said: Don't ask.

She got the Cokes from the vending machine, delivered them, shut the door. And got out before anyone could corner her with questions.

She shouldn't take the time, she told herself. She didn't *have* the time. But she got into the resort car, and took the shortest route to the ranch.

She went straight to the stables, grateful everyone was too busy to get in her way.

Sundown stood in his stall looking unhappy. He perked up when he saw her, poked his head out as far as it could reach.

"Where's your guy, huh? Is he as bored as you are?" She heard noises—scraping, jingling—glanced around. "He's back there? I'll go take a look."

When she reached the tack room, she saw Callen gathering up bridles, cinches, head collars. He looked as bored as his horse.

"Aren't you supposed to stay off that leg?"

"It's healing up, and I'm getting off it again in a minute. I can work on some tack, but if I work back here, Sundown's going to sulk."

"He's already sulking."

"See?"

"All right, I'll give you a hand. We'll set you up a workstation. You ought to leave his door open if you're going to be right there. It'll make him feel less confined."

"Good idea. What are you doing back here?"

"We'll get to that in a minute."

Together they dragged out a small table, a taller stool, a bucket of water, cloths, sponges, brushes, oils.

"What did Bickers say?"

"Healing clean. She doesn't want a saddle or anybody up on him for at least another week, and not until she clears it. But I can take him out, walk him around some. Already did. I got her list of dos and don'ts, and she'll come by again tomorrow."

"How about the two-legged stud?"

At least that got a fleeting smile out of him. "Pretty much the same as Sundown. I can go back to work Monday, maybe tomorrow for a few hours. She expects me not to be stupid and make her regret clearing that, and agreeing I don't need a people doctor. Now, did you come back just to see if we were being stupid?"

"No. Go on and sit down. You were limping more on that last haul. Tate's over at the BAC talking to Easy."

"Easy? About what?"

"About seeing Clintok riding his ATV yesterday, about an hour before you and Sundown were shot. Riding along Bear Paw."

"Is that so?" He said it slowly, coolly. But his eyes flashed hot blue under the storm gray. "How did Easy know it was Clintok?"

Staying steady, Bodine thought. For now. "He recognized him—goggles, no helmet. And the sheriff asked him to describe the ATV. I don't know Clintok's ATV, but I bet the sheriff does. Smaller than what we use, and a camo design. Easy was leading a trail ride. The guests saw him, too, and Tate, I expect, will talk to them, do the corroboration."

"Looks like I owe Easy more than a beer," Callen said, and began to take a bridle apart for cleaning.

"Curtis—that would be Deputy Curtis Bowie, you might remember him—is taking pictures where it happened. I can't say, but I think I know Tate well enough to speculate he's already talked to Clintok, and got a denial. But now there are witnesses who put Clintok on resort property, and in an area that leads up to where it makes good sense for sniping down on a horse and rider on Black Angus."

Nodding, as if they discussed casual dinner plans, Callen hung the bridle from a hook, began cleaning it with a clean, damp cloth. "It might be enough."

"I'd put money it's enough for Tate to fire him, and I hope it's enough to arrest him. I can say, because I know you well enough, if he's not behind bars you'll handle him yourself."

Callen said nothing, just kept cleaning tack.

"I'm going to ask you for one thing. Just one."

"I can try to give it to you."

"When you go to handle him, you tell me. I'll keep a beer cold for when you get back."

Setting the cloth down, Callen looked up now. "I've got a powerful feeling for you, Bodine. Knocks me sideways about half the time."

"It could be getting shot in the leg that does that."

"Nope." After moistening the saddle soap, wetting a sponge, he rubbed some into a light lather. "Want to go out to a fancy dinner?"

She started to push back her hat, then remembered she wasn't wearing it. "You're going from kicking the shit out of Clintok to fancy dinners?"

"I'm not much for them myself, but I find I want to see how I like having one with you." As he had with the cloth, Callen patiently, thoroughly soaped the leather. "Get all dressed up, maybe order some snooty French wine." His gaze flicked up to hers. "You wanna do that?"

"I've never been much for fancy dinners, either, but I wouldn't mind trying one with you. Once you're all the way healed up."

"That's a deal. If—all right, when—I decide to go after Clintok, I'll tell you."

Satisfied on all counts, Bodine squeezed his shoulder, gave Sundown a quick rub. "I've got to get back. Do you want me to have somebody bring you a cold drink?"

"I've got an invitation to lunch at the big house. We're fine till then."

He kept cleaning tack when she left, methodically, while Sundown watched.

"They might put him behind bars. They might put him behind them long enough to square it for us. If not, well, I'll square it for us." He reached up, rubbed Sundown's cheek. "That's a promise."

Tate got his statements, got his pictures, and however heavy it sat on him, accepted his duty.

He drove to Clintok's, the cabin tucked away on his family's ranch. Clintok's truck and ATV sat under an open shelter attached to the cabin, just as they'd been when Tate had gone by the night before.

And just as he had the night before, Clintok stepped out of the cabin onto the narrow porch.

He wore sweatpants, a sweatshirt ripped off at the elbows, and a skin of sweat. Tate concluded he'd been pumping iron for a while, one of Clintok's favorite pastimes.

"Garrett."

"Sheriff. Curtis," he added when the deputy got out the passenger door. "What can I do for you?"

"Well, Garrett, it's like this. You have the right to remain silent—"

"What the hell bullshit is this?"

Tate just continued reading off the Miranda warning.

"We all know you understand your rights, but do you want to confirm that?"

"Fuck you."

When Clintok turned away, yanked open the cabin door, Curtis moved in. "Come on now, Garrett, don't go making it harder than it is."

He made it harder by slamming a fist into Curtis's jaw. Cursing, Tate surged forward to help Curtis muscle Clintok to the ground.

"You're under goddamn arrest," Tate snapped. "Get those cuffs on him, Curtis, goddamn it. Resisting arrest, striking a police officer."

"I *am* a police officer."

"Not anymore you're not. You're under arrest for discharging a firearm on private property, and for attempted murder."

"You're out of your fucking mind."

"I got witnesses, for Christ's sake." Together they dragged Clintok to his feet. "I'm adding lying to a police officer to the list. When I came by here yesterday you said you hadn't had that ATV out in a week. And it was as clean as a whistle. Just washed clean. I've got witnesses, damn it to hell and back, Garrett, who saw you riding it on the resort, saw you heading it up on the road above Black Angus."

"Skinner's a goddamn liar."

"Six people saw you. Six. And we got the bullet Bickers dug out of that horse." That was a lie, but Tate was done with playing fair. "When we test your long guns, get ballistics done, what do you think we're going to find?"

He saw it, the panic, the flush of fury, the quick cut away of the eyes. "I want a lawyer. I want a lawyer now. I've got nothing to say."

"You'll get a lawyer. Get him in the back, Curtis. I can't

even look at him. One of my men, one of my own, trying to backshoot a man like that."

The accusation had Clintok kicking out, elbow jabbing. "Skinner killed those two women, and you do *nothing*. He kills them, and you suspend me for dogging him for it. He deserved having his horse shot out from under him. He deserved worse."

Tate's face looked like a mask of fury carved in stone before he shoved Clintok back against the truck. "You were aiming for the horse? Is that what you're claiming now?"

"You did nothing."

"I'm doing something now."

It tore up his gut, questioning one of his deputies—former—dealing with the pip-squeak of a lawyer. It didn't help the knotting and twisting that Clintok proved pitifully simple to trip up.

Maybe it soothed some to stand in the Longbows' kitchen and watch out the window as Alice carefully led the recovering horse around the paddock with Callen limping by her side.

"Her progress is really remarkable." Celia Minnow watched with him.

"Is she going to remember more about the captivity?"

"I wish I could tell you. I can tell you she's stronger, mind and body. I can tell you she seems to have forged a bond with him—with Callen Skinner. It's the horse in part. But it's also him. He left home, came back. So did she. Someone hurt him. Someone hurt her. Being here, surrounded by family, has helped give her a sense of safety, helped her throw off a lot of the indoctrination."

"But I still need to let her tell me as it comes to her."

"She has a lot of trust in you. Pushing too hard for answers could damage that. I know it's frustrating."

"I'm wondering if he's dead, and that's how she got away."

"If you're wondering if she caused his death, my opinion is she wouldn't have been capable. He dominated, she submitted. She speaks of him as alive. Her thought pattern often simplifies everything, as a child's would. It's coping. There's good and bad, mean and kind, soft and hard. And other times she's remarkably astute."

Celia gestured toward the window. "Cutting her hair? The courage of that, the symbolism of it? It was an act of self—recognition of self.

"She may slip back again, and everyone should prepare for that. But she's making good progress."

"I'm going to go out, talk to her, while she's with Cal and the horse. I'll keep it light and friendly."

Callen figured she'd have walked Sundown to Billings and back, and been happy about it. His own leg ached like a bitch, and he could only blame himself for skipping the afternoon Motrin. But he couldn't bring himself to ask her to stop.

"Can I braid his mane?"

"Ah . . ." Callen chanced a look back at Sundown, calculated the humiliation.

"I used to braid Venus's mane. And bring her carrots. I can bring him a carrot." Suddenly she stopped, looked around. "Where's Venus?"

"I don't know. Is that your horse?"

"She's mine. Grandpa let me pick her out. Pretty Venus. She's a buckskin, too, with a black mane and tail. And . . . that was a long time ago. I forget. It was a long time ago. She must have died like Grandpa when I was in the cellar or in the house. She must have died when I wasn't here."

"I had a horse before Sundown. I called him Charger. It was real hard for me when he died."

"But Sundown's getting better. He won't die."

"He's getting better."

"He's getting better," she repeated and began to walk. "When he's stronger, I can sit on him?"

"As soon as the doctor says."

"I talked to my doctor today, too. Both my doctors, the man and the woman. They said I was getting better, too. There's Tate. Bobby Tate. I know him. He's not mean."

"I know him, too."

"Alice Bodine," Tate said with a cheerful smile. "I sure like your hair."

"Bodine did it. That's her first name, that's my last name. This is Sundown. Somebody hurt him and Cal, but they're feeling better."

"So I see."

"You're the sheriff now. Bobby Tate's the sheriff. You have to find people who hurt people."

Tate nodded, took a chance. "You're right. I did find the person who hurt Sundown and Cal. I put him in jail."

Her eyes widened. "Does he have to stay there? Locked up? It's hard to be locked up. You can't get out. Nobody comes to let you out or hears when you scream." She pressed her face into Sundown's neck. "I didn't hurt anybody."

"No, you didn't, honey. But this man did, so the law has to decide what to do about it."

"You're the law. Bobby Tate's the law. Did you find Sir? Did you put him in jail?"

"I sure want to. I'm trying to."

She angled her head around again. "We used to kiss, didn't we?"

"We did."

"You don't kiss me now."

"Well, I got married." Tate tapped his wedding ring. "But before we kissed, after, too, we were friends. We are friends, Alice."

"Sir didn't kiss me. I didn't want him to, but he would have no matter that. But he didn't. We did other things. You did other things with me."

Tate cleared his throat as Callen looked discreetly away. "Well, yeah, we did."

"But you weren't mean. You weren't hurting. We laughed and laughed, and you walked on your hands. Sir doesn't laugh. He hurts. His hands are hard and mean, and he rapes me. Dr. Minnow says it's rape, not marital rights. He rapes me so it hurts, always." The words tumbled out, the pitch rising. "It's rape, Dr. Minnow says, even when I don't fight. If I fight he hits me and hits me and it's worse. Even when I just laid down and let him, she says it's raping. Is that the law? Is it? You're the law, is it the law?"

"It is. It's the law."

"If you find him, you'll lock him up? I want that." She surprised Callen by reaching out, gripping his hand. "I want him locked up where he can't get out, where nobody comes when he screams. I want that."

"I'm going to keep looking so that happens. I promise you, Alice. You said he had a beard all over, and dark eyes."

"Dark eyes. I close mine when he does it."

"Maybe you could tell me more about how he looks and we could draw him."

"I can't draw. Reenie can't, either. Even I can draw better, but I can't draw faces."

"I know somebody who can draw faces, if you want to try to tell me more of how he looks. How you remember."

"I don't know." Her hand tightened, a small vise, on Callen's. "I don't want to see his face. I'm going to make Cal a scarf. I'm going to ride Sundown when he's better."

"That's okay." Swallowing frustration, Tate kept his tone easy. "It's too pretty a day to worry about things. Maybe I'll come see you tomorrow, Alice, just to visit."

She nodded at Tate, then looked at Cal. "What would you do? You went away, you came back. Somebody hurt you and Sundown. Would you see his face so they could draw it?"

"I think sometimes if you look at something straight on, look it right in the eye, it doesn't seem as scary as it does when you close your eyes. And I think you're about the bravest person I know, so if you need more time with your eyes closed, you should take it."

"Bodine said I was brave, the doctor said I was brave. You said I'm brave, but I don't feel brave. I don't want to go back to the house, I don't want him to find me. I want to stay here. Can you come tomorrow," she said to Tate, "ask me again?"

"I sure can. It's good to see you, Alice. And you, Cal."

Callen hesitated as Tate started off. "Miss Alice, could you watch Sundown for a minute? I need to ask the sheriff something."

"We'll be right here."

Callen caught up with Tate at the gate. "Did he admit it?"

Tate leaned back against the gate. "He's changed his story half a dozen times. That hot head of his isn't helping him. Neither is lying to me about being on the property on that ATV—and he knows he's caught there. He's slipped up plenty, and trying to stick to shooting at a snake, not realizing the shot went wild and hit you and the horse. That won't hold. But in one of his slips, I think I got the truth. He wasn't shooting at you."

"Now, that's bullshit."

"He was shooting at your horse."

Callen rocked back on his heels, waited for his temper to peak and ebb. "He aimed at Sundown?"

"I'm going to say that's my opinion. I'm going to say it comes down to a goddamn dog and a goddamn poker game when you were kids. His father lost a dog to yours, and Garrett shot the dog out of spite. He was trying to kill your horse for the same reason. Pure spite."

Callen looked back to where Alice walked Sundown and chattered away to him. And could see it, see that wound across the belly, and how a few inches higher would have done the job.

"You'll take him down for it."

"That's going to be up to the prosecutor, the judge, and the jury. But I'll tell you, I'm going back at him, and I'll get him to say what he did. That I will do."

"All right."

"What you said to Alice, it's going to help me do my job for her, too. I'll do my job, Cal."

Cal nodded, but as he walked back to his horse he thought, sometimes, justice didn't have a damn thing to do with jobs.

CHAPTER TWENTY-SIX

By Sunday evening, with the crazy weekend behind her, Jessica drove to the ranch. Though just sleeping for a solid twelve hours held a lot of appeal, the invitation to Sunday dinner swayed her.

She enjoyed seeing Chase in his natural habitat, and had yet to connect with Callen since he and Sundown had been hurt. She accepted her Western transition as complete when she realized she wanted to see the horse as much as the people.

The transition didn't, and likely never would, include footwear. When she saw Sundown in the paddock and, to her delight, Chase spinning a rope—lariat, she corrected—she left the huckleberry crumble, which she'd made, in the car and walked over to watch.

Rory sat on the fence beside a woman with red hair pulled into a short tail. The woman clapped enthusiastically when Chase jumped in and out of the spinning rope.

When Chase gave Jessica a tip of the hat with his free hand, the woman glanced back. Though she'd heard about it, seeing Alice's transformation left her stunned.

"This is someone else," Alice murmured and reached for Rory's hand.

"You might not remember me, Alice. We only met for a minute a few weeks ago. I'm Jessica Baazov. I work for Bodine."

"Bodine's Reenie's girl. This is Rory. Not my Rory. He's Reenie's Rory. And Chase is Reenie's. He's putting on a show for me because I didn't get to see it."

"He's really good, isn't he?"

"Uncle Wayne did rope tricks. Chase said Uncle Wayne taught him. Sundown does tricks, too. Cal taught him. Cal's not just Reenie's. He's mine, too."

"I wanted to see Sundown and Cal."

"Grammy fussed at Cal and said he had to go in and put his leg up awhile. In a couple days I can sit on Sundown. He's much better, and the man who hurt him's locked up." Alice looked at Rory for confirmation. "He's locked up?"

"That's right. We don't have to worry about him anymore."

"Bobby Tate does his job." Alice applauded again as Chase took a bow. "It was a good show," she told him. "Jessica's here. I remember now. She's your girlfriend."

Chase lowered his head, concentrated on coiling the rope. "It's looking that way."

"He's shy," Alice told Jessica. "I never used to be shy, but I feel that way a lot now. We'll go help with dinner." Alice patted Rory's arm. "So Chase can be with his girlfriend."

Barely blocking a snicker, Rory hopped down, lifted Alice off the fence.

"I like your shoes," Alice said.

Jessica barely managed a "Thanks" before Alice

walked away with Rory. "I can't believe that's the same woman who came home from the hospital."

"It's spine." Chase looped his rope around a fence post. "That's Bodine spine. Dad told me she's going to work with an artist tomorrow, agreed to it, to try to get a picture of the man who took her."

He reached over the fence for her hand, tugged her so she climbed on the bottom rail. "Fancy shoes. Not for riding."

"I dressed for Sunday dinner." Then she laughed when Sundown moved up behind him, nudged him forward. "He's definitely himself again."

"Go on now, I don't need any help." To prove it, Chase cupped the back of Jessica's neck with one hand, lowered his mouth to hers.

Then he just stood there a moment, eyes on hers, fingers lightly rubbing her skin.

"Riding's out." He vaulted over the fence. "But we can take a walk."

"I haven't even gone in to say hello to your mother."

"Couple of minutes."

With her hand in his, the sun warm on her face, she walked with him.

She heard a cow lowing off in a field, and a chittering she knew came from some busy squirrel. And through an open kitchen window came laughter.

"You've put pansies in." She paused a moment, looking at the pots on the back porch steps. "My grandmother always put pansies in early, in the window box outside the kitchen window. She said they made her smile while she did dishes. Made her happy spring was coming around again."

"I didn't think you'd stay through the winter."

Genuinely surprised, she stared up at him. "Why?"

"I figure now it was my problem more than yours." He drew her around the front side of the house, and to the bench between the ginkgo trees. "I thought, just look at her, she'll run back to New York after her first Montana blizzard. But you didn't."

"You really saw me as that . . ." What was the word he'd used for Alice? *Spine*. "That spineless?"

"No. That was mostly me, and it wasn't my spine I was worried about. Can we sit a minute? I feel like I've got to finish this out."

"Yeah, maybe you should."

"Jessica. I'd say I saw you as this exotic bird. So pretty it hurt my eyes, and just out of my reach. Apt to fly off."

"Exotic bird, my *butt*. I've worked all my life, and worked hard. I—"

"More about me than you," he reminded her. "The first time I saw you, you were wearing a red suit, and your hair was coiled up, and you smelled like something mysterious blooming in a hothouse. You shook my hand, and said: 'Jessica Baazov, it's nice to meet you.' I could barely get my tongue to work. And all I could think was I hope like hell Bo doesn't hire this one."

"Well. That's nice to know."

He just put a hand heavy on her shoulder when she started to get up. "I told her it was a mistake when she did, and I've come around to seeing that was a lot more about me than you."

In a defensive gesture, she folded her arms under her breasts. "If you'd taken such an instant dislike to me, I'm surprised you didn't put a lot more pressure on Bodine."

"It wasn't dislike, and pressuring Bodine when her mind's made up's a waste of time. Taking your time's not wasting it."

And he took his time now.

"I thought it was a mistake, believed it was because I didn't see you staying. So pretty, so polished, I didn't see how you'd fit in. And since I was damn near struck deaf, dumb, and blind the first time I saw you in that red suit, it didn't bode well for me. I figured to keep my distance until Bo came home and said how I was right and you were leaving."

"Apparently you've been disappointed there."

"No, just wrong. I kept my distance as best I could because every time I saw you I wanted to touch you. And I knew if I touched you I'd want more. I knew when you left—even keeping my distance—I'd think of you. I wasn't going to cross that line. Then, well, I did."

She audibly sniffed, but softened. "I yanked you across that line."

"I was working my way across. It would've taken me longer, but I was working my way across. Then I knew, if you left I wouldn't just think of you. I'd never get over you. Any woman who came along after, I would put up against you—and she'd never measure up. She wouldn't have your face, or be as smart as you, have your grit under all that polish. There'd be nobody else."

He tugged her hand into his, studied it. "And I want a woman, and a family, a life we can grow into. I don't mind waiting for it, but without you, I'd wait forever."

"I . . . I watched *Tombstone*. I can ride a horse. I have a Stetson."

His lips curved as he pressed them to her fist. "I love you. I think I loved you before any of those things were true if love can hit that fast. I love knowing they're true now. I feel settled knowing you're happy here."

"I am happy here. There's nothing for me back in New York. I've built my life here. Friends, work, a life. I lost my family, Chase, when I lost my grandparents. And I've made a family here when I never thought to have one again. I've never had a friend like Bodine, and now Chelsea. And . . . everyone."

"I'm asking if you'd think about building onto that with me. If you could come to love me enough for that. For making a life and a family with me."

Marriage, good God, he was talking about marriage. The fast leap from a slow-moving man left her dumbfounded.

Sitting very still, barely breathing, she thought of her parents on one side. Selfish, careless, cold, abandoning her without a second thought. Then her grandparents. Kind, loving, giving, enfolding her into their lives without a second thought.

Then she thought of him.

"I don't know how I could love somebody so stupid he can't see I already love him more than enough already. But apparently I do."

Now he held her hand to his cheek, just held it there, before turning his head, pressing his lips into her palm. "Is that a fancy way of saying yes?"

"It wasn't fancy."

"It was a lot of words. How about I put it another way? Will you marry me sometime?"

"'Sometime' is pretty open-ended."

"You say yes. You say when."

"Give me a second." She looked out, over the land, to the mountains, to the sky that spread blue over everything. She felt him waiting, so steady and strong in his silence. She trusted him to wait until her head caught up with her heart.

"I say yes. I say October. After my first summer, before my next winter." Again, she laid a hand on his cheek.

"And saying yes, Chase, just saying yes, fills up little spaces in me I didn't know needed to be filled. You did that. You helped fill those little empty spaces."

He kissed her, sweet as a promise, held her close.

"You still got that red suit?"

"I'm not getting married in that red suit."

"I was thinking more of the honeymoon."

She laughed. Steady and strong, she thought again. And often surprising. "I've still got it."

While at the Bodine Ranch Sunday dinner turned into a celebration, the man known as Sir bumped his truck along the narrow road where winter had carved pits and shallow ditches. Every jolt rammed through his body.

He stopped, climbed out to unlock the gate posted with No Trespassing signs. The old metal shrieked as he shoved it open. He climbed back into the truck, drove through across the old cattle gate, got out again, dragged the gate closed, locked it, chained it.

A coughing fit seized him until he had to brace himself on the gate. He coughed up and spat out phlegm, caught his breath, then climbed back into the truck to jolt and bump his way back to the cabin.

Since he had to stop and rest often, it took him an hour to unload the supplies. He downed medicine first, the cough suppressant, the headache pills—he always seemed to have a headache these days—the decongestant, mixing them together in a kind of medicinal cocktail, downing them with the whisky-laced coffee he considered another element of his cure.

He'd picked up a meal, ate the two cheeseburgers slowly and without real appetite. He needed meat, good red meat, and forced it down bite by bite.

Breathing, wheezing, and whistling, he fell asleep in

the chair in front of the fire as the sweat slicking his skin went cold. He woke in the dark.

Cursing, he lit the oil lamps, got the fire going again.

He spent too much time sleeping, and needed to spend more planning.

He'd driven all the way to Missoula and back, proving to himself he was recovering from the damn plague Esther had cursed him with. He'd gotten medicine and supplies, even managed some scouting around.

He'd seen plenty of women. Women showing their bare legs, women with their breasts rising up under low tops. Their faces painted.

He'd thought one or two of them might suit him, might make a good wife once he broke them. But he lacked the strength—as yet—to take one.

So he'd take the medicine, eat red meat, and get his strength back. When he had, he'd hunt the back roads, haunt the dark places outside the dens of sin. The bars and cheap motels.

The right one would come along. God would provide.

Not another like Esther. Or the one he'd christened Miriam, who'd managed to hang herself with her bedsheet weeks after delivering a girl child.

Or Judith or Beryl.

He'd buried them all, all but Esther. Given them Christian burials, though they'd been sinners. Been disappointments.

He had to find another quickly. A strong, young, fertile woman, one who could be trained to obey. And to tend to him, as his illness had shown him he was no longer young.

He needed sons to carry on his legacy, to honor him as he aged. And he needed the woman to provide them.

The tourists would come soon—those parasites—they'd come, as would those needed to make their meals, make their beds. As he drifted to sleep again, he thought the coming weeks would offer opportunities.

Callen would rather have ridden horseback to work, and he sure as hell would rather have ridden Sundown. Since neither made a spot on the plate, he rode shotgun in Bodine's truck.

"I could've come in with Rory."

She spared him a glance. "Something wrong with my driving, Skinner?"

"I'd rather be behind the wheel."

"Take what you get." But she glanced again. "What's bothering you? The leg?"

"Christ, it got grazed. I didn't get gut shot."

She jerked her shoulder, maintained silence until she pulled up at the BAC. "Out, and take your crappy mood with you."

He sat another moment. "I've spent a lot of time with Alice the last few days."

"It's noted and appreciated."

"Careful you don't smack your head on a tree branch riding that high horse with your nose pointed at the sky. I liked the time with her—it took my mind off other things. And I feel like she got to trust me. I'm not going to be around today when she tries working with Tate and the artist."

"It's good of you to worry about her. I mean that. Nana and Grammy will be there, Dr. Minnow, too. And Dr. Grove said he's coming out to have a look at her."

She watched the sun break above the horizon in a thin line of bright, beaming gold. "You've helped take her mind off things, too. It may sound strange to say you picked a good time to get shot, but it worked out that way."

"That's one way to look at it." He shifted to her while

the eastern sky exploded. "How about that fancy dinner Saturday night?"

"Not only a fancy dinner, but a Saturday night fancy dinner?" Wide-eyed, she jiggled her shoulders back and forth. "I might have to buy a new dress."

"If you've got more than one, I haven't seen it anyway."

She laughed, kissed him. "Go on, get out, Skinner. You're on my clock." When he had, she leaned out the window. "If I get hung up, I'll have Rory come back and pick you up after work."

"I'll wait for you." He walked back to the window. "Come home with me tonight. I'll pick something up from the kitchen here for both of us. Come home with me."

"All right, but I'll get the food. I'm closer to the kitchen."

"Not fancy," he called out as she backed up. "That's for Saturday."

It occurred to Bodine as she turned, flicked a glance back at him in her rearview, they weren't just sleeping together. They were dating.

She did work longer than she'd hoped. Seasonals were dribbling back, others needed to be hired. New hires meant interviews, vetting, training, orientation.

"It's all a good thing," Bodine told Jessica as she packed her briefcase. "Bookings are up for spring right through to the first of the year, and they were solid last year. With us adding more activities and packages, it's only going to head up from there."

"You need a full-time assistant. I know how great Sal is, but you could use her full-time, or if you'd rather she run the front desk, you need somebody else. Having Chelsea's made a huge difference for events. You need the same."

Bodine frowned over it, over the simple truth of it. "I always get an itch in the middle of my back when I think of a formal assistant."

Jessica pointed with a perfectly polished pink fingernail. "That's your control button talking."

"I've heard that before. Maybe I'll talk to Sal. Maybe. Meanwhile, I've got an order to pick up from the kitchen. I have a date."

"Me, too. Apparently it's past time I saw *Silverado*. In exchange, Chase is going to try my lemon pasta with wilted arugula."

It struck Bodine again, and she stopped in her tracks. "My God, he's in love like Romeo. You're getting married."

"Yeah." Jessica patted a hand on her chest. "You'll be my maid of honor, won't you?"

"I can't believe it's taken you a damn day to ask!" After dancing forward, Bodine gave Jessica a squeeze. "I was my cousin Betsy's maid of honor, so I have some experience. And I trust you won't make me wear raspberry-pink organza with poufy shoulders."

"Blood oath on that one."

But as Jessica's smile struck Bodine as a little frantic, Bodine angled her head. "Don't tell me you're having second thoughts?"

"I've already had two dozen thoughts. They all circle back to I really love him. It's the marriage idea that scares me."

"He's going to eat wilted lettuce and you're going to watch a classic Western movie. In my book, you're already married. You just haven't had the party yet."

"As my maid of honor, will you keep saying things like that now and then over the next few months?"

"Absolutely. Now let's go round us up a couple of cowboys."

Shortly, as she drove home with two hearty chicken dinners in the back and Callen beside her, Bodine wondered out loud.

"Have you ever eaten wilted arugula?"

"Why would I?" Turning, he gave the containers in the back a suspicious study. "That's not in those take-home dinners, is it?"

"No. It's going to be on Chase's plate tonight at Jessica's."

"That man is sick in love," he said with some pity. "He doesn't much like unwilted lettuce."

"I was thinking the same. She's getting the better end of the deal, as for him eating it, she watches *Silverado*."

"Classic."

"And a visual feast for the female eye. We're having us some Cajun chicken, rosemary fingerling potatoes, and asparagus."

"You're making me glad I'm not in love with Jessica."

"Add on some huckleberry cheesecake."

"Maybe we should get married."

Laughing, she turned sparkling eyes at him. "Careful, Skinner, some women grab at straws. How about we watch *Silverado*? I've got my own DVD."

"Got popcorn?"

"I believe I can come up with that."

"I've got the beer." He reached over, touched her arm. "Alice is sitting out on the front porch."

Even as he spoke, Alice rose, her hands clutched together at her waist.

As if she'd been waiting for her cue, Cora stepped out.

Bodine pulled straight up.

"I faced it head-on," Alice said. "I looked in my head and I told Pete."

"Pete's the artist. The one Bob Tate brought here

today." Cora slipped an arm around Alice's shoulders. "Alice has been waiting to tell you."

"How do you feel about it?" Callen asked her.

"I'm glad it's over. It hurt." She pressed a hand to her belly. "I had to stop, and start and stop and start. I'm glad it's over. You have to look at it. We have one, and Bobby said everybody should look at it in case they know Sir. Ma?"

"I'll go get it."

"I like being outside. I like—" Alice stopped, tapped a finger to her lips.

"What is it?" Bodine asked.

"I keep wanting to say things over and over. I'm trying not to. I like being outside," she said carefully, "maybe because I had to be inside for so long. Coming out whenever I want makes me feel good."

Now she pressed her lips tight as Cora came out with the sketch.

"This is Sir. It doesn't look exactly right, but I can't explain better. His hair got gray like mine did, and his beard—sometimes he had it, sometimes he didn't. But most times he did. And his face got old like mine. This is how he looks, as best I can explain, now."

Bodine studied the sketch.

Were his eyes truly crazy, or did Alice only see them that way? In the sketch they had a wild, fierce look about them. The hair hung thin, unkempt, straggly. A grizzled beard covered the lower half of a thin, hard face. The mouth made a cruel, compressed line.

"Do you know him?" Alice demanded. "Do you know who he is? Bobby says he has a real name, not Sir. A real one."

"I don't think I do." Bodine looked up at Callen.

"I don't, but we know what he looks like now. It'll help

find him and stop him." Because he knew he could, he stepped up, hugged her. "You did really good, Alice."

On a sigh, she rested her head on his chest a moment before stepping back. "He's not as tall as you, but taller than Bobby. That's what I told Pete. His arms are strong. He has big hands, harder than Rory's or yours. He has a scar on his palm. This one." She tapped her left, slashed a line across it. "And one here, like that." She drew a curve on her left hip. "He's got a mark—"

She looked at her mother.

"Birthmark."

"A birthmark here." She touched her right outer thigh. "Like a smear. I said I'd remember when he locked me up, I said I'd remember when I got away. And I did remember. I remembered. Can we go see Sundown now? I don't want to think about it anymore."

"Sure we can. Did you keep an eye on him for me today?"

"I went out this morning, and I went out after I helped draw the face. I gave him a carrot, and one for Leo with the pretty blue eyes, too, and I brushed him and sang him a song."

"He sure likes when you sing. So do I. Maybe you can sing for us again when we see how he's doing."

He offered Alice his arm, made her grin.

"I can see her coming back, more and more," Cora told Bodine. "And today I watched her suffer through memories and fears. He looks like a monster. He looks like a monster and he had my girl all those years."

"He'll never have her again. Nana, he'll never touch her again."

"I don't believe in vengeance. The war took my husband, the boy I loved, the father of my babies. And I grieved, but I never felt hate in my heart. I feel it now. I feel it every day now. My girl's home, and coming back, and under the joy of that, I feel such hate, Bodine. It's black and it's bright, that hate."

"Nana, I don't think you'd be human if you didn't. I don't know if them finding him and locking him away for the rest of his miserable life will ease that for you."

"I don't know, either." Cora let out a long sigh. "I have to remember to look at her, to see her as she is, as she's coming back, and be grateful. But it doesn't stop me from wanting to cut his balls off with a rusty knife and hear him scream."

After shaking herself, Cora arched her eyebrows at Bodine. "That's not something most people would smile at."

"Most people aren't me."

"Oh, well. I'm going to put this ugly thing away." She took back the sketch. "Do you want to ask Cal to dinner?"

"Actually he asked me. I've got a couple of take-home dinners in the truck. We're going to watch a movie in the shack."

"Now I've got something to smile about."

"I'm just going to run up, grab the movie we're watching, and a couple bags of microwave popcorn from the pantry."

"Don't forget your toothbrush," Cora called out.

"Honestly, Nana." On a laugh, Bodine looked back. "Think who you're talking to. I've had a spare over there for weeks."

While Bodine ran upstairs, Callen checked Sundown's wound. Alice stroked the horse and sang "Jolene."

"You sure can sing," Callen said when she finished.

"I sang with Reenie, and I sang to my Rory, and I sang to myself. I couldn't have a radio or records or a TV.

Rory—Reenie's Rory—gave me a . . . It's little and has songs on it and you can put things in your ears and listen."

"An iPod."

"Yes! It's the nicest present. Rory is so good, he's such a good boy. The iPod is like magic. It has lots and lots of music, and I can listen to it when I can't sleep."

"Are you having trouble sleeping, Miss Alice?"

"Only sometimes now, not so much as before. And the music takes away the bad dreams. Even in the bad dreams I can't see him like he was when I got in the truck. I can't see him clear that way anymore. Was the truck blue, or was it red? I shouldn't have gotten in. I saw the snakes."

"In the truck? He had snakes in the truck?"

"Not real ones. The picture. The sticker thing. He's a sovereign citizen, a true patriot, and true patriots will rise up and overthrow the corrupt federalists. They'll take our country back."

"Did you tell the sheriff about the sticker?"

"Did I? I think. Maybe. True patriots will revolt because the tree of liberty needs to be watered with blood to bring the country back to the people, under God. A man needs sons to protect the land. I only gave him one that lived. One's not enough to fight and work and protect. I think he had more."

"More sons?"

"I don't know. I don't know. I don't know. More wives. Do you think I can sit on Sundown soon?"

"We'll ask Doc Bickers. Miss Alice, can you tell me why you think he had more wives?"

He prepared to back off. He could see the jerky way her hands moved, hear the anxiety in her voice. But she pressed her face to Sundown's.

"He said I didn't hear anything but the wind. I didn't

hear calling or crying or yelling. I imagined it, and shut up about it."

"It's okay."

"Sundown's almost better. You're almost better, too. You didn't limp today. Some things get better."

"You're a lot better yourself, Miss Alice."

"I'm better, things are better. I can go outside whenever I want to. Ma's teaching me how to crochet a sweater now. I heard his truck that night, I heard it. I wasn't sleeping. He took the baby away, he took my next baby away and the next. He took poor little Benjamin who went to heaven away, and I wasn't sleeping because I hurt inside and outside and in my head and in my heart."

Desperately sorry, Callen brushed a hand over her hand, laid it on her shoulder. She reached up, gripped it hard. "I heard the truck come back, and I was afraid, so afraid he'd come in and take his marital rights. And I heard the scream. It wasn't the wind, it wasn't an owl or a coyote. It wasn't the first time, but I heard it so clear that time, once, twice. I did. And I heard him, too. Shouting, cursing. And he didn't come for his marital rights that night or the next or the next."

"Were you in the house or the cellar?"

"The house. It was night, it was dark out my window. And once after, not the next or the next, but after, in the day. In the light, I heard calling. *Help, help, help!* I think. I couldn't hear it very well, but I *heard*. Then I didn't hear it anymore. But the crying once. I heard crying sometimes when I worked in the garden. Maybe it was the babies crying for me. I had to stop hearing the crying because I couldn't get to the babies. It's how I went crazy, I guess."

"You're not crazy."

She stepped back, smiled. "A little bit. I think I was more crazy then. I had to be or I'd have killed myself."

He went with his heart, with his gut, and framed her face with his hands, kissed her softly on the mouth. "You may be a little bit crazy, but you're still the sanest person I know."

Her eyes teared up even as she laughed. "You must know a lot of crazy people."

"Maybe I do."

When she left him, singing to herself, he pulled out his phone to call the sheriff. There might be more women locked up in some cellar being driven mad.

CHAPTER TWENTY-SEVEN

It took the best part of a week, with a delay of a solid day of soaking rain, but on a soft April evening, Callen saddled Sundown for what he billed as the Big Reveal.

"Maybe everybody shouldn't watch yet."

He turned, studied Alice in her new boots and buff-colored hat, her jeans and bright pink shirt. She'd added a brown leather vest he suspected was Bodine's.

"You sure look a picture."

She ducked her head, but he caught the smile.

"I'm going to be right with you," he reminded her. "But if you want to wait—"

"No, it's silly. I make myself silly. But you'll be with me."

"Every step. You ready?"

She gave a nod, put her foot in his hands for the boost. When she settled in the saddle, she let out a long, happy sigh. "It feels so good, like it did the first time. Not the first time ever, but since. Since you helped me sit on Sundown."

"Do you want the reins?"

"Not yet. Not yet. Most everybody's seen me sit on him now, and you walk me on him. You can just walk me on him, okay?"

He led her at a slow clip-clop toward the doors of the stables. "I used to ride so fast, so far."

"You will again when you want."

He led her out after a long workday where the Big Reveal included steaks on the grill, cornbread and beer, and a family who'd come together for something as simple, and as monumental, as a middle-aged woman sitting on the back of a horse.

Most of the ranch hands had gathered as well, and broke into applause.

Chase held the paddock gate open, closed it again behind them. Callen led them around in a full circle.

"We can just walk like this," he said to Alice. "You tell me if you're ready or you're not. It's all up to you."

"I'm not used to everybody looking at me," she confided. "My chest hurts some."

"That could be you feeling the pride in mine."

"You say nice things. I feel good when you talk to me. My Benjamin went to heaven, but maybe if he didn't he'd be like you."

The onlookers sat on the fence, or stood with a boot perched on a rung. She knew the faces, knew the names. But still, they all watched her.

"They're proud of you, too."

"Proud of me." She murmured that as well, as if letting it slide into her mind. "And happy to see Sundown's well again."

"That's right. You helped him get better."

"I helped. I can do it. I can do it, but you'll stay with me?"

"You know I will." He handed her the reins. "You go on and take a ride, Miss Alice."

She felt the leather in her hands, old memories and new ones, the feel of a good horse under her, the frisky spring breeze over her face. Sundown stood absolutely still until she nudged him into a walk.

Callen stayed close, but *she* rode. And it made her proud. It made her remember being young and safe and free. It brought that bubbling up inside her she knew now was happiness.

She looked down at Callen. "Can I?"

"Just let him know."

When she moved into a trot, all on her own, she heard the clapping, even some cheers. But she paid little attention to that. She *was* free.

"You didn't say anything about her learning to trot," Bodine said.

Callen just shrugged, stood by the fence. "You don't have to know everything."

When she stopped, face flushed, in front of the fence, she looked for Callen's nod. She took off her hat, held it high over her head as Sundown bowed.

When Callen helped her dismount, she threw her arms around Sundown's neck, then around Callen's waist. "Can I ride again tomorrow?"

"You can ride any and every day you want."

"Alice, I took a video." Rory held up his phone. "A movie of you riding."

"A movie! I want to see."

When she rushed over to Rory, Callen turned to Bodine and her mother. "I'd like to take her on an easy trail ride. When she's ready, I think Rosie would be a good ride for her. She's gentle and bright."

"I don't know if she'd ride away from the ranch," Maureen began.

"She would with Callen," Bodine put in. "Or Rory. Maybe with me. And Rosie's a good choice when she's ready to get up on a horse that's not Sundown."

"I'd want to talk to Celia first, and Ma."

"Reenie, come see! I'm a movie star!"

"She's just being careful." Bodine swung over the fence. "At this point Nana would let Alice ride to the moon and back if it put that happy look on her face. Mom's trying to balance that out."

"It's no problem. You might want to talk to the doctor about having her work with the horses here, then over at the BAC."

"The BAC?"

"An hour here and there, with me. I read up on some therapies, and a lot use animals. It's horses for Alice, though she likes the dogs, too. She grooms Sundown as if he's going to a beauty pageant. She could handle more of that."

"Maybe." Her mind hadn't gone there, but now that it had, she saw the benefits. "Maybe it would do her good to do some work, outside, in the stables. She's been helping Clem in the kitchen. You've got a brain, Skinner."

She gave him a friendly poke in the ribs.

"Sometimes I even use it."

"The work makes her feel useful, and feeling useful makes her feel normal. You should talk to Dad about it. See how she does here, then we'll talk about her spending a little time at the BAC, if she wants."

Alice obviously enjoyed the evening. She talked to her mother about the sweater she'd started, and, surprisingly, to Hec about the horses, watched Rory's little video countless times.

For himself, Callen bided his time. Under starlight with Chase slipping off to Jessica's, and Rory to a date with Chelsea, he sat with Sam on the front porch.

Cigars and whisky equaled a good way to end the day.

"You put in a lot of time with Alice," Sam said after a long stretch of easy silence.

"She put in a lot of time with me."

"Before we go into that, I've got something to ask you. I figure, since I don't remember a time you weren't, you'll be straight with me on it."

Callen felt the quick, slippery knot slide and twist in his belly. He'd been preparing for the boot to drop about Bodine, and had yet to formulate answers to questions her father might ask.

"There might've been a few times I slid under the straight line about things Chase and I got into."

"Not if I asked you direct."

"No, not if you asked me direct." Evasion? Well, that was just being cautious about something or other. Lying was lying.

"So I'm asking you direct: Are you planning to go after Garrett Clintok?"

The knot loosened. He found it a hell of a lot easier to answer that than a father's what-are-your-intentions-regarding-my-daughter.

"He's out on bail." Lazily now, Callen dragged on the cigar, watched the smoke trail off into the night. "I'm healed up. It's going to be up to him whether we have a conversation or something more . . . physical. But I can't let it go. It'll be harder if you ask me to let it go, but I still couldn't."

"What I'm going to ask is you don't go start that conversation alone. I don't doubt you can handle yourself, Cal, but you'd fight fair. It's how you're built. He won't, as that's not how he's built. He's got a streak in him, and always has."

Sam sipped some whisky. "And now he's ruined himself around here. Nobody's going to take his side on this. Can't say what the courts will do, but nobody's going to take his side. He'll never be a peace officer again wherever he goes—and go he will, if he doesn't end up in prison. He'll want to do more than bloody your nose."

Sam drew on his cigar, let the smoke go. "I'm going to ask you for that. Don't go for him alone. Take somebody you trust to bear witness to a fair fight."

It grated some, but the fact was Sam Longbow invariably talked plain sense. "I won't go alone."

"All right then. Now, why don't you tell me what you want to ask me about? If it's my daughter's hand, I'm likely to give it, but it's still going to twist up my heart."

The knot came back, slipperier than before. "I'm not . . . we're not going there right yet."

"All right. To save us the awkward moment when you are, consider it already given. We don't have to go back here."

"I don't have any land," Callen heard himself saying.

Sam angled his head, gave Callen a considering study. "Did you blow through all the money you made in California on whisky and wild women?"

"Only a small percentage of it."

"You're planning to keep working for a living, I expect."

"As long as you don't fire me, I'm good."

"Well, her grandmother didn't fire me when I slipped off with her daughter, so you're safe on that. Now, if you didn't want to talk to me about that, what's on your mind?"

"How would you feel about hiring on Alice?"

"Hiring Alice?"

"I was going to ask how you'd feel about letting her help some with the horses. Stable work. She's damn good at grooming, and she could muck. She's strong. The limp hampers her some, especially if she's tired, but she's strong. She's got a good way with horses. The dogs now, too. I guess it's animals altogether. But when I thought more on it, it seemed to me she'd get more pride out of it if she drew a little pay. Wouldn't have to be much."

As the night birds called, Sam contemplated his cigar. "I never thought of it."

"I said something to Maureen before, and I know she wants to talk to Nana and to the doctor. That'd be the right way, but you run the ranch, so . . ."

"It's a good thought, Cal. A good one. And judging from what I've seen the last couple weeks, the right one, too. We'll see if we can make it work. Somebody's coming."

Even before he saw the headlights, Sam heard the engine, off in the quiet of the night.

"Late for visiting," Sam added, but crossed his boots on his stretched-out legs, a man confident in his own.

"Sheriff Tate," Callen said quietly when the truck got close enough.

They waited as Tate stopped the truck, got out.

"Evening, Sam, Cal."

"Evening, Bob. You look tired out."

"Because I am."

"How about a chair, a whisky, and a cigar?"

"If I take the cigar, I'll pay for a week. You could have a hazmat team hose me down, my wife would still smell it. But the whisky I wouldn't mind. I'm off duty."

"Take the chair." Callen got to his feet. "I'll get the whisky."

"Appreciate that."

Before Callen could reach the door, Bodine opened it. "Sheriff."

"Evening, Bodine."

"I'm just getting him a whisky."

"I'll get it."

When she shut the door again, Callen picked up the cigar he'd set in the ashtray, leaned back against the porch rail.

"I was on my way home, and felt I should come on by, tell you where we're at. I've been talking to some people the last few days, pushing on the business Callen passed on that Alice passed to him. People we know are active or more than sympathetic to militias. True patriots being one. That's the phrase she used to you?"

"A couple times," Callen agreed.

He paused when Bodine came out. "Thanks. Long day." He took a slow sip. "Long, dry one. Those people dug into those groups aren't very likely to cooperate with a police investigation, especially with one who isn't what they call a 'constitutional sheriff.'"

He paused again, took a longer sip. "Still, we went out, talked, showed the sketch, made sure they heard what this individual we were asking about is being investigated for. Only the hard-liners are going to hold that line when a man's done what this one's done. Still, we didn't get much of anywhere on it. Until today."

At that Bodine walked over, stood by Callen.

"I got a call from somebody today. I won't say the name—couldn't say if you'd know it—but I've got to keep it confidential in any case. Says he recognized the face, has seen this man at the compound they have a few times. Doesn't know his name for sure. Says he goes by J.G. Says this man drills with them every few months—not regular.

Runs some supplies for them. Claims he hasn't seen this individual for months now. The compound's a good way east of here, but this character thinks our man has a patch of land around here, lives—as some of them do—off the grid. We're going to push on this, but carefully."

"Would a reward help?"

"Money never hurts," Bob told Sam.

"Fifty thousand, if he can lead you to the son of a bitch."

"Ten's enough for this type. You clear me to offer ten, he'll find out more than I think he already knows."

"Then you're clear for it."

"Saves me from asking." Bob drank again. "There's more, on the other information Alice passed to Callen. About there maybe being other women. The time she gave for hearing the screams, and the calls for help. Going after we figure he moved her into that shed. I did a search for missing persons, in the age span that makes the most sense. I've got one who's never been found. Nineteen-year-old girl, doing some hiking and photography on the trails in Lolo. Called her ma and her boyfriend from Stevensville on July sixteenth, fresh off the Bass Creek Trail. She planned, she said, to get some food, maybe another quick hike, then camp for the night. That's the last they heard from her. Last anybody did. Not a damn trace of her."

"He might have had more than Alice," Bodine offered. "He might have another woman locked up right now."

"I talked to the agent who has that case, that still open case. We'll talk again. I went to Stevensville, talked to the people he talked to back then who remembered seeing her. Still daylight when she walked off, and Alice says it was dark when she heard the scream. We're going to follow this through, try to narrow down when and where he grabbed her, if he did. I'm going to need to talk to Alice again, about when she might have heard the other sounds she told Cal about. Other things that might mean other women."

He let out a breath. "On the next, I need to tell you all we haven't got anything panning out on Billy Jean's or Karyn Allison's murders. The couple of leads we thought were viable, just weren't. We're still working it, but we don't have anything new, and it's been months now. Longer it goes, the colder it gets. I'm sick and sorry about it.

"And last." He lifted his gaze to Callen's. "You know Garrett's out on bail."

"I heard something like that."

"I'm telling you the prosecutor's going for him. Feels the evidence, and Garrett's own stupidity, mean a solid case. The lawyer might work out a plea, but he'll do time, Cal. He will do time, and he'll never carry a badge again."

"Glad to hear it."

"You ought to stay clear of him."

"I'm just having a cigar on the front porch."

Tate shook his head, rose. "You ought to stay clear. Thanks for the drink. I'm going to plan on talking to Alice tomorrow, but now I'm going home and hoping Lolly will warm up whatever she made for dinner."

He pushed up, started down the porch steps. Looked up.

"We got a clear night. You see something like that sky, no matter how long you've been the police, you just don't understand why people do what they do to people."

As Tate drove off, Sam picked up his empty glass, then Tate's. "I'd better tell your mother all of this."

"Do you want me to talk to her with you?"

He shook his head at Bodine. "I'll take care of this." He looked out where Tate's taillights grew small. "Long, hard day for some of us."

"I don't know what to do." Bodine lifted her hands, let them fall when her father went in. "What to do or think or feel."

"Nothing to do but take it as it comes. I need to say you know I've had an ear to the ground about Clintok. He's spending some time at the Step Up Bar. I'm going to take a drive over there in a few days."

"What's wrong with tomorrow?"

"I believe we have a date and a fancy dinner."

She flicked that away like a gnat. "We'll have the fancy dinner next Saturday. Get this done, Skinner. It'll eat at you until you do. We'll go tomorrow."

"Bodine, are you saying you'd rather go to a potential bar fight than a fancy restaurant?"

"I don't understand anyone who wouldn't."

Grinning, he held out a hand. "There come those powerful feelings again. Let's take a walk under this big sky."

He picked his wife. He had a plan. This time around there would be no mistake. Evenings most usually he worked on organizing, on preparing. Supplies and security.

A woman needed to be locked up tight until she understood the order of things. And even after that.

He had the leg irons bolted strong to the wall, added two more sturdy locks to the door. Thinking of the noise some of them could make, he took time to staple up strips of foam on the walls.

Not that anybody ever came around the cabin, but that sort of precaution should've been done long ago.

Once done, he took a good look around, imagined his wife in the bed. Stripped down, she'd be—he'd see to that—and ready for planting.

The image made him hard, so hard he was grateful he wouldn't have to wait much longer.

The long winter was over, and spring had come. The time for planting. To every time there was a season, he thought. And this was his.

The seed, his seed, would take. Grow inside the young, fertile womb. And then he'd make another change. Leave the son in the care of the mother. Honor thy father *and* mother. Yes, this time that would be done. He'd even bring the boy to her for visits, maybe some schooling as he grew. And do the same with the sons who came after the first.

They'd make a family, with him as the head, the woman as the helpmate, the sons as legacy.

Confident in his plans, in his choice, he lay down on the bed where he'd plow and plant. And considered how once that seed took hold, he might choose another wife, start another son.

He had room, could keep them separated until they learned to be sisters. Two to keep him pleasured, to grow the sons, to grow the crops, tend the stock, to clean and cook as time went on.

Two to see to the women's duties while he took on the men's work, pursued the men's interests.

He closed his eyes, building it all in his head. A kind of kingdom, he thought, and slept a little while to dream of it.

Callen planned to throw together a meal after work on Saturday, then drive out to the Step Up Bar about nine.

He'd put in a full day—spring weekends proved to be

packed tight at the resort—and had seen to Sundown's feeding and grooming himself.

And spent some time rubbing vitamin oil into the raw pink scar on his horse's belly. "Battle scar." He straightened, gave Sundown a couple of good strokes. "I can't balance the scales unless I shoot the bastard, and I just don't have that in me. Or don't want to act on it if I do. But I can add a couple of weights."

Sundown stomped his right front hoof twice, and though Callen understood the horse reacted to his tone, he went with it. "Yeah, one for each of us. Behave yourself," he ordered as he stepped out, latched the stall door. He crossed over to Leo, scratched Bodine's gelding between the ears where he liked it best. "Keep your eye on him."

He wound his way out, exchanging words with a couple of the hands, turning down an invite to poker. Since he'd taken longer with Sundown than he'd planned, he backpedaled cooking to tossing a sandwich together.

Then walked into the shack to the scent of cooking and the sight of Bodine at his stove.

"Woman, don't you have my supper on the table yet?"

"Funny," she said without turning around.

"Sort of was. What're you cooking? I didn't know you did much of that."

"I don't, but I can brown up some meat and pour some barbecue sauce on it, and fry up some potatoes. That's what you're getting."

It smelled a hell of a lot better than a cheese sandwich. "I'll take it and say thanks."

"Thought you would. Want a beer?" She glanced back to see him shake his head, nodded hers. "Saving that for after. While a few beers makes an interesting fight, a clear head's a smarter one. I wouldn't mind a Coke."

He got out two, opened both. "Bodine?"

"Callen?"

That made him smile and kiss the top of her head. "I've got words turning around in my head, looking for their right spots. When they get there, I've got things to say to you."

"Am I going to like hearing them?"

"Well, you'll have to let me know. I need to wash up. I've been with the horses."

"You've got about five, maybe ten minutes before this is on the table."

When he came back, she spooned generous portions of the sauced meat onto buns, scooped up fried potatoes, added a hefty portion of mixed vegetables.

"I stole the vegetables from Clementine. She had plenty done."

After she sat with her own plate, he two-handed the filled bun, sampled. "It's good. Got some bite to it."

"That's the hot sauce. I figured you could take it."

"Take it and like it. Meant to ask: Since we're not booked real heavy on Tuesday, I'd like to have my mother bring the kid in for a while again. Brody loves the horses, and he's been asking for another pony ride."

"You don't have to ask about that, Callen."

"I like checking with the boss."

"The boss says anytime you can work it out's fine. Text me when they get in. I'll come down and see them if I can."

"I'll do that. I told her they've started tearing down the old place."

"How'd she take it?"

"She was fine with it. Didn't matter. It didn't seem like she was putting that on, and I made a point of asking Savannah about it. She said the same, Ma's okay with it.

She really loves having the piece of flooring, especially since Justin made it into picture frames. And the rose-bushes, especially those. So it was the right thing to do."

"Was that weighing on you?"

"Some. Off and on. Now it's not. So, only this. Wouldn't you rather stay back here tonight while I go deal with Clintok?"

She stabbed some potatoes, looking at him with a little smile while she ate. "Clutching my pearls while I pace the floor? And having a ripped petticoat for bandages ready."

"Never seen you wear pearls, or a petticoat—though I imagine you'd look really good in both. And why do you assume I'd need bandages?"

"Grammy's pearls are set aside for me, and I could bor-row them if I wanted to clutch them. I don't own a petti-coat, so you'll do without bandages ripped from one. But I already tossed a bag of frozen peas in your freezer be-cause Clintok's big and he's a brawler. I may not have a doubt you'll kick his ass, but he'll land a few."

Watching him, she licked sauce off her finger. "But to answer your question, don't start thinking because I cooked you a meal I'll go full stereotypical female."

"You're not stereo or typical anything."

"Damn right. I'm going. Somebody's got to hold your coat, and nobody's robbing me of the pleasure of seeing you bloody him some."

"How about after our fancy dinner next Saturday we get a fancy hotel room?"

She polished off her sandwich, downed a little Coke. "Have you got money to burn, Skinner?"

"I've got it to spend."

"Looks like I'll be packing an overnight bag. Let's get these dishes done and get going."

"I was thinking I could eat another helping."

She poked a finger against his taut belly. "You'll regret that thinking if he lands those couple in your gut."

"Can't argue with that," he decided and pushed back from the table.

CHAPTER TWENTY-EIGHT

The Step Up Bar slouched beside a two-pump gas station that primarily stocked cigarettes, chewing tobacco, and ammo. You could buy coffee there if burning a layer from your stomach lining caused no concern, but the soft drink machine stuck out front offered the better bet on the rare occasions it was stocked.

Across the weedy, pitted gravel lot, a twenty-room motel with a reputation for dubious sanitary standards welcomed only the most desperate of travelers.

Still, some locals enjoyed the fuck-you ambiance and patronized the bar for some serious drinking. And occasionally, enough drinks lured a couple or two over to the motel for the nonadvertised hourly room rate.

The three enterprises largely stayed afloat due to bikers traveling through who preferred cheap drinks, a hard-eyed game of pool, and the occasional brawl over the niceties.

Before he'd taken off for California, Callen had dragged Chase in there with him for a couple of rounds of rebellious, underage drinking, as nobody in the place gave a New York rat's ass about checking IDs.

As Callen pulled in, passed the flickering vacancy sign for the One Shot Motel, he saw nothing much had changed.

He heard the insect buzz of the vacancy sign swatting at the still night air. Rising over it, the moon rode, a bite away from full, on a star-struck sky.

He steered away from the line of parked bikes, slid in next to a pickup. Shook his head.

Chase leaned back against the truck, Rory beside him, with Jessica and Chelsea flanking them.

"Didn't know we were having a party."

"That's how it goes," Bodine said as she climbed out.

Callen got out, walked over, scanned the lineup. "I appreciate the support, but it looks like I need an army to tend to my business here."

"I don't care how it looks." Chase pushed off the truck. "Clintok did what he did on our land. We won't get in his way or yours unless he tries something dirty."

"He's in there." Rory wagged his thumb behind him. "His truck's down there."

Callen tried one last time. "It's not the best place or circumstances to bring dates."

Now Rory grinned. "You brought one. Plus . . . tell him, Chelsea."

"I've got a black belt in tae kwon do." When she lowered into a fighting stance, Callen could only wonder. "I took it all through college."

"And I have a mighty and fatally accurate bitch slap," Jessica added.

Couldn't change it, Callen decided, so he'd trust the brothers would keep the women out of harm's way should harm rise up.

"All I need to do is punch him in the face. That'll square it for me."

Chase nodded. "Then you get that done, and we'll all be on our way."

Callen went in with what he thought of now as his damn entourage, and saw the interior hadn't changed much, either.

The decor ran heavy to taxidermy with bear and buck heads mounted, the Montana State flag framed beside the Gadsden. One new element? A sign reading:

GUNS DON'T KILL PEOPLE, I DO.

A couple of biker types smacked pool balls around, and a couple more drank bottled beer and watched.

The place held two booths. In one, a couple of old guys who looked permanently pissed off sat across from each other, working on their beers and playing cards.

He judged the second booth commandeered by the bikers, as empty bottles littered the table and leather jackets formed heaps on the seats.

Seven stools lined the bar, all full. At first glance he didn't recognize a soul but Clintok at the end, then felt a little tug of recognition for the big guy center bar, chomping down on beer nuts.

As the others filed in behind him, the balls stopped clattering, asses shifted on stools. Callen hoped to hell the fact the female population of the bar now numbered three didn't stir up trouble.

But he knew by the way Clintok straightened on his stool that at least one patron knew trouble had walked in.

"Skinner? That you?" The big guy gestured. "Kiss my ass, that's you, Cal Skinner. Heard you were back."

"Sandy Rhimes," Bodine muttered, and a lightbulb switched on.

"How you doing, Sandy?"

"Could complain, won't bother. Hey there, Chase, Rory, Bodine, ma'am, ma'am." He had a big, homely face and a sweet, almost angelic smile. "You bunch make a wrong turn somewhere?"

"Nope. I'm where I aimed for."

"Well, if you're having a beer, stick with the bottles. Slats here would tell you the same," he added, wagging his own bottle toward the hefty, bored-eyed bartender.

"We're not drinking right now. I've got some other business."

Sandy took a peer down the bar. "Clintok? If you got a beef with him, I'd . . . Wait." His mile-wide shoulders straightened, stiffened, and the sweet smile vanished. "He's the one who shot your horse? I heard about that." Sandy slapped down his beer, started to push his mighty girth out of the stool.

"It's okay." Christ, he didn't need to add another. "I've got this."

"Hope you do."

"Just stay back here," Callen told the rest, and walked down the bar to Clintok. "We've got business to finish."

"Fuck you, Skinner."

"I figure you're carrying, so I'm going to say if I see your hand go where I think your gun is, I'll break that hand at the wrist."

The red started creeping up into Clintok's face. "You're threatening a police officer?"

"I'm threatening an asshole, an unemployed one, I hear. I'm threatening a coward who hides up in the trees and shoots a horse. So you're going to want to keep those hands where I can see them."

Callen felt rather than saw the man on the stool behind him slide off, ease away.

"Coward?" Clintok pushed off the stool. "You're a murdering coward. You killed two women."

Now Callen sensed the bikers tuning in. "You want to believe that. You know different, but you want it to be true. What is true is: You shot my horse."

Clintok rammed a finger into Callen's chest; Callen let him. "I was shooting at a snake."

"Even your aim's not that bad."

"Same as you ever were." Eyes hot, teeth bared, Clintok jabbed the finger again. "No-good, no-good whelp from a loser who gambled away everything and hanged himself from the shame of it. And here you come? You come in here with the Longbow men, and women to hide behind."

"They're just here as audience for the ass-kicking. You want the ass-kicking in here or outside? That's your choice."

"You take it outside." The bartender brought out a bat, slapped it against his palm.

"Outside then," Callen said.

He saw the punch coming, made another decision to let it come. It landed hard enough to set his ears ringing, but he just wiped the blood from his lip.

"Keep coming." Callen backed up toward the door.

Clintok took two charging steps, and as Callen braced, Sandy flung out a beefy arm.

"Now, what're ya reaching for back there, Garrett?" He yanked the .32 out of its holster. "Man's a bushwhacker," he announced to the bar. "Shot this man's horse out from under him. We don't stand for that. Nosiree, we don't. We don't stand for trying to draw down on an unarmed man, neither."

He slapped the gun on the bar. "Best put that behind the bar, Slats. Now, are you walking outside to settle this on your own, Garrett, or do you want me to help you?"

"Keep your hands off me. Useless retard of a drunk."

"Get back there and keep the door open," Callen murmured to Chase. "I'll get him through it. Let's go, Clintok. If you try to run out the back, I bet I'm faster."

"Run from you?" Clintok charged forward. He grabbed a beer from the bar, smashed the bottle, continued to charge, slicing with the jagged glass.

Callen danced aside, let the momentum carry Clintok forward, and booted him hard enough in the ass to propel him through the door.

Chase grabbed Clintok's wrist, twisted. The broken bottle fell on the gravel.

"Thanks." Callen came roaring through. "Stay out of it."

He knocked the off-balance Clintok to the ground, had the pleasure of seeing him skid over the gravel and leave blood smeared on the stones.

Then stepped back, waited.

Bodine kicked the broken glass aside and like Callen watched as Clintok slowly gained his feet. His hands bled from their rude run over the gravel. Under the big moon and the snap and sizzle of the vacancy sign, she saw the darkening stain on the knees of his jeans from the spill.

And the hot blaze of rage in his eyes.

"Go get him," she murmured to Callen.

But to Callen's mind—remarkably cool at the moment—words delivered as sharp an insult as fists.

"Guns, broken bottles. Suits you, Clintok. Just like hiding out in the rocks and trees and shooting down at a horse. Just like putting a bullet in some helpless pup's head suits you."

"He shot a puppy?" This from one of the bikers as they filed out to watch the fight. "Son of a bitch!"

"That all suits you," Callen continued. "Like ambushes suit you, like having your friends hold a man down so you can beat on him. That one didn't work out so well for you as I recall. Time to see how you do one-to-one, in a straight-up fight."

"Should've put the bullet in you."

Callen smiled. "Which time? Back when we were kids and you killed that little dog, or now when you shot my horse?"

"Both." With that, Clintok charged.

Callen dodged the jab that flew as wild as any temper tantrum, followed it with a solid right cross, snapping Clintok's head back, bloodying his nose.

He'd told himself he'd be satisfied with this, with one bare-fisted punch that drew blood. But by God it lit a fire in him, one that had simmered for years.

Before he actively thought it through, his left hook landed on Clintok's jaw.

Maybe the two rapid blows cleared Clintok's head, or maybe he had instincts of his own. Either way Callen took a couple of punishing strikes to the ribs before he blackened his opponent's eye.

Behind them, Jessica closed her hand over Bodine's. "We should stop them."

"Oh, hell no."

Bodine winced when Callen took one to the face, jabbed her own free hand out when he delivered a pair of breath-stealing gut shots, followed it with a wicked uppercut.

Boots scraped over gravel as they lunged, as they circled. The metallic scent of blood wound around the smell of beer, of sweat, and surprisingly of the jerky Sandy gnawed on.

Animal grunts, the snap and crunch of knuckles meeting flesh, meeting bone. Beside her Jessica shifted, gave up, and put her hand over her eyes.

"Tell me when it's over."

"Nearly is."

Working all her life with cowboys, growing up with two brothers—not to mention Callen himself—Bodine figured she'd seen her share of fistfights and dustups. And she could judge them.

Clintok had the advantage of sheer power, but Callen had the weight on strategy. Then there was hot rage against cold fire.

Each time Callen landed a blow, Clintok's response grew sloppier. He's telegraphing, she thought. Come on, Skinner, can't you see . . . ouch.

Then she watched Callen return the glancing punch off his cheekbone with a jab fast and slick as a snake, a gut-punishing follow-up, and that vicious uppercut.

The last knocked Clintok off his feet, and Callen was on top of him. He didn't pummel his downed opponent, though she wouldn't have lost an ounce of respect for him if he had. The onlookers not only expected it but vocally encouraged it.

Instead, Callen pinned his man down, spoke clearly.

"It's done. You come back at me again, come back at any who matter to me, I won't just put you on the ground. I'll put you in it. Believe it." He shoved up. "Now get gone."

He walked away—leaning heavy on pride to keep from limping—taking from Bodine the hat that had flown off his head during the battle. Set it comfortably on his head.

"I guess I ought to buy everybody a drink."

"You're bleeding," Jessica said.

After a swipe of bruised knuckles over his bruised face, Callen shrugged. "Not much."

"Is it men?" Jessica wondered. "Is it men altogether, or is it men in hats?"

"We'll talk about it over a beer." Amused, Bodine started to give her friend a tug toward the door, then shouted a warning.

Clintok stumbled back into the light, a gun in his hand.

Callen shoved her clear, stepped quickly away from the group as Clintok raised the gun.

Her world stopped in an instant, slowed to an endless spin in that same snap of time. She heard shouting, like voices in a tunnel, felt someone drag her back as she tried to surge forward.

Then nothing.

She saw, horribly, she saw Clintok's finger pull the trigger. One, twice, a third time.

And nothing.

The baffled look on his face might have been funny if the ground hadn't undulated under her feet. As it did, Callen strode over it. The roundhouse was pure fury, sent Clintok flying back before he landed. And stayed down.

"You could've hit my woman, you miserable son of a bitch."

He picked up the gun, checked it. "Empty."

"Rory figured he had one in his truck." Pale but game, Chelsea gripped Rory's arm. "So he checked."

"A good salesman reads people." Moving easy, Rory walked to Callen, took the gun. "So I unloaded it."

"I owe you."

"Not a thing, but I'll take that drink."

Callen glanced back at Clintok, not just down, he noted, but out. "We've got to do something about that."

"I've done it." Holding up her phone, Jessica stepped back outside. "The sheriff's on his way."

"Oh, now, Jessie, why'd you go and do that?"

She only gaped at Callen. "Why? He tried to kill you."

"She's right." Chase reached out, drew her to his side. "I know how you feel, but she's right."

"She's damn right." It took all Bodine's willpower not to simply explode. "If Rory didn't have more sense than I've ever given him credit for, you'd be dead or close enough. He's not just an asshole, he's a crazy asshole. He's not just a coward, he's a murdering—"

Because he heard touches of hysteria, Callen moved to her, took her arms. "Okay. Okay. You probably want to take a breath or two."

"Don't tell me to take a breath."

"Or two." He kissed her, said, "Shit," when the contact stung, then leaned in to whisper. "Don't cry. You'll hate yourself."

"I'm fine."

"Drinks all around," Callen told the bartender while he kept his eyes on Bodine's. "I'm good for it."

"You'd better be." With a last look at Clintok, the bartender slapped his bat against his palm again. "He got what was coming to him."

Maybe so, but clearly Tate didn't look pleased when he pulled up some twenty minutes later.

He looked at Clintok, sitting on the ground, his hands secured behind his back with a zip tie, his face bloody. Looked over at Callen, leaning against the wall of the bar, sipping a beer along with Bodine, her brothers, and the other women.

He crouched down beside Clintok. "I told you to steer clear."

"I was having a drink, and he busted in with his god-damn posse and started it."

"And you decided to finish it by pulling a gun?"

"Wouldn't have had to if you'd done your job and locked that murdering bastard up."

"I've done my job right along, just like I'm going to do it now. You busted your bail carrying a gun in the first damn place. Curtis, lock him up in the back, and we'll take some statements, see what the hell's what here."

He walked over to Callen. "Told you to steer clear, too, didn't I?"

"We all decided to go out and have a drink," Bodine said. "We wanted to show Jessica some more of the local color."

After a long stare, Tate scrubbed his face with his hand. "Bodine, that's just insulting."

"It's not altogether untrue," Callen put in. "But it's also true I knew Clintok would probably be here, and it was surely true I planned to knock him on his ass."

"I could toss you in the back with him, charge you with assault."

"Well now, you could." Studying his beer, Chase spoke thoughtfully. "It's not going to stick real well seeing as Clintok threw the first punch, then went for his gun. You can ask the bunch in there if that's how it went down, and when you talk to Sandy Rhimes, he'll be sure to tell you he pulled Clintok's gun—the one he had on him—away from him before he could use it."

"Miss Baazov said Clintok had a gun aimed at Callen outside."

"He got that one out of his truck after Callen beat him in a fair fight. I unloaded that one," Rory added. "I had to figure he had one in his truck, and since he'd already shot

Callen once, tried to do the same again inside, it seemed prudent to take that precaution."

Now Tate used both hands to scrub at his face. "Jesus suffering Christ."

"You forgot about the broken glass. He smashed a bottle," Chelsea continued, "charged at Cal with it. He didn't fight fair till he had to, and even then."

"Does your ma know you're out here, getting in bar fights?" Tate demanded.

"She knows I'm with Rory. Or I expect she does. I live in the Village, but I talk to her most every day."

"A bunch of sass, that's what I get. Curtis, you go in, start with Sandy Rhimes. Get his statement. Miss Baazov—"

"Jessica."

"Jessica, we're going to take a walk over to the vending machine, since I can't have a good shot of whisky as I want. I'm going to assume you're the one standing here with the most sense. So you're going to tell me every step of what happened."

"I'd be glad to."

Callen took another pull on his beer as they crossed the lot. "He's going to be pissed awhile."

"He'll get over it." Bodine shrugged. "He knew you'd hunt Clintok down, and he knew he'd have done the same himself given the circumstances. What he'll be longer than pissed off is disappointed. Not in you, but in Clintok."

It took more than an hour, and by the end of it Callen felt every bruise and scrape. He thought fondly of the bag of peas Bodine had tossed in his freezer—and only wished she'd tossed in a half dozen.

Still, he considered every twinge, throb, and ache well

worth it. Garrett Clintok would look through bars for a very long time. He supposed Jessica's comment before they'd all gone their separate ways hit the mark, too.

Clintok needed some serious head shrinking.

If he gritted his teeth against the banging in his ribs when he got out of the truck, he could remind himself Clintok had worse.

"Do you want to go tell Sundown he's been avenged?"

"I'll tell him in the morning."

With some sympathy, Bodine put an arm around his waist. "You can lean on me." And looking up, she sighed at the moon. "I have to say this ranks as the prettiest night in my experience for a fight. Jessica got some strange and arty-type pictures of the Step Up and some of the patrons while Tate gave you the final lecture."

She opened the door, took off his hat, tossed it aside. Then brushed her fingers over his face as she surveyed the damage. "You won't look pretty for a few days, but you broke his nose."

"I thought so."

"Don't ever shove me aside like that again."

Now he arched his eyebrows—even that hurt. "I can guarantee you, should some fuckheaded asshole ever wave a gun around in your direction, I'll shove you aside again."

"Then next time I'll be ready, and shove you first." She gave him a little one, tugged him back to unbutton his shirt. "Let's have a look at the rest of you."

He gripped her hands. "It stopped my heart, shut it right down, the idea of you getting hit."

"It didn't do mine any good, either, when you stepped aside and gave him a clear shot at you. Damn Gary Coopering."

"Clint Eastwooding. Chase is more Gary Cooper."

He grabbed her face, kissed her hard so pain and lust and pleasure all burst and tangled.

Hot, so instantly hot, she gripped his shoulders, struggled to gentle her hold. "You're in no shape to get me revved up tonight, Skinner."

"I've got to get this done." Fast, he pulled off her shirt, shoved her back against the door. "I've got to have you. Just let me have you." He flicked open the catch of her bra, dragged it aside, filled his hands with her breasts. "Let me have you."

"I wanted to tear your clothes off since you threw the first punch." So she did, starting with his shirt. "Don't complain later when I hurt you."

When she crushed her mouth to his, he dragged her to the floor.

All the heat, all the fire, all the passion he'd banked to fight cold and clear surged into him. That need to pound flesh now burned as a need to possess it. Possess her.

And, with a madness, snapped free.

He felt pain as her hands, rough and greedy, pulled at his clothes, dug into muscle. But distant, almost unconnected, all but buried under this fresh, wild hunger.

He didn't wait for her, couldn't wait, but rammed himself into her as soon as he'd stripped her down far enough. Then he rode like his life depended on it.

She arched up on a breathless cry, gripping his hair like a rope to keep her from falling off a cliff. His eyes had gone green, reflecting hers, with an almost feral intensity that kept her gaze locked to them.

It tore through her, a wildfire, a lightning bolt, leaving her senses as scorched earth. She bucked under him, driving him harder, faster. If he plundered, she ravished. And when that bolt struck again, she rode the lightning until they burned themselves out.

Shuddering, slicked with sweat and some blood from wounds opened in the madness, she wheezed in air. His heart hammered against hers even as he lay—full weight—spent over her.

She thought of the moment Clintok had raised his gun—that spinning, the sensation of the ground shaking—and thought this was nearly the same.

"Here's what you're going to do."

"Bodine, I think there are multiple reasons I'm not going to be able to move right this minute."

"I warned you not to complain when I hurt you. What you're going to do is go in and take a hot shower. When you come out, you're going to take some Motrin, some whisky, and we're going to ice down what needs icing, treat and bandage what needs that."

"I'm fine right here."

"That's sex adrenaline, and it's going to pass really soon."

"Sex adrenaline." She felt his lips curve against her throat. "Ought to be bottled."

"You kicked ass that needed kicking tonight, and you topped that off with the best hot and crazy floor sex in my personal experience."

"Mine, too."

"That's about as manly a night as it gets, in my estimation. But you're hurt more than you might think. It'll be worse if we don't see to it."

Gently, almost tenderly, her hand stroked over his back. "Do that for me, Callen."

She never asked, not really, and never in that way, that soft way. So he had no choice.

And when he moved, the gasp and groan escaped before he could stop them.

"Your ribs took the worst. Left side."

"I know it." But for the first time he looked down, saw the spread of black-and-blue, hits of angry red. "Well, shit."

"It'll look and feel worse tomorrow, so let's get ahead of it." She yanked off the single boot he still wore, and the jeans that had been caught on it. Rising, she offered him a hand. "Come on, cowboy, hit the shower."

He gripped her arm, got slowly, painfully to his feet. Then just stood looking at her. "You've got to know what's coming."

Her heart stuttered a little. "Maybe, but I don't think it should come when you can barely stand and the standing we're doing is naked."

"You're probably right. It'll wait."

She pulled on her jeans again while he limped off to the shower. It would wait, she thought. She didn't need a lot of fuss, but if and when the man she now realized she'd been walking toward all her life told her he loved her, she'd at least like him to say so when he wasn't bleeding.

CHAPTER TWENTY-NINE

He didn't mind the black eye or the bruised jaw, the nicks and cuts or swollen knuckles. The ribs gave him some trouble, but after a day or two they didn't scream every time he moved wrong.

Since it struck close to the truth, he spun a tale for guests, especially the kids, of getting into a saloon fight with a bushwhacker.

And he talked Alice into taking a ride with him.

She lavished affection and attention on Rosie, and the young mare responded to it with utter devotion.

With Maureen, Alice planted the sister garden. In the kitchen, she cooked simple dishes with Clementine. With the weather warming, she often sat with the grannies on one of the porches crocheting.

The big day came when she agreed to drive with the grannies to Bodine House, to look it over, to consider if she'd be happy living there.

They stopped by the BAC—he learned later, at Alice's request. Even from a distance, he could spot her nerves, so he detoured and led the two horses he'd chosen for an upcoming trail ride toward the women.

"Ladies, and here I thought this was as pretty as a day could get. You proved me wrong."

"I do like a flirting man." Miss Fancy winked at him.

"We went to the house, the Bodine House. Ma and Grammy live there when they don't live at the ranch. I could live there. I could live there. I don't know."

"You don't have to decide now," Cora soothed. "We just wanted you to see it."

"There's a barn, it's just a little one. Rosie could stay there. Wouldn't she get lonely? It's hard to be alone."

"She'd have fine boys like these two to visit with all day long."

Alice studied the two horses, moved in to stroke them. "Lots of horses in the paddock. Lots. Who's that?"

He glanced back. "That's Carol. She works with me."

"With the horses. She has long hair, and she works with the horses. It doesn't look like it did." She looked all around, hugged her elbows. "I can hardly remember how it looked, but not like this. She works here. You work here. It's close to Bodine House."

"I like to sneak over and mooch lunch sometimes when your ma and Miss Fancy are around. Maybe if you decide to try living there, you'd come over here sometimes and help me out."

She stopped looking everywhere with those nervous eyes. "Come here, help out? With you? With the horses? Like I do for Sam and Chase at the ranch?"

"Yeah, like that. I can always use somebody who knows their way around horses like you do."

"I'm good with them. They're good with me. Who's that?"

"That's Easy. He works here, too."

"Is that a name? I don't know that name."

"It's Easy's name," Callen said and signaled him over. Alice immediately stepped back, grabbed Cora's hand. "I just want him to take these boys into the paddock over there. We've got people coming to ride them."

"Because he works here," Alice whispered, and clung to Cora's hand.

"Ladies." Easy tapped the brim of his hat.

"Easy, how about taking these two in, getting them saddled?"

"Sure thing, boss."

"Because you work here," Alice murmured, staring at him.

"I sure do, ma'am. Best job there is. Cal, Carol said she'll take Harmony on this ride. Wanted to ask if I should load Sundown up to trailer down to the center for the lesson you've got coming up."

"I'll ride him down. We can both use it."

"Sundown's here." Alice gestured. "I see him."

"That's one fine horse. Big boss coming," Easy added, and Alice tore her eyes from his face to look around.

"It's Bodine!" Alice's hand relaxed in Cora's. "Bodine works here, too. It's close to the Bodine House."

"I'll get these fellas saddled. Ladies." Easy tapped his brim again, led the horses away as Bodine strode up.

"Bodine. I went to see Bodine House. Nothing looks the same. Everything's different. It's big."

"It is big." Casually, she draped an arm around Alice's shoulders. "We like to think we have something for everybody who's looking for a Western experience. Maybe one day you'll take a ride around with me, see more of it. To my mind there's no better way to see Bodine Resort than on horseback."

"We can ride around?"

"That's right."

"Now?"

"I—"

"I'd like to ride now. I can take a ride with you."

"Um."

Callen grinned at her, knowing she'd be ticking off a half dozen things she'd planned to do. And none of them would be giving Alice a tour on horseback.

"Bodine must be so busy," Cora began.

"She's the big boss."

"You know, you're right. And the big boss can take an hour to show you around. Skinner, you pick out a good mount for my aunt."

"I can do that."

"You'll have Leo. I saw him over in the paddock. I'll have a new horse. I'm not afraid to ride a new one."

"You ought to come over with me, pick out one who looks good to you."

Obviously pleased, Alice took Callen's hand.

"I know you're busy, Bo," Cora said, watching Alice walk away with Callen.

"I like being busy. Why don't you and Grammy go on up, have some lunch, and I'll text you when we're back."

"You're a good girl, Bodine. Don't let anybody tell you different. Come on, Cora. I'm in the mood for a glass of wine with lunch."

She'd have to work late, Bodine thought as she saddled Leo. But she'd planned to anyway. Two events that night, she mused, and she wanted to lend a hand at least in getting them going.

Besides, she had that fancy dinner to look forward to tomorrow night. She figured Callen would get his words together by then. And if he didn't, she'd take that bull by the horns and say her own.

"Carol works here," Alice said so quietly Bodine barely heard. "She's taking those people out riding. She has blue-birds on her boots."

"She's taking them on a trail ride. I thought we'd ride more in the open, so you can get a good idea how things are laid out."

"We'll ride in the open. Easy works here. He's too thin. He must need a wife to cook for him."

"He could learn to cook for himself."

"He calls Cal boss, but you're the big boss."

"And she doesn't let us forget it." Callen moved in to check the cinches. "You picked a good one here with Jake. Want a leg up?"

"I don't need one anymore."

Alice swung into the saddle as if she'd done so every day of her life. And made him proud.

"You have a good ride, Miss Alice."

"I can, because you and Sundown taught me again. You've got a ma, but you're mine, too. You can be mine, too."

Touched Callen patted her knee. "We can be each other's."

"I'm Alice. You call me Alice. No more Miss Alice if we can be each other's."

"Alice it is."

With Bodine, she walked the horse through the gate Callen opened.

"We can ride toward the river," Bodine told her. "We'll see some cabins, and pretty country, and one of the camps."

"Camps."

"It's called 'glamping.' Glamour camping, because it's really fancy and plush, and we do it up right on the re-sort. Not like pitching a tent and pulling out a bedroll."

"Do we have to meet more people?"

"No." Recognizing her nerves, Bodine tried an easy smile. "I mean, we could go by somebody who'd say hi, but you don't have to talk to anybody if you don't want to."

"I get nervous when I do if I don't know them. I'm better. I think I'm better."

"Alice, you're so much better."

"I met Carol and Easy."

"And that's enough for one day."

Smiling, Bodine looked over, and saw tears standing in Alice's eyes. "What is it? What's wrong? Do you want to go back?"

"No. No. No. I was happy to see you. Happy to see Cal. I get happy to see Chase, and Rory. You're not mine. You're not mine. He took my babies away, all my babies. And they're not my babies now. They're my babies and not my babies. If Bobby found them, if I found them, they're not my babies. All grown up, and with another ma. A good ma would never, never tell them about their daddy. I can't have them back. I'd have to tell them. And they don't know me. I'm not the mother."

She let out a shuddering sigh. "I can say it, I can tell you when we're riding. It hurts in my heart, but it hurts more when I think of telling them. Cal says I'm brave. It's braver not to look, not to find, not to tell. But it hurts."

"I can't even imagine how much."

"Bobby put the man who shot Cal and Sundown in jail. He'll put Sir in jail when he finds him. But I have to tell him not to find my babies. I have to tell him that, and protect them."

"If I ever have a daughter, I'm going to name her Alice."

Alice gasped, and though tears shimmered in her eyes, they widened with stunned joy. "Alice? For me?"

"For my brave aunt, who'll get to spoil her."

"And rock her to sleep?" This time her sigh spoke of pleasure. "I can sing to her. Reenie and I can sing to her. She'll have a good ma, a good daddy." Settling, she looked around. "It is pretty country. It feels like home again. Every day it feels more like home again."

Whatever crunch it put her in, Bodine deemed it worth the hour or so she spent riding with Alice.

At sunset, she stepped out to check on the photography club holding their annual awards banquet, and was pleased to see the sky didn't disappoint.

All thirty-eight members worked to capture the brilliance of light and color, the billows and streams. A number of guests there for the first outdoor concert of the season did the same.

Satisfied, she went to check on their headliner, the musicians, ran into Chelsea and Jessica.

"Have the waitstaff light all the candles in about fifteen minutes," Jessica said. "I want the porches, the patios, the gardens to sparkle as soon as it's dark. And we need at least two waitstaff circling out here."

"On my list," Chelsea assured her.

"I was about to hunt you down, and here you are. Chelsea, did you pick up those samples for the summer setups? The napkins and rings and candles?"

"Yesterday. I left them on your . . ." She slapped a hand to her face. "Crap! I left them on my kitchen counter. I walked right out without them, and you wanted them today. I'll run home and get them right now."

"You've got a full list right now. It can wait."

"I'm sorry, Bo. I know you wanted to look them over, show them to your mother and your grannies, and I just— It won't take me ten minutes to get them and come back."

"You're going to be running around here nonstop in about five minutes," Jessica reminded her. "I can slip out in about an hour."

They weren't top priority, Bodine thought, but they were on the day's agenda. "Why don't we do this? I can just swing by and get them on my way home. I'm hoping to leave all this to both of you in about an hour. It's easy for me to go by the Village on the way home. If you don't mind giving me a key."

"I'll get it for you. I'm really sorry."

"It could wait, but I'm going to be showing it to a bunch of women. I want to give them time to argue about it."

"Two minutes. Just put it under the mat when you leave. I'll give the waitstaff a heads-up on the way."

"She'll kick herself for a week."

"She shouldn't," Bodine said. "She did me a favor picking them up when I was crunched for time. In any case, I'll be here for another hour, longer if you need. Just let me know if you need a hand with either group."

With Chelsea's key in her pocket, she circled around, slipping into the dining hall to check on setup, then over to the Mill to do the same.

She came back out to Callen standing with the horses under the rise of a full red moon.

The music started up with the lusty "Nothing On but the Radio."

She considered it perfect.

"I thought you'd have headed home by now."

"I'm about to," he said as she walked to him. "I wondered if I'd put it off long enough for you to be ready."

"Not for about an hour. You'll lead Leo home for me? I'm going to steal one of the Kias."

"Then I better give you these now." He pulled a clutch of flowers from his saddlebag.

"You bought me flowers?"

"I stole them from here and there on the way. I guess the sunset put me in the mood, and that moon did the rest. You said once you like getting flowers from a man."

"And I do." She took them, smiling at him. "That's something I wouldn't expect you to remember."

"I remember a lot when it comes to you. I've got those words."

"Oh, but—"

"I planned to put them together tomorrow, after that fancy dinner. That'd be more standard. But look at that moon, Bodine, that big, red moon hanging up there. It says more for people like you and me than champagne."

She looked up at the big brilliant ball in the endless sky. It did say more, to people like him and her. He knew her. She knew him.

"I want you to know what I'm going to say I haven't said to another woman. My mother, my sister, a few times. Not enough times, but I'm going to work on that. But never to a woman, not when I was here, not when I was gone, because saying it changes things, so I've been careful."

She looked down at the flowers—wild ones, she thought. Nothing hothouse, but flowers that came wild and free. And back up at him. His face still bruised, his eyes blue in the moonlight. "That's a lot of words already, Skinner."

"I'm working up to the important ones. When I came back, when I saw you again, it gave me a jolt. Not just that you'd grown up, gotten prettier, but seeing you made me realize I'd thought of you a lot when I was gone. Just little things, bits and pieces of my life here. The good ones. The good ones always seemed to have you in there, one way or the other. I didn't come back for you, but you made coming back right. All the way right.

"We felt something for each other, and maybe we

figured we'd jump into that, and that would be enough. It's not enough for me, and I'll do whatever it takes so it's not enough for you. I love you."

"There it is," she whispered, took a step closer.

Lifting a hand, he nudged her back. "I'm not finished. You're the first, you're going to be the last. You can have some time to get used to that, but that's how it is. Now I'm finished."

"I was going to say I love you back, but I'm going to need you to specify just what you're saying I have to get used to."

"A woman as smart as you ought to make that connection. We're getting married."

"We—what?" She took a deliberate step back.

"You can take some time on that, but—" He yanked her back. "Go back to the first part."

"You can't just leapfrog right over—"

He kissed her, drew it out. "Go back to the first part," he repeated.

"I love you back. But you can't tell me we're getting married."

"Just did. I'll get you a ring if you want one. I'll pick it out though."

"If I'm going to wear something I ought to have a say in—" This time she cut herself off, nudged him back. "Maybe I don't want to get married."

"A woman comes from what you do, sees what it can mean to make that promise? She'll be fine with it. I'm going to need your promise, Bodine, just like I'm going to need to give you mine. But you can take some time on it."

He kissed her again, hard, brief, final. "We can talk about it when you get home." With that, he took Leo's reins, swung up on Sundown. "I'll wait for you."

As he started to turn the horses, Sundown sent her a look. On a human face she'd have called it a smirk.

"You might have a long wait!"

"I don't think so," he said, and broke into an easy trot.

No doubt Bodine ran late because Callen had messed up her thought process. How was she supposed to concentrate on work, on questions from staff, on making sure the opening concert of the season got off to a smooth start when he'd effectively tossed marriage at her like a set of car keys and told her she'd be driving whether she was in the mood or not?

She'd prepared herself for the I-love-you, I-love-you-back portion—though by her schedule that should have been on Saturday's menu. But the leap straight to marriage didn't give her time to get her feet under her.

Still, she put his flowers in a vase, put the vase on her desk. She appreciated the flowers. She appreciated a lot when it came to Callen Skinner.

She didn't appreciate being told how she'd spend the rest of her life. Because he'd hit the bull's-eye on one element. She knew where she came from, and where she came from took marriage seriously. Not on a whim, not in a rush of hormones or dreamy feelings, but seriously, as the foundation for everything else.

With Chelsea's key in her pocket, she got behind the wheel of the little car she'd borrowed for the night. That's what she'd tell him, she decided. She wouldn't be told, and she took marriage seriously.

And she'd say just that when she damn well felt like it. He could wait.

She left the music, the lights, the guests, and the staff behind and drove into the quiet. She could use some quiet, some thinking time. As she pulled up in front of

Chelsea's apartment in the Village, she half wished she'd asked Jessica for her key, too. A little quiet and thinking time there, then a friend to listen.

Maybe she'd pick up the samples, take them back to her office. Or take a drive along the river. Or go home and close herself up in her room.

All of which, she admitted, struck like avoidance when she laid them out.

Hell with it.

She unlocked the door, propped it open with her hip to slip the key under the mat. And stepping in, reached out to switch on the lights.

The arm around her throat cut off her air and turned her shout into a garbled gasp. Instinct had her stomping down with her boot, jabbing back with an elbow. The quick, sharp bite in her biceps turned panic into terror so she dragged uselessly at the arm around her neck.

And felt herself falling, falling down a tunnel, limbs limp. Everything slowed down. Then everything stopped.

Though it was close to midnight before she drove into the Village, Jessica found herself revved. Everything had gone perfectly, and now she could leave the cleanup portion to Chelsea's—and Rory's, as he'd shown up— supervision.

While she expected Chase would be asleep—ranch life started early—she thought she'd text him so he'd hear from her the minute he woke in the morning.

Text him, she thought, after she'd shed her work clothes and poured a glass of wine.

With a smile on her face—it still amazed her anyone could be so ridiculously happy—she parked her car, got out. She'd taken two steps to her building when she noticed the Kia parked at the curb rather than in a slot. And in front of Chelsea's section.

Wondering why in the world Bodine would still be there more than an hour after she'd left, she wandered down, glanced in the car. Bodine's briefcase sat on the passenger seat.

Unsure, uneasy, she went to Chelsea's door, knocked. "Bo?"

Maybe she got caught up in the samples, she thought, but she couldn't see a single light reflecting in a window.

She lifted a corner of the mat, saw the key.

Shoving aside innate courtesy, Jessica picked it up, unlocked the door. "Bodine?"

She reached for the light switch, flipped it, but the dark remained. When she took another step, her foot hit something. Bending down, she picked up Bodine's hat.

The fact she made him wait didn't trouble Callen. She wouldn't be the woman he loved if she'd been biddable. Added to it, he liked knowing he'd knocked her off her stride some. The woman had damn good balance.

So he'd wait. A man could do worse than sit out on a pretty spring night, under that big red moon, waiting for his woman. He considered wandering back inside, getting a beer, maybe a book to while the time away.

Chase flew out of the house, and Callen surged to his feet. His heart had bounded straight into his throat before Chase said a word.

"Somebody's got Bo."

Something was wrong. Something was very wrong. Everything blurred, everything muffled. Her vision, her mind, her hearing. She wanted to call out, but couldn't form any words.

She felt no pain, felt no fear. Felt nothing.

Gradually she became aware of light, like a lamp with a dirty shade. And sound, an indistinct clicking. No color, no color, but shapes behind the dirty light. She couldn't think of names to go with the shapes. As she struggled to find them, the pain awoke with a vicious pounding in her head.

She felt the moan move in her throat as much as heard it. One of the shapes moved closer.

Man. Man. The shape was a man.

"You're not the one! That's not your house! It's your own fault. It's not my fault."

He moved away again, and through the ugly pounding in her head, the too-rapid beat of her heart, she began to make out other shapes, the names for them.

Walls, sink, hot plate, floor, door. Locks. God, God.

She tried to move, to push up, and the world rocked.

". . . for horses," she heard him say. "I didn't use too much. Just to keep you quiet, to get you here. But not you, wasn't supposed to be you."

Chelsea's apartment. Key under the mat. Dark inside.

She concentrated on moving her fingers, then her hands, then her feet. Something weighed on her left foot—left foot—and when she heard the rattle of a chain, she knew.

The trembling started deep inside, shuddered its way out.

Alice. Like Alice.

"Gotta make the best of it." He came back, sat on the cot beside her. "That's what we gotta do. You're young, and you're pretty."

She turned her head away when he rubbed her cheek.

"You got plenty of years of childbearing in you. We'll

make lots of sons. I know how to make you feel good while we're making them."

She pushed at him, still weak, when he trailed a hand over her breast.

"You don't want to be that way. You're my wife now, and you gotta please me."

"No, can't be your wife."

"A man chooses, and makes it so. Once I get you planted, you'll see. You'll see how it is."

"Can't." She pushed at his hands as he unbuttoned her jeans. "Sick. Water. Please. Can I have water?"

His hand stilled. On a heavy sigh he rose, went to the sink. "It's the horse sedative, I expect, but it'll pass. Either way, we're getting this started tonight. I've been waiting long enough."

She bore down, forced herself to think, think clearly through the fear and the pounding that made her sick, roiled in her belly, but she understood.

He had to lift her up so she could drink, and his touch revolted. But she drank, slowly.

"I can't be your wife."

He slapped her. "That's back talk, and I won't have it."

The sting only helped clear the rest of the muddle from her brain. "I can't be your wife because we're cousins." She used all she had to stay sitting up, to inch away from him. "Your mother and my mother are sisters. That makes us cousins, Easy."

"I don't want to hit you again, but I will if you keep lying and back talking."

"I'm not lying. Your mother is Alice Bodine, my aunt."

"My ma died giving me life. It's Eve's curse."

"Is that what your father told you? You heard about

Alice Bodine, how she came home after all those years. Years she spent right in this room."

"It's a house!"

"Right here, locked in, chained up just like you've got me. But you couldn't have done it. You're too young."

But not too young to have killed two women, she thought. Not too young to kill her if she set him off the wrong way.

"She named you Rory, and she talks about you a lot. How she sang to you and rocked you to sleep. How she loved you."

His eyes—hazel, she noted, just a hint of Bodine green in them—bore into hers.

"My ma's dead, been dead since my first breath."

"Your ma lived here for years after you were born. She told me all about this place. I know that foam on the walls is new. I know behind it, the walls are drywall, spackled, but not finished. And on the other side of that sheet hanging there is a toilet, a little shower. How would I know that if your ma hadn't told me?"

He scratched his head. "You're trying to confuse me."

"You met her. I think something in her recognized you. She started crying when she rode off with me after she met you. Crying and talking about you, and her other children. Babies your father took away from her. You must have seen her sometimes, around here. Working the garden. She said he chained her outside to work the garden. Did you ever see her?"

"That wasn't my ma. That wasn't that woman at the BAC neither."

"It was both. You weren't allowed to go out when she was out, were you? You weren't allowed to talk to her."

"Shut up."

"We're blood kin, Easy."

He slapped her again, harder, hard enough she tasted blood. But tears stood in his eyes. "He told you her name was Esther, but it's Alice. You know I'm not lying. He lied. He lied to you, and took you away from her."

"You just shut up!"

He shoved off the bed, began to pace.

"There was a dog, a mean dog, and a horse—swaybacked. A milk cow and some chickens. There's a cabin. He kept her there first, in the cellar. You were born in that cellar, lived there with her for about a year until he took you from her."

"He said she's dead, like the others."

Though her gut twisted at *the others*, Bodine fought her voice steady. "He lied, you know he lied. He made your life so hard, didn't he?"

"I took off when I was fifteen."

Sympathy now, she thought. Understanding now. "No wonder."

"Everything's rules, his rules, and he'd whip the skin off my bones if I broke one."

"I don't blame you for leaving." More sympathy, she told herself. Give him sympathy, understanding. Family feelings. "Your ma would've protected you, but he had her locked up."

"I came back. It's my land as much as his. I've got a right to it. I'm going to make a family. I'll have sons, and wives and a family."

"You've got family. I'm your cousin. You've got to let me go, Easy. I can take you to the ranch, to your ma."

"It's not gonna work that way. I'm not stupid. Maybe you're the liar. I gotta think." He went to the door, unlocked it. "If you're lying, I'm going to have to hurt you. Have to punish you for it."

"I'm not lying."

He went out, and she heard the locks *clunk*. For a moment she let herself fall apart, just crumble and shake and weep. Then she pushed off the bed, stood rocky, but stood.

She reached in her back pocket, but wasn't surprised he'd taken her phone. But from her front pocket, she pulled the little penknife she always carried, and sitting on the floor, tore back the foam. She began to dig around the bolt of the shackles.

CHAPTER THIRTY

He wouldn't allow panic; he wouldn't allow rage. Both lived inside him, but Callen kept them locked in as he stood in the Longbow kitchen.

The sheriff had come and gone. He knew Tate had every deputy out looking, had contacted the FBI, intended to push hard on the sources he'd been cultivating.

It didn't mean a damn to him.

He'd listened to Chelsea weep. She'd forgotten samples, and Bodine had gone by her place to get them. Nobody doubted whoever had Bodine had intended to take Chelsea.

But even when Chelsea had stopped weeping, she had no idea who had planned to abduct her.

Tate claimed they had an advantage, that with the timeline it couldn't have been much more than an hour between the time Bodine had been taken and when Jessica had found the car, the hat.

That didn't mean a damn to him, either.

What mattered was at first light he'd start where Alice had been found, start doing his own search.

He listened, and he studied the map Sam had spread out. And if he noticed Sam's fingers trembled now and then, he said nothing. Every soul on the ranch, others from the resort, they'd all take a section of that map and search in groups.

In trucks, on horseback, on ATVs.

He had his own section, and nothing would sway him.

"They've searched miles around there," Sam pointed out.

"Plenty of miles left. I'm damned if whoever took Alice isn't who took Bodine. I just need to borrow a trailer. I'll drive that far, and take Sundown from there. We can cover more ground."

"There are roads, gravel." Alice stood at the base of the back stairs, pale as the moon in her pajamas. "And fences, and places where the snow was so deep. I made a snow angel. I remember. Sir took Bodine. I heard you talking. He took Bodine."

"You don't need to worry now." Cora, so exhausted she had to lever up from the table, stood.

"Yes! Yes, I have to worry. Stop it, stop it, stop it." She pressed her hand to her mouth. "I can go back. If I could find it, I could go back. Will he let her go if I go back? I don't want him to hurt Bodine. She's mine, too. I'll go back if I can find it."

Maureen laid a hand on Cora's arm, then rose and went to Alice. Enfolded her. "I know you would, but we'll find her. We're going to find her."

"I love her, Reenie. I promise, I promise."

"I know."

"I shouldn't have left. He wouldn't have taken her if I hadn't left."

"No. That's not true, and don't ever, ever think it."

"Maybe Rory knows. Does he know how to get back?"

"We're going to look," Rory told her. "We're going to find her."

"Not Reenie's Rory. My Rory. Does he know?"

"Let's sit down now. Jessica, would you make tea? I just can't—"

"Of course."

"I don't want to sit. I don't need to sit. You sit! If Rory knows . . . I didn't want him to know. His father's evil. His father's mean. He shouldn't have to know. He was just a baby."

"Alice, please." Undone, Maureen dropped down, covered her face with her hands.

"I told Bodine. I told her I wouldn't tell them, any of my babies. Not my babies now. I told her. She said I was brave. But if he knows, he already knows. We have to ask if he knows or Sir will hurt her. He'll rape her and take her babies. He'll—"

"Stop it!" Maureen shoved up again, rounded on Alice. "Stop it."

But Callen nudged Maureen clear, laid both hands on Alice's shoulders. "How would we find him to see if he knows?"

"You know."

"I can't think of it right now, Alice. I can't get my mind clear. Help me out."

"He's good with the horses. He's polite and says ma'am. He has green in his eyes and some red in his hair, just a little. He calls you boss, and Bodine's the big boss. He'd help find Bodine if he can. He's a good boy."

It broke in him, broke over him. He had to lift his hands from her shoulders before they dug down to bone. "Yeah, that's right. Easy LaFoy," Callen said as he turned back to the table. "She's talking about Easy LaFoy."

The bolt went through the drywall and deep into the stud. Digging and hacking at the wood dulled the blade. Covered in sweat, fingertips bloody, she made herself stand, made herself search for something, anything she could use as a weapon or tool.

Plastic forks and spoons, plastic plates and cups. A cheap ceramic mug. She considered breaking it, hoping for a couple sharp shards, and put that aside for later, if necessary.

She studied the bathroom, the chain slapping behind her.

She turned, eyed the window, dark with night. If she could get the damn bolt out of the wall, she might find a way to pull herself up to it, break it. She'd be able to squeeze through, barely, but she'd squeeze through.

The problem remained that with a dull pocketknife it would take days, even longer to dig out the bolt.

She doubted she had days.

If Easy believed her, he couldn't use her. He might cut his losses there. If he didn't believe her, he'd use her.

People would look for her, and maybe they'd find her before she was dead or before she'd been beaten and raped, but she couldn't count on it.

She looked down at the pocketknife. Aim for his eye, she thought, cold as winter. It might be enough, but she'd still be chained to the wall.

She went back, sat on the floor again, and this time played the knife into the lock of the leg irons. She'd never picked a lock in her life, but if there'd ever been a time to learn, it was now.

Could she talk him into unlocking her? Play the blood

kin card? Hey, Easy, why don't you show me around the place?

She dropped her head to her knees, just breathed in, breathed out.

The man was crazy, as indoctrinated as Alice had been. And without the eighteen years Alice had had for foundation. No love for the father, she'd seen that. Could she use it?

Words could be a weapon just like a bullet or a blade.

"I'm not going to die here," she declared aloud. "I'm not going to be a victim here. I'm going to get out. I'm going to get home. Goddamn it, Callen, I'm going to marry you. I decided. I say that's it."

Furious with herself, she dashed away tears, blinked her eyes clear, and kept working.

At one point she dozed off, shocked herself awake. She'd sleep when she got home. Take a hot shower, drink a gallon of coffee. No, a gallon of Coke, cold, cold on her dry throat.

Eat a hot meal.

God, Alice. God, how did you survive?

Thinking of that, of the years Alice had done just that, survived, Bodine worked harder.

When she heard the *click*, her mind emptied. Every thought simply drained out. Her hands shook, dripped blood as she pried open the irons.

On legs that felt like rubber, she stood, calculating how to reach the window, heard the locks *thump* and *thud* on the door.

Scrambling, fresh fear sweat popping onto her skin, she slapped the foam back down, dragged the chain, stood beside the cot with her heart hammering and the dull pocketknife palmed in her hand.

She'd talk him down, she told herself. Somehow she'd talk him down, and if she couldn't? She'd fight.

The door opened, and her hammering heart jerked to a stop as she met the bitter eyes of the man who'd held Alice captive for twenty-six years.

She knew there would be no talking him down.

Callen unloaded Sundown from the trailer. Though he hadn't fired one in years, he had a gun on his hip. So did Chase.

They'd spread out, family, deputies, friends. A lot of ground to cover, he thought, but not as much as before. Easy had grown up south of Garnet, and Tate had confirmed the man they now knew as John Gerald LaFoy had a cabin somewhere south of Garnet.

He'd calculated in his head, as best he could, the most likely areas working back from where Alice had been found.

"Twenty-eight men out," Chase said as they both mounted. "A lot of rough country to cover, but twenty-eight men can cover it." He looked skyward. "FBI copter'll be up shortly."

The sun peeked, a hint of light, over the western peaks.

"I'm not waiting," Callen said, and rode.

Since LaFoy stayed off the grid, Callen figured he'd plant himself away from ranch houses and roads, use trees and the rise of the land for cover. But he'd need a way in and out.

They traveled the ranch road for a time, in silence, scanning.

"He's going to stay away from the ghost town, the tourists, the ATV routes." Chase lifted the field glasses that hung around his neck, peered through.

"The son of a bitch told Clintok we'd had a beer

together after work the night that college girl was killed. We didn't, but I didn't say otherwise. Figured he was covering for me, but he was covering for himself as much. I didn't see it in him, Chase. I never saw this in him."

"Nobody did."

"He wasn't after Bodine. I can't resolve if that means she's safe until he figures out what to do, or . . ."

"Just don't. She's alive. She can handle herself."

"She can handle herself," Callen echoed . . . because he needed to believe it. "I'm going to marry her."

"I thought that's how it was."

"That's how it is. I'm going west from here, off the road now. How about you keep north another quarter mile, then do the same? We're covered east."

"You see any sign, you signal."

On a nod, Callen led Sundown down a slope, up a rise, and into the trees. He saw signs, but of animal. Deer, bear, elk. Sam had taught him to track when he'd been a boy, just as he'd taught Chase, Bodine, Rory.

But Callen rode half a mile while the sun strengthened without seeing a single sign of human or machine.

He scented cattle, crossed into a pasture where they grazed, followed the fence line north until he could cross. Another ranch road, and since Alice had spoken of walking over more than one, he felt a twinge of hope.

He should've waited for her. Why hadn't he waited for her under that big red moon? Since those thoughts only brought on fear and despair, he blocked them out. Instead, he willed her to think of him. Maybe if she thought of him hard enough he'd know it, he'd sense it.

He came across a rancher mending fences, pulled up.

"You lost, son?" The man pushed up his hat, gave Callen and the gun on his hip a cool, hard stare.

"No, sir. This your land?"

"That's right. I expect you've got reason to be on it."

"I do. A woman was taken last night. We've got reason to believe she's being held in this area."

"You got a badge?"

"No, but others out looking for her do. She's my woman."

"Well, I ain't got her. Maybe she ran off."

"She didn't. Bodine Longbow."

The hard look shifted into concern. "I know the Longbows. Bodine's their girl? The one who runs the resort?"

"That's right. I'm looking for the LaFoy place. John Gerald LaFoy. He's got a son goes by Easy."

"Don't know it. Can't place that name."

"He's got a cabin, at least one outbuilding. An old horse, a dog, a milk cow, some chickens. Living off the grid. Has some business with the true patriots."

"Don't know the name LaFoy, but there's a place about a mile as the crow flies." He gestured northwest. "Mad Max—my boy called him that. My boy and his friends used to like riding up that way, till they got too close to that squatter—and he's nothing more than that—and he ran them off. I had some words with him about that, but that's ten years back easy. Sovereign citizen, half-crazy, you ask me, but live and let live. We steer clear of each other."

Hope, stronger, brighter, ran steady through Callen. "Have you got a phone on you?"

"I do."

"I need you to call Sheriff Tate, tell him what you told me, tell him where to find the cabin."

"You think he grabbed her up?"

"He's got a son, too, and yeah, they've got her."

"You wait for me to get a horse—quickest way to get there from here. I'll go with you."

"I can't wait. Call Tate," Callen said, kicking Sundown into a gallop.

He had to slow when the ground roughened, the trees thickened. As he rode, he dragged out his own phone, called Chase. He barked out the location.

"I'll be coming in from the north."

"I'm a half mile out," Callen said, and shoved the phone away.

He'd barely done so when he heard the gunshot.

LaFoy studied Bodine as he shut the door. Leaned on it, she noted—braced like he needed the support. His color looked sickly, his eyes red-rimmed. Easing her hand behind her thigh, she slid the dulled blade between her fingers.

She'd fight.

He had a gun on his hip, a knife sheath on his belt.

She'd fight.

"Knew he was up to something, sneaking in and out of here the way he's been. Insulated the walls, I see. Maybe he's not as stupid as he looks."

He cut his gaze to the bed, back to her. "Doesn't look like he's taken his rights yet, and that's for the best. The son honors the father. I'm the head of this house, the house I now provide for you. You're Myra, my wife. You'll call me Sir, and obey in all things. Take off your clothes and lie on the bed."

"You look sick. You look like you need a doctor." She needed him to come closer, close enough she could use the knife, get his gun.

"Take off your clothes," he repeated, starting toward her. "I will take my God-given rights, and you will bear me sons."

She stood her ground. If she backed up he'd see her leg

wasn't shackled. "Please." She let some of the fear show. "Please don't. Don't hurt me."

He grabbed her shirt in one hand, tearing it, back-handed her with the other. With her ears ringing, eyes watering from the blow, she struck out, jabbed the knife into the side of his throat.

The shock of it had him stumbling back a step, dragging her with him. As blood spurted and ran, she got her hand on the butt of his gun. A violent coughing fit pitched him forward. She went down under him, cursing, screaming, jabbing again as she fought to free the gun from his belt.

His hand closed around her throat, squeezing with shocking strength. She heard another shout, not her own, and the weight, the pressure released.

She saw Easy hurl his father against the wall.

"She's mine!"

"I'll beat you bloody, boy."

"You lied!" Now Easy's hands clamped on his father's throat. "I could've killed you in your sleep. I nearly did."

As she crawled, wheezing, she saw LaFoy's fist plow into Easy's face. And they set on each other like animals as she gained her feet and ran.

Rough ground, a swaybacked horse, an old cow that hadn't been milked, a chain spiked into the ground, and an old dog collar.

She thought of Alice, and in panic started to run toward the woods.

A cabin, and two trucks. She forced herself to change direction, to not give in to the visceral need to run, just run. One might have keys in it.

She heard the shout, kept running, but when she heard the sound of running behind her, she whirled, lifted the gun. She aimed it at Easy, center mass.

"I swear I'll shoot you. I won't think about it twice."

He stopped, his mouth bleeding, held up his hands. Actually smiled. "It's okay. It's okay now. I stopped him. He shouldn't've tried to take what's mine. It's okay for you to be my wife. I thought it all through. It's like Adam and Eve, the children of Adam and Eve. We're going to start a family. In a little while, I'll get Chelsea, too. She likes me. You'll have a sister wife."

"We're not, you're not. On your knees."

"I can make you feel good. I know how."

When he took another step, she braced herself to shoot, to kill if she must.

"Don't make me do this," she warned.

Then she swung the gun away from him, toward the man charging out of the prison with a knife in his hand and murder in his eyes.

"Honor thy father!" LaFoy shouted, and Bodine fired. Fired a second time when he barely slowed, and a third before he dropped to the ground.

"You shot him." His tone curious, his head angled, Easy stepped over, nudged his father with a boot. "I think he's dead."

"I'm sorry."

"He was a mean son of a bitch. It's why he couldn't keep a wife. Kept having to bury them. I didn't want to be mean to the two I picked out before. That wasn't my fault. I won't be mean to you."

"Please don't make me shoot you. Please don't." Her hand shook, shook so hard now she feared she wouldn't be able to steady it enough to pull the trigger.

He just smiled as he started toward her.

They both heard the horse coming, turned in time to see Callen pull the gun from his hip as Sundown sailed over the fence.

"On the ground, Easy. Facedown on the ground or I'll put you there bleeding."

Callen swung a leg over Sundown's neck, dropped lightly to the ground. "Now."

"It's my land now. I've got a right—"

Callen took the simple way. Two punishing lefts.

"Keep him there."

In response Sundown set one foot on Easy's back.

Leaving Easy facedown on the ground with the horse guarding him, Callen strode to Bodine.

"Let's have that." He took the gun from her shaking hand, stuck it in his belt. "Let me see, let me see where you're hurt."

"It's not my blood. It's not mine. I'm not hurt."

"You sure?" He shoved his gun in its holster, trailed his fingers over the bruise on her face.

"I shot—I shot—"

"Shh." He gathered her in. "You're all right now."

He heard the sirens, and the hoof strikes. "You're all right now," he repeated.

"My legs are going." Her knees didn't buckle, they evaporated.

"It's all right." He scooped her up. "I've got you now."

"I shot—I stabbed him. I stabbed him in the throat, I think the throat, with my pocketknife. Couldn't dig out the bolt, but I stabbed him. You gave me the knife and I stabbed him."

"Okay." Shocky, he thought—and no wonder. Her skin had gone pale as ice, and her pupils were the size of moons.

"Did I kill him? Is he dead?"

"I don't know. He's down and that's what counts. Look, here comes Chase. Your dad and Rory, they're coming, and Tate. Hear the sirens?"

"I was going to go out the window, but he came through the door. Sir, not Easy. I'm not making sense. I can't think straight."

"You can think later." Callen stayed where he was as Chase leaped off his horse, wrapped his arms around both of them.

"She's not hurt," Callen told him. "It's not her blood."

With a nod, Chase turned his head, looked at the two men on the ground. "Did you do that?" he asked Callen.

"I did one, she did the other." He glanced back as the sheriff's truck sped down the rutted road. "You don't have to talk to Tate yet. He'll wait until you're steadier."

"I'm okay. Better. I can probably get my legs under me now."

But Callen just carried her over to a chopping stump, sat with her in his lap. "We'll just sit here for a while."

"Good idea."

She talked to Tate, found the step-by-step retelling helped clear the fog out of her mind. And she watched Easy being led off, in handcuffs, still insisting he hadn't done anything wrong.

"He believes that," she said. "Taking me—though he meant to take Chelsea—that was just his right. Killing Billy Jean and Karyn Allison, those were just accidents and not his fault. He was raised to believe it. I forgot, God, I forgot, he said something about Sir—LaFoy—having to bury his wives. I think Alice was right. There were others."

"We're going to look into that."

"He was going to kill his own son. He came running out with the knife. He wouldn't stop. I had the gun. I had the gun, so I used it."

"Honey, you're not going to worry about that." Tate patted her knee. "It's clear as clear gets you were defending yourself, and more than likely saved the life of the man who got you into this."

"I stabbed him first—in the house. He came at me, he came at me when I wouldn't just strip and lie down like he told me. I needed him to get close. I'd been using the knife—you gave it to me," she said to Callen. "My twelfth birthday."

Callen stared for a moment, then laid his brow on hers. "You kept it all this time."

"It's a good knife. I want it back. Can I have it back?"

"We'll need it for evidence right now, but I'll get it back to you."

"It's pretty dull now. I used it to try to dig the bolt out of the wall, but it wasn't working, so I used it to pick the lock."

"That's what happened here?" Callen took her raw fingers, pressed them to his lips.

"It took forever, but I got the lock open, got out of the irons. I was figuring to get up to the window . . . Get out of the irons, get up to the window, break the window, get out the window. Run. Better if I could find a weapon somewhere in there, but I set that agenda."

"Bet you did," Callen reassured her, and just buried his face in her hair.

"Then he came in. Not Easy, LaFoy. He knocked me back, tore my shirt. Easy had slapped me a couple times, but I could talk him down. I knew I couldn't with LaFoy. He looked sick—forgot that, too. Like he'd been sick awhile. Had a coughing fit. I jabbed him a couple times, and he fell on me. I got his gun, was getting it when Easy came in and pulled him off me. I ran—skipped the going out the window part and ran. I saw the trucks, so I headed for them. Maybe I could get away in one of them, then Easy came running after me. I thought I'd have to shoot him, and what would I tell Alice? But then LaFoy came out with the knife. Then Callen rode up—after—when I thought I'd have to shoot Easy again."

"That's enough for now. I'm going to come out and see you after we're all done here. There's your dad now."

"I need to stand up, show him I'm okay."

Bare seconds after Callen let her up, Sam swept her off her feet again.

It would be harder to tell Alice. She knew it just as she knew it had to be done. And had to come from her. She drove home with her father—he needed it—and kept her hand in his the whole way.

All the women stood on the porch, her family, and Jessica, Clementine, Chelsea. She saw pale faces, shadowed eyes, fresh tears. Her mother sprinted to her, clutched her, wept as they rocked each other.

"We're going to take you inside, take you in, get you all cleaned up."

"Not yet. Can we all—all of you—sit on the porch first?" She looked at her father. "I need a little while with them."

"It's hard to let you out of my sight." But he kissed her, and signaled the others who drove up behind him to head around the back to unload the horses.

Bodine held each woman in turn, held hard. She saw the questions, the hope in Alice's eyes, felt her heart squeeze.

Clementine's chin wobbled, but she nearly managed to speak briskly. "I made a gallon jug of lemonade. I'm going to go get it."

"Clem, I'd sure like a Coke, if it's all the same."

"I'll get you one."

"I'll help you." Tears just rolled down Chelsea's cheeks.

Clementine put an arm around her shoulders. "I could use some help. You come on with me, sweetie pie."

"Alice." Needing it done, Bodine took her hand. "We're going to sit. I have some hard things to tell you."

"Did Sir hurt your face?"

"Yes, but that's all he hurt."

On a sigh, a sob, Alice lowered to sit on the porch steps. "You got away. You got away before he could hurt you more, before he could do all those things. I'm so glad, Bodine. I'm so glad. Now Bobby will put him in jail. Bobby's the law. Bobby's going to lock him up."

"He's dead, Alice."

Alice blinked at the tears, swiped at them. "Dead?"

"You're never going to have to see him again. He'll never hurt another soul. But, Alice, it wasn't Sir who took me, who locked me up."

"That's what Sir does." Now she groped for Bodine's hand, trembling.

"Callen told me you realized Easy was your Rory, the Rory Sir had taken away from you. That helped them find me, Alice. You helped them find me."

"I didn't want anything bad to happen to you."

"I know."

"Rory took you. My Rory. He took you and locked you up."

"LaFoy—Sir told him you were dead. He told him you died giving birth. He never knew he had a mother. And Sir taught him bad ways, bad things."

Cora sat now, stroked Alice's back.

"He tried to take two others before me, because that's what Sir taught him. And . . . they died."

"Sir's in him— What's his name, his real name?"

"John Gerald LaFoy."

"John Gerald LaFoy is in him, and he took him from

me before I could teach him right and wrong, before I could get enough of me—of us—in him. He was a sweet baby. I tried to take good care of him. He has to go to jail?"

"He will, but I think he needs help, too, and he'll get help."

"Like Dr. Minnow."

"That's what I think. And I think in a couple days, maybe sooner, they'll let you see him, talk to him."

On a strangled sound, Alice pressed a hand to her lips. "I don't want you to hate me."

"I never could."

"I . . . I want to see him, to tell him he's got a mother. He did terrible things, but he's got a mother. Ma—"

"I'll go with you."

"So will I," Miss Fancy told her, gripping Maureen's hand. "Reenie."

"I'll drive you. I can't go see him, Alice, I can't do that. But I'll drive you."

"Because you're my sister."

"Because I'm your sister."

Alice kissed Bodine's bruised cheek. "You get some ice on that. You go get your Coke, and let your ma help you get cleaned up. I love you."

"I love you, too."

Bodine rose, took her mother's hand, then reached for Jessica's. "We're next to sisters now, and I could use some help. Plus, you can tell me who the hell's running the resort."

"We've got it covered," Jessica assured her.

With a sigh, Miss Fancy lowered to the step on Alice's other side.

"I'm going to live in Bodine House with you. I'm going to live there and work sometimes at the resort with

Cal and the horses. I'm going to cook and crochet and try to be a mother to my Rory. We'll be three old ladies in our pretty little house."

"Who you calling old, girl?" Miss Fancy demanded, and Alice tipped her head to her shoulder.

"I'm going to keep my red hair, just like yours. I'm going to bake biscuits and ride at a gallop. I'm going to sing with my sister and not be afraid. Because I got away, and I came home."

She put an arm around her mother, drew her closer. And sat, content.

EPILOGUE

Bodine showered until the water ran cool. And though she'd intended to go back downstairs, she didn't object when her mother and Jessica tucked her into bed. She couldn't drum up an argument when Jessica ordered her to stay there, and take the next day off on top of it.

Though she had no intention of doing either, she fell asleep before they'd left the room. And slept five solid hours, unaware for one of them Callen stretched out beside her just to be close.

When she woke, she ate as if she'd been starved for a week.

As promised, Tate came to see her, talked her back through the entire ordeal. She remembered details she'd blurred over. Then surprised herself by dozing again on the sofa while he went off to talk to Alice.

Between sleeping and eating—including a big ranch meal outside so all the hands could join in—she hadn't managed five minutes alone with Callen.

And she had some things to say.

With that in mind, she announced she needed a good long ride. She sent him a look, crooked her finger.

They said little as they saddled the horses. She chose the route, as she had a purpose in mind.

"I never asked how you found me. I know about Alice's part in it, but—"

"I got lucky. Found a rancher who knew about the place. I was a good mile off, and about half a mile when I heard the shot."

"I'm going to have to go thank him in person. If you hadn't come when you did, I'd have killed two men instead of one."

"If you carry an ounce of guilt over that, you're plain stupid."

"I'm not stupid, and I don't carry any over LaFoy. It's not something I can just shrug off, but I'm not feeling guilty over it. I would've if I'd had to shoot Easy. He's not right, no matter what he did, he's not right. And he's Alice's son, so I'd have carried that weight. You came, and I don't have to. You saved me from that."

"You saved yourself with a goddamn pocketknife."

"I did, but it occurs to me you gave me that knife. You gave me the tool, and I used it. That's one more for you, Skinner. Let's walk a bit. I need to walk."

She swung off, waited for him to do the same.

Together they led the horses over land where the trees sighed in the wind, the grass waved in it, and wildflowers bloomed.

"I was so scared," she admitted.

"Me, too." Now he stopped, turned, yanked her to him. "Jesus, Bodine, I didn't know a man could be that scared and breathe." And he'd never, never in his life erase the image of her standing there, her shirt torn and bloody, her face pale and bruised.

"I knew you'd come, but I couldn't wait."

"You had an agenda."

Laughing, she kissed the side of his neck. "I did."

"Just like you, ticking off boxes. Thank God for it." He drew back, cupped her face, kissed her. "I'll make good on that fancy dinner, sooner or later."

"I'll make sure you do. Meanwhile . . . I like the land here. Can't beat the views." She gestured toward the mountains as the sun slowly slid through the wide blue sky toward them. "Plenty of room to spread out."

She walked over, looped Leo's reins around a branch. Curious enough, Callen did the same, and went with her as she wandered.

"Already got the ranch road—an easy ride, horse or truck, to work. I figure the house goes right about here, facing west for those sunsets. Barn over there, and a paddock. If and when you've a mind to do any serious ranching, you might want to add a bunkhouse. Good grazing here, horses or cattle. I wouldn't mind chickens," she added thoughtfully. "I've always found chickens oddly soothing."

Maybe his brain was still frazzled some, all things considered, but he had a hell of a time following her.

"You're talking about building a house here?"

"The house is your part—though I have several non-negotiable requirements for it. My part's the land. My parents promised each of us five hundred acres. More if we want it, but that's more than enough for me to start. If you did so well back in California, you ought to be able to pay for a house."

He was catching up now, and liked the direction just fine. "I did well enough."

"Good. I want a good wide porch, all the way around. Big windows, too. Fireplaces. I want one in the bedroom.

In fact, I saw a picture in a magazine of one in the master bathroom. I want one of those."

"You want a fireplace in the bathroom?"

"I do. And one of those big steam showers. I think double porches, though the top one wouldn't go all the way around. And . . . I'll make you a list."

"I bet you will. How many bedrooms am I building?"

"I think five would do."

He shook his head. "Six."

Eyebrows arched, she slanted him a cool look. "Do I look like a broodmare?"

"Six. And one of those rooms where you put up the biggest of big-ass TVs and watch movies."

Her eyebrows arched higher yet. "How well did you do in California?"

"You have to marry me to find out."

"I'm talking about building a house. I didn't say I'd marry you."

"You'd better." He only had to glance at Sundown to have the horse give her a solid head butt, sending her into his arms. "You're outnumbered. Let's build a house, Bodine. Let's make a family."

"I knew you'd come." She laid her hand on his cheek. "I was so scared, but I knew you'd come. I couldn't just sit and wait, but I knew. I wonder now if I always knew you'd come back. You'd come back home, and you'd come to me. I couldn't sit and wait, but I wonder if I knew. It's nice to think so. One thing's for certain: When I had the knife you'd given me all those years ago, and I worked on that lock, I knew when I got out, got away, I'd come back to you. I'd come to you, and marry you."

She wrapped around him for the kiss, swore she felt their roots planting together on that spot.

"I love you, Bodine. You'll know it every day."

"I love you back." She looked into his eyes. "I love you so much back."

"You hear that?" Callen swooped her up, gave her a spin.

Sundown gave a whinny of approval, hip-bumped Leo into a snort.

With a laugh, Bodine leaned her head on Callen's shoulder. "It's going to be a hell of a sunset."

"Every night."

"Speaking of nights. Five bedrooms."

"Six." He boosted her into her saddle. "And I'll throw in a hot tub on the top porch, for the master bedroom."

Bodine looked at the land, imagined the house. "A hot tub," she murmured.

Grinning, Callen swung into his own saddle so they could ride the land and talk of tomorrows while the sky turned to glory.

Read on for an excerpt from

UNDER CURRENTS

by Nora Roberts

Available July 2019 in hardcover from
St. Martin's Press

CHAPTER ONE

From the outside, the house in Lakeview Terrace looked perfect. The dignified three stories of pale brown brick boasted wide expanses of glass to open it to the view of Reflection Lake and the Blue Ridge Mountains. Two faux turrets capped in copper added a European charm and that quiet whisper of wealth.

Its lawn, a richly green skirt, sloped gently toward a trio of steps and the wide white veranda banked by azaleas that bloomed ruby red in spring.

In the rear a generous covered patio offered outdoor living space with a summer kitchen and those lovely lake views. The carefully maintained rose garden added a sweet, sophisticated scent. In season, a forty-two-foot sailing yacht floated serenely at the private dock.

Climbing roses softened the look of the long, vertical boards of the privacy fence.

The attached garage held a Mercedes SUV and sedan, two mountain bikes, ski equipment, and no clutter.

Inside, the ceilings soared. Both the formal living room and the great room offered fireplaces framed in the same golden brown brick as the exterior. The decor, tasteful—though some might whisper *studied*—reflected the vision of the couple in charge.

Quiet colors, coordinated fabrics, contemporary without edging over into stark.

Dr. Graham Bigelow purchased the lot in the projected development of Lakeview Terrace when his son was five, his daughter three. He chose the blueprint he felt suited him, and his family, made the necessary changes and additions, selected the finishes, the flooring, the tiles, the pavers, hired a decorator.

His wife, Eliza, happily left most of the choices and decisions to her husband. His taste, in her opinion, couldn't be faulted.

If and when she had an idea or suggestion, he would listen. If most often he pointed out why such an idea or suggestion wouldn't suit, he did—occasionally—include her input.

Like Graham, Eliza wanted the newness, the status offered by the small, exclusive community on the lake in North Carolina's High Country. She'd been born and raised in status—but the old sort, the sort she saw as creaky and boring. Like the house she'd grown up in across the lake.

She'd been happy to sell her share of the old house to her sister and use the money to help furnish—all new!— the house in Lakeview Terrace. She'd handed the cashier's check to Graham—he took care of things—without a second thought.

She'd never regretted it.

They'd lived there happily for nearly nine years, raising two bright, attractive children, hosting dinner parties, cocktail parties, garden parties. Eliza's job, as wife of the chief surgical resident of Mercy Hospital in nearby Asheville, was to look beautiful and stylish, to raise the children well, keep the house, entertain, and head committees.

As she had a housekeeper/cook three times a week, a weekly groundskeeper, and a sister who was more than happy to take the children if she and Graham needed an evening out or a little getaway, she had plenty of time to focus on her looks and wardrobe.

She never missed a school function, and in fact had served as PTA president for two years. She attended school plays, along with Graham if work didn't keep him away. She embraced fund-raising, both for the school and the hospital. At every ballet recital since Britt turned four, she'd sat front row center.

She sat through most of her son Zane's baseball games as well. And if she missed some, she excused it, as anyone who'd sat through the nightmare of tedium that youth baseball provided would understand.

Though she'd never admit it, Eliza favored her daughter. But Britt was such a beautiful, sweet-natured, obedient young girl. She never had to be prodded to do her homework or tidy her room, was unfailingly polite. In Zane, Eliza saw her sister, Emily. The tendency to argue or sulk, to go off on his own.

Still, he kept his grades up. If the boy wanted to play baseball, he made the honor roll. Obviously, his ambition to play professionally was just a teenage fantasy. He would, of course, study medicine like his father.

But for now, baseball served as the carrot so they all avoided the stick.

If Graham had to pull out that stick and punish the boy from time to time, it was for his own good. It helped build character, teach boundaries, ensure respect.

As Graham liked to say, the child is the father of the man, so the child had to learn to follow the rules.

Two days before Christmas, Eliza drove the plowed streets of Lakeview toward home. She'd had a lovely holiday lunch with friends—maybe just a couple sips more champagne than she should have. She'd burned that off shopping. On Boxing Day, the family would take its annual ski trip. Or Graham and the kids would ski while she made use of the spa. Now she had a pair of gorgeous new boots to pack along with some lingerie that would warm Graham up nicely after his time on the slopes.

She glanced around at the other homes, the holiday decorations. Really lovely, she thought—no tacky inflatable Santas allowed in Lakeview Terrace—by order of the homeowners' association.

But, no point being modest, their home outshined the rest. Graham gave her *carte blanche* on Christmas decorating, and she used it wisely and well.

The white lights would sparkle when dusk rolled in, she thought. Outlining the perfect lines of the house, twining around the potted firs on the front veranda. Gleaming inside the twin wreaths with their trailing red and silver ribbons on the double doors.

And of course the living room tree—all twelve feet—white lights, silver and red star ornaments. The great room tree, the same color scheme, but with angels. Of course the mantels, the formal dining table, all tasteful and perfect.

And new every year. No need to box and store when you could arrange for the rental company to come sweep it all away afterward.

She'd never understood her parents' and Emily's delight in digging out ancient glass balls or tacky wooden Santas. They could have all that with their visit to the old house and Emily. Eliza would host them all for

Christmas dinner, of course. Then, thank God, they'd head back to Savannah and their retirement.

Emily was their favorite, she thought as she hit the remote for the garage door. No question there.

It gave her a jolt to see Graham's car already in the garage, and she checked her watch. Let out a breath of relief. She wasn't late; he was home early.

Delighted, especially since someone else had the car pool, she pulled in beside her husband's car, gathered her shopping bags.

She went through the mudroom, hung her coat, folded her scarf, removed her boots before sliding into the black Prada flats she wore around the house.

When she stepped into the kitchen, Graham, still in his suit and tie, stood at the center island.

"You're home early!" After setting her bags on the wet bar, she moved quickly to him, kissed him lightly.

He smelled, lightly like the kiss, of *Eau Sauvage*—her favorite.

"Where were you?"

"Oh, I had that holiday lunch with Miranda and Jody, remember?" She gestured vaguely toward the family calendar in the activity nook. "We topped it off with a little shopping."

As she spoke, she walked to the refrigerator for a bottle of Perrier. "I can't believe how many people are still shopping for Christmas. Jody included," she said, adding a scoop of ice from the ice machine, pouring the sparkling water over it. "Honestly, Graham, she just never seems to get organized about—"

"Do you think I give a damn about Jody?"

His voice, calm, smooth, almost pleasant, set off alarm bells.

"Of course not, my darling. I'm just babbling." She kept

the smile on her face, but her eyes turned wary. "Why don't you sit down and relax? I'll freshen your drink, and we'll—"

He heaved the glass, smashing the crystal at her feet. A shard dug a shallow slice across her ankle with an added sting as scotch splattered over it.

The Baccarat, she thought with a little frisson of heat.

"Freshen that!" No longer calm and smooth, not nearly pleasant, the words slapped out at her. "I spend my day with my hands inside a human being, saving lives, and come home to an empty house?"

"I'm sorry. I—"

"*Sorry*?" He grabbed her arm, twisting as he slammed her back against the counter. "You're *sorry* you couldn't be bothered to be home? *Sorry* you frittered away the day, and my money, having lunch, shopping, gossiping with those idiot bitches while I spend six hours in the OR?"

Her breath began to hitch, her heart to pound. "I didn't know you'd be home early. If you'd called me, I would've come straight home."

"Now I have to report to you?"

She barely heard the rest of the words that hammered at her. *Ungrateful, respect, duty.* But she knew that look, that avenging angel look. The dark blond hair, perfectly groomed, the smooth, handsome face suffused with angry color. The rage in those bright blue eyes so cold, so cold.

The frisson of heat became electric snaps.

"It was on the calendar!" Her voice rose in pitch. "I told you only this morning."

"Do you think I have time to check your ridiculous calendar? You will be home when I walk in the door. Do you understand me?" He slammed her against the counter again, shooting a jolt of pain up her spine. "I'm responsible for everything you have. This home, the clothes on your back, the food you eat. I pay for someone to cook, to clean so you can be available to me when I say! I say. So you damn well will be home when I walk in the door. You'll damn well spread your legs when I want to fuck you."

To prove it, he rammed his erection against her.

She slapped him. Even knowing what was coming— maybe because of what was coming—she slapped him.

And that rage went from cold to hot. His lips peeled back.

He plowed his fist into her midsection.

He never hit her in the face.

At fourteen, Zane Bigelow's heart and soul centered on baseball. He liked girls—he liked looking at naked girls once his pal Micah showed him how to bypass the parental controls on his computer. But baseball still ranked number one.

Numero uno.

Tall for his age, gangly with it, he longed to get through school, be discovered by a scout for the Baltimore Orioles—he'd settle for any American League team, but that was his number one pick.

Totally *numero uno.*

He'd play shortstop—the amazing Cal Ripken would have retired by then. Besides, Iron Man Ripken was back at third.

This comprised Zane's ambitions. And actually seeing a naked girl in the—you know—flesh.

Nobody in the world could have been happier than Zane Bigelow as Mrs. Carter—Micah's mom—drove the car pool gang home in her Lexus SUV. Even if she had Cher singing about life after love playing.

He didn't have a passion for cars—yet—just a young male's innate knowledge. And he preferred rap (not that he could play it in the house).

But even with Cher singing, his sister and the other two girls squealing about Christmas, Micah deep into Donkey Kong on his Game Boy (Micah's desperate Christmas wish was the new Game Boy Color), Zane hit the highest note on the happy scale.

No school for ten whole days! Even the prospect of being pushed into skiing—not his favorite sport, especially when his father kept pointing out his little sister skied rings around him—couldn't dampen his mood.

No math, ten days. He hated math like he hated spinach salad, which was a lot.

Mrs. Carter pulled over to let Cecile Marlboro out. There was the usual shuffling, hauling of backpacks, the high-pitched squeal of girls.

They all had to hug, because Christmas vacation.

Sometimes they had to hug because it was, like, Tuesday or whatever. He'd never get it.

Everybody called out Merry Christmas—they'd called out Happy Holidays when dropping Pete Greene off, because he was Jewish.

Almost home, Zane thought, watching the houses go by. He figured to fix himself a snack, then—no homework, no freaking math—close up in his room and settle in with an hour on Triple Play on his PlayStation.

He knew Lois—off till like *après ski*—planned to make lasagna before she left for her own family holiday stuff. And Lois's lasagna was awesome.

Mom would actually have to turn on the oven to heat it up, but she could handle that much.

Better yet, Grams and Pop got in from Savannah tomorrow. He wished they could stay at his house instead of with his aunt Emily, but he planned to ride his bike over to the old lake house the next afternoon and hang awhile. He could talk Emily into baking cookies—wouldn't even have to talk hard for that.

And they were coming for Christmas dinner. Mom wouldn't even have to turn on the oven for that one. Catered.

After dinner Britt would play piano—he sucked at piano, which equaled another regular dig from his dad—and they'd do a sing-along.

Corny, totally corny, but he sort of liked it. Plus, he sang pretty good, so he didn't get ragged on.

As the car pulled over at his house, Zane exchanged fist bumps with Micah.

"Dude, Merry."

"Dude," Micah said. "Back atcha."

While Britt and Chloe hugged as if they wouldn't see each other for a year, Zane slid out. "Merry Christmas, Chloe. Merry Christmas, Mrs. Carter, and thanks for the ride."

"Merry Christmas, Zane, and you're always welcome." She shot him a smile, made eye contact. She was really pretty for a mom.

"Thank you, Mrs. Carter, and Merry Christmas." Britt practically sang it. "I'll call you, Chloe!"

Zane slung his backpack over one shoulder as Britt climbed out. "What are you calling her for? What could you have left to talk about? Y'all never shut up all the way home."

"We have plenty to talk about."

Britt, more than a full head shorter, shared his coloring. The dark hair—Britt's nearly to her waist and pinned back with reindeer barrettes—the same sharp green eyes. Her face was still sort of round and babyish while his had gone angular. Because, Em said, he was growing up.

Not that he was ready to shave or anything, though he did check carefully every day.

Because she was his sister, he felt honor bound to give her grief. "But y'all don't actually say anything. It's like: Ooooh, Justin Timberlake." He followed up with loud kissy noises, making her blush.

He knew Timberlake was her not-so-secret crush.

"Just shut up."

"You shut up."

"You shut up."

They back-and-forthed that until they reached the veranda—switched to snarling looks, as both knew if they went inside arguing and their mother heard, an endless lecture would follow.

Zane dug out his key, as his father decreed the house stayed locked whether or not anyone was home. The second the door cracked open, he heard it.

The snarl dropped from Britt's face. Her eyes went huge, filled with fear and tears. She slapped her hands over her ears.

"Go upstairs," Zane told her. "Go straight up to your room. Stay there."

"He's hurting her again. He's hurting her."

Instead of running to her room, Britt ran inside, ran back toward the great room, stood, hands still over her ears. "Stop!" She screamed it. "Stop, stop, stop, stop."

Zane saw blood smeared on the floor where his mother tried to crawl away. Her sweater was torn, one of her shoes missing.

"Go to your rooms!" Graham shouted it as he hauled Eliza up by her hair. "This is none of your business."

Britt just kept screaming, screaming, even when Zane tried to pull her back.

He saw his father's hate-filled eyes track over, latch on

his sister. And a new fear flashed hot inside him, burned something away.

He didn't think, didn't know what he intended to do. He shoved his sister back, stood between her and his father, a skinny kid who'd yet to grow into his feet. And with that flash of heat, he charged.

"Get away from her, you son of a bitch!"

He rammed straight into Graham. Surprise more than the power of the hit knocked Graham back a step. "Get the hell away."

Zane never saw it coming. He was fourteen, and the only fights he'd ever participated in consisted of a little pushy-shovey and insults. He'd felt his father's fist—a blow to the gut, sometimes the kidneys.

Where it didn't show.

This time the fists struck his face, and something behind his eyes exploded, blurred his vision. He felt two more before he dropped, the wild pain of them rising over the fear, the anger. His world went gray, and through the gray, lights sizzled and flashed.

With the taste of blood in his mouth, his sister's screams banging in his head, he passed out.

The next he knew, he realized his father had slung him over his shoulder, carrying him up the stairs. His ears rang, but he could hear Britt crying, hear his mother telling her to stop.

His father didn't lay him down on the bed, but shrugged him off his shoulder so Zane bounced on the mattress. Every inch of his body cried out in fresh pain.

"Disrespect me again, I'll do more than break your nose, blacken your eye. You're nothing, do you understand me? You're nothing until I say you are. Everything you have, including the breath in your body, is because of me."

He leaned close as he spoke, spoke in that smooth, calm tone. Zane saw two of him, couldn't even manage to nod. The shaking started, the teeth-chattering cold of shock.

"You will not leave this room until I permit it. You will speak to no one. You will tell no one the private business of this family or the punishment you forced me to levy today will seem like a picnic. No one would believe you. You're nothing. I'm everything. I could kill you in your sleep, and no one would notice. Remember that the next time you think about trying to be a big man."

He went out, closed the door.

Zane drifted again. It was easier to drift than to deal with the pain, to deal with the words his father had spoken that had fallen like more fists.

When he surfaced again, the light had changed. Not dark, but getting there.

He couldn't breathe through his nose. It felt clogged like he had a terrible cold. The sort of cold that made his head hammer with pain, had his eyes throbbing.

His gut hurt something terrible.

When he tried to sit up, the room spun, and he feared throwing up.

When he heard the lock click, he started to shake again. He prepared to beg, plead, grovel, anything that kept those fists from pounding on him again.

His mother came in, flipping the light as she did. The light exploded more pain, so he shut his eyes.

"Your father says you're to clean yourself up, then use this ice bag on your face."

Her voice, cool, matter-of-fact, hurt almost as much as his father's.

"Mom—"

"Your father says to keep your head elevated. You may

leave your bed only to use your bathroom. As you see, your father has removed your computer, your PlayStation, your television, items he's generously given you. You will see and speak to no one except your father or me. You will not participate in Christmas Eve or Christmas Day."

"But—"

"You have the flu."

He searched her face for some sign of pity, gratitude. Feeling. "I was trying to stop him from hurting you. I thought he might hurt Britt. I thought—"

"I didn't ask for or need your help." Her voice, clipped, cold, made his chest ache. "What's between me and your father is between me and your father. You have the next two days to consider your place in this family, and to earn back any privileges."

She turned toward the door. "Do as you're told."

When she went out, left him alone, he made himself sit up—had to close his eyes against the spinning and just breathe. On shaky legs, he stood, stumbled into the bathroom, vomited, nearly passed out again.

When he managed to gain his feet, he stared at his face in the mirror over the sink.

It didn't look like his face, he thought, oddly detached. The mouth swollen, bottom lip split. God, the nose like a red balloon. Both eyes black, one swollen half-shut. Dried blood everywhere.

He lifted a hand, touched his fingers to his nose, had pain blasting. Because he was afraid to take a shower—still dizzy—he used a washcloth to try to clean off some of the blood. He had to grit his teeth, had to hang on to the sink with one hand to stay upright, but he feared not doing what he'd been told more than the pain.

He cried, and wasn't ashamed. Nobody could see anyway. Nobody would care.

He inched his way back to bed, breathed out when he eased down to take off his shoes, his jeans. Every minute or two he had to stop, catch his breath again, wait for the dizziness to pass.

In his boxers and sweatshirt, he crawled into bed, took the ice bag his mother had left, and laid it as lightly as he could on his nose.

It hurt too much, just too much, so he switched to his eye. And that brought a little relief.

He lay there, full dark now, planning, planning. He'd run away. As soon as he could, he'd stuff his backpack with some clothes. He didn't have much money because his father banked all of it. But he had a little he'd hidden in a pair of socks. His saving-for-video-games money.

He could hitchhike—and that thought brought a thrill. Maybe to New York. He'd get away from this house where everything looked so clean, where ugly, ugly secrets hid like his video game money.

He'd get a job. He could get a job. No more school, he thought as he drifted again. That was something.

He woke again, heard the lock again, and pretended to sleep. But it wasn't his father's steps, or his mother's. He opened his eyes as Britt shined a little pink flashlight in his face.

"Don't."

"Shh," she warned him. "I can't turn the light on in case they wake up and see." She sat on the side of the bed, stroked a hand over his arm. "I brought you a PB&J. I couldn't get lasagna because they'd know if any was missing from the dish. You need to eat."

"Stomach's not so good, Britt."

"Just a little. Try a little."

"You need to go. If they catch you in here—"

"They're asleep. I made sure. I'm staying with you.

I'm going to stay with you until you can eat something. I'm so sorry, Zane."

"Don't cry."

"You're crying."

He let the tears roll. He just didn't have the strength to stop them.

Sniffling at her own tears, swiping at them, Britt reached down to stroke his arm. "I brought milk, too. They won't notice if a glass of milk is gone. I cleaned everything up, and when you're done, I'll wash the glass."

They spoke in whispers—they were used to it—but now her voice hitched.

"He hit you so hard, Zane. He hit you and hit you, and when you were on the ground, he kicked you in the stomach. I thought you were dead."

She laid her head on his chest, shoulders shaking. He stroked her hair.

"Did he hurt you?"

"No. He sort of squeezed my arms and shook me, yelled at me to shut up. So I did. I was afraid not to."

"That's good. You did the right thing."

"You did." Her whisper thickened with tears. "You tried to do the right thing. She didn't try to stop him from hurting you. She didn't say anything. And when he stopped, he told her to clean up the blood on the floor. There was glass broken in the kitchen, to clean it up, to clean herself up and have dinner on the table by six."

She sat up, held out half the sandwich she'd neatly cut in two. In that moment he loved her so much it hurt his heart.

He took it, tried a bite, and found it didn't threaten to come up again.

"We have to tell Emily and Grams and Pop you're sick. You got the flu, and you're contagious. You have to rest, and Dad's taking care of you. He won't let them come up to see you. Then we have to tell people at the resort you fell off your bike. He said all this at dinner. I had to eat or he'd get mad again. Then I threw up when I went upstairs."

He took another bite, reached for her hand in the dark. "I know how that feels."

"When we get back, we have to say you had a skiing accident. Fell. Dad took care of you."

"Yeah." The single word rang bitter, bitter. "He took care of me."

"He'll hurt you again if we don't. Maybe worse. I don't want him to hurt you again, Zane. You were trying to stop him from hitting Mom. You were protecting me, too. You thought he was going to hit me. So did I."

He felt her shift, saw in the faint light of the flashlight she'd set on the bed that she'd turned to stare toward the window. "One day I guess he will."

"No, no, he won't." Inside the pain, fury rose. "You won't give him any reason to. And I won't let him."

"He doesn't need a reason. You don't have to be a grown-up to understand that." Though her tone sounded adult, fresh tears leaked. "I think they don't love us. He couldn't love us and hurt us, make us lie. And she couldn't love us and let it keep happening. I think they don't love us."

He knew they didn't—had known for sure when his mother had come in, looked at him with nothing in her eyes. "We've got each other."

While she sat with him, making sure he ate, he understood he couldn't run away, couldn't run and leave Britt. He had to stay. He had to get stronger. He had to get strong enough to fight back.

Not to protect his mother, but his sister.

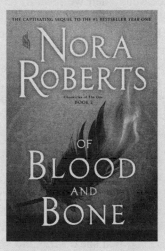
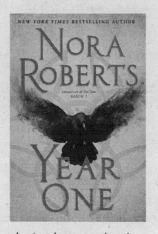